The Queen of the Fays
and Other Marvelous Tales

The Queen of the Fays
and Other Marvelous Tales

Edited, introduced and translated by
Brian Stableford

A Black Coat Press Book

ISBN 978-1-61227-814-8. First Printing. December 2018. Published by Black Coat Press, an imprint of Hollywood Comics.com, LLC, P.O. Box 17270, Encino, CA 91416. All rights reserved.
Printed in the United States of America.

TABLE OF CONTENTS

Introduction

In the late 1690s it became briefly fashionable in a small number of literary salons peripherally associated with the court of Louis XIV to write *contes de fées*: tales featuring enchantresses of a particular kind, adapted from ancient models but reconfigured in a distinctive way. Early English translators of the works of Madame d'Aulnoy translated the word *fées* as "fairies" and *contes de fées* as "fairy tales"—a name that they also applied to translations of Charles Perrault's didactic tales for children, although some of the stories in his first collection do not actually feature *fées*. The English appellation has survived to the present day, along with the assumption that it is not necessary for "fairy tales" actually to feature "fairies."

The translation in question inevitably produced further confusion because the word "fairy" had a long literary history in England, given particular *gravitas* by William Shakespeare, borrowing connotations from folklore that were quite different from the various ways in which the word *fée* had previously been used in French, both generally and in the more specific sense intended by the salon writers. The latter appear to have taken their primary inspiration from Mademoiselle L'Héritier de Villandon, although the three writers who produced such works most prolifically were Mademoiselle Caumont de La Force, her cousin Comtesse de Murat, and Baronne d'Aulnoy.[1]

---

[1] Collections of the work in question previously published by Black Coat Press, the introductions of which include more elaborate accounts of the process of its origin and development are *The Robe of Sincerity* by Marie-Jeanne L'Héritier de Villandon (ISBN 978-1-61227-732-5), *The Land of Delights* by Charlotte-Rose Caumont de La Force (ISBN 978-1-61227-760-8) and *The Palace of Vengeance* by Henriette-Julie de Murat (ISBN 978-1-61227-774-5).

Although it is sometimes claimed that the writers in question took their initial inspiration and their models from popular folktales, that is not true. Their primary reference-points were, in fact, to be found among the chivalric romances produced in France between the twelfth and fourteenth centuries. Mathurin de Lescure, whose introduction to his showcase anthology *Le Monde enchanté* (1883) was an early attempt to clarify what was by then a direly confused history, clouded by various misunderstandings and scholarly fantasies, scrupulously clarified the etymology of the word *fée*, and identified a crucial characterization in a thirteenth-century Arthurian romance that he titles *Lancelot du Lac*:[2]

"All women are called fays who know enchantments and charms, and who know the power of certain words, the virtue of stones and herbs; it is the fays who give wealth, beauty and youth."

It is in Arthurian romance that the two key models of *fées* as they were imagined by the salon writers are found, the first being an enchantress who crops up in numerous documents with a name rendered variously as Mourgue, Morgue and Morgaine, but who plays a particularly significant and central role in the fourteenth-century romance *Ogier le Danois* (tr. as *Ogier the Dane*), where she is called Mourgue la Faye. Her name was eventually standardized in English by Thomas Malory as Morgan le Fay, thus licensing my preferred translation of *fée* as "fay." The other Arthurian model is the enchanter Merlin's protégée, seductress and ultimate captor Viviane.

In the works of the writers who initiated the fashion, therefore, fays are human enchantresses rather than supernatural beings, and certainly not mischievous spirits like Shakespeare's Puck or Ariel—but the matter is not so simple, partly because the characters in Arthurian romance had implicit pre-

---

[2] The work in question is nowadays classified by scholars as part of a sequence of five linked works usually known as the "Lancelot-Grail cycle."

histories of their own that gave them a certain ambiguity, which the writers of romance felt free to vary as much as they liked. The character of Mourgue/Morgan is very variable, often being a human credited with a blood relationship to Arthur, but she also features in some romances as "the lady of the lake," and her name, although Lescure traces the second part all the way to the Latin root *fata* [fate], was more directly derived from Breton folklore, where a *morgen* is a kind of water-spirit. Viviane is identified in some romances as a daughter of the Roman goddess Diana, thus being akin to the nymphs of Graceo-Roman mythology.

The latter connection is partly maintained in the metaphysical context into which the salon writers fitted their fays, where there is almost no trace of the Judeao-Christian God or religion, but where Amour is ever-present and various other entities from the Graeco-Roman pantheon, including nymphs and Zephyr, also hang around in the wings, often confused with or supplemented by the four classes of "elemental spirits" described in *Liber de nymphis, sylphis, pygmaes et alamadris, et de caeteris spiritibus* (1566, falsely attributed to Paracelsus). That supernatural schema had been recently popularized in Parisian literary culture by the anonymous *Comte de Gabalis* (1670), a supposed guide-book to the magical invocation of spirits, probably written by one of Louis XIV's courtiers as a satire of occult science, but taken seriously by many of its readers.

Given that those confusions and ambiguities were inherent from the outset in what the salon writers were doing, it is hardly surprising that more ambiguities and embellishments proliferated instantly as soon as other writers began to adapt *contes de fées* to their own literary agendas—which makes the additional confusions introduced by the English translation seem less of an atrocity. The stories in the present anthology are by the first four writers who took it upon themselves, while the initial fashion was in full flow in the vicinity of the French court, deliberately to adapt the fundamental imagery of *contes de fées* to purposes markedly different from those initially embraced by L'Héritier, La Force, Aulnoy and Murat.

Catherine Bernard was a member of the salons in which *contes de fées* were invented, and was presumably present when that origination took place. It seems highly probably that *Inès de Cordoue, nouvelle espagnole* (here translated as "Inès de Cordova") offers a lightly-disguised account of how that initiation began: as a kind of playful exercise suggested to the members of a salon by one of its guides—almost certainly Mademoiselle L'Héritier, who was then the leading light of the salon hosted for many years by the aging Mademoiselle de Scudéry. Although that origination almost certainly took place in one of the weekly salons held in town houses in Paris, it was imported at some stage to Versailles, where it briefly became a popular fad at the very heart of the court, As to who it was that played the role at Versailles taken in *Inès de Cordoue* by Elisabeth de Valois we can only speculate, but the most likely candidate is the "dowager" Princess de Conti, the young widow of one of the leading "princes of the blood."

Although hardly anyone reads *Inès de Cordoue* nowadays and it is not yet reproduced on the Bibliothèque Nationale's *gallica* website at the time of writing, the brief passage in which Elisabeth's ladies-in-waiting specify the rules of the literary challenge that they pose to one another is often extracted and quoted as if it were a prospectus for *contes de fées*—as, in fact, something akin to it might well have been. Because of that, the two tales told within the text are frequently included in lists of *contes de fées*, although only one of them actually features a fay. Ironically, the title and basic theme of the other was appropriated by Charles Perrault, who dutifully inserted fays into his version, although the agent of enchantment in the original is the king of the gnomes.

Given that she was there at the beginning, and undoubtedly joined in with the game herself, Catherine Bernard (1662-1712) is clearly entitled to be considered one of the originators of *contes de fées*, and her contribution to the genre ought not to be reckoned trivial, no matter how slight it might be in terms of published wordage, but it ought also to be remembered and noted that the two tales included in her novella are closely adapted to their particular context, and they deliberately mirror the rhetoric of the whole. They adopt the fundamental strategy of the *conte de fées*, in fact, precisely to deny its most fundamental tacit assumption; they are renegade tales that deliberately subvert the narrative strategy not merely of *contes de fées* but the entire mythology of amour.

Bernard's anomalous tales did not serve as paradigms themselves; the key exemplars of salon *contes de fées* were undoubtedly provided by L'Héritier, La Force, Murat and Aulnoy, but *Inès de Cordoue* was not without influence among the salon writers. Madame d'Aulnoy wrote two *nouvelles espagnoles* [Spanish novellas] in which she similarly embedded shorter *conte*s as what she called *romances*, narrated by the characters, and seems to have intended those novellas to serve as packaging in order to get the tales into print, although the stratagem was overtaken by events when the floodgates of popularity were opened, and the novellas were then packaged themselves within a broader collection of *contes de fées* bearing that label proudly. It is probably not a coincidence that in each of Aulnoy's *nouvelles espagnoles* the first of the interpolated tales is a tragic variant, akin to Catherine's Bernard's, and atypical of Aulnoy's work in general. Aulnoy used the packaging stratagem again when she embedded some of the stories in her second collection of "*fées à la mode*" [fashionably fays] in a humorous novella set in provincial France, and the Comtesse de Murat did likewise in *Les Lutins du château de Kernosy*, which was probably written in the late 1690s, although it did not each print until 1710.

The significance of the description of the origin of *contes de fées* offered by Catherine Bernard is not so much in the specific rules suggested for the competition as the simple observation that there was a competitive aspect to the fad, overtly polite but covertly fervent. Not everyone who joined in with the game did so as a competitor, but even those who would have said, in effect, that they were not in it to win but merely for the fun of taking part, were nevertheless well aware that there was a competition going on. It must have been obvious from the very beginning that there were only two serious contenders for the purely symbolic prize—Aulnoy and Murat—and the evolution of their work is largely explicable in terms of the fact that they were consciously trying to outdo one another, but it needs to be borne in mind that the likes of Jean de Préchac and the Chevalier de Mailly were working in a competitive frame, and that awareness is not irrelevant to the nature and development of their work.

Bernard was not the only member of the initial coterie to introduce a note of skepticism in her works and deliberately to introduce a note of disenchantment into her tales of enchantment; the Comtesse de Murat did so too, but Murat did it subtly and delicately, as a slight coloration; Bernard, by contrast, is forthright and brutal, issuing a flat denial of the deceitful motto boldly proclaimed by the majority vote of literary romance: *amor vincit omnia* [love conquers all], Bernard's tales rarely feature in anthologies of *contes de fées*, where they would resemble acts of treason, although an interesting exception is noted below, but Perrault's carefully rewritten version of "Riquet à la houppe," which substitutes conventional saccharin for Bernard's bitter wormwood, inevitably does. That might be regarded, however, as a *trahison des clercs* in itself.

The fashionability of *contes de fées* did not last long. The opportunity for their works to reach publication was opened in 1697 by the enormous success of Charles Perrault's initial collection, although Mademoiselle L'Héritier and Catherine Bernard had sneaked their key works into print beforehand. As soon as Perrault had opened the door, however, printers rushed to apply for the royal privileges required for publication in order to issue collections of such tales by La Force, Aulnoy and Murat. The initial publications by all those writers must have consisted of tales already composed for reading in salons. Mademoiselle de La Force did not have the opportunity to do anymore; she had already been banished from the court before her collection appeared, imprisoned in a nunnery for the rest of her life by royal edict. Baronne d'Aulnoy and Comtesse de Murat did have a brief interval in which to write more tales with the possibility of publication in mind, but it was very brief indeed—a matter of months. Aulnoy had to leave Paris in 1699 for fear of arrest, and although Murat hung on until 1700, the delay did her no good; her pursuit by the king's Lieutenant-General of Police continued, and she was arrested in 1703 and confined to a state prison for eight years; by the time she was released, her health was ruined, and although she did return to writing when she could, the possibility of licit publication was long gone.

In fact, the possibility for anyone to obtain privileges for licit publication of *contes de fées* after 1699 was very remote, even though the collections that had already been licensed continued to sell in large quantities, remaining not merely popular but classic. Only one other writer who might have been a member of the initial coterie obtained such privilege after 1700 and she kept her identity secret, to the extent that she is nowadays known to history and bibliography by the entirely fictitious name of "Madame d'Auneuil," which presumably originated as a spelling mistake by someone attempting a misattribution to Madame d'Aulnoy.[3] Mademoiselle L'Héritier survived the purge and continued to publish collections of tales, albeit fugitively, but they did not feature fays, and even seemed to make strenuous efforts to avoid them. To all intents and purposes, the original coterie had been deliberately smashed, and it remained extremely difficult for newly-composed *contes de fées* to obtain royal privileges for more than half a century thereafter. The entire genre was effectively under interdiction, except for the collections that had already been licensed.

Why?

The simple answer is that nobody knows for sure. No formal ban was ever pronounced; no formal charges were ever

---

[3] *cf* the Black Coat Press collection *The Tyranny of the Fays Abolished* by Comtesse D.L. (ISBN 978-1-61227-792-9).

leveled at the authors who were banished or imprisoned, and no trials were held to examine such charges. Most histories of *contes de fées* and "fairy tales," therefore, remain blissfully unaware that any such proscription ever existed, although it undoubtedly did. Even the documentary evidence left in letters written by Comtesse de La Force protesting forcefully against the accusations that had led to her banishment do not spell out what the accusations in question actually were, but the Lieutenant-General's reports of Comtesse de Murat, although they do not contain a shred of what would nowadays be considered real evidence, at least report the rumors, mentioning confidentially what could not decently be said publicly. The two accusations cited therein are libertinism and lesbianism. The former is trivial; there is unlikely have been a single member of Louis XIV's court, including the many members of the royal family, who was not accused by covert gossip of libertinism, although accusations leveled against the "honor" of the female members could only be whispered in private. While it would not be impossible for a female courtier to be banished on the basis of secret reports of libertinism, it would have been highly unusual. Lesbianism was a different matter, protected by stronger taboos.

Given the circumstances in which aristocratic young women were brought up in seventeenth-century France, and the conventions of the society in which they lived, in which there was a measured but forceful sexual apartheid, it is not at all surprising that many women formed strong relationships of amity more intense than any relationships they formed with members of the opposite sex, especially in the marriages that were routinely made for them by their parents, and which often coupled very young women with very mature men for reasons of interest and status—a practice whose awful iniquity is one of the central obsessions of *contes de fées*. Madame d'Aulnoy had been a victim of an arranged marriage of that obnoxious kind at the age of sixteen, although the Comtesse de Murat had managed to hang on for a few more years before being bartered by her guardians.

As to what might have happened in private within the close relationships of female amity forged within that social cauldron we cannot know, and it is certainly the case that in such circumstances, misandry is easily explicable without having to hypothesize a strong sexual attraction between women, but we do know that the society of the court was perfectly well able to turn a blind eye to anything at which it did not want to look too closely. Mademoiselle de Scudéry never married and always referred to herself by the nickname Sapho; her protégée Mademoiselle L'Héritier never married either, but whatever suspicions other members of the court might have had about their relationship, those suspicions remained scrupulously unvoiced in public, and the "honor" of both women remained intact. Catherine Bernard, who also never married, similarly escaped overt censure, although she was rarely, if ever, present at Versailles.

That does not seem to have been the case with Mademoiselle de La Force, who similarly never married, and certainly was not the case with Comtesse de Murat and Baronne d'Aulnoy, both of whom had quit their forced marriages in a defiant fashion that had obliterated their "honor" *ipso facto*, regardless of anything they might have done thereafter. Whether they actually did anything of which their censorious peers would have felt entitled to disapprove or not, they were vulnerable, and they were victimized; and, in some measure, they took the genre whose development they had spearheaded with them, save for the exemplars for which they had already contrived to obtain privileges that were, in essence, irrevocable. They were not, however, unaided in bringing it into royal disrepute, because there was another scrupulously unmentioned factor in the prejudice that accumulated among the royal censors against *contes de fées* specifically and tales of enchantment in a more general sense.

The game in the context of which the invention of *contes de fées* presumably began was invented by women and it was played most assiduously by women, but the salons in which that occurred were not only attended by women; there were men in the audience too, and although most of those men were undoubtedly onlookers who would automatically have adopted the smugly patronizing stance of regarding the game as something essentially feminine, and hence beneath contempt, there were at least a few who saw it as something potentially adaptable to their own purposes—including, of course, Charles Perrault, whose *Histoires ou contes du temps passé* (1697; better known as *Contes de ma Mère l'Oye* and tr. as *Tales of Mother Goose*) thus claimed the lion's share of historical credit for pioneering the genre from similarly-sexist commentators, even though his work was largely parasitic and second-rate.

Only two other volumes published during the hectic rush into print of 1698, both issued anonymously, now appear to have been by male writers: *Contes moins contes que les autres* [Tales less tale-like than the others] and *Les Illustres fées, contes gallants dediés aux dames*, (here translated as "The Illustrious Fays") but their authors were not the only males to participate in the fad, and arguably not the most significant, especially in the context of the bad odor into which the genre soon fell. Even so, they might both have made a peripheral contribution to that disrepute, especially the former.

Contes moins contes que les autres, which contained only two stories, "Sans Parangon" (here translated and "Peerless") and "La Reine des fées" (tr. as "The Queen of the Fays") was eventually identified as the work of the prolific Jean de Préchac (1647-1720), who had been writing historical fiction, plays and poetry for twenty years, commencing with *L'Héroine mousquetaire, histoire véritable* [The Heroic Female Musketeer, a True Story—which, of course, it is not] (1678) Many of his subsequent prose works are in a similar slightly-salacious vein, their manner summed up by the title of his *Nouvelles galantes du temps et à la mode* [Fashionable Contemporary Gallant Stories] (1680).

Only three of Préchac's works—out of a total of at least twenty—are currently available on *gallica*, one of them an account of travels in Provence; only *L'Héroine mousquetaire* is available on *archive.org*, and of the four volumes in the

Hathi Trust catalogue at the time of writing, only the second volume of the *Nouvelles galantes* is available in full view, so it is difficult at present to form an overview of his work, but the impression given by that snapshot suggests that he had a very strong affection for the Béarn region of the Midi and that—as evidenced by the dedications of his works—he was an assiduous flatterer. Both of those impressions are confirmed by the two stories translated herein. *Contes moins contes que les autres* was never reprinted, but the two stories were reproduced in the illicitly-published 1717 compendium *Le Cabinet des Fées*, compiled by Estienne Roger, and were subsequently included in that collection's several successors.

Préchac's *contes de fées* are quite unlike those produced by the female writers, although both of them start out as if they intend to be, deploying the stock materials of the genre in a conventional fashion, much as Catherine Bernard's stories do; as they progress, however, they are transformed into something else entirely, becoming allegories of French history. "Sans Parangon" is the more straightforward of the two, becoming a transfiguration of the life and career of Louis XIV, represented as a relentless and ultimately hopeless quest to win the favor of Belle-Gloire (Beautiful Glory), here symbolized as an enchanted Chinese princess. "La Reine des fées" is more complicated and more enigmatic, and arguably more interesting and entertaining in consequence, although it suffers similarly from the endemic ailment of historical allegory, which is that, because history is essentially ongoing, it is difficult to contrive an ending for the story.

"Sans Paragon," inevitably, finds extra difficulty in concluding a disguised account of a career still in progress, which is tacitly addressed to the person in question by an author whose fate and status were entirely dependent on his whim. As to whether or not Louis XIV appreciated the egregious flattery laid on with a heavy brush in the story, we can only speculate, but there might be a hint to be gained from the fact that although Jean de Préchac lived for another twenty years after its publication he does not seem ever to have obtained another royal privilege to publish anything at all. It is entirely possible, therefore, that when Louis XIV was told about the story—probably by a rival flatterer with more expertise in the game—he reacted violently against the idea that he could be represented symbolically as a lovelorn fool engaged for life is an essentially absurd and hopeless quest to please an imaginary Chinese princess.

Whether that suggestion is reliable or not, history has left a much clearer indication of the king's reaction to the work of another male author who took enough inspiration from the game invented by the female salon writers to dabble in the production of *contes de fées* himself: François Fénelon (1651-1715), whose exploits might well have been a major factor involved in bringing the genre into royal disrepute.

Fénelon was a priest who became a missionary in his own country, specifically commissioned to strive for the conversion of Huguenots—French Protestants—to Catholicism. That mission took on a particular importance in 1685, when Louis XIV revoked the 1598 Edict of Nantes, by virtue of which his ancestor, Henri IV, had guaranteed tolerance for Protestantism in parts of France. Firmly committed to methods of mild persuasion and horrified by the forced conversions associated with "dragooning" (armed persecution, involving the removal of children from Huguenot families for Catholic indoctrination, under the threat of massacre), Fénelon's ardent preaching gained him friends and influence in aristocratic circles, which led to his appointment in 1689 as tutor to the Duc de Bourgogne, the eldest son of the Dauphin, then an unruly seven-year-old.

In order to aid in the formation of the character of his pupil, who was supposedly destined to inherit the French throne—which eventually passed to his younger son, whose father, grandfather and elder brother had all pre-deceased Louis XIV—Fénelon made use of his liking for stories, inventing moralistic fables and tales to illustrate and dramatize the principles of virtue and pacifism that he was attempting to inculcate. Many of the tales he invented for that purpose were animal fables similar to those adapted from Aesop and other ancient sources by the courtier Jean de La Fontaine, a close friend of Perrault, who was also an important influence in the latter's work. Others used imagery adapted from Classical history and mythology, including a long series of episodes mapping out the supposed adventures of Telemachus, the son of Ulysses, during his search for his absent father. At some stage, however, probably because the young Duc attended salons in which the game of *contes de fées* was being played, Fénelon borrowed that imaginative apparatus too, in the four tales translated in the present volume. They were presumably devised while he was gradually preparing *Les Aventures de Télémaque* for possible publication, at which stage it had to be submitted to the censors, and was brought to the attention of the king.

Fénelon was still in favor in 1696, when he obtained a royal nomination as Archbishop of Cambrai, having previously obtained a lucrative appointment as Abbot of Saint-Valéry and a seat in the Académie Française, but that favor came to an abrupt end in 1697. Whether the king actually read *Télémaque*, or was simply told about it by one of his advisors, we do not know, but of the fact that he disapproved of it very strongly there is no doubt. That is not entirely surprising, given that the rhetoric of the novel is extremely critical of the principle of absolute monarchy and the abuses facilitated thereby—in effect, preaching liberty, equality and fraternity in a work addressed explicitly to the heir to the throne.

Fénelon, because of his high status in the Church, could not be persecuted in the same brutal fashion as the Comtesse de Murat, and he continued to work within the Church as an advocate of political reform, but he was banished from Versailles with an effective order not to leave his diocese again, and he was not given a privilege to publish *Télémaque*, although some copies were printed in 1699 without that benefit. It was not until Louis XIV had died—shortly after Fénelon himself—in 1715, that the author's family reissued *Télémaque*, in 1716, and followed it up in 1718 with a volume of his fables and short stories, including the four featured herein, still without the benefit of a royal privilege. *Télémaque* became a best-seller anyway, and was rapidly hailed as a classic; some influential commentators considered it to be one of the most important philosophical works of its era; it was loudly touted as such by Rousseau, Montesquieu and other leading *philosophes*.

Télémaque probably did more than any other single text to demonstrate that the possession of a royal privilege for licit printing might be unnecessary in enabling a book to be widely ready, widely appreciated and let alone by the authorities authorized to attempt its suppression. Indeed, it probably played a major role in suggesting that a royal privilege might even be undesirable for an author who wanted to be read by the thinking people whose intellect the royal censors had the mission of circumscribing. In 1716 illicit publications were still a trickle, albeit a significant one, but they soon became a mighty flood, to such a extent that their persecution *en masse* became quite impossible, active suppression having to be concentrated on relatively few titles deemed particularly pernicious—although writers who issued their works outside legal channels inevitably found it politic to remain anonymous, and the printers issuing the books routinely employed false title pages claiming publication in Amsterdam, Brussels, The Hague, Geneva, or anywhere except the actual place of their publication, Paris.

Fénelon, being safely dead in 1716 and thus immune to persecution, was able to have his work posthumously attributed, but few others had that advantage, and that is why the attribution of so many *contes de fées*, especially those published after 1700, is so difficult. If Préchac's authorship of "Sans Parangon" did play some part, however minor, in bringing the genre into disrepute, it is perhaps not surprising that the author of *Les Illustres fées* was in no hurry to own up to its authorship. Even in the early nineteenth century the volume was misattributed by the bibliographer Antoine-Alexandre Barbier to Madame d'Aulnoy (everyone's favorite fallback attribution) although no one who had actually read the book could have mistaken it for her work for an instant. It was eventually linked to various other publications of "gallant" fiction, some of which were signed by initials that were decoded as "Monsieur le Chevalier de Mailly."

The problem of attribution did not stop there, however, the fecund Mailly family having numerous representatives in and around the court in the relevant era (although not as many as in a later era, when no less than three of its daughters were counted among Louis XV's mistresses). The catalogue of the Bibliothèque Nationale eventually declared positively that the guilty party was an illegitimate son, Louis de Mailly (1657-1724), who appears to have had a somewhat dubious reputation at court, related more to his behavior than his illegitimacy, but that attribution cannot be regarded as absolutely certain. However, Charles Mayer, compiler of the version of the version of *Le Cabinet des fées* issued in the late 1780s not only accepted the attribution of *Les Illustres fées* to the Chevalier de Mailly, but when he issued a new version of his *Cabinet* he belatedly attributed to Mailly an anonymous publication issued illicitly in 1718, entitled *Nouveaux contes de fées*.

It is not obvious why Mayer made that second speculative attribution, but it is possible that he recognized the second item in the collection, "Les Perroquets," as a slightly revised version of "La Princess couronnée par les fées" (tr. as "the Princes Crowned by the Fays") in *Les Illustres fées*, and drew the inference that the other stories in the collection might also by Mailly. He could not know, however, that "Le Buisson d'Épines fleuries" (tr. as "The Fay Princess" in *The Palace of Vengeance*) would later be attributed to the Comtesse de Murat, on the basis of a manuscript found among her papers. Had he read Catherine Bernard's *Inès de Cordoue*, he would also have recognized "Kadour" as a plagiarism of "Riquet à la houppe," with the names of the king of the gnomes and the princess he victimizes carefully altered in order to disguise the theft.

Had Mayer realized that those other two stories were stolen goods, he would surely have doubted his speculative at-

21

tribution of the collection to Mailly, and might well have formed the suspicion that the stories in it were all by different hands. It is not impossible that Mailly was the plagiarist, and that at least some of the other stories in the collection are his, but it seems likelier that he, Bernard and Murat, were all victims of theft by an unknown hand.

On purely stylistic grounds, it seems just about plausible that the author of the *Les Illustres fées* might have written one or more of three of the remaining stories in *Nouveaux contes de fées*, but it is beyond belief that he could possibly have been the author of any of the other four (readers will be able to form an independent judgment of that with the aid of the translations include herein). Whoever wrote them, however, they include some very interesting stories, and the collection was an important addition to the trickle of illicitly-published collections of *contes de fées*, almost simultaneous with the belated publication of Fénelon's contributions to the genre and following closely on the heels of Estienne Roger's eight-volume *Cabinet des fées* (1717). Roger's collection only included a single original item, all the rest being pirated from collections produced in the 1697-1698 boom, but the seven stories translated herein might all have been original to the later collection, unless they include other stolen goods that are harder to identify than the three cited.

If the seven stories translated here were original to the 1718 collection, however, that does not mean that they had been recently written. The likelihood is in fact, that, as with the Murat story, they were tales that had been produced in the course of the salon fad, which had missed the brief window of opportunity for publication and had been neglected until they were gleaned by the compiler of the collection—who might or might not have been the printer, speculating on his own behalf rather than working for a fee on behalf of some anonymous entrepreneur.

At any rate, it seemed to be worth including them here, as affiliates of the 1690s fad, rather than associating them with stories produced during the renaissance of the genre that oc-

22

curred during the 1730s and 1740s. Some of them, at least, are not trivial, although it is not obvious that the same claim can be confidently made about all the stories in *Les Illustres fées*.

Seen as a set, the translations included in the present volume might seem to be a fortuitous assembly of heterogenous materials, without anything resembling a common thread, but even as such they provide a useful illustration of the manner in which, as soon as *contes de fées* had been invented, the backcloth became available for adaptation to markedly different narrative purposes.

The very variety of the different purposes embraced by Bernard, Préchac and Fénelon is a striking illustration of the versatility of a format that seemed, at first glance, to be rather narrow. If the individual stories in *Les Ilustres fées* seem more stereotyped and imaginatively less ambitious, considered one by one, the spectrum they display is certainly not lacking in color and variety, and the more flamboyant stories in the 1718 collection, particularly "Le Navire Volant" (tr. as "The Flying Ship") and "Le Prince Perinet ou L'Origine de Pagodes" (tr. as "Prince Perinet; or, The Origin of Pagodas") make significant additions to the hectic imagery assembled by the core writers of the original fad. As well as rounding out the picture constructed by the Black Coat Press collections of the relevant works of those writers, therefore, the present collection gives a considerable insight into the potential that remained to be tapped and elaborated by further writers when a renaissance of the genre eventually became practicable, albeit in strange circumstances.

The translations of the stories by Jean de Préchac and the translation of *Les Illustres fées* were made from the copy of Volume 6 of the *Nouveaux Cabinet des fées* reproduced on *gallica*.

The translations of the stories by François Fénelon were made from volume 8 of the same set, and the translations of the stories from *Nouveaux contes de fées* from volume 14, as reproduced on the same website.

The translation of *Inès de Cordoue* was made from a facsimile reprint of the 1697 edition reproduced electronically in India by an unidentified publisher.

Brian Stableford

Catherine Bernard: *Ines de Cordova*

It was shortly after Philip II had married Elisabeth of France,[4] and although that prince was austere by nature, the love that he had for the queen, his wife, had taken away a part of his severity. His court had become elegant, and diversions were not banished therefrom.

As almost all of the young women who had come from France with the queen had been sent away she had been given many Spanish women, less in order to do her honor than to keep watch on her conduct, but as the Princess was amiable, they devoted themselves more to pleasing her than following the king's intentions. Among those for whom she had the most consideration, Ines de Cordova and Leonor de Silva held the first rank.

They were both beautiful, and the favor of the queen that they divided, combined with the competition of their beauty, distanced them from one another; However, nothing of that showed externally, and they were contenting themselves with harboring a secret envy when the young Marquis de Lerme, the son of the Duke of the same name, returned from the war

---

[4] This is not the Elisabeth de France (1602-1644) who was Louis XIV's sister and married Philip IV of Spain at the age of thirteen, but Elisabeth de Valois (1545-1568), who had earlier married Philip II of Spain—his third wife—in 1559, at the age of fourteen (he was thirty-two). The marriage had previously featured peripherally in Madame de La Fayette's *La Princesse de Clèves* (1678), nowadays considered to be the first true French novel by virtue of its naturalism and psychological focus, and is presumably the model that Bernard had in mind in her own novella. Later references place the action of the story in the mid-1560s.

in Flanders, where he had signaled himself by means of striking deeds.

The young lord was born to please, and being the best looking and wittiest man in the court were not his finest qualities. The grandeur of his courage had already distinguished him at twenty-two years of age, and the most tender and passionate soul there ever was attracted other sentiments to him than universal approval.

Leonor de Silva was the first person with whom he had entered into some commerce, because of her brother, the Baron de Silva, who had come back with him from Flanders. Although the Baron was of scant merit and for that reason could not be in perfect liaison, a long habit of seeing him had held them in a kind of amity. Silva introduced him to his sister in the queen's apartment, where the ladies had the liberty of speaking to the cavaliers when she held a circle. As the Marquis de Lerme was gallant and Leonor was beautiful, he immediately said flattering things to her, which she interpreted so favorably that she acquired in advance the sentiments that she desired to inspire in him.

A slight indisposition prevented Ines de Cordova from showing herself in the court for some time; that was a favor that fortune did for Leonor, but which did not last long. Ines eventually appeared on an occasion in which her intelligence seconded her beauty; it was not possible to resist the charms of both at once.

The queen, who was French, had conserved the liking for conversation; she had a certain passion in her own soul that caused her to love verses, music, and everything connected with gallantry. In the afternoons, she retired for four or five hours to her cabinet with the ladies of her court that she chose for that kind of retreat. She proposed, in order to create a new amusement for herself, making up gallant tales.

The order was received with pleasure by all the ladies who composed the little court; rules were agreed for those sorts of stories, of which the two principal ones were that the adventures should always counter plausibility and the sentiments should always be natural. It was judged that the charm of the tales should only consist of making visible what was happening in the heart, and that there should also be a kind of merit in the marvelous imaginations, which would not be retained by the appearances of verity.

Lots were drawn in order to see which of her ladies would speak first, and when the lot had fallen to Ines, Prince Don Carlos[5] arrived, to whom the queen explained the project. He wanted to be present for the story that Ines would tell, which the queen could not refuse him, and Ines was given the rest of the day to invent the tale that she would tell the following day.

Don Carlos was assiduous in the company of the queen, his mother-in-law. As he had been destined to marry her before the king had thought of marrying her himself, he could not help regretting that he had lost her when he saw her, and he sought her out incessantly, although it augmented his dolor.

The Princess of Eboli,[6] the wife of the prime minister, did not quit the queen, because of a secret interest she had in Don Carlos, which was no less fatal to the queen than to him.

The day destined to hear Ines arrived. The Marquis de Lerme, who had hard mention of her beauty, begged Don Carlos to allow him to go with him to the queen's apartment, and the prince permitted him to do so. Leonor flattered herself, on seeing him, that he had come in search of her to the place where the queen's favorites were, but as soon as he had seen Ines, he disillusioned Leonor, whose illusion had been her sole delight.

---

[5] Elisabeth de Valois had previously been betrothed to Philip's son, Carlos, Prince of Asturias, who was likewise fourteen years old in 1559, but political reasons had dictated the substitution.

[6] Ana de Mendoza, the wife of Philip's chief councilor, Ruy Gomez de Silva, whom she had married at the age of thirteen (he was thirty-seven), was nineteen when the story is set.

Prince Don Carlos, the Princess of Eboli and two or three ladies of the court sat down and the queen having ordered her to speak, Ines began her story as follows.

The Rose-Bush Prince

The queen of a realm that is not found on the map, being the widow of a king she had loved tenderly, lived in a dolor proportionate to the amour she had had. A daughter, the unique fruit of their marriage, gave her an occupation of sorts capable of dissipating her chagrin, but Florinde—that was the daughter's name—was to cause her some in her turn.

One day, when all the queen's women were in her room with the princess, a little ivory chariot appeared drawn by six butterflies with wings painted in a thousand colors. A person whose stature corresponded to the carriage, and whom they suspected to be a fay, after having circled them in the chariot several times, threw this note:

> Florinde was born with many charms,
> But her misfortune will be extreme
> If she has to love one day
> A lover whom she cannot see.

The fay disappeared, and left a great surprise in all minds. The queen was more disturbed by it than she ought reasonably to have been; the eccentricity, and even the apparent impossibility, of that misfortune, did not reassure her against the caprices of amour and those of destiny combined. She thought of forestalling them, and did not wait until Florinde had reached the age of amour to make her known to all those who might be potential suitors.

Among the neighboring princes there was one hidden from the eyes of the world, but Florinde's portrait did not fail to reach him by way of the fays, for whom nothing is impossible. The king, his father, being the widower of a wife who had made him suffer all the horrors of jealousy, had married a second one unlikely to inspire it but born to feel it. She took the caprices of her passion so far that the prince in question knew that he had only exchanged troubles, and did not know which of his woes was the greater. In that uncertainty he had concluded that marriage was a frightful bond, and he resolved to keep the only son he had far from commerce with all women. He had him brought up in a magnificent castle, and delivered him to all the diversions of his age.

The young prince was taught all the sciences that could not instruct him of what it was desired to keep hidden from him. In sum, all his amusements were lavish, except the one for which he was born; but amour allows nothing to escape.

The prince, who found Florinde's portrait under his feet, initially looked at it in surprise. Admiration followed close behind, accompanied by a disturbance unknown to a young man accustomed to exercises and reflections that had nothing in common with those sentiments.

His first desire was to see the original of the portrait; it was a face more delicate than those he had seen until then, and, either because of the instinct of a mystery natural to amour or because he realized that something was being hidden from him, he did not communicate to anyone the design he had to quit a place that had always appeared agreeable to him, but which he began to regard as a prison as soon as he wanted to leave it.

He was able to escape his surveillance, and he set forth without knowing where he was going. He had only taken a few steps when he encountered the fay that we have already mentioned.

"Where are you going, unfortunate prince?" she said to him. "You're running toward all the misfortunes that your father wanted to enable you to avoid, but you can't escape your destiny."

Meanwhile, Florinde's mother ordered a magnificent tourney, which attracted to her court all the princes of the neighboring realms. They wanted to show off their handsome faces and their skill splendidly; but, although Florinde could not help holding them in esteem, amour did not enable a choice, and a pity that was cruel to all of them prevented her from determining in favor of any of them. They had acquired for her the sentiments that her beauty was bound to inspire, and she would have made too many of them miserable if she had made one of them happy.

The queen sent away those princes dolorously; her daughter did not like any that he had seen, so half of the prophecy had been fulfilled, and the rest remained to be dreaded.

Sometime after that, Florinde, weary of the court and having nothing to keep her there, obtained permission from her mother to retire to a country house. It was an agreeable place, appropriate to amuse a young person free of the cares of amour.

One day, while she was walking in a flower-garden, she perceived a rose-bush that was greener and more florid than the others, which curbed its little branches as she approached, seemingly giving her approval in its fashion.

An action so novel in a rose-bush surprised the princess; the prodigy made in her favor pleased her; it was a kind of homage by which she was touched. She went around the flower-bed several times; the rose-bush bowed every time she went past. She wanted to pick a rose that seemed to her to be very red, but she pricked her finger painfully.

The sting of the wound prevented her from sleeping at night, and the next morning she got up earlier than usual, and went to walk in the flower-garden.

The rose-bush redoubled its reverences with an urgency that delighted the princess and made her forget the pain, only to think about the marvel. Finally, while musing, she approached the rose-bush too closely, and found herself caught on it without being able to free herself. As she tried to pull away she felt an extraordinary resistance.

She struggled nevertheless, but she heard a sound emanating from the leaves that resembled sighs.

"What!" she exclaimed. "A rose-bush can sigh?"

"It can do more, Madame," it said to her, "and you have the power to make it talk. Permit it to tell you its sad story.

"I am a prince," it went on. "The most precious thing in the world had been hidden from me. I lived without seeing you, and this is what it has cost me to come in search of you. A fay has given me this form, and told me that I would keep it until the day when I would be loved by the most beautiful person in the world; but what I see here must be reserved for the gods, and I am running the risk of always being a rose-bush."

The princess made to reply. Something serious took the place of the joy that the reverences of the rose-bush had given her; she even thought it too bold in having dared to embrace her with its branches. She quit it, but not without looking toward the flower-bed more than once.

Her night was agitated by sentiments that were quite similar, although she thought that they were different. The animated rose-bush caused her astonishment; the prince it concealed caused her pity; she felt a sort of anger because it had had the audacity to speak to her about amour, but in the end, she pardoned the lover in favor of the bush. How can one be angry with a rose-bush?

The princess returned to the flower-garden the next day. In truth, she took care to keep her distance from the rose-bush, but she could be perceived by it, and could even hear its plaints. After circling it several times she drew nearer to it, and tried to console it for its metamorphosis, without answering for anything else.

A few days later, seeing that it was too exposed to the insults of the atmosphere, she had a little marble cabinet built for it, sustained by pilasters, where she went to visit it frequently.

Gradually, she became accustomed to giving it a human face in her mind, and even a pleasant face. Little by little, she permitted it to speak to her about amour. It seemed to her that the discourse of a tree could not be dangerous.

The rose-bush was able to take advantage of that favorable disposition; it said a great deal, but it made it understood that it was suppressing even more; and by means of a disorder above eloquence, it convinced her that she was loved very tenderly.

The princess thought so often about the prodigy of the rose-bush that she no longer thought about anything else. The marble cabinet was the place to which her steps naturally conducted her; it even escaped her to say excessively tender things to the prince, for whom she felt a great compassion, but the fay's menacing oracle could not be effaced from her mind, Perhaps she already loved what she had not seen, but she doubted it as long as she only saw a tree; she was afraid of returning its original form, but sometimes wished it involuntarily.

For its part, the rose-bush found room for laments amid the most flattering words that the princess said to it. "If I can believe your words and your cares," it said to her, "I excite your pity, but you do not have enough if you give me nothing more; and that mild sentiment of the most beautiful person in the world cannot give me back my form."

Meanwhile, the queen could no longer support the absence of her daughter, and gave her an order to return immediately. That was a thunderbolt for the princess; it was necessary to separate from the rose-bush, for which she found, at that moment, that she had a veritable passion. She shed a quantity of tears over its leaves, which could not be washed by them without sensing their virtue.

Immediately, the rose-bush disappeared, and Florinde no longer saw anything at her feet but a charming prince. He embraced her knees with all the certainty of being loved: a pleasure that is almost never sure for other lovers, all the ordinary evidence being suspect by comparison with that marvelous event. Thus, the idea of his happiness transported him to such a point that he lost, so to speak, the usage of his senses; when he recovered them, he seemed by virtue of his immobility still to retain something of the tree that had hidden him.

At the sight of such a lovable prince, Florinde's amour was augmented, but her modesty increased proportionately; she regretted the veils that had hidden her own sentiments from herself.

She returned to court, and the prince went with her. The queen, who did not know anything about the adventure of the rose-bush, and who only knew the birth of the prince, permitted him to be a suitor for her daughter.

He saw his mistress every day, but it was no longer without witnesses, and he often regretted his tree-bark; it had constrained him less than all the decorum that was required of him.

The prince pressed for his marriage, but Florinde, frightened by the prodigy of her amour, which gave her reason to fear the fay's oracle, engaged the queen to agree that she send that lover away in order to make sure of his constancy before giving herself to him.

She summoned the prince and said to him: "Prince, you know that I love you, and in accordance with that word I have the right to dispose of you. The prediction of my misfortunes frightens me; everything that ought to make me fear them has happened. If you were not sure of being loved infinitely, my alarms can convince you of it; if you were less so, I would anticipate my disgrace by breaking with you, but in spite of my terrors, I cannot, and it is better that, in giving me certain marks of your fidelity, you belie the oracle. You had only seen me when you loved me. Perhaps I was only able to please you by virtue of the novelty. It is necessary to test you; go and live on the Isle of Youth until I recall you. Go; I want to flatter myself that the more charming the abode is, the more the voyage will afflict you."

What a proposition for a beloved lover! Since he had known amour he had always seen the person he loved, and he had never had the idea of absence. To live far from Florinde seemed so terrible to him that he thought his last moment had come. He did not have the strength to complain; his tears flowed without him sensing them, and his action marked such

a great amour that the princess, judging that she could not resist such a great passion, fled to the queen's apartment. From
there she sent an order to her lover that he obey her without
seeing her again, that he simply leave, and that she would take
care of soothing her woes.

The prince set forth with a submission of which few examples have been seen since. He was ill when he arrived on
the Isle of Youth, and thought he would find physicians there,
but there had never been any need for them on an island of
that name. Laughters, Games and Amours welcomed him by
throwing roses at him; immediately he breathed an air that
restored his health, and at the same time, all the charms that
dolor had caused him to lose.

He was taken to the palace of the queen of the realm by
way of a path covered with the flowers that are born with the
commencement of spring. He saw a person who had all the
graces of beauty with all the naivety and joy of childhood; she
was only fourteen years old. She was sitting on a jasmine
throne; a thousand Amours were playing around her, some of
them enchaining her with orange-blossom and others spreading it over her head; others were undoing her hair and allowing the tresses to fall over a nascent cleavage. She was ex-
changing badinage with her women and throwing them flowers with a marvelous grace.

That spectacle had the wherewithal to distract him from
his sentiments for Florinde. The Queen of Youth was not married, because she wanted a husband of her own age, and gallant, whom she had not been able to encounter. The prince was
twenty-four and bearded. A few of the followers of youth
asked him for news of past centuries, but the queen began to
look at him favorably. The century of ten years that distinguished their ages disappeared because of all the charms with
which the prince was replete

The queen did not neglect anything to engage him: gazes, flattering words and little teasing actions, the meaning of
which is very serious, everything was put to use, and everything was understood, although the prince, who was cleverer

than her, pretended not to pay any attention to it. She explained herself more overtly, and made him proposals of marriage, with the advantages most capable of touching an amiable man, such as always being his, and possessing forever and without interruption all the goods without which the others are nothing, all the graces and all the pleasures.

It was difficult for the prince to refuse the dowry that the she was offering to bring him. Gradually, he forgot Florinde, and it was just in time that she forced him to remember that she was still in the world.

Scarcely had she spent a day without seeing the prince than she had sensed the horror of living without the person one loves; however, she strove to vanquish her sentiments; she had already loved without seeing; she did not want to marry without knowing that she was loved constantly. A fortnight passed in those agitations, but she was about to succumb to them, dread and jealousy coming to join the dolors of absence. It was necessary to sacrifice reflections to amour, and she sent for the prince, who was given this letter on her behalf:

If you are suffering as much as me, you have much of which to complain. I cannot support my dolors and yours; I cannot risk losing you for having wanted too much to make sure of you; it is enough, you are already worthy of being recompensed for having obeyed the cruelest of all orders. Alas, I did not know their rigor very well, but I have felt it, and I judge that you cannot sustain it. Depart and come back; why are you not here?

That note arrived very appropriately; the prince, to whom his solitude had given a severe education, had not yet had the leisure to be spoiled by society; he believed that it was not permitted to him to be inconstant, and in spite of the liking that he had for the Queen of Youth, he left the island. As he drew away slowly from a place that had charms for him, however, he read the news of his proscription on a few placards that he encountered on his road. The queen promised anyone who delivered her fugitive, dead or alive, the same favors that she had offered him.

It did not require any more to cure the prince. He hastened his flight, and he arrived at Florinde's feet; seeing him return, she did not have the strength to examine whether he had been faithful.

They were married, and, the prince having become king by virtue of the death of his father, he took his wife to his own estates, where the marriage, in accordance with custom, ended all the charms of their life. Fortunate are those who live therein in honest indifference, but people accustomed to love are not as reasonable as others, and hardly ever provide an example of good households.

The prince, by virtue of idleness, told Florinde that he had had a slight weakness for the Queen of Youth. Florinde made him as many reproaches as if she had not been his wife; he was shocked and importuned by them; he wanted to lament them and console himself with the ladies of the court; she spied on him, surprised him, and heaped him with insults.

Finally, persecuted by her furies, he asked the fays to become a rose-bush again, and obtained that as a favor.

For her part, the jealous Florinde had a head so weak that she could not bear the odor of a flower that reminded her of her amour; it is since that time that roses have always caused the vapors.

The queen applauded Ines's story. Don Carlos gave her excessive praise, and the Marquis de Lerme made it understood by the silence he maintained that he was thinking something above praise. Leonor, who had thought that she alone would attract his gaze, perceived that it was going in another direction. She asked Ines several questions about her tale with as much malice as bitterness. Ines replied to them with a mildness that completed making her appear a perfect person.

The next day, Leonor prepared to narrate a fable, and she neglected nothing in order to prevail, if she could, over Ines. Her story commenced as follows.

Riquet With The Crest

A great lord of Granada, in possession of riches worthy of his birth, had a domestic chagrin that poisoned all the wealth with which his fortune was heaped. His only daughter, born with all the features that constitute beauty, was so stupid that even beauty only served to render her disagreeable. Her actions had nothing of that which creates grace; her figure, although slender, was heavy, because her body lacked a soul.

Mama—that was the daughter's name—did not have enough intelligence to know that she had none, but she sensed nevertheless that she was disdained, although she could not figure out why.

One day, when she was walking alone—which was ordinarily the case—she saw a man emerging from the earth, who was hideous enough to appear monstrous. The sight of him made her want to flee, but his speech called Mama back.

"Stop," he said to her. "I have distressing things to tell you, but I have agreeable things to promise you. In spite of your beauty there is something about you that makes you disregarded; it is because you have no thought; and without boasting, that defect puts you far below me, who is in the same situation by virtue of the body as you are by virtue of the mind.

"That is the cruel thing I had to say to you, but by the stupid way in which you are looking at me, I judge that I did you too much honor when I feared offending you, which makes me despair of the subject of my proposition. However, I shall risk making it to you. Would you like to be intelligent?"

"Yes," replied Mama, with the same expression with which she might have said *no*.

"Well," he continued, "this is the means. It's necessary to love Riquet with the Crest—that is my name. It is necessary to marry me in a year's time; that is the condition I impose on you; think about it if you can. If not, repeat the words that I'll teach you; they'll teach you to think eventually. Adieu for a year. These are the words that will chase away your indolence, and cure your imbecility at the same time:

Amour who can animate anything,
If, in order not to be so crass,
One only needs to be able to sing,
Your praises, I'm ready to pass.

As Mama pronounced those lines, her figure relaxed, her expression became more lively and her stride freer. She repeated them.

She went to see her father, and said coherent things to him, and then sensate ones, and finally intelligent ones. Such a great and prompt metamorphosis could not be unobserved by those who were most interested in her. Lovers arrived in a crowd; Mama was no longer solitary, either at balls or when out walking; she soon made many infidel and jealous; there was no talk any longer about anything but her, and in her favor.

Among all those who found her lovable it was impossible for her to find no one better looking than Riquet with the Crest; the intelligence that he had given her did poor service to her benefactor. The words that she repeated faithfully inspired amour in her, but with an effect contrary to the intentions of the author: it was not for him.

The best looking of those who sighed for her had her preference. He was not the most fortunate as regards wealth, so her father and her mother, seeing that they had wished misfortune on their daughter in wanting her to be intelligent, but being unable to take it away from her, at least gave her lessons against amour. To forbid a young and pretty woman to love, however, is like forbidding a tree to bear leaves in May; she only loved Arada—that was her lover's name—a little more.

She refrained carefully from telling anyone about the adventure by which reason had come to her. Her vanity had an interest in keeping the secret, and she now had enough intelligence to understand the importance of concealing the mystery of how she had acquired it.

Meanwhile, the year that Riquet with the Crest had given her in which to learn to think and to resolve to marry him, had almost elapsed. She saw the due date approaching with an extreme dolor; her intelligence, which was becoming a fatal gift, did not let any afflicting circumstance escape her. Losing her lover forever, and being in the power of someone of whom she knew nothing but his deformity—which might not be the least of his defects—but in any case, someone she was engaged to marry by virtue of accepting gifts from him that she did not want to return: those were her reflections.

One day, when she was thinking about her cruel destiny, and wandered off on her own, she heard a loud noise, and subterranean voices singing the words that Riquet with the Crest had made her learn. She shivered; it was the signal of her misfortune.

Immediately, the earth opened up. She descended into it gradually, and saw Riquet with the Crest there, surrounded by men as deformed as him. What a spectacle for someone who had been followed by all that was most lovable in her own land! Her dolor was even greater than her surprise; she shed a torrent of tears without speaking; that was the only use she made then of the intelligence that Riquet with the Crest had given her.

He looked at her sadly in his turn. "Madame," he said to her, "it isn't difficult for me to see that I'm even more disagreeable to you than the first time I appeared to your eyes, and that I've doomed myself by giving you intelligence. But after all, you're still free, and you have the choice of either marrying me or reverting to your original state. I can send you back to your father as I found you, or render you mistress of my kingdom. I'm the King of the Gnomes, and you'll be their queen; and if you want to forgive me my form and sacrifice the pleasure of your eyes, all the other pleasures will be lavished upon you. I posses the treasures contained in the earth;

39

you'll be their mistress; and with gold and intelligence, who can be unhappy, or merit being?

"I'm afraid that you might have some false delicacy; I'm afraid that in the midst of all my treasures I might appear to be inconvenient; but if my treasures, with me, don't suit you, speak; I'll take you far away from here, where I don't want anything that can disturb my happiness. You can have two days to get to know this place, and to decide between my fortune and yours."

Riquet with the Crest left her, after having conducted her to a magnificent apartment; she was served there by gnomes of her own sex, whose ugliness wounded her less than that of the males. She was served a magnificent meal, in which nothing was lacking except good company. Afterwards, she saw a comedy, in which the deformed actors prevented her from being interested in the subject. In the evening there was a ball, but she had no desire to please there, so she felt a mortal disgust that would not have made her hesitate to refuse Riquet with the Crest, his riches and his pleasures, if the threat of stupidity had not stopped her.

In order to liberate herself from an odious spouse she would have resumed stupidity without difficulty, if she had not had a lover, but it would have meant losing that lover in the cruelest fashion. It is true, however, that she would be lost to him by marrying the gnome. She would never be able to see Arada again, nor speak to him, nor even give him news of her; he would be able to suspect her of infidelity. In sum, she would have a husband who, in taking her away from the man she loved, would always have been odious to her even if he had been likeable, but was also a monster. Thus, the resolution was difficult to make.

When the two days had passed, she was no less uncertain. She told the gnome that it was impossible for her to make a choice.

"That is to decide against me," he told her, "so I'll return you to your original state if you dare not choose."

She trembled; the idea of losing her lover by virtue of the scorn that he would have for her touched her sharply enough to make her renounce him.

"Well," she said to the gnome, "you've settled it; it's necessary to be yours."

Riquet with the Crest did not make any difficulty. He married her, and Mama's intelligence was further augmented by that marriage, but her unhappiness was augmented in proportion to her intelligence; she was frightened by having given herself to a monster, and she could not understand how she would be able to spend another moment with him.

The gnome perceived his wife's hatred clearly, and was wounded by it, although he was offended on behalf of his intelligence. That aversion reproached him incessantly for his deformity, and made him detest women, marriage and the curiosity that had led him away from his home.

He often left Mama alone, and as she was reduced to thinking, she thought that it was necessary to convince Arada by means of his own eyes that she was not inconstant. He could reach the place where she was, since she had reached it; it was at least necessary to give him news of her, and excuse herself for her absence by means of the gnome who had abducted her, the sight of whom would answer to him for her fidelity.

Nothing is impossible for an intelligent woman who is in love. She bribed a gnome, who took news of her to Arada. Fortunately, the time of faithful lovers still endured; he was in despair at Mama's forgetfulness without being embittered by it; insulting suspicions never entered his head; he was lamenting; he was dying without having a single thought that could offend his mistress, and without seeking to cure himself.

It is not difficult to believe that, with those sentiments, he went to find Mama, at the peril of his days, as soon as he knew where she was and she had not forbidden him to come.

He arrived in the subterranean realm where Mama lived. He saw her; he threw himself at her feet. She said things to him that were even more tender than intelligent. He obtained permission from her to renounce the world in order to live underground, and she made him beg for it, although she had no other desire than to engage him to make that decision.

Mama's gaiety gradually returned, and her beauty was all the more perfect for it, but the gnome's amour was alarmed by that; he had too much intelligence and he was too well aware of Mama's disgust to believe that the habitude of being his could have lessened her distress. Mama had the imprudence to adorn herself; the gnome did himself too much justice to think himself worthy of it, and soon deduced that there was a good-looking man hiding in his palace.

He needed no more than that; he meditated a vengeance finer that merely getting out of it. He summoned Mama.

"I don't amuse myself lamenting and making reproaches," he told her. "I leave that to humans. When I gave you intelligence, I intended to enjoy it. You have made use of it against me, but I can't take it away from you completely; you have subjected yourself to the law that was imposed on you. But if you have not broken our treaty, you have not obeyed it rigorously. Let's split the difference. You'll have intelligence by night—I don't want a stupid wife—but you'll be stupid by day for whoever has pleased you."

At that moment, Mama sensed a mental heaviness, which she soon could not even feel any longer.

That night her ideas reawakened; she reflected on her misfortune; she wept, and could not resolve herself to be consoled, not to seek the expedients that enlightenment might have been able to furnish her.

The following night, she perceived that her husband was profoundly asleep. She put under his nose a herb that augmented his slumber, and made it last as long as she wished, She got up in order to draw away from the object of her wrath. Conducted by her reveries, she went to the place where Arada was lodged, not so much to look for him, as perhaps to flatter herself that he was looking for her. She found him in a pathway where they had often met, and where he asked her what was happening. Mama told him the story of her misfortunes, and they were soothed by the pleasure she had in relating them to him.

The following night they met again in the same place, without being seen, and those tacit rendezvous continued for so long that their disgrace only enabled them to savor a new kind of happiness. Mama's intelligence and amour furnished a thousand expedients in order to be agreeable, and to enable Arada to forget that she lacked intelligence for half the time.

When the lovers sensed day approaching, Mama went to wake the gnome; she took care to remove the soporific herbs as soon as she was beside him. When day came she became an imbecile again, but she spent the time sleeping.

A passably happy state of affairs cannot last forever; the leaf that caused sleep also caused snoring. A gnome domestic who was neither fully asleep nor fully awake thought he heard his master groaning; he ran to him, perceived the herbs that had been put under his nose, and took them away, believing that they were inconveniencing him—an attention that was triply unfortunate.

The gnome saw that he was alone; he searched for his wife furiously, and hazard or his evil design took him to the place where to two lovers never wearied of searing eternal amour to one another.

He did not say anything, but he touched the lover with a wand that gave him a form similar to his own; and when he had made a few turns with him, Mama could no longer distinguish him from her husband.

She saw that she had two husbands instead of one, and never knew to whom to address her complaints, for fear of mistaking the object of her hatred from the object of her amour; but perhaps she scarcely lost by it. Lovers always turn into husbands at length.

Leonor concluded her tale thus, and although it was not without artistry, and her narration was not without wit, "The Rose-bush Prince" prevailed considerably with the Marquis de Lerme; it would not have taken much for him to exempt himself from comparing them. No praise emerged from his mouth; it seemed to him that he owed it all to Ines, and that he would have been stealing from her that which he owed to others.

Outraged by his silence, and with good reason, Leonor resolved to avenge herself on him by preventing him from talking to Ines. She succeeded in that, by means of her application. He found her everywhere; as soon as he began to speak to Ines she approached them and interrupted them.

Lerme's passion was, however, augmented by the obstacle he found to declaring it, and although Ines owed the first impression she made to her charms, she owed at least a part to her rival's ardor to be importunate.

It was not possible for such a violent passion to be unknown to the person who inspired it. The Marquis de Lerme came to the queen's apartment every day; his eyes and his urgency revealed his passion even to those who had no interest in it. He was amiable; they both were, on condition of both being present; they were prevented from explaining their thinking to one another, but they compensated themselves for their silence with the vivacity of their sentiments.

They were under that constraint for some time, but finally, Don Luis de Cordova, Ines's father, arrived at court, and it was a kind of relief to Lerme to think that he would at least be able to explain himself to him. However, hazard soon gave him an opportunity to talk to Ines herself, although it was in unfortunate circumstances.

Don Luis de Cordova, whom the king had sent to Portugal, came back with the queen, the sister of Philip II,[7] who had no other design than to see her brother and Queen Elisabeth, whose beauty was causing considerable rumor. The king received his sister with an extraordinary magnificence, and added pleasures to the honors that he rendered her. He gave her a magnificent fête at Aranjuez, to which the whole court was

---

[7] Philip's sister, Juana of Austria, married Juan Manuel, Prince of Portugal in 1552; he died in 1554 when she was pregnant with the future Portuguese king Sebastian I.

invited; the ladies went there very elegantly dressed, in carriages drawn by Neapolitan horses.

Leonor and Ines were with their governess in one of the carriages; the cavaliers were on horseback and were chatting to the ladies through the carriage windows. Lerme, seeing a cavalier who was talking to Leonor on one side, went to the other in order to talk to Ines; but Leonor, more intent on what her companion was saying than what the cavalier was saying, caused an embarrassment in the conversation that prevented them all from realizing that they were near to the river that leads to Aranjuez, and that the horses, in spite of the skill of the coachman, had already entered into it at a point other than that where it was fordable. Ines was troubled by that, which put her in a danger that she wanted to avoid, and, uttering a cry, she leapt out of the carriage and fell into the river. Lerme, prompt to help her, jumped in after her and pulled her out.

The coachman, meanwhile, was able to manipulate the reins of the horses with so much skill that he get them out of the river, but when they were out, they ran with such fury that he was no longer their master, and Leonor, who was in the carriage, found herself in a peril as great as her companion, without anyone to get her out of it, because the cavalier who had been talking to her could not get ahead of the horses in order to stop them.

Ines had fainted because of the fright she had had and the water she had swallowed, but a few men having arrived, she was carried to a house that was not far away, and she was brought round by means of cares.

As soon as she was in a state to distinguish objects, saw Lerme at her feet, and thought that it was evidently him who had extracted her from peril, the joy of being obliged to a man for whom she had such an amorous penchant was her first emotion, but the same thought caused her anxiety.

Lerme, who noticed her embarrassment, and did not dare to speak for some time, finally broke the silence.

"I'm very unfortunate, Madame," he said to her. "I ask no other recompense than your consent to the pleasure I have had, but you're refusing it to me."

"I owe you my life with pleasure," she told him, "but I'm embarrassed to find myself alone here."

"Well, Madame," he said, "you are with a man who adores you, and who has never been able to tell you so. I might perhaps attract your anger by telling you; I'm trembling, and find myself in a peril greater than the one you have just escaped. Don't leave me in this uncertainty."

"I can't reply to you," she told him, "while I'm in this place."

"Well, Madame," he cried, "when will you be able to speak? Elsewhere, a thousand obstacles oppose it, and I do not see you disposed to suffer that I explain myself with people who cannot fail to approve of my passion for you. On whom, does my happiness depend, if I cannot make it depend on you alone?"

"I'm not forbidding you anything," she said to him, "except remaining with me any longer."

Lerme quit her with a dolor mingled with joy; it seemed to him that she approved of his designs for marriage, but that it was without passion on her part, and the extreme modesty that she was showing him appeared too incompatible with amour.

Lerme left her in order to search for a means of taking her back to Madrid, to which she wanted to return because she was not in a state to appear at the fête; but Don Luis having learned that she had fallen, came back to look for her and take her back there himself.

For his part, he had helped Leonor by putting himself in the passage of the hordes, which he had stopped. Leonor's gratitude had been equal to the danger that she had run; her disturbance had augmented her beauty, and he had not been insensible to it. He returned to Aranjuez, where he spent the rest of the day talking to her, and Leonor, conceiving the hope of avenging herself on Ines and Lerme if she rendered Don

Luis amorous, employed all the artifice she had in her mind to render herself mistress of his.

Don Luis had a penchant for amour that fifty years had not been able to weaken, and he had a sufficient fortune to be able to expect a fortunate success in his designs.

The Marquis easily obtained permission from him to become his daughter's suitor, but as soon as Leonor heard that news she turned Don Luis's head with so much art that he deliberated for a long time over the marriage after having approved it. The delay appeared to be lovers to be a bad augury, but in the meantime they talked to one another in the queen's apartment; at least they had the relief of being afflicted together.

By virtue of the marriage, Ines became accustomed to hearing talk of amour; she had even learned to reply in the same language. Leonor did not interrupt her discourse as much, because Don Luis occupied her and, wanting to take possession of his mind in order to harm them, she had long conversations with him.

At the court, people only respired joy and only sought pleasures. The queen's maids of honor invented a game that led to new ones; they consulted one another in whispers regarding one of the company, each giving her own, and if a cavalier was encountered with the same idea as a lady, he was obliged to give her a fête. Advice was asked for Ines, and Leonor, curious about what would happen, thought about matching herself, if possible, with the Marquis de Lerme.

She advised Ines to love the man who loved her most; that was the opinion of the Marquis, and according to the rules of the game, he gave Leonor a fête; the fête was magnificent and elegant; a part of the court was there, but he could not constrain himself to the extent of not giving all the honors to Ines, although Leonor had reason to expect them, so she was not the mistress of her chagrin.

"In truth," she said to Lerme, "if I had been asked for advice for you, I would have advised you to give a fête for Ines rather than me."

"One ought to pardon a lover anything," he told her. "You're not unaware that I love Ines, and she's here."

He could talk about his amour, since Don Luis had given him permission to pretend to his daughter, but he was talking about it to a lover. The preference he had given to Ines had never been so sensible to her, and although she had no doubt about it, he had not one as far as declaring it to her; she even found an incivility in telling one young woman that he was in love with another. Afterwards, he did not seem to pay any attention to the reproach she made him of acquitting himself poorly in the fête in her regard. He only spoke to Ines, and Leonor no longer retained any measure; neither love nor hatred stops half way.

Leonor had not accepted the proposals of marriage the Don Luis had made her; a residue of tenderness that she still felt for Lerme left in her heart, involuntarily, the hope of marrying him if he could be deterred by the obstacles she brought to his marriage with Ines, but finally, chagrin took possession of her mind and no longer left her with anything but the desire to avenge herself,

The next day she told Don Luis that she would marry him, on condition that he declared overtly to Lerme that their alliance was no longer agreeable to him and that he engage Ines to Baron de Silva, her brother.

That Baron, whose mind and heart had no delicacy, could not be insensible to Ines's beauty. The thought of marrying such a charming person gave birth in his soul to a sort of amour that was nothing but desire.

Don Luis was too much in love not to accept the proposition that was put to him, with the result that he forbade his daughter to speak to the Marquis de Lerme and commanded her to regard the Baron de Silva as the man that he destined for her husband.

No dolor ever equaled that which Ines felt at that reversal. The order was so terrible that she had the strength to disobey it in part, and although she believed that she was resolved not to see the Marquis de Lerme again, she felt that she could never resolve herself to marry the Baron de Silva. It was not that the first of those misfortunes did not appear to her to be very great, but she still hoped to find some consolation in the merit of her constancy.

After having spent the night in tears, Ines was obliged to go to the queen's apartment, and while traversing a gallery that led there, she found the Marquis de Lerme, to whom Don Luis had made is intentions known. He had come there in the hope of meeting her and in order to learn her final resolution.

Sadness was painted equally on their faces; they looked at one another in a manner that expressed their woe and the sentiments that they had.

"It's necessary for us to say adieu forever," Ines said to him, shedding tears, "and we have even greater evils to fear. They want me to marry Baron de Silva,"

"Baron de Silva!" cried the Marquis, dolorously. "I have nothing to say to you," he added, with a great deal of respect, "except that I will love you forever."

"It is prescribed to me what I have to do," Ines said to him, "And you will see the extent to which my fidelity will go."

With that, she quit him, unable to remain any longer in that place without the danger of being surprised there.

Ines threw herself at the queen's feet, and begged her to make use of her authority to prevent her from marrying the Baron de Silva, but Leonor had prejudiced her in favor of her brother, and it was only by shedding a torrent of tears that Ines obtained from the queen that, in favor of her first engagement, she would obliged Don Luis to grant her a delay of a few months.

Lerme and Ines, no longer being able to speak to one another, found the means to write to one another by means of a maid named Matilde, who was absolutely devoted to Ines, but that innocent pleasure produced an unfortunate adventure.

Prince Don Juan de Austria, who had previously been held to be a son of Luis de Quijada, was recognized by Philip

II as the son of Charles V.[8] That recognition was made at Valladolid. The king, who was hunting, summoned him and embraced him as his brother in the presence of the entire court. They spent a few days together and returned to Madrid. The queen had remained there because of her pregnancy, and she was walking in the garden when someone came to tell her that the king was arriving with Don Juan. She went to the gate to receive them, and, everyone having followed her, people hastened to look at the new prince.

During that confusion, the young woman who carried Ines's letters to Lerme thought that she could hand him one without being noticed, with the result that, having advanced toward him and spoken to him, she gave it to him. He took it and put it in his pocket hastily, until he could leave in order to read it; but Barn de Silva, who was not far away, and who examined all his actions with application, approached him, and when the crowd became denser, he removed the note adroitly from Lerme's pocket.

The Marquis got out as soon as he could escape from the crush, and went into a path in the garden in order to read Ines's letter, but his dolor was immense when he could no longer find it.

Baron de Silva, who has taken it, was reading it in another path, and found these words therein:

I always find in your letters a gratitude that wounds me, and which only permits me a feeble idea of your passion. It is true that for you I have resisted the will of my father and you always appear to me to be surprised by that. How cruel it would be for me to have done so much, if you had not expected it of me! If you are so obliged to me for my conduct, you do not share my sentiments sufficiently, and it is even necessary that you do not know them; you do not sense how much I am

---

[8] The Holy Roman Emperor Charles V was Philip's father, so this acknowledgement was a recognition of Don Juan as his brother.

opposed to what might prevent me from being yours. I am even more offended by your fears for the future. Why want Baron de Silva to decide something that I have already decided in your favor? Can you not assure yourself of my heart and your courage? Leave me the care of avoiding this marriage without it costing you anything; you will have more pleasure in being proud of me than I will in having one more obligation to you.

The Marquis de Lerme, who was in a furious anxiety at not finding that letter, retraced his steps, and encountered Baron de Silva as he was reading it with a great deal of application and anger. Lerme, approaching him quietly, took him by surprise; he was close enough to him to recognize Ines's handwriting, and he demanded to know who had put that letter in his hands.

The Baron, who was reading the passage in which there as mention of him, replied to Lerme that he accepted the challenge of which Ines was afraid. Lerme, to whom it was of the utmost importance to recover Ines's letter, snatched it from his hand and told him afterwards that he was ready to give him reason in a place appropriate for fighting; but Silva, beside himself with wrath, drew his sword, and in spite of respect for the place, struck him a mighty blow before he could protect himself.

Lerme still had strength enough to draw his sword, however, and to pierce the Baron's right arm; the latter dropped his own sword because of the pain he felt. Lerme tried to pick it up, but he was so weakened by the blood he had lost that he fell, in such a manner that it was hidden beneath him. He still had his own sword in his hand, and Silva, trying to snatch if from him, received a blow in the face that caused him to enter into an extreme fury.

The combat could only have had deadly consequences if many people had not come running and obliged the Baron to flee. He had commenced the combat, and would not have been excusable with regard to the king for having fought in his palace and almost under his eyes; with the result that Don Luis, who was one of those who had been drawn by the noise, let him escape through a small door that he found open.

As everyone had followed Prince Don Juan and Don Luis's house was not far way, it was easy for Baron de Silva to go there without being seen by many people. Initial dressings were put on his wounds, which were not dangerous, and in the evening he was transported to a less well-known place.

Meanwhile, the Marquis de Lerme, having lost a lot of blood, remained lying where he was, and the rumor ran around that he was dead. Ines, whose chagrins had not ceased for a long time, could not sustain that final attack, and fainted in the arms of one of the queen's maids of honor. Even Leonor was not insensible to the news, and was fortunate that learning that her brother had been wounded enabled her to hide her disturbance.

The Marquis de Lerme was carried away, and it was perceived that he was not lifeless. The king was extremely angry that swords had been drawn so close to him. He ordered the Duke de Lerme, his father, to answer for his person until he was healed. The physicians did not think his wound dangerous and his friends tried to soothe the king's wrath by representing to him that his only crime had been to defend himself.

Prince Don Juan, who had known Lerme in Toledo, employed himself on his behalf with a great deal of ardor, but he could not prevent the king from exiling the Marquis to Alcala.

Baron de Silva, knowing full well that he was the more guilty, left Madrid in secret, where a search had been mounted for him, and went to Seville, where he married a young woman with whom he fell in love, whose birth was very disproportionate to his. As what he had felt for Ines was less a passion than a design to marry her, that design, although formed, had not been able to sustain itself against absence.

Leonor was in despair at that marriage; she could no longer see any means of avenging herself on Lerme, and she deferred marrying Don Luis.

Lerme was rid of a rival, but the displeasure of being distanced from Ines would not allow him to savor that repose. Every man appeared to him to be a rival, and might have been. He thought many a time that Ines shared the chagrin of his absence, but that was not seeing her.

Prince Don Juan came as far as Alcala to visit him, and the amity of that prince would have consoled him, if a lover could be consoled apart from his mistress. The liaison between Don Juan and the Marquis had commenced in their childhood; they had learned their exercises together in Toledo, the school of all the young noblemen of the court. Don Juan, who was still believed at that time to be the son of Quijada, was honored by the fact that Lerme had distinguished him from the others in befriending him, and since he had been recognized as the son of Charles V, he had only wanted to be regarded on the same footing.

After Lerme had been in Alcala for five or six months, it was discovered that new rebellions were being fomented in Flanders. Prince Don Carlos had an extreme desire to go there at the head of the troops that were to be sent, but the king, who did not want to render him the master of so many forces, for fear that he might abuse his power, gave command of the troops to the Duke of Alba.[9]

The Marquis de Lerme had already signaled his valor in several encounters; is fens, and Prince Don Juan above all, took that opportunity to ask for mercy for him, and had no difficulty obtaining it.

---

[9] Fernando Alvarez de Toledo, third Duke of Alba, became known as the Iron Duke because of his military exploits in the Netherlands. He had represented Philip as his proxy in the marriage to Elisabeth. The Duke of Alba went to Brussels at the head of an army in order to put down unrest associated with Calvinist iconoclasm, sand remained there until 1567; the other events cited in the story in this passage occurred in 1568.

Ines saw her lover again for a few days, but the prohibitions on speaking to him were redoubled, and after having been such a long time without seeing him, it was a species of hindrance for her, less cruel, in truth, than absence, but crueler than all her other woes. He tried to see her in private; she wanted that, contrary to the common run of amour. That was not enough; fortune did not favor them.

Lerme departed with the Duke of Alba, and was fortunate in all the employments that the general gave him. The rebellions in Flanders were calmed for some time by the severity of the Duke of Alba, who had the Counts of Horn and Egmont, the leaders of the revolt, arrested.

The Duke of Alba having established a kind of tranquility, sent the Marquis de Lerme back with a few troops and remained in Flanders to maintain what he had done.

Lerme returned to Madrid and found sad changes there.

The Princess of Eboli, no longer being able to suffer the indifference of Don Carlos, had commenced to hate him cruelly, and took care to inspire that hatred in her husband. He already had a strong desire to harm the prince because, having been his tutor, he had always treated him so harshly that he would have dreaded having him for a master. They conspired to doom him, and convinced the king that the prince had criminal liaisons with the queen, and as everyone knows, Philip II, who was violent and pitiless by nature, condemned that only son to death, who chose for a method of execution having his veins cut in a bath. A short time afterwards, he had the queen—who, as one can imagine, was not exempt from his fury—poisoned, even though she was pregnant.[10]

---

[10] Generally-accepted history asserts that the mentally-defective Carlos died of natural causes and that Elisabeth died as a result of a miscarriage, but the idea that Philip had caused both deaths, especially the former, became an element of the anti-Spanish propaganda later dubbed the "Black Legend," which was primarily an English hate-campaign, but also spread to France.

The Marquis de Lerme arrived on the day of that death; he found Philip II in a sufficiently tranquil state to give him a audience and to discuss with him everything that had happened in Flanders; he was even so unfortunate in that conference that it pleased his master, who, being obliged to send news of Lisa's death to France, to honor him with that employment. He also charged him with making a secret treaty with Charles IX and Catherine de Medici against the Huguenots, who had considerable persons for leaders.

Lerme received that mark of esteem with a dolor that he was constrained to hide beneath an external gratitude. It was necessary to go away from Ines again; he put at the same rank his past disgrace and the honors that had followed it, and they appeared to him to be a long sequence of misfortunes.

The disorder into which everything had been thrown by the queen's death enabled him to find a means of seeing Ines on the eve of his departure; in the evening he slipped into the cabinet where she was alone. To begin with, Ines was surprised to see Lerme in that place, and the unfortunate consequences that the meeting might have for her reputation were presented to her mind, but those reflection ceded to the pleasure of seeing him and speaking to him.

They gave one another an exact account of all the sentiments they had had in their disgrace, and saw very clearly by the manner in which they loved one another that they would love one another forever, but they did not fail nevertheless to ask one another for mutual assurances.

"You cannot doubt the sincerity of my heart, and I cannot doubt the sincerity of yours," the Marquis said to Ines. "But after all, tell me that I will never lose it. There will be other Barons de Silva; will you always be able to resist the will of a father? Answer to me for events; remember that I am the most unfortunate of all men. I love you, but I never see you, and a cruel presentiment makes me fear my return as much as I wish for it."

"When one is loved as you are, what does one have to fear?" replied Ines.

"It is my happiness that causes my anxiety," he told her. "I know what you are worth; I have attached myself to you without reserve, and if it is necessary for me to separate myself from you, what would remain of me? What happiness could I promise myself, if I were to lose the least of your sentiments?"

"You will have these alarms for a long time," she said to him, "if you have them as long as you are loved, but know me; trust in my heart, in my sentiments, and more than anything, in yourself. Who could I love, except for the Marquis de Lerme? Is there anyone in the world who could not reassure him? If it is only necessary to answer to you for events, believe that your absence has made me know only too well the torture of living without you, and if I did not have the hope of one day being yours, I would renounce life. Do you not see that I can never change, and that the present is a pledge of the future?"

They talked for a lot longer, and had the leisure to explain all their thoughts to one another. However, when they had parted, they discovered many things that they had forgotten to say. Lerme left without being seen by anyone, and the next day, he left for France.

The queen was given a magnificent funeral, and all the maids of honor were dismissed. Ines returned to the house of Don Luis; he treated her as a disobedient daughter, and gave her a room for a prison. She did not see anyone to whom she could confide her dolors, but what fortified her passion was that, in removing all help from her, she thought about it incessantly, and had never loved Lerme as much as when she no longer heard any mention of him. She remained in that state for several months

Meanwhile, Leonor having been unable to conclude avenging herself on the Marquis de Lerme, still conserved the desire to do so. Although she found advantages in regard to fortune in marrying Don Luis, she had always deferred the marriage for fear of seeing the love of a husband relent, and being less able to make him do everything that she appeared to wish.

She had not dared to press him to make his daughter marry while the queen had been able to protect her, but the queen no longer being there, she made him understand that she was finally resolved to marry him, provided that he thought of an establishment for Ines before marrying herself, because it was not possible for her always to have before her eyes a person she blamed for all her brother's misfortunes.

Don Luis, still in love, did not fail to approve those reasons, and thought of ridding himself as soon as possible of any subject of delay. He cast his eyes upon the Count of Medina de Las Torres,[11] recently arrived at the court, and who was already advanced in age. He had known Lerme since the last war, but having always been out of Madrid, he was unaware of his passion for Ines.

Don Luis took him to his daughter's room, and told her that he destined him for her husband. La Torres saw her without looking at her, and half the charms of her face were lost on him; it was not that he feared being too attached to beauty; on the contrary, one could say that the scant knowledge he had of that peril, guaranteed him against it.

Ines emerged from the sad repose of which she had made a habit. Retreat had enabled her to savor a certain mildness that she believed would no longer be troubled, and she had hoped at least to have nothing more to regret than the absence of the Marquis de Lerme, but Don Luis's harshness went as far as not even allowing her that dolorous pleasure in all its purity, and she had to mingle with it the dread of no longer appearing to be as faithful to him as she had promised. She asked for time to resolve herself to the marriage, and as she was only given a week, she sought a means of employing it to reach a place of safety. A convent appeared to her to be the only refuge from her father. That was, it is true, to renounce he

---

[11] This title did not exist in the 1560s; Philip IV was subsequently to create the title of Duke of Medina de Las Torres in the seventeenth century.

Marquis forever, but she would not belong to anyone else, and she wrote him this letter:

The authority of my father is prevailing over my promises but not over my passion; he wants to force me to marry. In order to avoid such a cruel destiny, I have made the resolution to retire to a place where I will have no other possession than thinking of you in liberty, and I prefer that to all the other possessions in the world,

Seeing that her tears and pleas were futile, Ines pretended to accept the party who had been proposed to her, in order to have more liberty to follow her design, and on the eve of the day destined for her marriage to the Count of Las Torres she left with Elvire, one of the maids that had already been given to her to serve her, and whom she had won over by her mildness. They went to a house of nuns whose abbess was the sister of Don Luis.

Ines's aunt had always testified a particular amity to her, and, on seeing her come to her in tears to as for her protection, she did not refuse it.

Elvire went to tell the Count that her mistress had resolved not to return, and to become a nun. Las Torres was surprised, and went immediately to look for Don Luis in order to tell him the news. The father, who wanted to be obeyed, was beside himself with anger, Leonor was in despair; the mark of constancy that Ines was about to give the Marquis de Lerme in renouncing everything for him would engage him to love her forever. Ines even had a year to deliberate before taking her vows. That was too long a delay for Leonor's vengeance, and even for the amour of Don Luis, to whom she had protested that she would never marry him until Ines was married.

An opportunity to intimidate Ines soon presented itself. The Marquis de Lerme could not remain firm in his duty on learning that she was about to be lost to him. His reason abandoned him; he left France, putting all is affairs in the hands of a man he trusted, and without considering that he was committing a crime against the state, he only listened to his amour.

The diligence with which he made his journey was what prevented him from arriving soon enough. Fatigue and chagrin caused him to fall ill, and the news of his departure preceded him by several days. Philip II, who was too severe to pardon a fault of that nature, combining anger with his natal harshness, had him arrested near Madrid and had him tried by the Council of State. Don Luis de Cordova was the president, Las Torres held the second rank, and their authority, with their credit, rendered them masters of his destiny. His death or perpetual imprisonment were the penalties that could be imposed on him. Death was proportionate to the severity of the master and would frighten those who might have been capable of failing in their duty. Perpetual imprisonment was proportionate to the crime; so those two decisions were, in a sense, at the choice of the judges.

Don Luis let his daughter know that there was a means of saving the life of the Marquis de Lerme, whose enemy he only was because she loved him; that if she resolved to marry the Count of Las Torres, they would join forces to lessen the sentence that would be rendered against Lerme.

Ines was not proof against such threats. Her resistance was at an end, and although she thought that her constancy, mortal as it would be for Lerme, would be more agreeable to her than the life she wanted to conserve for him, her more pressing duty was, however, to save him.

She told her father that since he had contributed himself to giving birth to her inclination for Lerme, she confessed to him that the sole view of extracting him from peril could determine her and that, in order to marry Las Torres she would wait until Lerme's life was safe.

Leonor did not hate Lerme enough to want his death. His long imprisonment, which was the only mercy that could be granted to him, made it impossible for her to think of a marriage with him, so she gave her word to Don Luis that she would marry him on the same day that Ines married Las Torres.

The Council was held; a few judges opined for death, but thanks to Don Luis and Las Torres, the majority of the votes were in favor of perpetual imprisonment.

Don Luis married Leonor, and Ines married Las Torres, whose heart, having never known amour, was engaged by the marriage. As he had only ever had feeble desires, they were augmented by his happiness.

When Ines had married the Count of Las Torres and she saw herself beyond any possibility of ever belonging to Lerme, or even thinking about him without scruple she was surprised to have thrown herself into that abyss. The difference between her present misfortune and her past misfortune appeared very great; everything importuned her mind and everything seemed to her to be a new obstacle to her sentiments.

She even found herself constrained in a way by Elvire, who was entirely hers and whom the Count of Las Torres had returned to her. Her dolor was ashamed of appearing in other eyes with so much violence and so much transport. The dread she had of explaining herself made her sense so keenly how much the movements of her heart must seem suspect. If she had only been by herself she would never have thought that such an unfortunate amour could be a crime. Vanquished, however, by the pleas of Elvire, to whom she had never disclosed her sentiments and who could not sustain the sight of her tears, and pressed by her inclination to talk about Lerme, she confessed to her, excusing herself in a manner that made it appear that she was not entirely excusable.

The Marquis de Lerme had been taken to Madrid; he was a prisoner there, and was guarded with the utmost rigor; he was not allowed to speak to anyone or receive any letter, with the result that the destiny of Ines was absolutely unknown to him. The uncertainty regarding his mistress was a cruel redoubling of his woes. For her part, the Countess of Las Torres was mortally afflicted by the pains that he was suffering for her, and her eyes were always bathed with tears.

Elvire, with whom she was accustomed to talk about her passion, sought everything that might console her, and opportunities to serve her soon presented themselves. Elvire's brother was appointed as Lerme's guard in the absence of the lieutenant of the castle where he was interned. However, she did not commence by telling the Countess that news, but represented to her that Lerme was worthy of being given some relief by means of her letters, assuring her that nothing was impossible, provided that the will was not lacking.

That discourse astonished the virtue of the Countess at first; she even rejected it as chimerical; then she became accustomed to suffering it as such. The misfortunes to which Lerme had been reduced for having loved her demanded that she soften them, out of pity and justice, even if amour had not had a part to play.

Gradually, she succeeded in no longer being embarrassed by the difficulty of success; then Elvire told her that her brother was able to render her the service. The facility of failing in her duty was another new obstacle for Ines, but as the project had pleased her when it was impossible, it finally pleased her when it became easy.

She wanted to write to Lerme, but where could she begin? How could she tell him, in the midst of all that he was suffering, that she had been unable to avoid belonging to another? Could a letter be sufficient to excuse her in such a conjuncture?

"What will he say, my dear Elvire," she cried, "to the fact that I have not been able to keep my promises? He'll believe me to be weak and light, no matter what I write to him. Can I find reasonable terms to accord my marriage with my sentiments?"

Seeing by that embarrassment that she had more desire to see Lerme than to write to him, Elvire only sought to favor that.

After having agreed with herself that a letter would only put Lerme in a crueler state than the one from which she wanted to remove him, the Countess resolved to see him in the prison if she could; he merited that favor as much by his misfortunes as the sentiments that she had for him. He had letters from her that she told herself that it was her duty to ask to be returned. In sum, she found virtuous reasons for that which amour alone made her undertake.

Elvire got her brother to consent to everything she asked of him, because he saw little risk for himself in letting Lerme see women who had to keep the secret for their own sake, and because care had been taken to gain him with considerable bribes.

Elvire told the Countess of the success of the negotiations—who, seeing that it was in her power to tell Lerme that she was married, only looked forward to that moment with terror.

"This is the last day that he will love me!" she cried. "I am going to take all hope away from him, and yet I cannot suffer the slightest diminution of his tenderness; it's quite sufficient that my duty forces me to combat mine."

She sent Elvire with a letter that prepared him to see her, which did not inform him of her marriage.

Meanwhile, changes had arrived in Lerme's fortune.

Prince Don Juan, who had only applied himself to means of serving him, had allowed the initial transports of Philip II's wrath to pass, and in order to act more surely had remained inactive for some time. He had even pretended to forget his friend and to share the king's anger, in order to have more facility to cause him to lose it.

The conjuncture arrived. Don Juan gave birth in the king to the desire to converse himself with the prisoner regarding the negotiations he had begun in France, and gradually, he came to excuse him for the violence of passions that merited the pardon of faults in a man who was committing them for the first time. Lerme's passion for Ines was not unknown, and he had no doubt that amour was entirely responsible for his crime. The king had always liked the young man, so his mercy was taken to him and he was be freed at when he least expected it.

At that moment, Elvire came on the part of the Countess. Lerme's first concern was to ask her whether Ines was married and where she was—in sum, whether she still loved him. Elvire, who knew that her mistress was reserving it to herself to give him such cruel news, which could only be announced by a dear person, told him that he had reason to be content with amour, and finally, when he pressed her on the matter of Ines's marriage and not responding would have been a confession, she told him that Ines could still be his.

That word having reassured him, he no longer thought of anything but seeing her.

As the Countess of Las Torres had resolved to speak to him during the day, Elvire asked Lerme if he could go with her to the place she indicated to him, which was not far away. Lerme having assured her that his only concern was to see Ines, he sent word to Prince Don Juan, who had told him that he would take him to the feet of Philip II in the afternoon, also to give him the morning in order to be more in a state to appear before him. He allowed Elvire to conduct him to an apartment that was at her disposal because the master was absent.

One of his domestics, from whom he had never had any secrets, with the consent of Ines, had orders to take note of the place and to come and find him at the hour prescribed by Don Juan.

When Elvire was sure of the Marquis de Lerme and she had told the Countess of Las Torres that he was waiting for her and that she was the mistress of finding him, all the latter's combats were redoubled, and on the point of departing, she realized that she was not yet resolved.

That step seemed terrible to her, and a presentiment of disgrace combined with the timidity that amour and virtue produce delayed her for such a long time that the Count of Las Torres returned home before she had gone out. He told her that he was going that day to give a few orders on the king's behalf to the man who was supervising the buildings of the Escorial.

That house is seven leagues from Madrid, so he assured her that he would not return until the following day, and left her the mistress of giving the Marquis de Lerme more time than she had thought that she would be able to give him. Scruples returned in a host to the mind of the Countess, but she felt drawn by them before having vanquished them, and before being fully determined to depart she left, hidden under Elvire's garments.

She walked, alone and trembling, toward the place here the Marquis de Lerme was.

Elvire remained in her mistress's room, in order to tell the Count, if he returned for some unexpected reason, that the Countess was asleep in her cabinet.

Fortunately, the Countess had not been recognized by anyone, and she arrived at the indicated house. But she had delayed for so long that it was the time when Lerme had to go to the palace, and she found the man who had come to warn him that Prince Don Juan was waiting for him in order to present him to the king.

Seeing the error she had made by her delays, the Countess wanted to repair it by obliging Lerme to depart promptly. She could dispose of the rest of the day. How could she tell Lerme, in a word, that she was married to Las Torres? How could she deprive herself of the pleasure of lamenting it and consoling him for it, since she owed it to him to speak for the last time?

She told him to go, and, seeing that he was frightened by the proposition, that he persisted in remaining, that he assured her that in his view nothing could compare with the pleasure of seeing her, and that he had even sent away the man who had come to see him on behalf of Don Juan, she told him that if he left instantly, she would wait for him in that place.

He still resisted, and could not resolve to abandon her. Finally, charmed by that tenderness, she feared that he might fall back into some inconvenience and that Don Juan might get tired of waiting. She protested that if he did not go to see the king right away, she would leave the house and never see him again.

He implored her at least to say something to console him. She told him, albeit with timidity, that she was taking a great enough step to be dispensed of assuring him of her sentiments.

Elvire had made him understand that Ines was not married; he was content with that, and he was about to go see the king with a sort of satisfaction, but they immediately found an obstacle that nearly defeated all their plans.

The Countess of Las Torres, who wanted to remain in the apartment for a part of the day, found that the doors there could only be unlocked from the inside by a secret mechanism unknown to her, which was only known to the master of the house. That is common enough among the Spaniards, whom jealousy obliges to take extreme precautions against their wives.

She hesitated as to whether she ought to remain, but her misfortunes did not stop there, and one runs before one's destiny. She did not have the leisure to make a mature deliberation. If the opportunity were lost it could not be recovered; the greatest step was taken, with the consequence that, determined by her heart, she told the Marquis to take the key to the apartment and hurry to return. It was not necessary for her to order him to do that, and he flew, so to speak, to see the king in order to be able to return sooner.

Meanwhile, the Countess remained in a state that cannot be described. As soon as she no longer saw the Marquis and she was able to make reflections she thought a part of what she had already thought before coming, but there is a difference between thinking about steps when they are to be taken and when they are done. She was already leaning toward repentance.

The moments seemed to her to be insupportably long. She feared that Lerme might not be the master of returning, as their desires and the pressure of circumstance had persuaded them, and she also feared that absence might have relented Lerme's passion, and that it might no longer have the same urgency, although she had been convinced of the contrary by his eyes.

Unfortunate lovers are not unfortunate enough if they only have veritable woes. Her imagination forgot nothing of all that could make it despair.

Don Juan presented Lerme to the king, who, after having pardoned him, nevertheless received him with a severe expression. Lerme had thought that he would be able to leave promptly, but the king told him that he was retaining him for the whole day because he wanted to talk to him in depth about French affairs.

"Come into my cabinet," he said, with a grave smile. "I don't believe that, on emerging from prison, it will be difficult for you to spend an afternoon locked up with me."

Lerme shivered at that order; death would have been less cruel for him. He did not know how to get out of the difficulty. The Countess had told him to come back promptly and she could not get out of the place where she was unless he opened the door. To resist Philip II and be arrested was not a means of getting out of it; pretexts were impossible to find in the disturbance he was in, and would not have been received; the truth could not be spoken without indiscretion; everyone knew the person with whom he was in love.

In that extremity he looked in all directions to see whether Don Juan had gone, and, not being able to see him any longer, nor any of his friends, except for the Count of Las Torres, who had returned to see the king before going to the Escorial, he addressed himself to him. He embraced him while the king's head was turned and put the key in his hands, imploring him by everything he held most dear to go to the house that he indicated to him and merely open the door of the apartment of which he had given him the key and not to ask any questions.

Lerme did not know the name of the person that Ines had been afraid of marrying; she had not identified him when she had written to him because she had resolved to enter a convent.

The Count of Las Torres assured him that he would render him that service as he desired. Services of that sort are sometimes rendered in Spain with sufficient fidelity; he was more appropriate than another for that employment, and the scant vivacity of his mind removed his curiosity regarding amorous intrigues. He was the only man in the court to whom Lerme believed that Ines was unknown, because he was not in Spain when she was in the queen's household. In sum, not allowing himself to foresee unfortunate consequences for his amour in informing his mistress of the reasons that obliged him to take that eccentric step, had set his mind somewhat at rest in having found, in that pressing need, a means of setting her free.

The Countess, equally tormented by remorse and dread, had stationed herself at a small window and was looking it impatiently to see whether Lerme was coming back. She perceived her husband in the distance, and that sight made her go pale; but how her fear redoubled when she saw him stop and enter the house where she was. What did she not think then? What state even approaches that one in which she found herself?

Meanwhile, a natural sentiment urging her to avoid his wrath, she searched in all directions and saw a small door, which she pushed rudely, and which, being poorly sealed, opened. She closed it again behind her and went into another apartment, which was that of the master of the house. She found no one there but a woman, whom she implored to save her life and to enable her to get out of the place. The woman, touched by the state in which she saw such a beautiful person, conducted her into a back street, where Elvire's mother lived, to whose home she went.

The Count of Las Torres had reflected on the disorder of the Marquis and the urgent manner in which he had come to beg him to open that door. All the difficulties that he had found in his marriage to Ines had not permitted him to be unaware of the passion they had had for one another, and he feared that she might have a part in this adventure. In that case, however, the Marquis would not have chosen him for such an employment; in consequence, that circumstance could have reassured him; but he feared it, even though he did not believe it. Lerme had asked him to take discretion as far as having no curiosity; all that caused him umbrage, because he had a extreme passion for his wife.

In sum, however, it is understandable that on this occasion, the instinct of verity prevailed over the appearances that were perhaps contrary to it; he went into the apartment to which Lerme had given him the key without discriminating the sentiment that as making him act. He visited the whole house and, not finding the Countess there, he went to his own house to see whether she was there.

As soon as she had recovered from the fear that she had been in for her life, the uncertainty of what would become of her became a thousand time crueler. She had he leisure to sense all her misfortunes and to see their cause. She was able to think that the Marquis de Lerme, having learned of her marriage to Las Torres, had not been able to contain his fury at first, and had delivered her to her husband himself, but that idea seemed so cruel that she no longer found it plausible. Finally, she imagined something like the truth, and, thinking about the calamity of precautions that fortune does not second, she sank into mortal ideas from which she could not escape.

Constrained by the state she was in to confide in someone, she begged Elvire's mother to go to the Count of Las Torres's house and find out what was happening there.

The Marquis de Lerme had satisfied the king in regard to all the questions he had asked him, and toward the end of the day, having got away from him, he ran to the place where he had left Ines in order to discover whether she had got out of it and whether, by a good fortune that he dared not expect, she might have left an address of the place where she had gone; but he found nothing that could give him the slightest indication.

That adventure afflicted him greatly; he did not know what Ines would think of him; she did not know the reasons that had retained him with the king; she might cause him of negligence, perhaps of infidelity or scorn. Everything could appear plausible to a person who had made such a considerable step and who found himself left thus, and although he had almost expected what had happened to him at that moment, he was not prepared for it.

He set forth for the Count of Las Torres's house, in order to ask him whether he had done what he promised.

Everything there was in an extreme disorder. The Count, having come home in order to calm his suspicions, had asked for his wife; Elvire had replied to him that she was asleep in her cabinet, but he was not content with that response; he had demanded the key, with the consequence that Elvire, pretending to go to fetch it, had gone out in order to inform her mistress of what had happened; but had not found her. After having searched in all the places that seemed to her to be most probable, she encountered the Marquis de Lerme, who was going to the Las Torres house.

She told the lover about the disorder that everything was in at the Count's house because he had not found his wife, letting him know by that all that he still did not know about Ines's marriage.

He was no longer master of his despair; he understood what he had done, and he discovered so many misfortunes at once that, unable to sustain all his thoughts, he drew his sword and stabbed himself before Elvire realized his intention. She called people to help her, and he was carried to his father's house, where the wound, contrary to his intention, was not found to be mortal.

Meanwhile, Elvire, not finding her mistress and not daring to return to the Las Torres house, went to her mother's house, where she found her. She told her the sad news about her master's fury and the Marquis de Lerme's despair.

Ines was in a state of collapse that rendered her almost insensible to her woes; they were too great to be sensed. However, she could not remain for long in that state. She sent Elvire to obtain news of the Marquis's wound, and, having learned that it was curable, she found that she was till susceptible to joy; but it was necessary to seek a remedy for her other troubles, and there was a new one, which was the embarrassment of finding a safer retreat; she feared, with reason, that the place where she was might be discovered, and that Elvire's mother, who had withdrawn, might be exposed to some violence.

She could not see any security in Madrid, with the consequence that, after much uncertainty, she determined to follow the fortune of Elvire's widowed mother, who was not without some wealth. She had the design of spending the rest of her days in a house in the country she owned, not far from Seville. She offered it as a retreat to the Countess of Las Torres, and the Countess bought, by means of the gift of a few precious stones she had about her person, a refuge appropriate to her means.

Elvire, being in peril in Madrid, left that same night with the Countess of Las Torres, who disguised herself so well that she arrived at Elvire's mother's house without obstacle.

There, she made it a duty to forget everything; that was the only remedy for her woes. Her published adventure had destroyed her reputation; her father did not love her; her husband no longer had any esteem for her; and finally, she was separated forever from her lover. So many reasons or quitting the world—but that lover had wanted to die for the love he had for her. How difficult it was to forget that!

It was only by means of a kind of forgetfulness of herself that she could go on to the end.

She never abandoned Elvire, and, their house being isolated on the edge of a forest, they had not made any acquaintance. The Countess did not even know the names of their neighbors; they had heard it said that the houses of a few noblemen were not far away, but for her that was a reason to remain hidden and to avoid any sort of encounter.

They sometimes went for walks in the forest. That solitude was their only pleasure; with the consequence that, by dint of reflections on the embarrassment and on the chagrin even in the greatest sweetness of life, they succeeded in no longer doing anything, and enjoyed a repose that they had never found in society.

Before leaving Madrid, the Countess of Las Torres had left a letter with Elvire's mother and had begged her to ensure that the Count of Las Torres could read it. The woman, with her veil lowered, had given it the next day to one of the Count's domestics to give to him, without telling him who she was.

That letter contained a sincere confession of the sentiments that Ines had had for the Marquis de Lerme, which had been authorized by Don Luis before acquiring so much force. She gave him an account of the last step she had made for him, and which reason had partly inspired. Finally, she told him that, criminal by virtue of the failure of her project, she did not dare appear before him; that, even so, he might finally be persuaded of the innocence of her conduct, that what he learned by that about her sentiments would give him chagrin, and her confusion; and that he was not to search for her, that he would not find her, but that at least she was lost to the rest of the word and to herself, since she was to him.

At first, that letter did not have the effect that she expected of it. He made further searches for his wife in all the houses of Madrid and the surrounding area; but, not finding her, the thought of losing such a beautiful person forever forced him to regret her. The Marquis de Lerme's wound and the languor in which he remained made him think that he was unfortunate; the ingenuousness he had had in giving him the keys to the place where Ines was locked obliged him to find that what she had said in the letter was true.

Time, which causes the greatest anger to relent, enabled the Count of Las Torres to make all these reflections, but he might perhaps have been cured of his passion in the end, if an adventure had not forced him to remember his wife.

She was walking with Elvire one evening in the grounds of their house, surrounded by a living hedge, when they saw a man on horseback enter though a breach, whose appearance as that of a person of quality. The Countess of Las Torres even thought that she remarked in him features that she knew. As she did not have her veil, she turned her head, and Elvire went to meet him.

He asked pardon for his enterprise, and told her that he had been attacked by thieves, one of whom he had killed with a pistol shot. He had fled from the rest of the band, and had been on the point of falling into their hands when he had discovered the breach by which he had entered the place. He asked for permission to go out on the other side. The thieves, having seen him disappear and seeing the houses, feared having gone too far and turned back.

Meanwhile, the Countess of Las Torres had retired into the house for fear of being recognized by the man, whom she dreaded was the Baron de Silva.

Elvire, having given him the means to get out, came to find her. They discussed together the misfortune of unexpected encounters that rendered precautions futile, and thought about the peril that the Countess of Las Torres would have in being recognized. She was anxious about it all night, but in the end, she was not entirely sure that it was Baron de Silva, and the necessity of staying in the refuge forced her to calm down.

It was, indeed, the Baron, slightly changed by the wound he had received in the face from the Marquis de Lerme. The king, in response to Leonor's solicitation, had pardoned him for having fought in his palace, but the fact of his wife not being of a birth to appear at court engaged him to remain almost perpetually in Seville. He had gone astray that evening while hunting, and that had caused his latest adventure.

He had known from Leonor the entire story of the Countess of Las Torres, and her face had truck him immediately; her prompt retreat had confirmed that thought that it was her, with the consequence that he had not doubted it for a moment. He had loved her enough to hate her and he did not waste that opportunity to harm her. He wrote to Leonor the next day that he had found the Countess of Las Torres.

Leonor, whose hatred had not been soothed by all her rival's misfortunes, did not delay in informing the Count of Las Torres; and, giving that retreat the blackest colors that she could, she put his mind in a cruel situation. He left for Seville without having examined closely what he wanted to do. If he believed his desires, the Countess of Las Torres was scarcely culpable, but she appeared much more so if he believed Leonor.

Baron de Silva, who informed him of the place where the Countess of Las Torres was, inspired in him the sentiments of vengeance that he had himself, with the consequence that the husband entered her house full of fury. He was alone; Baron de Silva had quit him on the threshold.

He asked for the Countess of Las Torres, and a domestic who did not know her by that name told him that he had apparently mistaken the house for another. He entered without listening and, opening a door violently, he came into the room where she was with his sword in his hand.

The Countess, whose troubles had detached her from life, received him with sufficient firmness; nevertheless, the surprise of seeing her husband in that place, and a kind of agitation inseparable from the idea of death, even when one is scornful of it, cast a fire in her eyes and colored her complexion in a manner very advantageous to her beauty.

The Count of Las Torres dropped his sword.

"Oh, if you believe me culpable," she said to him, picking it up and returning it to him, "why spare me in the state to which I am reduced? There is less cruelty in taking my life than in conserving it."

She could not retain her tears as she spoke those words.

The Count of Las Torres did not have the strength to reply to her. He looked at her in a manner that enabled her to judge that he only saw that she was beautiful.

Then, finally, without raising his eyes to her face, he said: "Who could not believe you innocent, Madame? For myself, I don't know whether you're deceiving me, but I can't think so, and I don't want to do you any more harm."

With that, they shed a torrent of tears. The Countess of Las Torres told her husband everything that had happened, without disguising anything. He showed her so much tenderness that, in spite of the sentiment of her own woes, she could not refuse him her compassion. He told her everything that had happened since she had left Madrid.

As Leonor and Baron de Silva had solicited him to vengeance, and he was in one of those moments of the overflow of the heart in which one cannot hide anything, he begged her to return to Madrid, and told her that since he was sure of her virtue, it was necessary to let everyone know it. But she did not want to reestablish herself in the opinion; he was more scornful of it than she was. In addition, she feared for the tranquility of her heart; it appeared dangerous to her to be within range of seeing the Marquis, and even if she did not encounter him, the mere thought that it might be possible to encounter him at any moment would be sufficient to trouble her. She begged her husband to allow her to enjoy the peace that a long series of disgraces and reflections had acquired for her, and her pleas, as much as her arguments, made him consent to her remaining in the country.

The king had given him a rather important employment that obliged him to return to Flanders, and he only engaged the Countess to change location and to establish herself near Madrid in one of his lands, where she could exist in a manner more appropriate to her quality. She accepted the offer.

Elvire accompanied her, with her husband's consent; he could not refuse that consolation to a wife whose virtue he recognized involuntarily. As soon as she was established in the place of her solitude, he went to Flanders, and left her there in a state different from the one in which he had found her. She was no longer a person detached from passions of any sort, and her tenderness for Lerme had reawakened while she was trying to justify herself to her husband. She found herself innocent, since he had judged her thus. Her scruples weakened every day, and a tender melancholy reigned in her soul, which was not without a sort of dolor.

The Duchess of Feria[12] had a country house not far from that of the Count of Las Torres; she stayed there almost permanently, and curiosity had obliged her to come and visit the Countess on the rumor of her adventure. The Countess returned her visits, and as they had no other neighbors, they saw one another often.

Meanwhile, the rumor of the return of the Countess spread in Madrid. The Marquis de Lerme, who did not know what she had thought since he had, so to speak, delivered her to her husband, came quite often in disguise to prowl around the house, in the attempt to encounter her.

One day, when she had gone to see the Duchess de Feria, she got down from her carriage momentarily in order to take a walk. She was leaning on Elvire, and her domestics were following her at a distance. She saw a man enveloped in a cloak, who removed it a soon as he saw her; although her veil was lowered he judged by her appearance that it was the Countess of Las Torres. It did not take her long, either, to recognize the Marquis de Lerme, in spite of the pallor of his complexion.

The surprise of the Countess, at that unexpected sight, was extreme, and her disturbance was so great that it caused a kind of tremor. She was constrained to sit down on a heap of grass that was nearby. Elvire lifted up her veil slightly in order to give her a little air, and she saw Lerme, who dared not approach, gazing at her in a timid and respectful fashion, which augmented her disturbance,. She could not help shedding a few tears, and she had a desire to speak to him. However, the same reason that made her want that prevented her from doing

---

[12] Jane Dormer, Duchess of Feria (1538-1612) had been a lady-in-waiting to Queen Mary before marrying Gomez Suarez de Figuroa, Duke of Feria; when he died in 1571 she took over the management of his estates. The daughter Casilde with whom the story credits her is, however, entirely fictitious.

so, for the moment, and gave her such a great timidity that, without knowing what she ought to do, she retraced her steps as soon as she had the strength to walk; but it was not without darting a glance at Lerme that made him reparation for her flight.

Lerme, who had the same timidity, combined with respect and the dread of giving some suspicion to the domestics who were following her, let her depart without daring to approach her. The misfortunes that he had caused her rendered him even more circumspect.

When she was back home, and saw that there was no possibility of seeing the Marquis, she was surprised that she had avoided him.

Would I have compromised my virtue, she asked herself, *if I had heard from an unfortunate person the confirmation of his innocence? I could have told him the reasons that had obliged me to marry someone else, and I could have begged him to cease to love me, and I would have been more tranquil for it. What must he have thought of the promptitude with which I fled him? The pallor that I remarked in his face did not cause me to hazard a word of consolation; perhaps he believed that it was an effect of the indifference that I have acquired by mans of solitude.*

Alas, she added, *I wish to Heaven that I had reached that point, but since that cannot be, at least may he not believe it.*

There was, however, enough reason to judge the matter thus for that thought not to quit her and it afflicted her excessively that she sometimes resolved to find a means of talking to Lerme, however perilous it might be, but she believed that she had lost the opportunity by her own fault, and that he would no longer look for her after having seen her avoid him.

In addition, in spite of her penchant, she dreaded that such a step might be too contrary to her duty; her husband had testified so much amour and generosity to her that she was engaged to sacrifice that residue of inclination to him, but after all, she could not vanquish it, and only sought to reconcile it with her virtue.

For his part, Lerme had remarked all the tenderness and all the rigor of the Countess. He was torn between dolor and a kind of joy; he had found in the gaze of the Countess the wherewithal to maintain his passion, even though her conduct robbed him of all hope.

He searched hard for opportunities to see her again. He knew that she often went to see the Duchess of Feria, and the Duc de Lerme, his father, who was the first Gentlemen of the King's Chamber, rendered a considerable service to the Duchess, which gave the Marquis a reason to enter into some liaison with her.

She came to Madrid to thank the king for the favor he had done her, and, knowing that the Duke de Lerme had made a considerable contribution to it, she marked her gratitude in the terms that the office merited. He had the design to marry his son to Casilde, the daughter of the duchess, and it was with that in view that he had rendered her the service.

The Marquis, to whom he communicated his design, did not want to ruin by too much sincerity the only means he had of seeing the Countess of Las Torres; he allowed him to hope that he might resolve himself to it, on condition that he was allowed to know the character of Casilde particularly before any proposition of marriage was made.

The Duchess of Feria soon returned to her country house; the Duc de Lerme came to visit her there, and the Marquis, having obtained permission from her, went there. She had enough obligation to them not to refuse to see them.

The Countess of Las Torres had had a slight disposition since the return of the Duchess de Feria, which had prevented her from going there for a few days. The first time she returned, she had scarcely entered than the Marquis de Lerme arrived. The liberty of the country allowed the Duchess de Feria to receive the Marquis in the room where the ladies were.

Although the Countess had resolved, after a fashion, to speak to him, that sight embarrassed her to the highest degree; she had never expected to find him in the Duchess's home, and she was on the point of leaving as soon as she perceived him. However, as she had just come in, she could not leave so promptly without an affectation for which she would have been obliged to account to the Duchess, and the necessity enabled her to vanquish her embarrassment. She tried to speak as if the Marquis had not been there.

Soon, another lady who was there with her having indicated that she wanted to peak to the Duchess in private, the Countess got up to leave, but the Duchess begged her to stay and to permit her to go into her cabinet. One of the maidservants was with Elvire at the far end of the room, so it was not contrary to decency to be there with a cavalier.

The Countess still made every effort to leave. The opportunity to speak to Lerme was so present that she dreaded it as much as she desired it; in the end, however, she still wanted it enough to vanquish all her scruples, with the result that, the Duchess of Feria having strongly indicated that she would be pleased to spend the day with her, she no longer resisted.

The Duchess of Feria went into her cabinet and Lerme remained with the Countess of Las Torres.

"Madame," he said to her, "it has not depended your rigor that I have not lost the opportunity once again to justify myself for something of which I am only culpable because I was ignorant of the greatest of my woes; but I have no complaint to make; I appear to you as criminal, and I am sufficiently so, unfortunately, even without it being my fault."

"I haven't accused you of anything," the Countess said to him, "And I would have taken your defense against myself, even if I had not known of your innocence. I do not know if I have had in you a similar guarantee of my fidelity, but you must have believed that it was not by virtue of inconstancy that I married the Count of Las Torres."

With that, she told Lerme all the things that had forced her to do it.

"Oh, Madame," he said, "what cruelty to have conserved my life while you deprived me of yours; death is less cruel than despair."

"Since this is the last time that I shall speak to you in private," she said. "I dare to confess that my unhappiness has always equaled yours. After this, avoid me; that is the price of the confession I have just made you."

"What, Madame!" he said. "Avoid you when, in order to encounter you in the presence of a thousand witnesses, I am deceiving my father by allowing him to hope that I might marry Casilde! No, Madame, I can no longer live without seeing you, and my woes, so long and so cruel, have acquired me the right to disobey you on this occasion."

The Duchess of Feria emerged from her cabinet as he finished speaking. He stayed or a few more hours, but it was with a mind so occupied that the Duchess did not need much penetration to know the truth.

As soon as the Countess was alone with Elvire, she told her about the conversation that she had not been able to overhear from so far away, and everything the Marquis de Lerme had told her about his father's designs; and she confessed to her that that news had not troubled her as much as she would have thought, either because it was a opportunity to cure herself in seeing him attached to another, or because Casilde's scant charms did not frighten her at all.

In truth, that young woman could not be regarded as a rival; she only inspired disdain, and if anything were capable of maintaining a catastrophic passion, it was comparing Casilde with the Countess. However, she regarded that marriage as a port in which, it seemed to her, her reason would be secure.

"So long as Lerme is free," she said to Elvire, "I shall sense in my soul a secret pleasure that amour maintains there; it I necessary that I tear out even the slightest root."

But she did not discern that the hope of seeing Lerme in another form than that of her lover in the eyes of the world, and even seeing him frequently, was slipping insensibly into her heart.

A few days later, the Duc de Lerme having spoken about the marriage to the Duchess of Feria in spite of the pleas that his son had made him to defer the proposition, she acted with all the vivacity necessary to conclude it. Seeing that the Marquis de Lerme did not bring to it the same disposition as his father, she believed that she ought to engage the Countess of Las Torres, by mean of a few artifices, to bring him round to it.

She knew the passion that they had for one another, and the delicate sentiments that the Countess had regarding her reputation, so, by means of a feigned confidence, she sympathized with her for not being happy in the midst of honors and riches, since they are only wealth when they give one all that one can desire; that she had desired the marriage of her daughter with the Marquis de Lerme for a long time, and that the Duc de Lerme wanted it as much as she did, but that there was an opposition in the mind or the heart of the Marquis that afflicted them sensibly.

"Let us discover," she added, "whether he does not love elsewhere, for if he has a fortunate passion, it is not just to contain it."

Those words struck their target. The Countess of Las Torres saw that her reputation would be at risk if she did not engage Lerme to act like a man devoid of passion. She only sought a means of speaking to him, and the Duchess soon furnished one by leaving them together for a second time.

"You're surprised," the Countess said to him, "that I am not fleeing you today, but you will be more so by what I have to say to you."

"I know, Madame," he said to her, "that I ought not to flatter myself, and I tremble at the favor you are doing me in remaining here."

"I intend," she said, "to give you my advice, but if you do not follow it, it will be necessary to resolve yourself to never seeing me again."

"You have the right to command, Madame," he replied, "after which I await our cruel orders."

"It is necessary," she said, "that you marry Casilde. Respond to your father's expectation; save my reputation, which your resistance is rendering suspect."

"Me, Madame, marry Casilde!" he exclaimed. "Have you forgotten that I love you?"

"I will regard this marriage," she replied, "as an effect of the power that I have over you. I know that it will require more passion for you obey me in this occasion than to remain mine; but in sum, I shall flee you so long as you are not engaged, I swear, and I shall no longer come here. Whatever harm your absence might do me, your presence would do me harm. Make everyone believe that you are detached from me, and if possible, make me believe it myself."

"So, Madame," he interrupted, "if by an excess of amour of which there has never been an example, I am able to obey you, you will see me with an indifferent eye. To be regarded solely as Casilde's husband will be the recompense for having sacrificed myself to your will."

On that, flattering things escaped the Countess of Las Torres, which caused the horror of the proposition to disappear in her lover's eyes. He no longer saw anything but the price.

"Well, Madame," he exclaimed, "persuade me and don't constrain me. Assure me at least that your sentiments will be proportionate to my unhappiness. I have never had need of hope in order to love you, but I need it to resolve to marry Casilde, and it's necessary that you regard me as no longer being yours."

"Remember," she said to him, "that I can only see you with propriety if you if you can no longer give rise to the thought that I'm preventing you from belonging to another. Don't see any other interest than the one about which I have spoken; it ought to be considerable enough, and I'm even ashamed of having had to speak to you about it."

"Oh, Madame," he said, "don't repent of what pity makes you say, even if you are driving me to despair. Can you not permit me to seek other opportunities to see you without it costing me such a terrible engagement?"

"What are you proposing to me?" she interrupted. "I have said too much, and your boldness is forcing me to repent of it."

"I can see, Madame," he said, "that I am as unfortunate in your sentiments as in your orders."

Someone came in at that moment and she went away.

A week later, the Countess of La Torres seeing that the marriage had not been concluded, went out when Lerme came in. He left shortly afterwards, overwhelmed by dolor.

From that day on, he sensed that the rigor of the Countess of Las Torres would force him to obey her. However, his repugnance for the marriage was extreme, and he did not surrender yet. When he saw that she continued the same conduct, however, and that the Duchess of Feria was making it understood that only the Countess of Las Torres could oppose the marriage, he was defeated. He could not live without seeing her, and he could not bear the suspicions that were being raised against such a perfect virtue.

He went to tell the Duc de Lerme that he was ready to marry Casilde, but he reproached himself for the injustice that he was doing that young woman by marrying her even though he had another inclination. The Countess commanded it, however, and his amour made him vanquish his scruples.

The Duc de Lerme was glad that his son was agreeable to the marriage. He took advantage of that disposition and took the news to the Duchess the following day, whose haste to conclude it responded to the Duc's wishes. As soon as it was settled, the Duchess of Feria went to see the Countess of Las Torres in order to inform her, and told her that the ceremony would be celebrated the following day.

The Countess was not at all content with that news, although she had wanted it. She found at that moment a sort of repugnance for it that it was impossible for her to vanquish. Her only consolation was the thought that the repugnance was equal on the part of the Marquis de Lerme. The Duchess of Feria invited her to a ball that was to be held the day after the wedding, and she could not dispense with promising to be there.

On the day of the wedding she received the news that the Count of Las Torres had died in Flanders. That news afflicted her; he had shown her a great deal of amity, and gratitude obliged her to have some pity for his destiny. She found herself free again, but it was at the time when she had forced Lerme to marry. It is true that he was not yet married and that he only ought to be that day, but she found difficulty in making him break his word to the Duchess. She learned of her husband's death at the very moment when she was telling herself that it was necessary for the sake of amour that she suppress all other thoughts.

All in all, she would have liked Lerme to be aware of her condition without her contributing to letting him know it.

The death of Las Torres had not yet been published. The king might know it already, but Lerme was not in Madrid because of his marriage. The Countess of Las Torres sent word to the Duchess de Feria that she could not see her the following day because of the death of her husband; that was an indirect way of getting the news to the Marquis, but the Duchess, who received the message, did not find it convenient to inform him. The tenderness that he had for the Countess of La Torres might suddenly prevail over his promises, and the Duchess of Feria did not want to commit her designs o the caprices of a lover.

She even thought that the Countess might talk to him or write to him; she had him watched and gave precise orders to prevent anything reaching him. The wedding was to take place in private; only the Duc de Lerme was there, who had the same interest as the Duchess in preventing his son from hearing the news.

Elvire, who knew that the Duchess alone had received it, and who was also aware of the scruples of her mistress, departed without telling her, in order to go and find the Marquis de Lerme, but it was futile. The Duchess de Feria had hastened the marriage ceremony, which was taking place in her home, and it was impossible to reach the Marquis.

Meanwhile, the Countess of Las Torres had felt some relief when she had sent word to the Duchess of Feria regarding her widowhood, which ought to delay or break the Marquis's marriage. It seemed to her that she had some shame and chagrin about that, but she had no doubt that it would not happen.

When she heard that the Duchess alone had received the news, she dreaded that the Marquis might learn it too late, and, telling herself after the first movements of modesty that she was free and that she would be responsible all her life to Lerme and herself for her timidity, she summoned Elvire to obtain her advice. She was told that the maid had gone to the Duchess of Feria's house, and flattered herself that Lerme would be informed by her of where she stood.

Finally, seeing that Elvire as taking too long to return, she got up several times from where she was sitting, and although she knew that the agitation was getting her no further forward, she went to the door and came back with an extraordinary anxiety. Finally, she wrote to the Marquis de Lerme, but she had scarcely begun the letter when she learned that the marriage ceremony had taken place.

She did not have the strength to lament; she remained in an immobility caused by the excess of her disturbance.

As soon as she saw Elvire return she begged her not to say anything, but, in spite of her prohibition, the maid told her everything about her attempts to speak to the Marquis, and the invincible obstacles she had found.

"Let's go," said the Countess. "I have nothing more to do in this world. Let us at least profit from our misfortunes."

She returned to the same convent that she had chosen once before as a refuge against the marriage to which her father wanted to constrain her; it served her now against her own passion.

The Marquis de Lerme learned of the death of the Count of Las Torres the day after his wedding. What a thunderbolt for him! He was not the master of his despair.

He went to the convent where the Countess of La Torres was, but he was unable either to see her or write to her, and, his languor having not discontinued since his wound, he caught a fever of which he died a few days later.

Jean de Préchac: *Peerless*

There was once a king and a queen who led a very particular life; a young prince and a very lovable princess were the fruit of their marriage. The little princess was named Belle-main, because she did indeed have the most beautiful hands that it was possible to see.

It was the custom in those days to implore the help of the fays at the birth of great princesses; however, the king, who scorned their enchantments and knew how dangerous it is to penetrate the future, had never wanted to suffer that the fays should be consulted about the destiny of Belle-main, which had irritated the fays greatly.

The queen, who loved her daughter with an extreme tenderness, fell into a profound melancholy every time she thought that it would be necessary someday to be separated from that lovable princess by a marriage. That thought gave her so much anxiety that she imagined that she would never have any repose if she were not enlightened as to the destiny of her dear daughter, which caused her to resolve, in spite of the king's prohibitions, secretly to see a fay who lived in the neighboring mountains, whose name as Ligourde.

The fay, who was very malevolent and who was seeking to avenge herself for the fact that the queen had not invited her to the birth of her children, received her in an enchanted palace paneled with gold and azure. After the queen had explained the reason for her journey and had asked her very politely to tell her Belle-main's destiny, Ligourde replied to her, with a great deal of pride, that she would torment herself pointlessly trying to render her daughter happy; that she would give her another princess in exchange; that both of them would be very unhappy, with the difference that Belle-main's woes would last much longer; that she would be married to a prince who would be very fond of birds, particularly one red bird, which would cause the princess much chagrin; that he would be exposed to all the scorn of a long sterility; that her subjects would revolt against her; that her relatives would make war on her; and finally, that a monster would rip out her entrails and devour her.

All the fay's words were as many dagger-blows for the unfortunate queen, who fell in a faint at Ligourde's feet. The fay, without taking the trouble to bring her round, did nothing but transport her in that state to the bed of her husband, the king.

That prince, who had not yet perceived the queen's absence, was very surprised to see her unconscious. He called for help, and she recovered her senses, with difficulty. He asked her very urgently the cause of her illness, but instead of replying, the queen shed a torrent of tears and gave the king to understand, in the midst of sobs, that she wished with all her heart that her daughter had never been born. Then she informed him of everything the fay had said.

The king scoffed at that, assuring the queen that she must have dreamed everything that she had just told him. But the queen, who remembered distinctly all that the fay had told her, remained inconsolable, and having summoned Belle-main, she embraced her, with her eyes bathed in tears, and implored her to promise her never to marry.

The princess assured her that she would always be submissive to her will. The queen, holding her in an embrace, talked to her with a great deal of tenderness; she made her the confidence of some of the misfortunes with which the malevolent Ligourde had threatened her, and added that she could easily avoid them by always remaining unmarried.

Several great kings, informed of the beauty and the surprising qualities of Princess Belle-main, sent ambassadors to ask for her in marriage, but the queen always gave rise to obstacles, and remained inexorable to the entreaties that were made to her on all sides.

The princess, who had a great deal of the humor of her father, the king, and who was not convinced that the predictions of fays were infallible, made futile efforts to disabuse the queen, and finally determined to make the acquaintance of another fay, named Clairance, who had the reputation of not being malevolent, in order to try by her own means to learn their secrets and deflect, if possible, the fatal destiny with which Ligourde had threatened her.

She had heard it said that the fays scorn riches, and that it is easier to win them over by means of very simple presents than with gold or silver, which obliged her to choose nine packets of the finest flax that it was possible to find, with nine distaffs and nine cedar-wood spindles; she added to that thirteen ivory thimbles, and charged her nurse with taking that present to the fay, making her a thousand amities on her behalf, and neglecting nothing to engage her to come and see her in the palace.

The nurse, who was very clever, carried out the commission marvelously, with the consequence that Clairance, touched by the present and the confidence that the princess was testifying to her, sent the nurse back, promising that she would go to see Princess Belle-main when she least expected it.

Satisfied with her nurse's negotiation, the princess was awaiting the arrival of Clairance with impatience when, while walking in a garden one day with her mother, the queen, she noticed an old woman in a corner, who was spinning, and who asked them for alms. The queen was annoyed, and complained loudly that someone had allowed that old woman to come into her garden, but the princess, who was charitable, gave her a gold coin.

Then the old woman, waving her distaff, made three circles, and in an instant, the garden was metamorphosed into another, much more beautiful, filled with an infinity of flowers, with broad pathways lined by orange trees, as far as the eye could see, with waterfalls and fountains.

"I am very glad," said the old woman, "to recompense the princess for her liberality and to let the queen know that she can spare herself the trouble of getting angry because someone let me into the garden."

The poor queen, astonished by that transformation and that speech, judged correctly that the old woman was a fay and begged her pardon a thousand times for her ignorance.

"I am the fay Clairance," said the old woman. "I have come to see Belle-main, who seems to me to be worthy of a better fortune than the malevolent Ligourde promises her."

The queen, delighted to hear her, threw her arms around her in order to embrace her, and Clairance, having examined the eyes, the facial features and the hands of the princess very attentively, said to her: "Ligourde is a very skillful fay, but she must not have explained herself very well, or you didn't understand her very well; for I can assure you that Belle-main will marry a great king. She will, in truth, have a few chagrins, but those chagrins will turn to her glory and her advantage; she will have a son, who will be a prodigy. You only have to fear the traps of the cruel Ligourde, who will try to make him perish in his youth.

The mother and daughter implored the fay to have pity on them and to protect them against the malice of Ligourde. Belle-main was able to flatter her so much and ask for her help with so much confidence and entreaties so pressing, that the fay promised never to abandon her; then she disappeared, as did the beautiful garden. The queen and the princes withdrew, wonderstruck and surprised by such an extraordinary adventure.

Some time afterwards, ambassadors arrived at the court to ask the king for Princess Belle-main on behalf of a powerful neighboring monarch, who testified a great deal of eagerness to marry her. The queen, who dreaded the misfortunes with which the princess had been menaced, could never resolve to let her marry, but the king, who had learned that his aspirant son-in-law had a very well-made sister, desired that his son, the prince, should marry her. As soon as it was said, it was done, for the amorous king, only thinking about possessing

Belle-main, who had been refused to so many other monarchs, gave his content to his sister's marriage.[13]

So much magnificence had never been seen as that of the double wedding. Ligourde, who was not asleep, cast several spells on the king's daughter-in-law as soon as the wedding night, so that she was immediately very unfortunate, but when she tried to do as much to Princess Belle-main, whom we shall henceforth call Queen, Clairance, who was beside her, incognito, prevented her from doing so.

The two fays had had a great contest, and as they both agreed that the new queen would soon become pregnant with a prince, Ligourde, for fear that Clairance might forestall her, immediately made three predictions for the prince to whom Belle-main would give birth. The first was that he would suffer serious maladies in his youth, the second that he would have many enemies, and the third that he would have a mistress so difficult that he would spend the best part of his life trying to content her.

"Stop, malevolent fay," Clairance interrupted, "and wait until I have given my three predictions. The first is that he will have a long life, the second that he will always be victorious over his enemies and the third that he will have great wealth."

Ligourde seemed offended that Clairance had given predictions so opposed to hers, and could not help telling her that time would decide which of the two would be able to sustain their predictions better. Clairance appeared to reply to her with adequate modesty, still trying to deflect the evil designs that she was meditating against the queen. The two fays withdrew, grumbling.

---

[13] When Louis XIII married Anne of Austria in 1615 (they were both fourteen years of age), his sister, Elisabeth de France married Anne's brother, Philip IV of Spain. Anne had a long series of miscarriages and stillbirths before giving birth to Louis XIV in 1638, which licensed the unusual plot-development featured in the novelette.

Belle-main was received in the estates of the king her husband, with unusual acclamations and applause; as it was the custom to kiss the queen's hand and no princess had ever been so beautiful, that attracted the admiration of her subjects to her.

The king, who was very fond of hunting, had a large number of very rare birds he showed them all to the queen, and exaggerated particularly the good qualities of one red bird that had a high head and a very dangerous beak and claws.[14] The queen remembered Ligourde's threats then, and although she was persuaded of the good qualities of the red bird, she nevertheless always feared it, and only looked at it with difficulty.

As soon as the first year of the queen's marriage there was some suspicion of her pregnancy; she was uncertain herself when, one day, as she was alone in her cabinet, one of her women came in to propose the purchase of a parrot that spoke several languages, especially that of the queen's homeland. That last circumstance excited all her curiosity and she ordered that the bird be brought to her, which made her a beautiful speech in her native tongue. The queen having then asked it several different questions, the bird replied to them very precisely.

It is incredible how much joy the parrot gave the queen, who imagined that she would not be able to become bored henceforth having that marvelous bird beside her. The entire court admired it as a prodigy, and the king often came to the queen's cabinet in order to hear the parrot speak, which finally wearied of all the questions that were put to it and no longer wanted to reply. The queen, fearing that it might be ill, was chagrined by its silence, and gave it all the caresses that she could imagine.

Touched by the queen's dolor, and sensible to the marks of amity she gave it, the parrot spoke to her in these terms: "Cease to be afflicted, beautiful queen; I am your good friend

---

[14] Cardinal Richelieu.

91

Clairance, who has taken the form of a parrot in order to be able to converse with you more conveniently without anyone having any suspicion of it. You are certainly pregnant, and the wicked Ligourde is already mediating strangling your child in his cradle; I have come to save him, and I shall see it through. If you have the strength to keep the secret and you have enough confidence in me to give me your child, I will save him from Ligourde's ambushes and give him an education worthy of his birth, quite different from that ordinarily given to princes. But as the first spell that Ligourde has cast on him will last until he is twenty-one, it's necessary for you to confide him to me and have the patience to wait until that long time has passed before seeing the dear child again."

Although the queen was penetrated by the obliging cares of the good fay, it was nevertheless impossible for her to suspend her dolor. She shed a torrent of tears without being able to respond with a single word.

"Will you at least consider confiding him to me?" the fay continued.

"Alas," said the queen, "you know that I have abandoned myself to your advice, but I fear that the king and his people will never give their consent to that."

"Yours will suffice for me," said Clairance, "for I'll render your pregnancy invisible. I'll even enable you to give birth without knowing it, and you can count on my taking care of your child like the apple of my eye. After the fatal time has passed I'll return him to you and you can give birth again in the eyes of the world, but above all, keep the secret, and make your decision soon, without being alarmed by all the chagrins to which you'll be exposed by a long sterility. I also promise you that after the birth of that dear son, whom I want to name Peerless, because no prince will ever be able to compare with him, you will be consoled by a second son, whom you will love tenderly and for whom I am meditating a spell in order that he will be loved by everyone who comes near him, and that his entire life, which will be long, will be nothing but a continuous sequence of pleasures and glory.

The queen was so convinced of Clairance's good intentions that she gladly gave her consent to everything that she proposed to her, savoring in advance all the joy of a second fecundity. She had just finished imploring her to take good care of the scion of so many heroes when the king came into her cabinet. The parrot started to sing a very agreeable song, which gave the king a great deal of pleasure; then it leapt out of a window and flew away. The queen pretended to be very alarmed and sent people in all directions to try to catch it; it was published throughout the realm that five hundred pistoles would be given to anyone who could give news of it, but it was impossible to discover anything. It is affirmed that the king, who loved the bird passionately, testified far more chagrin than the queen.

Meanwhile, the queen's pregnancy was unknown to anyone, and she gave birth without anyone perceiving it. Clairance took Peerless away, and as her art informed her of the great things that the prince would achieve in the future she took a great pleasure in bringing him up well. She paid particular attention to preparing a very clean and healthy apartment for him, and as the fay knew that children often take after their nurse, she chose for his nurse an enchanted queen who had a good temperament, with very noble inclinations. Several enchanted graces and amours were ordered to rock the baby. It would be easy for me to make a description of his cradle and swaddling clothes, but one only has to picture everything that can be imagined of the richest and in best taste in an enchanted palace, and that would still be far below Peerless's cradle and swaddling-clothes.

The good fay, who could never see enough of him, having noticed that he had difficulty going back to sleep once he was woken up, remembered that the princess of China who was incontrovertibly the most beautiful and also the proudest princess on earth, and who was enchanted for several centuries, had the most beautiful voice that any mortal had ever had; the fay ordered her to remain beside the child and lull him to sleep with her songs when he woke up.

The extreme beauty of that princess had generated so much rumor with her enchantment that the greatest princes on earth considered themselves only too fortunate to risk their lives to merit her esteem, and although she had very flattering and insinuations manners, she had such a high opinion of her own merit that the most generous actions seemed to her to be more than adequately recompensed by a single one of her glances. She only tolerated heroes in her service, and demanded that they accomplish extraordinary, and often impossible, things for love of her; if they succeeded, she permitted them, as their sole recompense, to continue to serve her, and if thy succumbed, it seemed to her that their destiny was worthy of envy, since they were dying in her service. Her great pride occasioned her to be named Beautiful Glory. The fays, jealous of her extreme beauty, resolved to abduct her and to enchant her for three thousand years; Clairance opposed that for a long time, but, seeing that she was causing an infinite number of heroes to perish to satisfy her caprices, without her having any liking for them, she consented to her enchantment, but demanded nevertheless that the princess would not age during that long interval of time and that she would always have the same beauty as on the day of her abduction.

She had been given as a task winding eleven thousand balls of thread per day, but Clairance liberated her from that painful occupation in favor of the little prince and ordered her to sing every time he woke up until he went back to sleep. That occupation appeared so pleasant to her, after the difficult employment that she had just quit, that it contributed more than a little to give birth to the inclination that she had thereafter for young Peerless, who was always content every time he heard Beautiful Glory sing. Clairance, who idolized the young prince, seeing that Beautiful Glory acquitted her commission with so much success, said a few obliging words to her and enabled her to hope that she might leave her in Peerless's service for a long time.

From the age of seven, the fay had Peerless taught several languages; when he was strong enough to commence his exercises she chose skillful masters for him. As she wanted to render him very robust she only gave him one sort of meat in his meals and never put any herb into his soup except sage, although she sometimes had him served little betony salads. Beautiful Glory obtained such a furious ascendancy over his mind that he always became irritated everywhere that he did not see her; she was so satisfied by the young prince's heart and the nobility of his sentiments that she never resisted always being with him and amusing him as agreeably as she possibly could.

From his most tender youth, the prince had so much inclination for war that he often armed the women who served him with pikes and muskets and commanded their exercises with a great deal of skill, only intending in everything to please Beautiful Glory. As he advanced in age, however, the proud princess did not render to him so assiduously, and even hid the secret inclination that she had for him.

Admiring the strong passion that the prince had for arms, the fay wanted to give him the means of exercising that noble ardor, and made him a present of a little ivory whistle, with which he could make a thousand armed men emerge every time he blew it; in consequence, he could have armies of several thousand men in a single morning, which he dispersed in various places, and always made them act without any confusion.

The fay also desired that he become a politician and learn the art of ruling, and it was in that view that she gave him a council composed of several great men, in which all sorts of important matters were discussed. At first, the prince had some difficulty constraining himself to enter the council, but in the end, the complaisance he had for the fay prevailed and he went to it very assiduously. It was there that he began to know justice, to disentangle the true from the false and, eventually, to penetrate into the depths of the human heart.

Those military and political occupations being insufficient to occupy his vast genius, he also took pleasure in the fine arts, and although Clairance's palace as grandiose and superb, he found faults there and made her see that symmetry had not been properly observed. He had a particular taste for the gardens, and for everything that was appropriate to embellish them.

The fay, delighted to find so many talents and good dispositions in him, gave him a wand with which to exercise them; he only had to tap with it three times to make anything he imagined appear. The virtue of the wand did not remain unexploited, for the prince, giving free reign to his imagination, built a palace of prodigious extent, in which he could accommodate, if necessary, most of the officers of his troops. It had very spacious courtyards; the staircases were marble and jasper, with all the embellishments that art can furnish; one entered into a series of apartments, magnificently furnished and ornamented with an infinite number of excellent paintings; finally, one admired the gold, the azure, the embroideries, the beautiful paintings and the crystals less than the manner in which all those ornaments were disposed. One passed then into a grand gallery ornamented with mirrors and beautiful marble and marble statues, with marvelous paintings, in which one remarked heroic actions so prodigious that nothing similar had ever been seen, even in fable.

Gold was so common in that superb palace that everything was covered with it, including the roof, and if anything could claim the attention after having seen so much richness, it was the magnificent garden, into which one entered on emerging from the palace; one encountered huge fountains of white marble with jets of water, pools, sprays and cascades. Finally, there were streams that, instead of snaking as they do elsewhere, rose up into the sky and sprang as far as the clouds. At the same time, one saw charming flower beds and beautiful avenues of orange trees, with the consequence that one was always spoiled for choice as to where to commence one's walk, because one would have liked to see everything at once. Anyone who wanted to retire to some corner, in order to dream there at their ease, found agreeable springs surrounded by seats of marble and grass.

Animals of every species were seen there, which were only there to please spectators: the lions, tigers and leopards were deprived of their ferocity, the snakes had no venom, and people did not even fear the dragons, the mere sight of which was so terrible everywhere else. If, by chance, one wearied of strolling, one encountered, at the extremity of the gardens, an arm of the sea in the form of a canal, and also a large number of mariners with boats and richly ornamented galleys, offering new pleasures on the water.

One day, the fay having ordered Beautiful Glory to accompany the prince on an excursion on the beautiful canal, Peerless had the curiosity of asking her sentiment regarding everything she had just seen, but the princess replied coldly that riches were so common in the Empire of China that her father the Emperor always preferred simple and neat houses to superb palaces. Peerless found himself at the far end of the canal when Beautiful Glory said that, and as he had a particular attention to everything that might please the princess, he leapt ashore and struck the ground three times with his wand. A castle entirely made of porcelain appeared, surrounded by a flower bed filled with jasmines, with an infinity of little jets of water, and the complete ensemble had he most agreeable effect that could be seen.

Although the prince's gallantry and the desire that he testified to want to conform in all things to Beautiful Glory's taste gave the princess pleasure, she nevertheless hid her joy and did not make anything evident. Clairance, however, having examined the magnificence of the palace and the neatness of the gardens with pleasure, admired the prince's good taste and ordered, in order to give him pleasure, that for three hours every day all the enchanted individuals would have an entire liberty to walk in the apartments of the beautiful palace; that there would be charming music there; that all sorts of games could be played there; and that there would even be magnificent collations in which everyone would find something to satisfy their taste.

Peerless was deeply touched by that favor, with regard to the pleasure that he judged that it might give to Beautiful Glory, but the humor of that princess was so extraordinary that one never knew where one was with her, and the efforts that one made to please her only caused her chagrin. She imagined that the prince's curiosity had engaged him to ask Clairance for those amusements in order to have an opportunity to see and converse more conveniently to the beautiful enchanted women who were in the palace, and even though all sorts of immoderate desires were banished from the enchanted places and jealousy was unknown to anyone these, Beautiful Glory could not abide the prince paying the slightest attention to anyone but her, convinced that she alone merited all his attachment and that everything else was unworthy of him. Peerless, who was very fond of music, never missed an opportunity to hear it, but, Beautiful Glory having testified that she did not like it, he did not hesitate to make her that sacrifice and deprive himself of music.

While Peerless, who was already only twenty-one years old, attached himself uniquely to pleasing Beautiful Glory and perfected himself in all sorts of exercises, his mother, the queen, was waiting with extreme impatience for the effect of the good fay's promises, and flattered herself that her dear child would be returned to her any day. That great princess suffered with an unexampled virtue the persecutions of her enemies and listened without being moved to the murmurs of the people, who cried loudly that it was necessary to send her back to her own country and give the king a more fecund princess, it being unreasonable that a great kingdom should lack heirs because of the sterility of the queen, when it would be easy to find others very glad to take her place who would infallibly produce successors to the crown. Her great virtue enabled her to suffer all those murmurs with a great deal of patience, always waiting for the term of twenty-one years to expire.

She was not mistaken, for the fay, seeing that the fatal time of Ligourde's threats had passed, declared to the prince that his enchantment was concluded and that it was time to go and console his parents. Peerless, who had believed himself to be the son of the fay, was alarmed by that discourse, especially when he understood that it was necessary to leave Beautiful Glory, but, the fay having explained to him all the mystery of his birth, he showed great docility and asked Clairance as a final favor that she would come to see him as often as possible, begging her, above all, always to bring Beautiful Glory with her. The fay, who could not refuse him anything, promised him everything he wished, and when she had made use of her enchantments, the prince disappeared and the queen found herself pregnant, to the great contentment of the king and his people.

She gave birth some time later, and as no prince had ever been desired as much as that one, it is not astonishing that his birth cased universal joy. Everyone was surprised to find him larger and more formed than children ordinarily are at birth, but what caused even more astonishment, and nearly spoiled everything, was when it was perceived that he had teeth, the fay having neglected to enchant them. In fact, they had all the difficulty in the world finding nurses, because he wounded them with his teeth and scratched their breasts. The extreme joy that everyone had at his birth prevented anyone from pausing to examine that prodigy; there was public and private rejoicing everywhere, and everyone tried to distinguish themselves by means of demonstrations of a veritable joy.

The queen still wanted him to be called Peerless; she loved him with so much tenderness that she suffered painfully when he was taken away from her for a few hours a day in order to begin his education. As he advanced in age, however, the idea of what he had learned in Clairance's palace grew, and he learned all things easily, often remembering that he already knew them. From birth, he also had a complaisance for all beautiful women, by virtue of the habitude he had acquired of pleasing Beautiful Glory, of whom he only any longer had a confused idea. It was noticed, meanwhile, that he only laughed at agreeable things and that he did not say very much, but what was more surprising was that he only gave his applause to sensate things and already knew how to refuse it appropriately. The memory of Beautiful Glory was insensibly renewed in his mind, and his complaisance for the ladies was augmented at the same time. The queen, who rarely lost sight of him, rejoiced in finding him so mild in humor and so inclined to goodness.

The king, his father, having died while Peerless was still very young, his reign commenced with the winning of a battle that was fought by his generals, which appeared to everyone to be a good augury. The queen being unable to sustain the weight of government alone, chose a famous druid,[15] very experienced in affairs, to aid her with his advice, but that choice divided the court and caused great disorder throughout the realm. Finding the occasion favorable to stir up trouble, Ligourde insinuated to several noblemen that it was doing them a great injustice to distance them from the government of affairs. Several of them formed an alliance and took up arms, with the consequence that the queen required all her prudence and her great virtue to break up their cabals and maintain the druid in the position that she had given him.

Peerless, who had more penetration than it was permissible to have at his age, and who already knew the druid's good intelligence, always listened to his advice with a great deal of docility, and as he had the same inclinations that he had had in the enchanted palace, he was very fond of soldiers and it gave him great pleasure to see them performing exercises that he often commanded himself. Although he no longer had a whistle to make as many armed men as he would have liked emerge, he took particular care of those in his service, giving orders that they should never lack anything, As he was retained by the sage advice of the druid, which prevented him from following all the impulse of his noble ardor, he contented himself with disciplining his troops well and often passing them in review. He only gave his favor to those who did their

---

[15] Cardinal Mazarin.

duty better than the others, and favored the officers particularly when their troops were in good condition, which made everyone work hard for that end, and it is certain that no prince ever took better care of his soldiers than Peerless.

The prince was meditating several great designs when the malevolent Ligourde, who could not understand how he had avoided, at his young age, the fate that she had given him, found a means of slipping one of her handmaidens into the prince' palace, whom she named Fever, and whose malignity nearly caused the young prince to die. However, Clairance, having been warned, came running, expelled the handmaiden and cured the prince. The fay, who had discovered that Beautiful Glory was the capricious mistress with whom Ligourde had threatened the prince, and who foresaw the embarrassment into which she might throw him, expressly avoided appearing before him for fear of being obliged to keep her word and bringing Beautiful Glory to him, but the extreme peril that Peerless was in caused her to pass over all sorts of considerations.

Addressing herself to the queen, she said: "These, Madame, are the last efforts of your enemy. I have rendered them futile and I can answer to you for the fact that in future, Peerless will enjoy a long life."

The queen was sensible to the fay's cares, and did not neglect anything to mark her gratitude. She introduced her to the king, her son, exaggerating the great obligations that he had to her. Peerless, who was very grateful, had an appreciable joy in seeing his benefactress, and at that moment everything that he had learned in her home returned to his mind. He took her hands to kiss them, made her a thousand amities and gave evidence, in every way he could discover, of the satisfaction he had in seeing her. As he knew the taste of fays perfectly, he ordered that a collation be brought composed of hazelnuts, brown bread, honey and fresh water. The fay was very appreciative of his attentions, and although she never ate outside her palace, she allowed herself, to oblige the prince, to sample his collation.

It was then that all the charms of Beautiful Glory presented themselves to Peerless's mind; he was dying of the desire to ask the fay for news of her but he did not dare, for fear that she might think that he was reproaching her adroitly for not having kept her word. Clairance divined his thought.

"The state that you were in," she told him, "did not permit me to bring you the Chinese princess. It's true that I realized a trifle belatedly that I had engaged myself too lightly, but alas, you'll see her all too soon. I won't tell you any more, for it's pointless to argue about things that can't be avoided; it's the fate that the malevolent Ligourde has given you; but since I don't have the power to protect you from it, at least you'll dispense me from authorizing by my presence her dangerous advice and the chimerical hopes with which she'll amuse you. You'll see her, since I've promised you that, every time that the sun passes from one sign of the Zodiac to another, and I'll render her invisible to everyone but you, for fear that your subjects, on seeing her, might become as many rivals, it not being possible for a feeble mortal to prevent himself serving her when he has only seen her once. All I can do for love of you is to hide her from everyone's eyes, and to inspire in other men the same desire to serve you that you will have to please Beautiful Glory."

The fay disappeared on finishing that speech, and the prince, without paying any attention to anything that she had just said against Beautiful Glory, was only occupied by the desire to see her again. He waited with an extreme impatience for the sun to change house, and, far from being chagrined by what Clairance had just said to him, he felt a secret joy in thinking that he alone would be permitted to see and serve that incomparable princess.

Finally, the much desired transition of the sun arrived and that same day, Beautiful Glory appeared in the prince's cabinet in a chariot in the form of a throne, decorated with emeralds and laurels, harnessed to a dozen swans. I shall not talk about her attire, because it was effaced by her extreme beauty and the splendor of her eyes, which would have dazzled everyone if she had not been invisible.

The prince immediately threw himself at her feet, and seemed transported by joy in seeing her; in spite of her great beauty, however, she inspired so much respect that Peerless dared not even kiss the hem of her dress.

"I'm very glad," she said, "that, now you are on a real throne and that you're no longer enchanted, you have the same sentiments for me as you had in the fay's palace, for if you have enough virtue to serve me in my fashion and to sacrifice everything for me, perhaps the term of my enchantment will end soon and I will find myself in a state to add several more crowns to the one you have inherited from your forefathers."

Formidable words pronounced by a beautiful person always make a deep impression on a lover, but Beautiful Glory seasoned them with so much grace, and a tone of voice so touching, that it is necessary not to be surprised if the young prince was sharply penetrated by them. He assured her of an eternal attachment and made her a thousand protestations that he would never find any difficulty when it was a matter of winning her esteem.

Beautiful Glory dared not make a long visit, for fear that the fay, in order to punish her, might give her some tedious occupation, but she promised nevertheless to take advantage of the permission that had been granted to her to return once a month. Peerless, who was charmed to see her, tried to let her know, with all imaginable politeness and respect, that he would have been very glad to retain her for a few more moments, but she was inexorable, and released the tether of her swans, which rose into the air instantly. The king suffered that departure very impatiently, but he was so submissive to Beautiful Glory's orders that he dared not even complain.

That agreeable visit nevertheless gave him an extreme joy, and inspired him with a vivacity that he had not yet experienced. The entire court perceived that change in him, which was followed by several fêtes and gallantries that the prince made in favor of the ladies; for, relating everything to his amour, he judged that he owed that homage to the sex of his adorable mistress.

Gradually, the sun passed from one sign to another, and the princess returned to the king's cabinet.

"It is time," she said, "that you renounced amusements unsuitable for a prince who calls himself Peerless and who is devoted to Beautiful Glory. You have done nothing thus far to render yourself worthy of the name you bear, and if I did not know your great heart and I judged you by your actions, I would have difficulty believing that you want to devote yourself to me, as you have promised. It is not enough for Beautiful Glory to wear a crown; I want it to be ornamented with laurels; your courtiers assure you that you are gallant, young and handsome, and the ladies treat you as a hero when your exercise your soldiers on peaceful fields; I need victims mingled with blood and laurels. In a word, remember that you were born for Beautiful Glory."

As she finished speaking she released the tether of her swans, without waiting for the response of the king, who remained very ashamed of a reproach that he had not merited, because his extreme youth and the deference he had always had for the druid who aided him with his advice to govern his kingdom had prevented him from following the impulsion of his courage. However, that reproach did not fail to sting him and caused him to meditate great designs, the execution of which he judged might please his princess. The visits that she rendered him animated him even more, and he tried in the meantime to render himself worthy of her in all the respects that depended on him, for he was extremely polite, very gallant, very liberal and loved probity above all else.

The aged druid having died,[16] Peerless resolved to govern his estates and to take care of his affairs himself, but for fear that the princess might interpret his tranquility poorly, he took account of the situation he was in and the necessity in which he found himself of devoting himself entirely to affairs

---

[16] Mazarin died in 1661.

of state before undertaking any foreign war, no longer having the enchanted wand in order to produce armed soldiers and needing considerable sums so sustain the wars he was projecting.

Beautiful Glory approved of his reasons, and even said that it was the veritable path to render himself worthy of her. It required no more to engage Peerless to attempt the impossible. He applied himself forcefully to affairs and rendered assiduously to all the councils; he began in that occasion to put into practice everything he had learned in the fay's abode; his application, his assiduity and his admirable discernment surprised everyone, and it is certain that, by his cares, he disentangled in very little time a chaos of very difficult intrigue-ridden affairs, and put himself in a state to follow the noble sentiments of his heart. Beautiful Glory, who judged by that difficult labor that he was capable of all great things, spoke to him more obligingly than she had ever done, and her words were as many enchantments redoubling the prince's ardor.

Shortly thereafter, Peerless put himself at the head of a fine army, and rendered himself master of several important fortified places in spite of the resistance of the besieged, who had put all their troops in those places to defend them.

Beautiful Glory, who had never doubted the prince's, courage did not appear very satisfied with that first campaign, and told him, in one of her visits, that there was nothing very extraordinary about a bellicose prince with fine troops and in the fine season taking places, but that a prince named Peerless, who was seeking to please Beautiful Glory, ought to launch attacks in the middle of winter, through the ice and he frost, without even waiting for all his troops to be assembled.

That terrible discourse did not astonish the prince, for he found nothing difficult when it was a question of winning the esteem of his mistress; he set forth a few days later in the middle of winter and attacked with a small number of troops, in spite of the snow and the ice, a large province where there were several heavily-fortified places, of which he finally rendered himself the master by means of incredible labors and after an infinity of heroic actions. It was then that Beautiful Glory, sensible to so many marks of valor, permitted him to kiss the hem of her dress for the first time.

Flattered by such a particular favor, Peerless raised new troops and was making arrangements to enter into campaign as soon as possible, already promising himself to conquer several provinces, when Beautiful Glory, having come to the king's cabinet, spoke to him in these terms:

"I'm satisfied with your courage and I release you from the obligation of taking any more places; I'm even convinced there are none to be found that could resist you, especially when your enemies have no army to dispute the campaign with you. Similar conquests will have no merit with me, I don't like easy victories; if you want to please me, you'll suspend your noble ardor and wait until your enemies, having recovered from their astonishment, are in a state to oppose you with forces similar in number to your own."

Peerless needed all his moderation to renounce the conquests he had promised himself to make; nevertheless, as he had only taken up arms to please Beautiful Glory, it was necessary to submit to her will.

That sacrifice was nevertheless very agreeable to her, and she thanked him for it in very obliging terms. As the prince was continually occupied with an ardent desire to do something to the liking of his charming mistress, and he no longer had the opportunity to distinguish himself by means of arms, he abridged the laws, and reformed a great many abuses that had slipped into the administration of justice. Beautiful Glory gave her praise to his vigilance and his application, but she asked him for a new proof of his attachment, which threw the prince into great embarrassment.

"You know," she said, "the hope I have of soon ending my enchantment. You have dared to raise our prayers as far as me; you're not unaware that I like beautiful palaces, and yet you have none in which you can receive me."

Peerless assured her that she would soon be satisfied, and, having summoned the most skillful architects in the world, he had built in the capital of his estates one of the finest palaces in the world, with very agreeable gardens proportionate to the magnificence of the palace.

That great work was almost finished when Beautiful Glory, having come to visit the prince, as usual, made him know that did not like living in cities, and that if he wanted to give her a veritable testimony of his attachment and his complaisance for her he would have a place and gardens built in the country similar to those that he had imagined in Clairance's abode by means of the virtue of his wand.

Frightened by such an extravagant proposal, Peerless represented to her that the fay's palace was only an illusion, and that all the marble on earth, or all the gold in Peru, would not be sufficient for such an edifice.

"You know very well," said Beautiful Glory, "that ordinary things don't suit me, and that I only like those that approach the impossible. I've told you what I desire; it's up to you to examine whether you have enough courage and enough desire to please me to undertake it."

She did not wait for a response, and disappeared.

There was never been an embarrassment similar to that of the prince, who would a thousand times rather have died than displease his princess. However, although he thought the execution of that grand design impossible, in order to mark his submission to Beautiful Glory's orders, he decided to attempt it, without flattering himself that he might succeed. He traced a plan himself, as close to the fay's palace as might be possible for him, scarcely gave himself time to consult the architects and commenced, without losing a moment, to build the palace and to have the gardens marked out, with the result that in two years, the great work was very advanced. [17]

---

[17] Louis XIV began the massive redevelopment of Versailles, previously his favorite hunting lodge, in 1683, after the death of his wife, Maria Theresa of Spain—who has no equivalent in the story—with the aid of the architect Jules Hardouin-Mansart.

That diligence pleased the princess greatly. Peerless, without having perceived that, redoubled his efforts, and never had any rest until the palace and the gardens were in their perfection. Gold was everywhere with so much profusion that the roofs were covered with it, and although he was only trying to imitate what the fay had already done, it is still the case that it surpassed the enchanted palace in many respects.

Flattering himself that the princess would be content with her palace, Peerless waited impatiently until she had seen it to ask her what she thought; but he was extremely surprised to see a new planet presiding over the hemisphere without Beautiful Glory appearing. That gave him cruel anxieties, by which he was overwhelmed until the following day, when the princess arrived.

She told him that the swans of her chariot, having been dazzled by the reflection of the sunlight from the roofs, had flown into the canal instead of entering his cabinet, and, their wings having got wet, it had been impossible for them to resume their flight; that the fay, having come running, had condemned them to remain there for life; and, having taken her back to her palace, had kept her there until now, when she had given her a team of eagles to draw her chariot in future.

She then testified much gratitude to him for the urgency he had had in finishing the magnificent palace, and promised him never to forget it. As she was invisible to everyone else, Peerless begged her to cast her eyes momentarily over the arrangement of the apartments; she consented to that, and after having examined them well, she assured him that she found more magnificence there, a more excellent music and a much better company than in the fay's.

In another visit the prince begged her to take an excursion on the canal, and pointed out the agreeable porcelain castle to her, which appeared at the extremity. She found that it bore a striking resemblance to the one in China, and agreed without difficulty that Peerless's was more elegant and more perfect than the other. But either because that very fact caused her some jealousy or because her taste had changed, she asked the king to have it demolished and build another of marble and jasper in its place, which was done a few days later.

The superb edifice, as well as the rich furniture with which it was ornamented, augmented the reputation that Peerless had already acquired by his conquests. Strangers arrived from all parts of his kingdom and admired those great riches and an infinite number of different curiosities, and more than anything else, the surprising qualities of the monarch—who, however would have preferred a single glance from his mistress to the unanimous applause of the entire universe.

In the impatience he always had to do something great to win her esteem, he complained one day to the princess that she no longer gave him any occasion to display the pleasure he had in obeying her.

"Alas," she said, "you've made me admire the canal in your garden as a very extraordinary endeavor, and yet I perceive that several individuals have as much in their country houses; you know that I don't like the commonplace. but if you really want to please me and veritably want to convince me that you're only thinking of rendering yourself worthy of me, I'd like you to make me a canal that would traverse the land from sea to sea, which, by connecting the two, would give me the pleasure, when I'm no longer enchanted, of passing from the Ocean to the Mediterranean without exposing myself to the hazards or difficulties of a long navigation."

"That enterprise," said the prince, "would be the work of a fay rather than that of a prince like me."

"What!" said the princess, angrily. "You have the temerity to aspire to my esteem, and such a enterprise astonishes you!"

"Nothing is capable of astonishing me," Peerless continued, "when it's a matter of the service of Beautiful Glory, and since you absolutely desire that canal, I'll build it, or die trying."

The princess withdrew, very satisfied with Peerless's resolution, although he doubted himself whether he could ever succeed in an enterprise so new and so bold. He commenced work with infinite care and expenditure; any prince other than Peerless would have been put off by the impossibility he saw of continuing it, but the monarch, who knew that great difficulties were as many means of pleasing Beautiful Glory, still continued his enterprise, and finally achieved it, with a patience and labors that approached those of Hercules.[18]

The princess was in the utmost astonishment at seeing such a difficult enterprise concluded; as soon as her first visit, she assured Peerless that he alone appeared worthy of her esteem, but that she desired that he return to collect new laurels on the field of Mars.

Peerless, delighted by an order so in conformity with his desires, assembled numerous troops with an extraordinary diligence and commenced his campaign with a famous siege. The besieged defended themselves rather vigorously, but it was necessary to cede to the efforts of Peerless. Perceiving the facility with which he had made his conquests, Beautiful Glory told him one day that other heroes took places by force of time, and that if he wanted to distinguish himself and give her a new spectacle, it would be necessary to take a new fortress every day.

Scarcely had she finished speaking than Peerless entered enemy territory like a torrent, and took a new fortress every day. The rapidity of so many conquests astonished several neighboring potentates, who believed nevertheless that they were secure, because Peerless, not finding any more places to conquer, would be obliged, if he wanted to go any further, to cross a great and profound river, and as armies do not cross rivers as easily as birds, it would take a long time to construct bridges there. Peerless, always seeking to please his princess by means of extraordinary actions, decided, without being embarrassed by the peril or the difficulties, that his army would swim across.

---

[18] The royal edict that launched the construction of what was initially known as the Canal royal en Languedoc was issued in 1661, and the project was completed in 1681.

The novelty of that great action disconcerted his enemy so much that all the neighboring countries ran to submit to the victor, who would easily have rendered himself master of several great estates if Beautiful Glory, astonished by how far he had surpassed her hopes, had not represented to him that, fining nothing but terror everywhere, and no enemies, she no longer credited to his account conquests that he might make over people who surrendered without fighting. Peerless, who was only thinking of pleasing his charming mistress, made that sacrifice to her again, and retired to his estates.

Ligourde, jealous of the prince's prosperities, seeing the astonishment and consternation of his enemies, enabled them to perceive that they had in their lands a yellow bird,[19] to which she had given several spells, and although it was still young and did not have strong enough wings to go very far, she assured them that it might serve them usefully in future. That advice caused them to pay a great deal of attention to the yellow bird, and to rally their courage, but all that was futile, for, Beautiful Glory having visited Peerless on his return from his campaign, she testified to him the satisfaction she had with everything he had just done for her service. She made him understand that it was for his generosity to scorn easy conquests, and that he ought to content himself with having reduced his enemies to the consternation and confusion they were in, without waning to profit from their disorder. Peerless, only too happy to be able to please Beautiful Glory, consented to that without hesitation. That noble procedure, in circumstances so favorable, attracted several obliging words on the part of his mistress.

Peerless, who was always thinking in his greatest repose of anything that might do more to please is princess, applied himself anew to protecting the sciences and the arts, by establishing several manufactures and academies of painting and sculpture in various parts of his realm. Beautiful Glory having visited him some time afterwards, spoke to him in these terms:

---

[19] William of Orange, future King of England.

"You have performed an infinite number of fine actions, I confess, but it appears to me that you have scarcely paid any attention to what concerns me personally, since you haven't even thought of putting yourself in a state to be able to send an ambassador to my father, the Emperor of China, to ask when my enchantment will be ended. Where are your ports? Where are your naval armies?"

Peerless was delighted that his mistress was thinking herself about means of being his, and although he already had ports and ships, he built a new port and constructed several great ships, with care, at immense expense. Beautiful Glory seemed very content with that, but she said to the prince nevertheless that, the voyage to China being long and difficult, it would be good to make some establishment in America in advance, to serve as a staging post in case his ambassadors needed to retreat without running the risk of being lost in a long navigation. No sooner was it said than done: Peerless gave such good orders that he made sure shortly afterwards of several ports in the New World, and established companies that had a continual commerce with India and America.

Beautiful Glory, who had already been served by several great heroes, was obliged to concede that she had never found one who had entered as generously into everything that gave her pleasure with as much application and as much success as Peerless.

"It's necessary to agree," she said to him, "that you have great wealth, fine armies, magnificent palaces and delightful gardens, but you still lack a treasure of inestimable price, which my father the Emperor holds in higher esteem that his crown, and that is a faithful friend. I've often heard him say that he greatly lamented the condition of kings, who were surrounded by a crowd of adorers, who had every complaisance for all their desires, but rarely had faithful friends who talked to them frankly and without some particular agenda. He had one who was very disinterested, who had a great deal of intelligence, great mildness, an infinite penetration, who reasoned accurately in all sorts of matters, who never flattered him, and who loved my father independently of the Emperor."

That portrait, which struck the prince, was so much to his liking and so much in conformity with his inclinations that he deemed himself unfortunate in the midst of his riches, since he did not have a friend of that character. He thanked the princess for her advice, and, the eagles having taken off, as usual, the prince remained very thoughtful, making serious reflections on everything that he had just heard.

From then on he observed those who were close to him; he examined their minds and hearts, always seeking a resemblance to the portrait that the princess had just painted for him. Finally, after many different proofs, he was fortunate enough to find a person of rare virtue and extraordinary merit, who had precisely the qualities of the portrait.[20]

Peerless, who had previously delivered himself to passionate courtiers who often attached one another, found himself so relieved in being able to talk about everything with an open heart and without fear that anyone would speak evil of him, that he never lost an opportunity to converse with him every time that his great occupations permitted it.

However, Beautiful Glory did not like to see him tranquil for long; not long hereafter she inspired him to undertake further wars. The yellow bird that Ligourde had enchanted, and which had become much accredited since, fluttered continually, and made several attempts to halt Peerless's progress, but its efforts did not prevent the prince from continuing to make war with the same success, for to appear on the battlefield and to make conquests were the same thing for him. All seasons were the same to him; he laid sieges in winter as in summer, indifferently; he camped in the snow as in a meadow covered in flowers. His enemies, having joined forces thanks to the efforts of the yellow bird, made new efforts, and marched at the head of a powerful army to oppose his conquests, but that did not prevent him from taking several places before them,

---

[20] Madame de Maintenon with a diplomatic sex-change.

and their presence only served to give more witnesses to his victories.

Seeing that nothing could rest the incomparable prince, Beautiful Glory suggested to him that he lay down his arms again, and made him known that since he could to longer find enemies worthy of him, she wanted him to attach himself to embellishing his houses and his gardens, which he did with a magnificence that is easier to imagine than to write.

Beautiful Glory having recognized by several experiences that the prince, far from ever resting, was giving everything to the public whenever the requirements of war permitted him to take some relaxation, said to him one day that she could not understand how he could sustain the embarrassment of a continuous sequence of affairs; that her father, the Emperor of China, had much better taste, since, after devoting a part of the week to imperial duties, he became a private individual for the rest of the time and retired to a agreeable palace surrounded by delightful gardens, where everything was surprisingly clean. An infinite number of curious things were to be seen there, which were pleasant to behold, particularly a river that was precipitated from the top of a mountain, which made a cascade so extraordinary that on fine days the reflection of the sunlight from the waterfall fell back on the palace and illuminated all the apartments. It was in that fine abode that he lived without constraint, far from the crowd, accompanied by a small number of chosen people, who only talked to him about agreeable things, without ever discussing their particular affairs with him. Peerless admired the good taste of the Emperor of China and assured Beautiful Glory that he would profit from the example.

The reputation of Peerless, his heroic actions and his great virtues, went as far as the light of the sun. Several great potentates, from the extremities of the earth, sent ambassadors to him with rich presents. His realm was a seed-bed of illustrious individuals; all the nations were well-received there and people came to it from all directions in order to admire the incomparable prince and to learn politeness and the practice of virtues from his example. Beautiful Glory, who had put him to all sorts of proofs, assured him during her visits that she was only waiting for the end of her enchantment to show him her gratitude, but the prince still feared not having done enough for her, and sought continually for new opportunities to gain her esteem.

Although the fay Clairance had enabled him to evade, by her cares, one of Ligourde curses, and had rendered him a perfect health, his encampments in the snow and the other fatigues of war were causing him an irritating discomfort, the consequences of which appeared to be very dangerous, but Peerless, only consulting his courage, without giving his subjects time to perceive that great peril, had iron and fire applied to it, and was cured. That surprising firmness gave admiration to the whole world. Beautiful Glory assured him, in her first visit thereafter, that she had been very touched by the great resolution he had shown, and that she found it very worthy of him.

Although Peerless had no knowledge of the time when the enchantment of the princess was due to end, it was nevertheless easy to observe that he was always thinking about it, and to give her very sensible evidence of that, by sending ships to the extremities of the earth, and very close to China, in order by that means to accustom his subjects to the knowledge of distant seas, to anticipate in good time the difficulties that might oppose the long navigation he was meditating, when he would end envoys to China to ask for her hand.

That foresight pleased Beautiful Glory greatly, who could hardly think of any more new marks of his attachment to demand of her lover; she had exhausted the supply in war and in peace, in the perfect discipline of his troops, in the reformation of the law, in the establishment of commerce and navigation, in the good order of finance, in the protection of sciences and arts, in the magnificence of buildings, in the embellishment of gardens, in actions of firmness, in the practice of all sorts of virtues, and, generally, in everything imaginable that might be appropriate to a great hero.

The prince found means, by his valor and his perfect moderation, not to have any enemies, but his great actions, which renown published all over the world attracted an infinite amount of envy. He had a dream at that time that gave him some anxiety. He saw a cock attacked by an eagle, a peacock and several turkeys, and by a great number of ducks that surrounded him on all sides and pressed him hard. The inequality of the combat did not prevent the cock from defending itself vigorously against all of the, giving them such rude pecks with its beak that it sometimes ripped away feathers. The generous Peerless, fast asleep as he was, wanted to go to the aid of the cock, and woke up.

As he was the least superstitious prince in the world, he paid no attention to that dream, but having learned shortly thereafter that several great potentates were conspiring against him, he remembered the dream, which caused him some anguish, because his awakening had prevented him from seeing the denouement of the combat. Nevertheless, sure of himself and also delighted to find new opportunities to please his princess, he was not embarrassed by all the public rumors.

The dream, however, was only too veritable, for Peerless was informed that the yellow bird, which was beginning to try its wings, was fluttering everywhere and had finally engaged a large number of emperors, kings, republics and other sovereigns to form a league against Peerless, and was even soliciting his friends and enemies to enter into that formidable league.[21] The noise of the great storm that was forming against him never astonished him, nevertheless he was careful to remain on his guard and to assemble his troops.

Beautiful Glory, who learned that so many great powers were conspiring against Peerless and were ready to fall upon his estates, congratulated him on it instead of lamenting it, and as she knew the prince's great courage perfectly, she inspired him to forestall his enemies without waiting for them to have the audacity to attack him.

---

[21] The Grand Alliance or League of Augsburg.

Firstly, the prince marched on the frontier and seized, in spite of the numerous troops of his enemies, a place that they might have used as a passage to enter his estates. That wise foresight broke all their measures, and they were obliged to await another campaign in order to commence some enterprise.

However, the wings of the yellow bird had become so strong that it passed over the sea in a single flight; the joy that it had in succeeding in that bold project, or the difficulty that it had in landing, caused its plumage to change, and a red crest emerged on its head similar to that of a cock, which gave it a great relief. It was because of its pressing entreaties that its allies equipped a large number of ships and sent prodigious armies on campaign.

In one of her visits, Beautiful Glory spoke to the prince in these terms: "It is time, brave Peerless, to harvest laurels; if I were not counting more on your courage than your forces, I would fear for you greatly. The kings, your predecessors, who had only one enemy to face, had need of all their valor to sustain the war; consider that you have several powers to combat, a hydra with an infinite number of heads. Your treasury is exhausted because of the complaisance you have had for me, whereas your enemies, who have not yet made any expense, have no lack of gold or silver. I dread that you might succumb, and that the great numbers might overwhelm you, and what causes me even more pain is that my enchantment is such that, in spite of everything you have already done for me, if some other hero, even though he has never seen me, becomes your conqueror, I shall forget you and I would become his recompense. So, think once again that it is a matter of losing Beautiful Glory or of making sure of her forever."

Peerless, who did not fear his enemies and who sensed that he had enough courage to defend himself against all of them, was offended by the princess's speech; but, making the reflection that the interest she was taking in his person gave her that anxiety, he forgave her for her remonstrations. Shortly thereafter, he set forth on campaign, and notwithstanding the futile efforts of so many powers in league against him and the numerous armies that opposed him, he fought them and he won a great battle against them. The sea was no more fortunate for them, for their fleet was also defeated by Peerless's naval army, and no one doubted that the league, which was composed of several potentates who had so many different interests to look after, and who were also defeated everywhere, would soon disintegrate, having no appearance that it could subsist for long.

Beautiful Glory was not the last to congratulate Peerless on so much fortunate success, but it did not have the effect that had been expected, for, far from being deterred, they attacked in several different places simultaneously, convinced that they could vanquish him more easily when his forces were divided; but his vigilance and his valor were equal to everything, and he was always victorious. However, neither the important places he took from them nor the battles he won ever decided anything; their number was so great that they always found themselves in a state to repair their loss and renew their troops.

Beautiful Glory admired the conduct, the valor and the foresight of the prince equally, in sustaining such a difficult war so courageously, always believing himself very well recompensed in his travails by the satisfaction that the princess showed him. His unique fear was of not having done enough for her, and he was continually occupied in seeking new opportunities to merit her esteem.

Filled with that thought, and thinking to draw his enemies in order to engage them in a general and decisive battle, he waited until all their troops were on campaign and went to attack, in their presence, an impregnable rock of which the name alone spread terror in all the neighboring countries. Such a surprising resolution astonished the allies so much that they set a hundred thousand men to defend the place, although they were convinced that it could not be taken in the time that Peerless was pressing it urgently.

The wicked Ligourde, after having excited all the elements, also infiltrated the price's household with one of her handmaidens, named Goute, and one of her couriers, named Badnews. Anyone but Peerless would have been very embarrassed by a conjunction as delicate as that, but the hero only sought assistance in his firmness, and, forgetting his illness, he only consulted his courage; he had himself taken to the tail of the trench, and animated everything so well by his presence and his example that the enemy was repelled and the place taken.

In order to mark how agreeable that great action was to her, Beautiful Glory gave him her hand to kiss for the first time in his life, which was such a signal favor for him that he would have been sorry, on that occasion, not to have had as many enemies and as many affairs as he had.

The allied powers persisted in their obstinacy, always convinced that their union and their perseverance would eventually exhaust the strength of Peerless, who was alone against them, but his courage never relented, and he defeated them several more times in the following campaigns. Astonished by Peerless's firmness, which she found far above the heroes who had served her, and remarking that he was enjoying the war, Beautiful Glory resolved to put him to a new proof, which was no less difficult than all the others.

One day, she told him that the important services that he had rendered to her made her desire to be disenchanted soon, in order to be in a state to recompense him, but that, reflecting on the name of Peerless and that of Beautiful Glory, she did not believe that there as a fabric in the world worthy to serve as a royal cloak on the wedding day; that she had once heard mention of the golden fleece, and that she would dearly like to have it for the great ceremony; and that he hoped that he would be kind enough to send a well-equipped fleet to India in order to steal that fleece and bring it back for her.

The prince was utterly astonished to hear such an extraordinary proposition. He represented to her that he would never hesitate to attempt anything when it was a matter of pleasing her, that she might remember his conquests, his magnificent palaces, the junction of the two seas and many other things that he had done for her, but that, India being so far away, and the fleece so difficult to find, and his enemies much stronger than him on the sea, he could not see any appearance of making a success of that project.

Beautiful Glory, who had the humor of the majority of persons of her sex, unwilling to brook any argument when they want something very much, thought it very bad that Peerless was raising all those difficulties.

"There is no need," she said, "to recapitulate what you have done for me, since I have not forgotten it, and you have been able to remark that I was not insensible to it; and it is precisely the facility that you have always found in carrying out everything that might please me that engages me to make a request so new. I have a good enough opinion of you to believe that, since I desire it, it will not be impossible for you.

Peerless, confused by the honor that the princess was doing him, did not hesitate to attempt that ridiculous project, cast his eyes upon a captain whose valor and experience gave him every hope, and sent him to India with a beautiful fleet. He arrived there after a long and difficult navigation; he discovered, by his cares, a fortress where the fleet was being kept but he discovered that it was being defended by Cyclopes, the number of whom was superior to his fleet. He attacked them regardless, and he perceived, shortly thereafter, that the reputation of Peerless was as well-known in the new world as in his own estates, and that fear of his name alone had intimidated the Cyclopes, whom he forced to hand over the fleece. He brought it back to Peerless.

The prince laid it at the feet of Beautiful Glory, who was charmed by that rich present and was even more to her taste than a much more considerable conquest. The praise that she gave him engaged him to seek new opportunities to please him, in trying to draw the army of the allies into a battle. Again, he besieged an important place in their presence, which he took without their making any move to oppose him. Then he decided to enter deep into enemy territory and besiege, by sea and by land, a famous fortress that served as the rampart of a great kingdom, and was guarded by troops as numerous as those of the besiegers.

That enterprise seemed very reckless, but the general conducting the siege, animated by the same blood as Peerless and fortified by the orders and great courage of the prince, pressed the besieged so hard that, after a thousand surprising actions on either side, the place was finally forced to capitulate and surrender to the victor.

Beautiful Glory was transported by joy by that, and remained convinced that nothing could resist Peerless in future. "The measure is complete," she told him, "and my mind, fertile in proofs, cannot furnish me with anything more to exercise your great courage; the experiments that I have already made convince me sufficiently, and enable me to judge your capability. I want you to surprise our enemies with an entirely new victory. Everyone is so accustomed to seeing you capture places that there is no longer any merit for you in that, but since you are seeking to perform extraordinary actions worthy of Peerless, surrender to your enemies the famous fortresses that give them so much anxiety, and which they would never be able to retake from you."

"It's for love of you that I took them, charming princess," Peerless replied. "I find myself fully recompensed, since I am fortunate enough to please you by returning them."

That surprising moderation surprised Beautiful Glory greatly, especially at a time when Peerless found himself in a state to dictate the law everywhere if he had wanted to take advantage of so many favorable circumstances. That also disarmed the confederated powers, which all hastened to gain the benevolence of the prince, and even repented of having made war on him, as they got to know him, and his merit and his rare virtues, more in intimately.

It was then that Beautiful Glory sensed the misfortune of her enchantment most keenly, not knowing when it would end, and seeing herself unable to crown Peerless. She did not hide that from the prince, and testified to him the chagrin that it caused her, letting him know that in her uncertainty as to whether the enchantment would end soon or whether it would last several more centuries, his great courage and the extraordinary things that she had seen him do, had inspired a thought that appeared extravagant, but which she thought worthy of Peerless.

"You have disarmed the powers of the earth," she said to him, "by means of your valor and your virtue. What prevents you from now attacking the hells and making war on the fays, who, with the aid of demons, case so much disorder on the earth? I admit that the arms that you employ in your military expeditions are not appropriate to that; very different ones will be required for that war, but I am sure that you will find them of you care to apply yourself to seeking them, and it will only depend on you to break my enchantment."

Although that great project was very much in conformity with Peerless's sentiments, and he was very touched by Beautiful Glory's arguments, especially the pleasure of disenchanting her, the memory of the great obligations he had to the good fay being present in his imagination, his gratitude prevented him from savoring all the pleasure that he would have had solely in the idea of liberating his charming princess.

But Beautiful Glory, who knew his generous heart, having perceived his embarrassment, disabused him by informing him of all the mysteries as to which she had been enlightened by the several centuries that she had spent in Clairance's palace. She had never dared to reveal them for fear of the cruel tortures that she would have been made to suffer, but she was beginning to scorn them, in the hope she had that the prince would soon be able to liberate her. She told him that the good fay and the evil fay were the same person, who employed those different personalities in order to impose herself more effectively on the public; that all the enchantments, and even the rich palaces, of the fays were only an illusion; that in order to issue the predictions by means of which they rendered themselves so redoubtable to humans, they took advantage of the knowledge that the demons gave them of the future; and that although they had no power to change the destiny of anyone at birth, they nevertheless made predictions that which they regulated in accordance with the knowledge they had of what everyone would become.[22]

Surprised to learn such a curious detail, which he found very plausible, Peerless was very glad to be disabused, and he assured Beautiful Glory that, since she was content with him and he no longer had any enemies, he would devote all his efforts to the difficult discovery of arms with which to undertake the new war that she had just proposed to him.

The princess was preparing to reply to him when the eagles of her chariot appeared abruptly, without waiting for her orders. It was the fay herself who was drawing the chariot, disguised as the eagles, and she was terribly irritated by Beautiful Glory's boldness and the reckless designs that she had inspired in the prince. She did not want the princess to continue her visits any longer, and would have prepared to make her suffer horrible tortures if she had not perceived that Peerless, no longer seeing his princess, would apply himself very seriously to her liberation. The dread that she had that the redoubtable monarch, whose great courage she knew, might also vanquish the infernal powers, made her suspend the execution of her cruelties and dissimulate her anger.

On the contrary, she affected to treat Beautiful Glory well, by informing her that she had an interest herself in deflecting the price away from that reckless enterprise. Since, if he succeeded in it and broke her enchantment, she would no

_____

[22] This is a very unusual narrative move; nowhere else in the *corpus* of *contes de fées* are demons added to metaphysical context of fays, but it does represent the view of orthodox Churchmen that if enchantresses were not demonic in themselves they could only be devil-led witches, among whom no distinction could be drawn between "good" and "bad," any involvement with whom would have tainted Peerless/Louis XIV with Satanism.

longer be anything but a simple mortal, and that it would even be dangerous if the prince did not attach himself, once and for all, to a more solid glory and scorned all the rest.

The princess, who mistrusted the artifices of the enchant-ress, and who judged that the prince's enterprise was not impossible, since the fay was afraid of it, thanked her proudly for her advice, and waited, with a great deal of confidence, for Peerless to set out to break her enchantment.

The Queen of the Fays

There was once a king who was known as King Guillemot. He was the best prince on earth, who asked for nothing but love and simplicity; it is even affirmed that he wiped his nose on the sleeve of his doublet. He was in no hurry to get married. However, as the Guillemot race was very ancient, his people wanted him to give them successors. There had been talk of several different marriages, but he had always found invincible difficulties in them.

A neighboring princess, whose name as Urraca, had estates that were much to the liking of King Guillemot, but Urraca had always shown a marked repugnance for marriage and a great deal of insensibility to the efforts that several sovereigns, particularly Comte d'Urgel, had made to please her. Her dominant passion was astrology, and she was determined not to marry until she had read in the stars that she would be the mother of a perfect princess, who would be a prodigy of beauty and virtue, who would do infinite good, and would have no other concern than relieving the afflicted.

That knowledge obliged her to listen to the proposals that came to her from all directions. Her nurse often spoke to her in favor of Comte d'Urgel, who had put her in his interests by means of great liberalities, but Urraca, who had the same humor as most other women in being sensible to distinguished ranks, would rather have been a queen than Comtesse d'Urgel.

King Guillemot, informed of the dispositions of the princess, sent an ambassador with an authority to marry her on his behalf, and sent her at the same time a gilded belt, a packet of pins, a small knife and a pair of scissors—ordinary presents in those days. The marriage was soon concluded, and the wedding ceremony too.

The new queen requested that the king should come to find her himself and stay for a time in her estates before taking her back to his kingdom, but King Guillemot rejected that proposal and insisted that the queen come to find him.

The proud Urraca could not reconcile herself to such an absolute order, and the malevolent nurse, who had not received any present from the Guillemots, animated the mind of her mistress in such a way that they spent more than a year in that situation.

Comte d'Urgel, who had found means of seeing the queen without her perceiving him, had fallen passionately in love with her, and still continued to heap the nurse with presents, in order to be informed of the sentiments and the slightest occupations of the queen.

The pride of the princess left him nothing for which to hope, but his amour did not permit him to be disabused, and he believed that he might be able to achieve anything by means of the advice of the deceitful nurse. Although those early times were far from the corruption of the present century, Amour, who has always been subtle and full of inventions, inspired the comte to engage the nurse to introduce him to the queen's presence, persuading her that he was King Guillemot, who was coming see her incognito. That appeared to him to be all the easier because the queen had never seen her husband. He proposed it to the nurse, and presented her at the same time with a purse full of gold guillemots, which were then very rare.

The nurse, dazzled by such a rich present, promised him everything and they agreed together that the comte would dress as a page in King Guillemot's livery; that the page would bring a garland of flowers to the queen, and would tell her that, his council not having wanted to permit him to go to see her in the apparel of a king, he desired to enter her presence secretly, and had sent her to ask for her permission.

That project was carried out in its full extent, and the nurse did not fail to make much of the gallantry of King Guillemot, with the result that the poor queen found herself pregnant and gave birth after nine months to a beautiful princess without her having heard any further mention of King Guillemot. She nevertheless sent a courier to him to inform him of the birth of his daughter.

King Guillemot became very angry on learning that news, and wanted to put the courier to death, but his council prevented him from doing so, and sent him back with a very piquant letter against the honor of the queen.

As the race of Guillemots was very ancient had had for a motto *Rather death than dishonor*, the entire house was mortified by that insult, especially the king, who was inconsolable and threatened his subjects with allowing himself to die of hunger. It was a primitive century, in which husbands, less polished than those of today, had the simplicity of punishing themselves for their wives' faults.

King Guillemot, having nearly gone mad, was walking along a pathway one day when he heard a voice that followed him, crying *cuckoo, cuckoo*, which was in those days the greatest insult that one could address to a married man. The king flew into a fury, called his guards, and commanded that the reckless individual be hacked to pieces. In spite of all his threats, the voice did not stop. The king was informed, in order to calm him down, that it was a bird, but that only served to irritate him further, convincing him that the entire world was laughing at his adventure, even the birds, which were saying aloud what people were only thinking.

In his wrath, he ordered that all the birds in his kingdom should be exterminated. His vengeance not being satisfied by that cruel massacre, he also wanted them to be eaten. All the courtiers ate some, in order to be obliging, and found them so good that people have continued to do so ever since, although they had previously been horrified by any human who ate a bird, and the pleasure that King Guillemot had in avenging himself caused him to change the resolution he had made to allow himself to die of hunger.

While King Guillemot was exterminating innocent poultry, the queen, who was waiting the return of her courier, nursed the little princess herself, fearing that if she drank the milk of an ordinary nurse, she might also absorb any bad inclinations she might have. As the fays meddled with everything in those days, she sent word to a fay named Belsunsine, one of her friends, who lived in the Pyrenees, asking her to be godmother to the princess.

The fay, sensible to such a great honor, endowed her with an infinite number of good qualities and named her Meridiana. The queen gave a magnificent fête in order to do more honor to the fay, which would have continued for several days but for the arrival of the courier bringing King Guillemot's outraged letter. The poor queen, who had acted in good faith, nearly died when she learned that King Guillemot disavowed the child and as treating her with the utmost indignity.

In her despair, she found no better remedy than to assemble her council; she explained the entire affair to them as it had happened, assuring them that the nurse was a reliable witness to all her conduct. Then she demanded justice against the bad conduct of King Guillemot. It was resolved with a common voice that war should be declared, and although King Guillemot's estates were of far greater extent than Queen Urraca's, her subjects were so convinced of the perfidy of King Guillemot and the innocence of the queen that they all swore to risk their wealth and their lives for the reparation of the insult.

War was declared on King Guillemot, and troops were levied everywhere; serious preparations for battle were made and everyone debated such an extraordinary adventure. Those who knew of the simplicity of King Guillemot and his scant urgency for women judged that the child was not his, knowing full well that he was incapable of making such a voyage or of performing a similar gallantry. The queen had the reputation of being the most virtuous princess on earth, the more her actions were examined, the less occasion was found, or even any pretext, for suspecting her conduct.

Several neighboring potentates wanted to involve themselves in mediation, but the Guillemots, jealous of the point of honor, rejected all the propositions that were made to him to recognize the child, and the queen, who believed that she had been abused under the faith of marriage, preferred to perish with all her subjects if King Guillemot would not admit the fact and beg her pardon for his perfidy.

Comte d'Urgel was one of those who pressed hardest for that element, and as he still loved the queen and did not think much of the Guillemots, he proposed, in order to spare the blood of so many people, to settle the matter in single combat, offering to defend the honor of the queen in the capacity of her champion.

King Guillemot would not accept that challenge, but Prince Guilledin, his brother, who had a courage worthy of the ancient Guillemots, begged the assembled estates of the realm to permit him to fight Comte d'Urgel. As it was a matter of nothing less than the loss of the kingdom, the estates permitted the combat, with great acclamations, and having rendered on the appointed day to the capital city of the queen's estates they found Comte d'Urgel there, who testified much scorn for a champion that he believed to be far beneath his courage.

The combat took place in the presence of the queen and her council, and either because Prince Guilledin was more adroit than Comte d'Urgel or because victory is always declared for the truth, the Prince felled the Comte with a thrust of his lance, which wounded him mortally.

The judges having run to him, he declared before dying that he had deceived the queen with the help of the nurse. The wicked woman was arrested and did not have the strength to contradict what the Comte had just said.

The unfortunate queen, enlightened as to a mystery that, in spite of her good faith, made her appear culpable, would have died of dolor if, on the advice of Belsunsine, she had not suspended her despair for love of Meridiana. She nevertheless ordered that the nurse should be handed over to Prince Guilledin, and that the gilded belt, the pins, the little knife and the scissors that King Guillemot had sent her should be returned to him.

Prince Guilledin returned victorious, and was received in his brother's estates with extraordinary applause. The nurse, imprisoned in an iron cage, was dragged through the streets for a long time, and then thrown into the sea. King Guillemot, who had refused Comte d'Urgel's challenge, was deposed and imprisoned, and Prince Guilledin mounted the throne.

Urraca, ashamed of her misfortunes, did not have the courage to suffer the sight of any of her subjects and retired, with her dear daughter and the fay Belsunsine, to a mountain in the Pyrenees, the highest of all, which is named the Pic du Midi. She put all her application into educating Meridiana well, inspiring her with scorn for all men, and teaching her everything she knew about astrology.

The young person in question was becoming more lovable every day, and already had more intelligence and reason than is usual for children of her age. Belsunsine loved her as tenderly as her own mother, and while Urraca made her party to her science, the fay revealed her supernatural secrets to her. She remembered everything she was told once, and had a nature so mild that she always obeyed without question everything that was demanded of her.

Meridiana's great beauty, her docility and the continuous progress that she made in the sciences and all the secrets of the fays consoled her sad mother greatly, but as all the happiness in life is of short duration, another fay, whose name was Balbasta, jealous of the beauty and the extraordinary talents of the young princess, abducted her secretly. For fear that Belsunsine might discover her retreat she burned juniper and other berries in all the places through which she passed, and imprisoned the princess in a high tower in the Château de Pau, which is at the foot of the Pyrenees. She gave her the task of drawing water from a very deep well, putting it in a sieve, and then climbing five hundred steps, in order to take it to the top of a tower where the fay had a little garden that she made her water.

Queen Urraca, already overwhelmed by misfortunes, was unable to survive the loss of her dear daughter, and died not long after Meridiana's abduction, without the amity that Belsunsine testified for her, or all the assurances that she gave her of taking no repose until she had discovered her retreat, being able to console her.

Meanwhile, Meridiana, far from complaining about her difficult task, acquitted it with a great deal of success, aided by the secrets that Belsunsine had already taught her, without Balbasta ever perceiving it, with the consequence that every time the evil fay appeared, the princess received her very graciously, always begging her to order her to do something more difficult, assuring her that she would never be able to take enough trouble to please such a benevolent fay.

Balbasta, surprised by the rude labor and patience of the princess, nevertheless gave her new occupations every day, the latest of which were always more difficult than the previous ones, all the way to making her pick up a bushel of millet, one seed at a time, threatening to make her suffer horrible tortures if she missed a single one and if she could not tell her how many seeds here were in the bushel.

Meridiana always acquitted herself in the same manner, and never failed to thank Balbasta for her generosity. The fay, vanquished by the docility of the princess, finally wearied of persecuting her, and, having visited Belsunsine one day, whom she found very afflicted, she asked her the subject of her chagrin.

The good fay naturally told her the source of her affliction, exaggerating the beauty, the good nature and the admirable talents of Meridiana; she dissolved in tears in telling her the story. Balbasta, who was convinced of the princess's merits, allowed herself to be softened by her companion's tears, and promised her to discover her retreat and bring her back to the Pic du Midi, on condition that she engaged the charming princess to love her.

Belsunsine, delighted by the mere thought of seeing her dear Meridiana again, promised everything.. The next day, Balbasta returned to the Pic du Midi and presented the princess to Belsunsine, who almost died of joy on seeing her again. She tried to console her for the death of her mother, and the two fays, having embraced her tenderly, both promised her to serve as her mother and not to hide any of their secrets from her. They gave her, in advance, a ring that shielded her from any insults that other jealous fays might make her.

It was a long time before she was able console herself for the death of her mother. She built her a magnificent mausoleum on top of the mountain, and that death did not fail to engage her in further meditations on the unfortunate condition of mortals, who are exposed to so many different miseries, without great princes being dispensed from that fatal vicissitude. She was confirmed then in the resolution she had already made, which her mother the queen had so often inspired in her, to practice virtue, to renounce commerce with humans, to apply herself anew to the knowledge of the stars, and to profit from the goodwill that the fays had for her. Filled with those sentiments, she attached herself strongly to Belsunsine, who finished teaching her everything she knew.

Balbasta, who loved her no less than her companion, made her party to all her secrets; Meridiana attended several assemblies of fays, where she was much admired and applauded. As they remarked that she was informed of all their secrets, and that she was entirely detached from life, they resolved to receive her among the number of fays. She seemed touched by the honor that was being offered to her, but when, in the ceremony, it was proposed that she take the form of a dragon, in order to have the gift of illusions, and to be able to make a magnificent palace appear where there was nothing but smoke, she forbade it, and affirmed that she did not want to deceive anyone. Many of the fays murmured against that delicacy, but it was passed by a majority vote, because of her beauty and her high birth.

As soon as she was a fay she thought of nothing but using her power of enchantment to relieve a hoist of oppressed individuals. She chose for her dwelling a grotto in the Pyrenees, which she ornamented with a large number of beautiful statues, and which is known today as Meridiana's Espalungue.

She traveled to all the countries in the world under the pretext of visiting her companions the fays, to whom she gave rich presents, although she only undertook the voyage in order to acquaint herself with the mores of all nations. She recognized, however, that there was malice, infidelity and weakness everywhere, and that the majority of humans had almost the same faults in whatever country they lived. She did not find any who were perfectly happy and did not desire anything more; that knowledge gave her a great deal of compassion for their miseries, and fortified her in the resolution she had made always to relieve the unfortunate.

Throughout her voyage, she never missed an opportunity to do good. Having arrived in India, at the home of the fay Mamelec, she remarked in her palace a young woman of surprising beauty, who was occupied in cutting stubble to make litter for fifty camels.

Judging that there might be something extraordinary in that, Meridiana asked her who she was. The beauty admitted that she was the daughter of the king of Monomotapa, and told her that her stepmother, seeking to avenge herself for the fact that she had not wanted to marry one of her brothers, had asked the fay Mamelec to abduct her, and that the fay had enchanted her for three hundred years, of which only two hundred had passed as yet. She started to weep as she finished speaking, and begged Meridiana not to distract her from her labor, because if she did not finish by the marked time, four old women who were her overseers would take turns to beat her; the first would give her fifty strokes of a rod on the soles of her feet, the second as many on her shoulders and the other two twenty-five each, half on her belly and half on her buttocks.

Meridiana, moved by the story of so many cruelties, tapped a stone with her wand, and the camel stables were furnished with litter in an instant. The beautiful Indian woman, astonished by that marvel, judged that Meridiana was a great divinity and implored her, her eyes bathed with tears, to have pity on her misery. The fay consoled her and promised to employ herself in her service; she spoke about her to Mamelec, and asked her with such great entreaties for mercy for the beautiful princess that it was granted to her with a good heart.

Meridiana ran to the princess and assured her, while presenting her with a white rose, that in an hour she would find herself in the room from which she had been abducted, in the same garments, with the same youth and beauty that she had had on the day of her abduction.

It is true that she arrived in the palace of her father, the king, but as the kingdom had passed to another house in such a long interval of time, no one recognized her. The king, who had several children, was very surprised to see the princess; her great beauty was admired, but as it was a matter of ceding the kingdom to her, no one dared declare themselves in her favor. The archives were examined, and it was found that it was true that a princess of the royal blood had been abducted by the fays, but what appearance was there that she had returned after two hundred years? In brief, the king did not find it appropriate to get to the bottom of a question that might have cost him his throne.

As all peoples like novelty, and those of Monomotapa were very curious to see such an extraordinary person, the king was led to fear that there might be an uprising in favor of the princess, and he was told that, in order to set his mind at rest and assure his children of the crown, it was necessary, as a matter of good politics, to put her to death. Others, less cruel, suggested that he marry the princess to his eldest son, but the king, who was miserly and hoped to make enough money from the prince's marriage to marry his two daughters, rejected the latter advice and resolved to put the princess to death, accusing her of seducing his people.

She was arrested, but during her trial, the king's eldest son, touched by the charms of the beautiful person, went to declare to his father that if he put the princess to death he would throw himself on the same pyre that had been built to burn her. The king was so offended by his son's declaration that he hastened the execution of the unfortunate princess, but the fay Meridiana, who had foreseen what would happen, went to visit her in her prison and found her much more afflicted by the resolution that the prince had made to die with her than her own misfortune.

The fay approved of the gratitude she had for the young prince, and after having promised her never to abandon her, she told her that her father had hidden a rich treasure in a place that she indicated to her, assuring her that the reigning king would let her marry his son gladly if she revealed that treasure to him. Then she went to the king's cabinet, spoke to him in a menacing tone and called him cruel and a usurper, adding that he was very fortunate to be able to assure the kingdom to his children by means of the marriage of the beautiful princess, who had more treasure than all the other princes of India put together.

She disappeared after saying that, and the king, frightened by that vision, was agitated by a host of confused and various thoughts. His avarice prevailing over all those impulses, however, he resolved to obtain clarification from the princess herself as to whether she had treasure, and, judging that the queen would be better able than him to extract that secret, he charged her with that commission.

The queen, as cunning as all Indians, flattered her and caressed her, already addressing her as her dear daughter-in-law and exaggerating the strong passion that her son had for her, since he wanted to die for her service. The princess, who had already seen the prince several times and knew the obligations she had to him, assured the queen that she would be delighted to conserve that dear son, and told her that if the rights she already had over the crown were not sufficient, she would give her a treasure of inestimable price. The queen embraced her a thousand times, and, that treasure having been found in the place that the fay had indicated, the marriage was made with extraordinary magnificence and the reciprocal satisfaction of the two lovers.

Delighted to have finished such a great favor, Meridiana returned to her grotto in the Pyrenees. Her vigilance and her good heart did not permit her to remain tranquil for long; she was at the childbirth of all the queens, and, not content with preventing the tricks of other fays, she endowed the princess with an extreme beauty and the princes with great valor, and even sometimes rendered them invulnerable. The consequence of that was that in past centuries, the children of kings had no need of their sword to conquer several kingdoms. Meridiana's reputation extended throughout the world, and whatever envy the other fays had against her, she treated them with so much civility and was able to make them such agreeable little presents and speeches that she hardly had any enemies, and was greatly esteemed in all the corps of fays.

The help that she gave crowned heads did not prevent her from rendering services to people of mediocre condition, and if she found a poor shepherdess who did not have the strength to defend her sheep against a hungry wolf, she flew to her aid and took her to a good pasture, which the wolves would not have dared to approach. If a sleeping woodcutter had lost his ax, she did not disdain to bring it back to him, and if a poor traveler fell into the hands of thieves she came to his defense and protected him from their cruelties. In sum, everyone who appealed to the fay Meridiana was sure of being helped promptly. It was by such actions that she won the hearts of persons of all conditions, finding all her pleasure in procuring good and preventing evil.

As there is no one who does not approve of good deeds, although not everyone had the strength to do them, the fays were delighted by all the good they heard said of their companion, and perceived with pleasure that the terror they had once inspired was turning to affection, that they were welcome everywhere and summoned to all the councils of kings, even of particular families. Belsunsine and Balbasta published everywhere the obligation they had to the beautiful Meridiana, and the other fays did not contradict them.

The ambition that slips into all sorts of estates caused the fays to judge that if they chose a queen their corps would become much more considerable, since that queen would be ranked among the other crowned heads. That project having been applauded by all the fays, they met one day in order to hold the election. Having rendered to the market place, the affair was discussed. It was proposed that the power of the person elected should be limited, but, the choice having fallen on Meridiana, all the fays had so much esteem for her and so much confidence in her probity that they gave her a boundless authority, to the point of being able to interdict those who displeased her.

Meridiana was then crowned, in spite of her resistance, and notwithstanding the reasons that she gave the assembly for preferring Princess Merlusine to her. However, she did not abuse her authority, and had even more regard for the fays than she had had before. That good conduct charmed them to such an extent that they had no difficulty in obeying her.

The new queen having firmly established her monarchy, sent the fays away with the order to inform her regularly of everything that was happening in the different countries in which they lived, and she retired herself to her grotto in the Pyrenees, where she received several ambassadors on the part of a large number of sovereigns who had obligations to her, and who congratulated her on her new dignity.

Her elevation gave her new cares, and did not spare her any. Always eager to find, in all the places that she went, that she could be useful to someone, she suffered with impatience anyone thanking her for a benefit, assuring them that she had far more pleasure in giving it than they had in receiving it. She criticized the great for the scant attention they paid to the fortune of their inferiors, since it cost them so little; she excused the faults of everyone, and did not understand how one could resolve to return a bad deed or do any harm to anyone. In sum, there never was anyone who honored virtue more, or who had so much indulgence for human weakness.

She sometimes allowed herself to be seen in her grotto, sometimes on the Pic du Midi, and often in different places, where she listened to all those who wanted to speak to her, even making use of treasures that she discovered for the indigent, giving a princess to be married a bushel of gold as liberally as she gave a modest sum to a shepherdess to repair the loss of a ewe that had died.

A marquise who has been married for a long time without having children was finally fortunate enough to become pregnant; she chose a woman of confidence who had already served as nurse to her son. That nurse having very subtly exchanged her own child with the son of the marquise, the young man had inclinations so base, and gave a thousand chagrins to his supposed parents, to the point that the marquis accused his wife of infidelity, it not being possible that he was the father of such a bad lot. The marquise, who had nothing for which to reproach herself, groaned and wept continually because, as the false marquis grew older, his bad inclinations were further revealed. She had heard mention of the Queen of the Fays and her marvels; that obliged her to undertake a journey to the Pyrenees to implore her aid.

The marquise threw herself at the feet of the fay, imploring her to enable her to die or to change the inclinations of her son. The fay lifted her up very graciously, and told her that she had no reason to lament either for her son or herself, since that son resembled her in body and mind. Mortified and shamed by a response that seemed so disobliging, the marquise was already disposed to leave when Meridiana embraced her and told her how her son had be exchanged by the nurse, how it was easy to prove that by means of a little yellow mark that he had on his left arm. The marquise remembered that immediately, and was impatient to quit the fay in order to go in search of her son. Meridiana, who perceived that, judged that the journey to return to her husband and tell him that good news would be very long, made her a present of two horses that could cover a hundred leagues in an hour, and sent her away very content.

The marquis, who could not console himself for having a heir so unworthy, nearly died of joy on hearing his wife's story. His first impulse was to kill the wicked nurse, but the marquise calmed him down and they went to see the nurse together, who lived on one of their lands. First they asked her for news of her son; she replied, weeping, that he was the worst son in the entire regions, that he had lost their flock, that he spent entire days hunting, adding that he would make a better marquis than a shepherd.

"Would you like to exchange him with ours?" the marquise asked her.

"You think you're joking," retorted the malign shepherdess. "Perhaps you'll do him as much honor as yours, but do better and take charge of both of them."

During that dialogue the young hunter arrived, laden with game, which he presented to the marquis with a politeness worthy of his birth. The marquise, who thought she was looking into a mirror on looking at the young man, who resembled her very closely, could not retain the impulses of nature for long and embraced him several times, her eyes bathed with tears.

"We're talking," the marquis said to him, "of making an exchange of you for my son. Would you be sorry?"

"If that could be," replied the young man, "without doing any wrong to your son, I feel that I have enough courage to sustain such an illustrious rank."

"Yes," the father continued, "but it's necessary, in order to be a marquis, to have a yellow mark on the left arm."

The young man immediately rolled up his sleeve and showed his yellow mark. The marquis and his wife, unable to doubt the truth, embraced him again, and the nurse, seeing the mystery discovered, did not have the strength to maintain her imposture and admitted everything.

It was by similar actions that the Queen of the Fays acquired the esteem and veneration of a infinite number of people, Her generosity was admired by all the fays, but very few were found who wanted to imitate her; on the contrary, the majority made use of their power to cause a thousand woes to humans, either out of envy or malice; they ordinarily devoted themselves to persecuting beautiful women, especially great princesses, which caused Queen Meridiana a great deal of pain. She would have liked to be everywhere, in order to remedy that. She tried several times to give them a horror of evil and inspire noble sentiments in them, but it was futile. There were old hunchbacks who only nourished themselves on the tears and sobs of persecuted princesses, and who would rather have died than cease their malice.

Seeing that bad habits had got the upper hand, and that the matter could not be remedied, Meridiana finally resolved to make use of her authority and the power she had to forbid them the use of their functions as fays for as long as she wished. She assembled them all and expressed to them the sensible displeasure she had in seeing that the fays, who might be honored as divinities if they applied themselves to good, were only thinking, for the most part, of tormenting illustrious persons; that humans were unfortunate enough, by virtue of their short lives, maladies, the lack of possessions and an infinity of unexpected accidents that happened to them on a daily basis, without the fays putting all their industry into persecuting them; that that seemed to her so unjust that she had resolved to prohibit it for three centuries, and only to allow them the liberty to do good, in order that they might have time to apply themselves to exercises of virtue and correct their inveterate malice.

She ordered them thereafter to come, in the final years of the third century, to the hall of the Château de Montargis, which was large and spacious, in order to render her an account of the progress they had made, promising to reestablish in their functions all those whose conduct had been benevolent and who had some good deed in their favor.

That fulminating sentence made the entire troop murmur, but it was necessary to obey. The majority of the fays abandoned the mountains and almost all of them retired to old châteaux, where they amused themselves spinning and waiting for the end of their interdiction, and since that time no more mention has been heard, of abductions or other similar vexations that the fays used to make, and the memory of them would have been lost if their tales did not remain to us.

Queen Meridiana, always applied to good, made a voyage to Fortunate Arabia, from which she brought back cinchona, sage, betony and several other herbs that have the virtue of prolonging life. She planted them in the Pyrenees, where they are still found today, and established a marvelous flower garden, garnished with all sorts of flowers, on the heights of the Pic du Midi, without time having been able to destroy that agreeable flower garden, which still subsists and which curiosity-seekers can see with pleasure. Then she devoted herself, for several years, to studying the crystalline waters that emerged from the Pyrenees, and, having perceived that those waters have several different virtues, she judged that if she could make them pass throughout the mines of gold, lead and sulfur that there are in those mountains, the waters would take on the virtues of those minerals, and would be a great help for the relief of humans. She examined their sources, caused them to flow through new conduits, and mingled them so well that those waters cure all sorts of maladies. It is to the cares of that illustrious fay that we owe the waters of Bagnères, for fevers and various other maladies; those of Bares, for all sorts of wounds; those of Cautères, for indigestions; Aigue-bonne, for ulcers; and Aigue-caure, for rheumatisms.

Although Meridiana was a benefactress for the whole world, she had a particular predilection for her homeland, and, thinking that the majority of kings in those times were cowards or imbeciles, she was touched with compassion by seeing people governed by such princes. The opinion she had that the people of her homeland were all borne to goodness, and the knowledge she had of their intelligence, often made her hope that a prince of Béarn might reign one day in the beautiful realm of France, but as she was a enemy of injustices and that could not be one without dethroning the legitimate kings, she deferred the execution of that project for a long time. Finally, she found an opportunity by virtue of the marriage of Antoine de Bourbon with Jeanne d'Albret, heir to Navarre and Béarn;[23] the fay disposed minds so well that the affair succeeded.

The queen gave birth to four different children, whom the fay, who had long views, abandoned to destinies, not finding that they had the qualities necessary to fulfill her project. But in the end, the queen having become pregnant for a fifth time, the fay endowed the child with a good mind and great valor, and then enabled him to be brought up without any delicacy, just like the children of commoners; and it was him who succeeded to the crown of France by virtue of his merit, and perhaps also the help of the fay.

That prince had a son whom the fay endowed with a great deal of intelligence, valor and justice, but having forgotten to endow those first two with a long life, and perceiving that humans had need of examples who would be present for a long time in order to excite them to virtue, she resolved to repair that fault at the first opportunity; in fact, she gave the sin of the latter prince the justice of his father and the valor of his grandfather, and also added a great piety and a long life.

Satisfied with so many good deeds, and above all in thinking that the Béarnais, for whom she had a great deal of esteem, would have the opportunity in future to make use of their talents and their intelligence, by the favor of the kings that would be their compatriots, she wanted to efface from human minds the memory of the fays and retire to her grotto, where she would remain for several years without seeing anyone.

It was only about two years before the three centuries of the fays' interdiction would elapse when their queen, who had assigned them to the Château de Montargis, perceived that it was in too much disorder to receive such good company. Nevertheless, as the situation of the castle was very advantageous, there was a very spacious hall there, a charming view, a great

---

[23] Antoine de Bourbon married Jeanne d'Albret in 1548; their son succeeded to the French throne as Henri IV.

forest and a beautiful river, Meridiana wanted the assembly to be held there.

Not wanting to make use of her art to reestablish it, however, she remembered that the great prince who was its master took his origin from the region of the Pyrenees, and she was informed that he was able to embellish houses with the same facility as he won battles. She made use appropriately of that knowledge and insinuated to that prince the desire to reestablish the Château de Montargis, which was executed with as much diligence as if the fays had done the work, with the result that the house, abandoned for several years, was soon in a state to lodge several great princesses comfortably.[24] Meridiana having arrived there, all the other fays, impatient to have their interdiction lifted, also went there.

The queen, having received them very favorably, testified the joy that she had in seeing them again, and was the first to render an account of her occupations during the three centuries of their absence. Her modesty caused her to pass succinctly over all the good things she had procured, and she only spoke about the impatience she had had to see them gain, convinced that each of her sisters had done well and had conducted herself much better than she had.

Merlusine, having made a profound reverence, assured the queen that she had never missed an opportunity to do good to those of her house and to many others, and although she had been living for a long time in the mountains of Dauphiné, she had cede her retreat to the Chartreux and retired to the Château de Sassenage, where she did all the good of which she was capable secretly, without any other motive than the satisfaction that well-born souls find in practicing virtue. The queen treated her very civilly, and after having done her much honor and given her great praise, she lifted her interdiction.

---

[24] The restoration of the Château de Montargis in the 1560s was actually carried out by Princesse Renée de France, the younger daughter of Louis XII.

An old fay, bleary-eyed and poorly-built, presented herself before he queen and told her that she had retired to the Château de Pierre-Encise, where she had prevented the prisoners receiving letters from anyone, and, none of them having escaped from that rude prison, demanded for recompense that the queen permit her to perform enchantments as she had before. The queen replied that since the employment of jailer was so much to her taste she ordered her to continue in it, without meddling in anything else. That judgment was applauded, and the poor old fay was jeered loudly.

Then a tall good-looking fay advanced before the queen and told her that she had chosen for her retreat the Château de Moncalieri on the Po; that she had found a duchesse in childbed, who was about to be on a par with queens, that she had endowed the little princess to whom she had given birth with a great deal of intelligence, solid virtue, the most beautiful eyes in the world, a beautiful complexion and even god conduct, very premature, because as soon as she was born she had destined her to occupy the most august throne on earth. She added that her confidence in the good qualities of that amiable princess had gone so far that she had persuaded he duchesse, her mother, to put her to proof for a year, assured that the better one knew her, the more one would love her, which had succeeded, as she had said.

The fay then wanted to talk about many other advantages that she had procured for her homeland, but the queen, seeing that she was entering into details that were too delicate, interrupted her and assured her that what she had done for the charming princess was more than sufficient to merit that she continued to employ enchantment with the same liberty that she had had before her interdiction, and in order to mark how much her conduct was agreeable to her she also lifted in her favor the interdiction of another fay, one of her friends, who had done nothing to merit that favor.

Another fay appeared who had a very composed manner; she told the fay that she had retired a long time ago to the Castello Ferrara; that she had prevented neighboring princes rendering themselves masters of it on several occasions and that her zeal for the religion had engaged her to make that beautiful duchy fall into the hands of the Pope. The queen, without entering into any detail, criticized her for allowing the house of the ancient Dukes of Ferrara become extinct, and dismissed her.

Then another fay presented herself who wore a black velvet toque on her head, and told the queen that she lived in the Château de Boussu in Flanders, and that in order to imitate the good deeds of the Queen of the Fays she had thought that she could not do better than to purge the world of a large quantity of libertines; that in order to succeed in that she had attracted to the château several thousand men of all sorts of nations, and had caused a large proportion of them to perish. The good queen was horrified by that great cruelty, and, having reproached her for the death of several heroes, she forbade her ever to appear in her presence again.

Another fay in hunting costume presented herself before the queen and told her that she had lived in the Château de Fontainebleau a long time before François I had augmented the building; that she had been exposed to an infinity of slanders; thus far, she had been made to pass for a phantom under the pretext that she sometimes hunted in the forest; that she assured Her Majesty that she had never done any harm to anyone, even avoiding frightening shepherds; and that she had had the satisfaction of being present at the first childbirth of a sage queen and had given her child all the virtues of a hero and, above all, a generosity similar to that of the queen, his mother, and that she saw with pleasure that the prince had never told any lie, whether his father had put him at the head of his armies, had summoned him to his council or charged him with other cares. The queen, who was very interested in the prince that the fay had just mentioned, lifted her interdiction and even praised her.

Another fay, who appeared after the one from Fontainebleau, threw herself at the queen's feet and told her that she lived in the Château de Chambord, where she had had almost no opportunity to do good or evil;[25] that she had never-theless had good will; and that, unable to do any better, she had often prevented the foxes from eating the pheasants; she even admitted that the only malice she had ever done was to present herself to a hunter in the form of a fox, made him fire several rifle shots and come back in the same form to ask the hunter whether he had seen two of her little comrades go by. The entire company laughed, including the queen. The fay begged the queen, however, to reestablish her prerogatives as a fay; the queen consented to that, but limited her to doing harm to foxes, wolves, cats and other animals that eat game.

Another fay, who had a very intelligent appearance, pre-sented herself before the queen and said that she had retired to the Château de Chantilly, where she had contributed a great deal to the education of several great heroes; that in recent times she had taken particular care to embellish the house and gardens, and that she had had the skill to attract a princess there who was so charming that she alone, without the help of the waters and the gardens sufficed to render the château the most agreeable abode on earth. The queen, who liked actions in which virtue and industry appeared, permitted her to en-chant as before.

A new fay presented herself, with rather extraordinary garments, and told he queen that she had once lived in Heidel-berg Castle; that other fays, enemies of the house Palatine, had been at the childbed of the Electress and had given several nasty predictions to the princes and princesses born there; that she had only been here once, by chance, at the time when the Electress gave birth to a princess whom she had endowed with great virtue, a good mind, much probity and elevation and a very noble souls; that she had not even neglected to give her beautiful teeth and beautiful hair; but that princess having

---

[25] After the death in 1547 of François I, who had it built as a hunting lodge but hardly used it, the Château de Chambord was abandoned until Louis XIV ordered its restoration in the mid-17th century, but he abandoned it to in 1685.

passed into other states and the electorate into distant branches, in which she did not know anyone, she was resolved no longer to return to Heidelberg, begging the queen to assign her another mansion for her dwelling. The queen, satisfied with the good faith of the German fay, reestablished her former privileges and assigned for the Château de Montargis and its forest for her ordinary dwelling.

Another fay, very replete, prostrated herself before the queen and told her that she lived in the Château d'Amboise and its forest, that once when she was bathing in the Loire she had prevented a boat from capsizing, and that that action alone merited he restoration of her privileges; but the queen remembered that the fay had been part of the conspiracy that had once been woven around the Château d'Amboise, and dismissed her without listening to her any further.[26]

The fay of the Château de Blois presented herself before the queen and told her that she had taken care to conserve in Bois fine language and fine cream, asking to the reestablished in her rights, but the queen, who remembered that she had given occasion to everything that had happened in the last estates of Blois and had a more recent memory of pernicious advice that she had inspired not long ago in a great prince who lived in the château, ordered her to work perfecting Blois cream, and forbade her to meddle in anything else.

Another fay was presented, simply clad, who said to the queen that she was one of the oldest fays in the world, that she lived in the Château de Pons in Saintonge, that she had seen it change master several times, dolorously, and, dreading that it might finally fall into the hands of a bad master, she had procured its possession by a prince who was no less commendable by his intelligence and a host of good qualities than for his

---

[26] The Amboise conspiracy of 1560 was an alleged Huguenot plot to abduct François II and seize political control of the realm.

high birth.[27] The queen, in favor of that good action, permitted the fay to continue to work enchantments as of old.

Another fay came forward, who told the queen that she lived in the Château d'Epagny in Bourgogne, of which she had procured the possession by a great princess, who, by virtue of her extreme beauty, her majestic air and her good conduct merited being compared to the Queen of the Fays, since her reputation was known throughout the world, to the point that peoples of the extremities of the earth had made her their divinity; the fay asked that her privileges be reestablished, and even added that she had never done other malice than once breaking the drawbridge of the château in order to retain for longer the most august company in the world, which she had attracted there. The queen found that she had good taste and lifted her interdiction.

One appeared who had a very serious expression, and said that she lived in the Château de Nancy, that she had seen with a great deal of regret the absence of her prince, that if anything had contributed to console her for that, it was the alliance he had made with a queen of august blood who had a great deal of virtue and piety; that she had abandoned the Château de Nancy for some time to attend the first childbirth of that queen and had endowed the child with a handsome face, great valor and a strong inclination o return to his estates; that, the prince having reached an age to be married, she had conducted his affairs so well that she had procured him a young princess who only counted kings and emperors among her ancestors, but much less considerable by her high birth than her docility, her intelligence and her noble manners. "I flatter myself, great Queen," the fay continued, "that in favor of that illustrious couple, you will reestablish me in my former rights, in the assurance that I give out that the first child born to that marriage will not fail to be endowed very advantageously." The queen started laughing, and lifted the interdiction.

---

[27] The Château de Pons was besieged and destroyed by Louis XIII in 1621.

Another fay presented herself, who spoke a corrupt French and told the queen that she lived in the Château de Ryswick, to which she had attracted by means of her skill the ambassadors of the greatest princes on earth, and after several conferences, had finally obliged them to conclude a good peace.[28] Then she wanted to talk about the merit of the princes of the house of Nassau, to whom the house belonged, but the queen, who was fully convinced, told her that she did not need any other reasons to engage her to lift her interdiction. She praised her zeal highly and not only reestablished all her ancient functions, but accorded her the same favor for another fay, whom she could choose.

A very decrepit fay appeared before the queen, and told her that she had lived in the Château de Loches for a long time, where nothing had very happened against the service of the princess; that even the English, having besieged the castle, which they thought they would take by famine, and having reduced the besieged to the last extremity for want of food, she had imitated the squeal of a pig and started crying night and day on the ramparts, with the result that the English, convinced that here were still abundant provisions within the castle, lifted the siege. In addition, she had exercised such delicacy in the choice of governors of the place that she had only ever suffered persons of great merit and known probity, and that in recent times, when the castle no longer had a garrison or fortifications, she had never relented on the probity of the governor. The queen, who admired actions of honor, reestablished her privileges as a fay.

Another fay presented herself, who told the queen that she lived in the castle of Barcelona, that she had always loved fine actions; that in spite of whatever predilection she might have had for her homeland, she had been so touched by the extreme valor of the two princes who had attacked its ramparts

---

[28] The Treaty of Ryswick, signed in September-October 1697, can only have been concluded very shortly before the story, published in 1698, was written.

that she had not been able to refuse them entry to her castle. The queen replied that all women were virtuous if they were touched by someone's merit, that since she had paid more attention to the valor of the two heroes than to her duty, she ordered her to leave the castle of Barcelona and go to that of Aner, where she could watch over the establishment of that house; she left her the liberty of all her former privileges for that.

The queen was trying to end the session when another fay appeared, dressed in the Turkish style, who said that she had lived for a long time in the castle of Andrinople, where she had often changed the condition of a slave into that of a sultana and that, in order to conform with the character of the Queen of the Fays, she had watched over the conservation of the Ottoman princes, and had even prompted the abolition of the barbaric custom of strangling they younger ones for the security of the eldest. By virtue of that, three brothers had ruled successively, and then the son of the first had succeeded his father and his uncles.

The queen lifted her interdiction, gave great praise to the vigilance of the fay, and said that it was to be wished that all fays had the same attention and watched continuously over the conservation of great princes, lamenting that none had been found to go into Spain to watch over the royal house; but the fays responded that they only chose old castles for their retreat and Her Majesty knew very well that there were no castles in Spain.

Several foreign fays then presented themselves, but the queen, who was convinced of great vexations that they had caused in the countries where they lived, did not want to listen to them, and after having made a very eloquent speech, to exhort those who remained under interdiction to apply themselves to virtue, she closed the session after having signed them to return in three centuries to the hall in the Château de Pau to render her an account of the progress they had made in the exercise of virtue.

François Fénelon: *The Story of Rosimond and Braminte*

There was once a young man more handsome than the day named Rosimond, who had as much intelligence as virtue, whereas his elder brother Braminte was ugly, disagreeable, brutal and malevolent. Their mother, who had a horror of her elder son, only had eyes to see the younger.

The elder, who was jealous, invented a horrible calumny to doom his brother. He told his father than Rosimond often went to see a neighbor who was his enemy, in order to report to him everything that was happening in the house and to give him the means of poisoning his father.

The father, who was very angry, beat his son cruelly, leaving him covered in blood, and then kept him imprisoned for three days without nourishment. Then he threw him out of the house, threatening to kill him if he ever came back. The frightened mother dared not say anything; she only moaned.

The child went away weeping, and, not knowing where to go, he traversed a large wood in the evening. Night surprised him at the foot of a rock. He sat down at the entrance to a cavern on a carpet of moss, where a clear stream ran, and went to sleep, overwhelmed by lassitude.

When he woke up, at daybreak, he saw a beautiful woman mounted on a gray horse with a horse-blanket embroidered with gold. She seemed to be going hunting.

"Have you seen a stag and dogs pass this way?" she asked him.

He replied that he had not.

Then she said to him: "It seems to me that you're afflicted. What's the matter? Look, here's a ring that will render you the most fortunate and the most powerful of men, provided that you don't abuse it. When you turn the diamond inwards, you'll immediately become invisible. As soon as you turn it outwards, you'll appear again. If you put the ring on your little finger, you'll appear to be the son of a king, followed by a magnificent court."

The young man understood immediately that it was a fay who was speaking to him.

After those words, she plunged into the woods. As for him, he returned immediately to his father's house, impatient to try out his ring.

He saw and heard everything, without being discovered. He wanted to avenge himself on his brother without exposing himself to any danger. He only showed himself to his mother, embraced her, and told her all about his marvelous adventure. Afterwards, putting the enchanted ring on his little finger he suddenly appeared as a prince, the son of the king, with a hundred beautiful horses and a large number of richly clad officers.

His father was very astonished to see the king's son in his little house. He was embarrassed, not knowing what respects he ought to render him.

Then Rosimond asked him: "How many sons do you have?"

"Two," replied the father.

"I want to see them. Have them come right away," Rosimond said to him. "I want to take them both to court, to make their fortune."

The timid father replied, hesitantly: "Here's the elder one, whom I present to you."

"Where is the younger one, then?" said Rosimond.

"He isn't here," set the father. "I punished him for a fault, and he's quit me."

The Rosimond said to him: "It was necessary to instruct him, but not to expel him. Give me the elder one anyway, let him come with me. And you, go with these two guards, who will take you to a place I indicate to them."

Immediately, two guards took the father away, and the fay we mentioned, having found him in the forest, struck him with a golden rod and made him enter a dark and profound cavern, where he remained enchanted.

"Stay here," she said to him, "until your son comes to take you away."

Meanwhile, the elder son went to the king's court, at a time when the young prince had embarked to go to war in a distant island. He had been carried away by the winds to unknown coasts where, after a shipwreck, he had been captured by a savage people.

Rosimond appeared in the court as if he were the prince who had been thought to be lost. He said that he had returned thanks to the help of a few merchants, but for whom he would have perished; that caused public joy. The king seemed so delighted that he could not speak, and he never wearied of embracing the son he had believed to be dead. The queen was even more emotional. There was great rejoicing throughout the kingdom.

One day, the person who was passing for the prince said to his veritable brother: "Braminte, you see that I've taken you out of your village in order to make your fortune, but I know that you're a liar, and by your impostures, you've caused the misfortunate of your brother Rosimond. He's hidden here. I want you to talk to him, in order for him to reproach you for your impostures.

Trembling, Braminte threw himself at his feet and confessed his fault.

"It doesn't matter," said Rosimond. "I want you to talk to your brother and ask for his pardon. He'll be very generous if he forgives you; you don't deserve it. He's in my cabinet, where I'll take you shortly. I'll go into a neighboring room, however, in order to let you speak freely with him."

Obediently, Braminte went into the cabinet. Immediately, Rosimond changed his ring, left the room and then came into the cabinet through another door, wearing his natural face. Braminte was very ashamed to see him. He begged his pardon and promised to repair all his faults.

Rosimond embraced him, weeping, forgave him, and said to him: "I'm in full favor with the prince. It only depends on me to make you perish or to keep you in prison for life, but I want to be as good to you as you've been malevolent to me."

Braminte, ashamed and confounded, replied to him submissively, not daring to raise his eyes or to call him brother.

Afterwards, Rosimond made the semblance of undertaking a secret voyage in order to go and marry a princess of a neighboring kingdom, but, under that pretext, he went to see his mother, to whom he related everything that he had done at court, and gave her a little money, the help of which she needed. The king let him take whatever he wanted, but he never took very much.

Meanwhile, a furious war erupted between the king and a neighboring king, who was unjust and broke his word.

Rosimond went to the court of the enemy king, and entered by means of his ring into all that prince's secret councils, always remaining invisible. He took advantage of everything he learned about the enemy's measures. He anticipated them and thwarted them all.

He commanded the army against them, defeated them entirely in a great battle, and soon concluded a glorious peace with them on equitable conditions.

The king thought of nothing but marrying him to a princess, the heiress of a neighboring realm and more beautiful than the graces; but one day, while Rosimond was hunting in the same forest where he had once met the fay, she presented herself to him.

"Refrain carefully from marrying," she said to him, "as if you were the prince. It's necessary not to deceive anyone; it's only just that the prince for whom you are mistaken, returns to succeed his father. Go search for him on an island, to which the winds I send in order to swell the sails of your ship will take you without difficulty. Hasten to render that service to your master, against what might flatter your ambition, and think about reentering your natural condition as a good man. If you don't do that you'll be unjust and unfortunate; I'll abandon you to your former misfortunes."

Rosimond had no difficulty profiting from such sage advice. Under the pretext of a secret negotiation with a neighboring state, he embarked on a ship, and the winds took him first to the island where the fay had told him that the true son of the king was.

The prince was a captive among a savage people, where he was made to guard livestock. Rosimond went invisibly to take him away from the pastures to which he guided his animals, and, covering him with his cloak, which was invisible, like him, he liberated him from the hands of those cruel people.

They embarked together. Other winds obedient to the fay brought them back.

They arrived together in the king's chamber. Rosimond introduced himself and said to him: "You believed me to be your son; I'm not, but I'm returning him to you; look, here he is."

The astonished king addressed himself to his son and said: "Wasn't it you, my son, who vanquished my enemies and made peace gloriously? Or is it really true that you were shipwrecked and taken prisoner, and that Rosimond has rescued you?"

"Yes, Father," he replied. "He's the one who came to the land where I was captive. He took me away. I owe him my liberty and the pleasure of seeing you again. It's to him and not to me that you owe the victory."

The king could not believe what he was being told, but Rosimond changed his ring and appeared to him under the features of the prince. The frightened king saw two men at the same time, who both appeared to be his son.

Then he offered immense sums for so many services to Rosimond, who refused them. He only asked the king for the favor of keeping his brother Braminte in his employment in the court. For himself, he feared the inconstancy of fortune, the envy of men and his own fragility. He wanted to retire to his village with his mother, where he would set about cultivating the land.

The fay, whom he saw again in the woods, showed him the cavern where his father was, and told him the words that it was necessary to pronounce in order to release him. He pronounced them with a very sensible joy.

He freed his father, whom he had been impatient to liberate for a long time, and gave him what he needed to spend his old age comfortably. Rosimond was thus the benefactor of his entire family, and he had the pleasure of doing good to those who had wanted to do him harm.

After having done the greatest things for the court, he only wanted the liberty to live far from its corruption. To complete his wisdom, he feared that his ring might tempt him to emerge from his solitude and engage himself again in great affairs.

He returned to the wood where the fay had appeared to him so favorably. He went every day to the cavern where he had once had the good fortune to see her, in the hope of seeing her there again. Finally, she appeared before him, and he returned the enchanted ring to her.

"I'm returning to you," he said, "a gift of great value, but very dangerous, and which it would be very easy to abuse. I shall only believe myself to be safe when I no longer have the means to emerge from my solitude, with such means of contenting all my passions."

While Rosimond was retuning the ring, Braminte, whose natural malevolence was not corrected, abandoned himself to all his passions, and wanted to engage the young prince, who had become king, to treat Rosimond unworthily.

The fay said to Rosimond: "Your brother, ever the impostor, has attempted to render you suspect to the new king and to doom you. He deserves to be punished, and it's necessary that he perish. I'm going to give him the ring that you're returning to me."

Rosimond wept for his brother's misfortune, but then he said to the fay: "How can you claim to be punishing him by means of such a marvelous present? He'll abuse it in order to persecute all the good people, and to have limitless power."

"The same things," the fay replied, "are a salutary remedy to some and a mortal poison to others. Prosperity is the source of all ills for the wicked. When one wants to punish a rascal, it's only necessary to make him very powerful to make him perish soon."

She went to the palace then. She showed herself to Braminte in the form of an old woman clad in rags, and said to him: "I've withdrawn from your brother's hands the ring I lent him, with which he acquired so much glory. Receive it from me and think hard about the use that you will make of it."

Braminte replied, laughing: "I won't do what my brother did, who was insensate enough to go and look for the prince instead of reigning in his stead."

With the ring, Braminte only thought about discovering the secrets of all the families, committing treasons, murders and infamies, listening to the king's councils and stealing the wealth of individuals. His invisible crimes astonished everyone. The king, seeing so many secrets discovered, did not know to what to attribute that inconvenience, but the limitless prosperity and insolence of Braminte caused him to suspect that he had his brother's enchanted ring. In order to discover him, he made use of a foreigner from an enemy nation, to whom he gave a large sum of money. The man came by night to offer Braminte immense wealth and honors on behalf of the enemy king, if he would let him know via spies all that he could learn about the good king's secrets.

Braminte promised everything, and went to a place where he was given a vast sum to commence his recompense. He boasted about having a ring that rendered him invisible. The next day, the king sent for him; several papers were found on him that proved his crimes.

Rosimond came to the court to ask or mercy for his brother, but it was refused. Braminte was put to death; the ring was deadlier to him than it had been useful to his brother.

In order to console Rosimond for Braminte's punishment, the king returned the ring to him as a treasure of infinite price. The afflicted Rosimond did not judge it likewise; he went to look for the fay in the woods.

"Here's your ring," he said to her. "My brother's experienced has made me understand what I didn't fully understand at first when you told me. Keep this fatal instrument of my brother's doom. Alas, if he were still alive he would not have covered the old age of my father and mother with shame; perhaps he would be sage and happy, if he had never had what he needed to content his desires. How dangerous it is to have more power than other men! Take back your ring. Woe betide those to whom you give it! The only favor I ask of you is never to give it to anyone in whom I have an interest."

The Story of Florise

A peasant woman knew a fay who lived nearby. She asked her to come to one of her childbeds, where she had had a daughter. First the fay took the child in her arms and said to the mother: "Choose: she will be, if you wish, as beautiful as the day, with an intelligence even more charming than her beauty, and the queen of a great realm, but unhappy; or she will be ugly and a peasant, like you, but content in her condition."

The peasant woman immediately chose beauty and intelligence, with a crown, for the child, at the risk of some unhappiness.

So there was the little girl, whose beauty was already commencing to outshine all those that had ever been seen before. Her intelligence was mild, polite and insinuating; she learned everything that anyone wanted to teach her, and soon knew better than those who had taught her. She danced on the grass on feast days with more grace than any of her companions. Her voice was more touching than any musical instrument, and she made up the songs she sang herself.

At first she did not know that she was beautiful, but while playing with her companions on the edge of a clear spring, she saw herself, and noticed how different she was from the others. She admired herself. The whole country, from which people came in crowds to see her, made her even more aware of her charms. Her mother, who was counting on the fay's predictions, already regarded her as a queen, and spoiled her with her complaisance. The young girl did not want to spin, sew or look after the sheep; she amused herself picking flowers, ornamenting her head, singing and dancing in the shade of the woods.

The king of the country was very powerful; he had only one son, named Rosimond, whom he wanted to marry. He could never resolve to hear mention of any princess of neighboring estates, because a fay had assured him that he would find a peasant more beautiful and more perfect than all the princesses in the world. He made the resolution to assemble all the village girls in his realm below the age of eighteen, in order to choose the one who was most worthy.

An innumerable quantity of young women who were only of mediocre beauty were excluded right away, and thirty were separated out who surpassed all the rest infinitely. Florise—that was the name of our young woman—had no difficulty in being among that number.

The thirty young women were lined up in the middle of a great hall, in a kind of amphitheater where the king and his son were able to look at them all at the same time. Immediately, Florise appeared in the midst of all the others like a beautiful anemone among marigolds, or a flowering orange tree in the midst of wild bushes. The king cried that she merited the crown.

Rosimond thought himself fortunate to possess Florise. Her village clothes were taken away; she was given others embroidered with gold. In an instant, she was covered in pearls and diamonds. A large number of ladies were occupied in serving her. Everyone only thought about divining what might please her, in order to give it to her before she went to the trouble of asking for it. She was lodged in a magnificent apartment in the palace, which only had, instead of tapestries, large glass mirrors as tall as the rooms and he cabinets, in order that she should have the pleasure of seeing her beauty multiplied in all directions, and the prince could admire her wherever he cast his eyes.

Rosimond had given up hunting, gambling and all physical exercise in order to be with her incessantly, and as his father died shortly after the marriage it was the sage Florise, having become queen, whose advice determined all matters of state.

The queen, mother of the new king, whose name was Gronipote, was jealous of her daughter-in-law. She was cun-

ning, malign and cruel. Old age had added a frightful deformity to her natural ugliness, and she resembled a fury. Florise's
beauty made her appear even more hideous, and irritated her
continually; she could not tolerate such a beautiful person dis-
figuring her; she also feared her intelligence, and abandoned
herself to all the furies of envy.

"You have no heart," she often said to her son, "for having wanted to marry that little peasant, and you have the base-
ness to make her your idol. She's proud, as if she were born in
the place where she is. When the king your father wanted to
marry, he preferred me to any other because I was the daughter of a king equal to him. That's what you should have done.
Send that little shepherdess back to her village and think about
some young princess whose birth is appropriate to you."

Rosimond resisted his mother, but one day, Gronipote
stole a note that Florise had written to the king and gave it to a
young man of the court, whom she obliged to take it to the
king, as if Florise has testified to him all the amity that she
owed to the king alone.

Rosimond, blinded by jealousy, and by virtue of the malign advice given to him by his mother, had Florise imprisoned
for life in a high tower built on the point of a rock that rose up
over the sea. There she wept night and day, not knowing by
what injustice the king, who had loved her so much, treated
her so unworthily. She was only permitted to see an old woman to whose care Gronipote had confided her, and who insulted her continually in that prison.

Then Florise remembered her village, her cabin and all
her rural pleasures.

One day, while she was overwhelmed with dolor and deploring the blindness of her mother, who had preferred that
she be a beautiful and unhappy queen rather than an ugly
shepherdess content with her lot, the old woman who treated
her so badly came to tell her that the king was sending an executioner to cut off her head and that she had nothing more to
do than to resolve herself to die. Florise declared that she was
ready to receive the blow.

In fact, the executioner sent by order of the king, on Gronipote's advice, was holding a huge cutlass for the execution when a woman appeared who said that she had come to say a few words in secret to Florise before her death. The old woman allowed her to speak to her, because the person seemed to her to be one of the ladies of the palace, but it was the fay who had predicted Florise's misfortunes at her birth, and who had taken on the features of the queen mother's lady-in-waiting. She spoke to Florise in private, taking her away from everyone else.

"Would you like," she said to her, "to renounce the beauty that has been so fatal to you? Would you like to quit the title of queen, resume your old clothes and return to your village?"

Florise was delighted to accept that offer. The fay applied an enchanted mask to her face; immediately, her facial features became coarse and lost their proportion; she became as ugly as she had been beautiful and agreeable. In that state, she was unrecognizable, and she passed without difficulty through all the people who had come to witness her execution.

She followed the fay and went with her to her homeland.

They searched hard for Florise, but could not find her anywhere in the tower. The news was taken to the king and Gronipote, who mounted further searches throughout the kingdom, by fruitlessly. The fay had returned her to her mother, who would not have known her after such a great change had she not been warned.

Florise was content to live, ugly, poor and unknown, in her village, where she looked after her sheep. She heard people every day recounting her adventures and deploring her misfortunes. Songs had been invented about her, which made everyone weep; she took pleasure in singing them with her companions, and she wept at them like the others, but she thought that she was happy looking after her flock, and never wanted to tell anyone who she was.

The Story of King Alfaroute and Clariphile

There was a king named Alfaroute who was feared by all his neighbors and loved by all his subjects. He was wise, good, just, valiant and clever; nothing was lacking in him. A fay came to find him and told him that great misfortunes would soon befall him if he did not make use of the ring that she put on his finger. When he turned the diamond of the ring inside his hand, he immediately became invisible, and as soon as he turned it outwards again, he was visible, as before.

That ring was very convenient for him and gave him great pleasure. When he was suspicious of one of his subjects, he went into the man's cabinet with his diamond turned inwards; he heard and saw all domestic secrets without being perceived. If he feared the designs of some neighboring king, he went to all his most secret councils, where he learned everything without ever being discovered. Thus, he anticipated without difficulty everything that anyone wanted to do against him; he thwarted several conspiracies formed against his person, and disconcerted the enemies who wanted to crush him.

He was, however, not content with his ring, and he asked the fay for a means of transporting himself in an instant from one country to another, in order to be able to make prompter and more convenient use of the ring that rendered him invisible.

"You're asking too much," the fay replied, with a sigh. "Fear that the last gift might be harmful to you."

He did not listen, and still pressed her to grant it to him.

"Well," she said, "it's necessary, then, for me to give you, reluctantly, what you'll repent of having."

Then she rubbed his shoulder with an odorous liquid. Immediately, he felt two small wings born on his back. Those little wings would not show under his clothing, but when he had resolved to fly, he had only to touch them with his hand;

they would immediately become so long that he would be able to surpass infinitely the rapid flight of an eagle. As soon as he no longer wanted to fly, he had only to touch his wings again; they would shrink immediately, in such a way that they could no longer be perceived under his garments.

By that means, the king could go anywhere in a matter of moments; he knew everything, and no one could imagine how he divined so many things, for he shut himself away and appeared to remain in his cabinet almost all day long, without anyone daring to enter it. As soon as he was there he rendered himself invisible by means of his ring, extended his wings by touching them and traveled immense distances.

By that means he engaged in great wars, in which he won all the victories he wanted, but as he saw the secrets of men incessantly he knew that they were so wicked and deceptive that he no longer dared to trust anyone.

The more powerful and redoubtable he became, the less he was loved, and he saw that he was not loved even by those to whom he had given the greatest wealth. In order to console himself, he resolved to go into all the countries in the world to search for a perfect woman whom he could marry, by whom he could be loved, and by means of whom he could render himself happy.

He searched for a long time, and as he saw everything without being seen, he knew the most impenetrable secrets. He went into all courts; he found deceptive women everywhere, who wanted to be loved but who loved themselves too much to love a husband in good faith. He went into all private houses. One woman had a light an inconstant mind, another was hypocritical, another arrogant, another eccentric; almost all were false, vain and idolaters of their own person.

He descended as far as the lowest conditions, and finally found the daughter of a poor laborer, as beautiful as the day, but simple and ingenuous in her beauty, which she counted for nothing, and which was, in fact, the least of her qualities, for she had an intelligence and a virtue that surpassed all her personal graces. All the youth of her neighborhood hastened to see her, and every young man believed that he would assure the happiness of his life by marrying her.

King Alfaroute could not see her without being impassioned by her. He asked her father for her, who was transported with joy to see that his daughter would be a great queen.

Clariphile—that was her name—passed from her cabin into a rich palace, where a numerous court received her. She was not dazzled by it; she conserved her simplicity, her modesty and her virtue, and she did not forget where she had come from when she was heaped with honors.

The king's tenderness for her was redoubled, and he finally believed that he would succeed in being happy. It would not have taken much for him to be happy already, so proud was he commencing to be of his queen's good heart. He rendered himself invisible continually in order to observe her and to surprise her secrets, but he did not discover anything in her that was not worthy of admiration. He no longer had any but a residuum of jealousy and suspicion that still troubled him slightly in his amity.

The fay who had predicted the fatal consequences of her last gift warned him frequently, and he was importuned by her. He gave orders that she was no longer to be allowed to enter the palace, and told the queen that he forbade her to receive her. The queen promised to obey, with a great deal of difficulty, because she liked the good fay very much.

One day, the fay, wanting to instruct the queen with regard to her future, entered her apartment in the guise of an officer, and told the queen who she was. Immediately, the queen embraced her tenderly. The king, who was then invisible, perceived it, and was transported by jealousy to the point of fury. He drew his sword and ran the queen through, who fell into his arms, dying.

At that moment, the fay resumed her veritable form. The king recognized her, and understood the queen's innocence. Then he tried to kill himself. The fay stopped the thrust and tried to console him.

As she died, the queen said to him: "Although I am dying by your hand, I am dying entirely yours."

Alfaroute deplored his misfortune in having wanted, in spite of the fay, a gift that was so deadly. He returned her ring and begged her to take away his wings. He spent the rest of his days in bitterness and dolor. He had no other consolation than going to weep over Clariphile's tomb.

The Story of an Old Queen and a Young Peasant Girl

There was once a queen so old, so very old, that she had neither teeth nor hair. Her head shook like leaves stirred by the wind; she could no longer see, even with spectacles; the tip of her nose and that of her chin touched one another. She had shrunk by half, and all in a ball, with a back so curbed that one might have thought that she had always been deformed.

A fay who had been present at her birth accosted her and said to her "Would you like to be rejuvenated?"

"Willingly," replied the queen. "I'd give all my jewels to be no older than twenty years."

"It's necessary, then," the fay went on, "to give your old age to someone else, whose youth and health you'll take. To whom will you give your years?"

The queen searched everywhere for someone who wanted to be old in order to rejuvenate her.

Many beggars came forward who wanted to be old in order to be rich, but when they had seen the queen cough, spit, gasp and live on broth, dirty, hideous, stinking, suffering and gibbering a little, they no longer wanted to be charged with her years; they preferred begging and wearing rags.

Ambitious men also came, to whom she promised high rank and great honors. "But what would we do with rank?" they said, after having seen her. "We wouldn't dare show ourselves, being so disgusting and so horrible."

Finally, a young village girl presented herself, as beautiful as the day, who asked for a crown as the price of her youth. Her name was Petronelle. The queen was annoyed at first, but what could she do? What was the point of getting annoyed? She wanted to be rejuvenated.

"Let's share my realm," she said to Petronelle. "You can have half of it and I'll have the other. That's quite enough for you, who are a little peasant girl."

"No," replied the girl, "That isn't enough for me; I want it all. Leave me my condition of a peasant with my flowery complexion, and I'll leave you your hundred years with your wrinkles and the death that has you in its claws."

"But what will I do, if I have no realm?" the queen responded.

"You'll laugh, you'll dance and you'll sing, like me," said the girl. As she spoke, she started to laugh, to dace and to sing.

The queen, who was far from being able to do as much, said to her: "What would you do in my place? You're not accustomed to old age."

"I don't know what I'll do," said the peasant girl, "but I'd like to try, for I've always heard it said that it's a fine thing to be a queen."

While they were bargaining, the fay arrived, and said to the peasant girl: "Would you like to make your apprenticeship as an old queen, to see whether the métier would suit you?"

"Why not?" said the girl.

In an instant, wrinkles covered her face, her hair went white, she became grumpy and sullen; her head shook, and all her teeth too; she was already a hundred years old. The fay opened a little box and took out a host of officers and richly-dressed courtiers, who grew as they emerged and rendered a thousand respects to the new queen.

A great feast was served, but she had no appetite and could not chew; she was ashamed and astonished; she did not know what to say or do; she coughed as if she were about to come apart; she drooled over her chin; she had sticky mucus hanging from her nose, which she wiped away with her sleeve; she looked at herself in a mirror and found herself uglier than a she-ape.

Meanwhile, the veritable queen was in a corner, laughing and beginning to become pretty; her hair came back, and her teeth too; she recovered a good complexion, fresh and pink; she straightened up, with a thousand little affectations; but she was dirty, short-skirted, with dirty garments that seemed to have been dragged through ashes. She was not accustomed to that attire, and the guards, mistaking her for some scullion, wanted to throw her out of the palace.

Then Petronelle said to her: "Now you're embarrassed by no longer being queen, and I'm even more so. Look, here's your crown, give me back my gray smock."

The exchange was immediately made; the queen grew old again and the peasant was rejuvenated. Scarcely had the change been made than they had both repented of it, but it was too late; the fay condemned each of them to remain in her condition.

The queen wept every day as soon as she had a pain in the tip of a finger; she said: "Alas, if I were Petronelle, at the present moment, I'd be lodged in a cottage and living on chestnuts, but I could dance under the elm-trees with shepherds to the sound of a flute. What's the use of a good bed, where I do nothing but suffer, and so many people, who can't soothe me?"

That chagrin augmented her woes; the physicians, a dozen of whom were incessantly around her, also augmented them.

Eventually, after two months, she died.

Petronelle made a round dance along a clear stream with her companions when she learned of the queen's death; then she recognized that she had been luckier than wise in having lost her royalty.

The fay came back to see her and gave her a choice of three husbands. One was old, chagrined, disagreeable, jealous and cruel, but rich, powerful and a great lord who could not do without her beside him night and day; another was good-looking, mild, obliging, amiable and of noble birth, but poor and unfortunate in everything; the last was a peasant like her, who was neither handsome not ugly, who would not love her either too much or too little, and who would be neither rich nor poor.

She did not know which to choose, for, naturally, she liked the fine clothes, carriages and great honors very much; but the fay said to her: "Get away, you're a fool. Do you see that peasant? That's the husband you need. You'd love the second too much; you'd be loved too much by the first; both of them would make you unhappy; it's quite enough that the third won't beat you. It's better to dance on the grass, or in the bracken, than in a palace, and to be Petronelle in the village than an unhappy lady in high society. Provided that you have no regret for grandeurs, you'll be happy all your life with your laborer."

Chevalier de Mailly: *The Illustrious Fays*

Blanche-Belle

Lamberie, Marquis de Montserrat, governed his estates with a great prosperity; everything succeeded for him as he wished. With the exception of a single item that he desired passionately, he possessed everything that makes for human felicity; but he had never been able to have children, for which reason the marquise, his wife, as in great affliction.

The marquise had heard mention of the birth of Romulus, which antiquity attributes to a simple conversation that Rhea, his mother, had had with a sylph. She wished a thousand times to have such an adventure, and in any manner whatsoever, she desired to efface the shame of not having been able to be a mother.

One day, when she was alone in an arbor in her garden, her imagination being full of the power of sylphs, she fell asleep, and was occupied during her sleep by a dream that gave her great pleasure. She thought she had spent a very agreeable night with a sylph as beautiful as Amour, and she woke of firmly convinced that she was pregnant.

She was not mistaken; she gave birth nine months later to a daughter who seemed, at birth, to be marvelously beautiful.

As husbands have the eccentricity of not approving of their wives having mysterious conversations, even with sylphs, the marquise kept her dream secret and allowed the marquis to flatter himself that he was the father of the charming little princess, who was named Blanche-Belle.

In a few years she became the marvel of marvels by virtue of her beauty; she was brought up with so much care that she was soon seen to have the admiration of all Montserrat. The rumor having spread throughout Italy that there had never been a person so perfect, there was no potentate who did not aspire to her conquest. Apart from the charms that rendered her so desirable she obtained from the sylph to whom she owed the light of day a gift of infinite price, for every time she opened her eyes when she woke up a pearl emerged from each of them, and the first word she spoke every day was accompanied by a ruby that fell from her mouth; that was the source of an immense wealth.

Knowing that she had such a fine means of amassing great wealth, the marquis found the choice of the prince whose felicity she would be very difficult. He thought, before being separated from her, of making use of such a fine opportunity to put his house in a very flourishing state, and he accumulated such great treasures that nothing could any longer be lacking in the course of his life.

Having taken that prudent precaution he decided to examine which of all the princes who aspired to Blanche-Belle's hand was the most worthy to possess such beauty and such grandeur. He even consulted the charming daughter whom he loved so tenderly, and having learned that she did not have any inclination to marriage as yet, and that none of those who had sighed for her had touched her heart, he did not press her to determine herself, in the hope that, with the merits and the admirable secrets that she had, she could always choose whoever pleased her when the desire to engage herself had come to her.

She had been in that state of nonchalance for a long time when the most lovable prince that the sun had ever illuminated appeared at the court of Casal; that was Fernandin, King of Naples, who, wanting to visit all the courts of Italy, having commenced with Milan and then come to Casal, limited his curiosity there. As soon as he had seen Blanche-Belle all his projects were converted into that of pleasing her. The princess, for her part, found him so lovable that, the marquis having asked her how he seemed to her, she confessed frankly that she would not be sorry if a prince of his sort wanted to think about her, and declared to her father that she would be entirely ready to obey if he commanded her to listen to him favorably when he made her the offer of his heart.

At the same time, the King of Naples meditated the means of rendering himself agreeable to the marquis and his daughter, and had no difficulty in succeeding; the dispositions were so great on either side for that alliance that it was concluded as soon as it was proposed. The marriage was celebrated with great pomp. The marquis was satisfied to have found such a great king for a son-in-law, and the princess, his daughter, charmed by the merit of the king, her husband, believed herself to be the most fortunate person in the world.

The king wanted to show all his subjects the lovely princess that made his happiness. She appeared in Naples, utterly brilliant in her beauty, and her garments were decorated everywhere by pearls and rubies. The people, dazzled by so much splendor, went as far as adoration for their incomparable queen, and the king's contentment was inexpressible, in possessing, in the midst of the applause of a great city, the loveliest princess in the world. As there has not yet been any eternal happiness, however, it is not surprising that his was troubled.

The King of Tunis, having learned that Fernandin was the master of such a rare treasure, resolved to steal it from him. Keenly affected by the account that had been given to him of the beauty of Queen Blanche-Belle and the gift that she had of producing pearls and rubies every day, he prepared great armaments in order to make war on Fernandin, who, having as much care to conserve his dear Blanche-Belle as his crown, sent her to a castle he had in the depths of the woods and asked his father's widow, and a daughter she had from a previous marriage, to keep her company.

They agreed to do that willingly, glad to have the opportunity to carry out an evil design that they had been meditating against Queen Blanche-Belle since the first day she had appeared in Naples. The old queen hated her mortally, because she occupied a place that she had intended to have her daughter fill, King Fernandin having showed her some good will while his father was alive, to the extent of making her hope that he would marry her when he was king.

Neither the old queen nor her daughter had made any complaint about the king's infidelity, but they were no less to be feared in consequence. The king ought to have realized that a dissimulated hatred is all the more dangerous for it, and that a woman abandoned for another rarely pardons the affront that she considers has been offered to her. Blanche-Belle's adventure provided a famous example of that.

As soon as the old queen had that charming person at her disposition in a castle of which she was the mistress, she thought of nothing but her undoing, and putting her daughter in her place. But how could the king be deceived and the queen put in a place where he would never be able to find her? For, wicked as the old queen was, she was not wicked enough to kill a person who gave her a thousand caresses every day, or perhaps she did not want to render the king irreconcilable if he discovered the trick she had played on him.

In all the embarrassments of such a great design, the old queen thought that she could not do better than take advantage of the help and advice of an illustrious fay who had contributed a great deal, by means of her art, to making her queen, and had always taken a particular care of whatever concerned her since her childhood. She went to find her, therefore. The fay's palace was in the densest part of the wood. The old queen went there, only taking her daughter with her.

After having consulted her carefully, and taken good measures, she said one day to Queen Blanche-Belle that she wanted to take her to the most beautiful place that she had ever seen. It was, she said, a beautiful meadow surrounded by canals in which ran the most beautiful water one could ever see, and which was filled with all kinds of fish. At one end of the meadow, she also said, there was a castle where one of her old friends lived, to whom she would be pleased to introduce her, and who could only be seen at home because she had been ill and had only just recovered. To give the young queen even more curiosity, she told her that her friend was knowledgeable, like the fays, and that by looking at her hand she would be able to tell her what would become of the enterprise of the King of Tunis, and all the most considerable things that would happen to her in the course of her life.

What curiosity does a young woman not have who knows that her husband, whom she loves tenderly, is exposed to the uncertain events of war? Has one ever been seen who neglected to know the future? It is not astonishing, therefore, that the young queen allowed herself to be seduced and led to a place where she would have spent her life miserably if the sylph who had presided over her birth had not had the power to take her out of it. The sylph was the son of a fay more powerful than the old queen's friend, who had never refused anything to the sylph, the most accomplished of her children.

The old queen, who thought that Blanche-Belle would never find a means of getting out of the hands of her friend the fay, took her boldly to her home, where, as soon as the charming queen had arrived, she found herself imprisoned in an apartment in the palace. The queen told her that it was a just punishment for the infidelity that she had caused the king to commit against her daughter, whom he had promised to marry, but that no other accident would befall her than the loss of a lover who did not belong to her, and that she would be served in her apartment in a manner that would leave her nothing to desire.

Blanche-Belle found herself in a remote place, at the mercy of an aged individual whom she did not know and who appeared to her to be omnipotent in that place, by virtue of the quantity of black men and dwarfs who all wore collars like slaves. It is not surprising that a young person would be frightened in such circumstances and that she had recourse to submission and prayers as she tried to conserve her life. The fay assured her that she had nothing to fear, and even promised to do everything possible to render her captivity supportable.

It is true that, in addition to having Blanche-Belle served with great respect in her apartment, she gave her very good food, and even gave her the pleasure every day of music and having books brought to her. She ameliorated her solitude in that way, but she had placed pitiless guards at the door of her apartment, with the consequence that she could never go out.

The old queen had returned to her castle with her daughter, to whom her friend the fay, by means of the art of enchantment, had given such a perfect resemblance to Blanche-Belle that everyone was deceived by it. The queen said that she had left her daughter with her friend, who had asked for her to keep her company, and that she had left her there all the more willingly because she had promised to make her the heiress of her castle and al her wealth.

There was nothing more to desire than to be able to accustom the new princess to all the mannerisms of Blanche-Belle, in order for the resemblance she had to be perfect. The queen took care to instruct her, and hoped that the king would be satisfied. There was only one defect for which there could be no remedy; the fay did not have the power to grant her the gift of pearls and rubies that Blanche-Belle had; but as the queen had taken care to accumulate a great quantity while Blanche-Belle produced them, she believed that would be a means of deceiving the king for a long time. She knew, in any case, that he had never cared a great deal about that sort of wealth, and there was reason to think that he would regard it with even more nonchalance if he came back, as there was every appearance that he would, victorious over the King of Tunis.

The king did indeed return to Naples soon, after a complete victory, and sent in all diligence for his charming Blanche-Belle. The old queen set forth immediately with such great confidence in the measures she had taken to make her daughter queen that she had no doubt that she would see her fill that place for life.

The deceit had been so cleverly carried out that the king believed, in the first days, that he possessed his lovely

Blanche-Belle; he found, however, something lacking and believed that she had lost part of her charms; gradually, that thought threw him into a distaste so great that it was soon followed by a sadness and melancholy, by which he was gripped without being about to say precisely why. Finally, that melancholy extended so far that, no longer taking any pleasure in his court, he resolved to go hunting with only a few companions. He chose the castle in the forest where he had asked that the queen be taken during the war.

He hunted there for several days in succession, and the hunt always took him within sight of a castle that he did not know; but he was so nonchalant that he did not reflect greatly about that. He was so detached from everything that he had no curiosity; even the hunting occupied him without giving him any pleasure.

That was the insipid state into which the king had fallen when he was suddenly extracted from it by a voice that was audible at a window of the castle, which he thought he recognized. Unable to determine precisely who it was, he approached, and saw someone extending her arms to him and asking for help, in a voice that penetrated all the way to the depths of his heart. He moved a little closer, and suddenly felt reborn all the vivacity of the initial ardor he had had for Blanche-Belle. He finally recognized that he was seeing the veritable object of his passion, but he was in a strange surprise on seeing in the castle someone he believed to be in Naples, and having reflected on the sudden change that had occurred in his heart, he did not know whether what he saw might be a dream.

His surprise was even greater when he saw the person in mid-air. She descended a moment later to alight gently beside him. His heart told him that it was his veritable Blanche-Belle. He jumped to the ground and, having embraced her tenderly, they were unable to speak or to quit one another for several moments. When the first transports of joy had passed, Blanche-Belle gave the king an account of her adventure, and how she had felt herself lifted up and carried through the air by an unknown power.

She was obliged for that to the sylph that had presided over her birth; he had come to deliver her from a captivity to which she had thought herself condemned for life and allow her to find again the perfect felicity the loss of which she had regretted a thousand times more than her liberty.

The king, more passionate than he had ever been, deferred the care of his vengeance in order not to think about anything but taking his charming Blanche-Belle back to the castle where he had his petty court and getting away from a place he did not know, where there was so much for her to fear.

He assembled his council the following day, where he exposed the wickedness of the old queen and the trick that she and her daughter had played on him. He also explained the grounds he had to complain of the fay who had lent her power to it. After having heard the advice of everyone, all of whom favored severe punishment, he ordered, on his own impulse, the sole penalty of banishment against the old queen and her daughter, and that the fay's castle be demolished.

The queen and her daughter had already retired before having heard the judgment pronounced against them, however, and the fay's castle was sought in vain by those sent to raze it. It appeared that it had been transported elsewhere, and wherever it was, it served as a retreat for the old queen and her daughter, who went to spend their lives there in the regret of having committed a futile crime. They left King Fernandin the happiest of all princes, with the charming Blanche-Belle, for whom his passion augmented every day during the course of a long life: a marvel of which no example had ever been seen before.

The Magician King

There was once a king who was powerful as much by virtue of the extent of his domination as the secrets of magic that he possessed. After having spent the years of his youth in all the pleasures that a rich magician prince could not lack, he encountered a princess of great beauty who fixed his fickle humor, for he had always flown from beauty to beauty before. He asked for her in marriage, and having obtained her, he thought himself the most fortunate of men in possessing such a lovable person, by whom he was loved perfectly.

Before the end of the year that beauty gave birth to a son worthy of his heritage, for he appeared as soon as he entered the world so marvelously beautiful that he won the admiration of the whole court. As soon as the queen, his mother, thought she was strong enough to undertake a short journey, she used the pretext of taking him for some fresh air to carry him secretly to the home of a fay who was her godmother. I say secretly because the fay had warned the queen that the king was a magician, and as there has always been a fierce war between sorcerers and fays, the king would not have approved of anyone having commerce with the latter.

The queen's godmother had a palace in a forest that was not far from the court. The queen, as I said, took her son there in order that he might receive the gifts of faerie, so useful in the adventures for which princes are destined.

The fay, who was particularly interested in everything concerning the queen, and who found the young prince very pretty, gave him the art of pleasing everyone, so to speak, from the cradle, and in the fullness of time, a marvelous facility to learn everything that might render him a accomplished prince one day. He made such rapid progress therein that all those charged with his education were charmed to see that he surpassed their expectations every day.

The prince, for whom so much was hoped, was not very old when he lost the queen, his mother, who gave him, as a final item of advice, as she died, to resolve nothing of consequence without having asked the opinion of the fay who had taken him under her protection.

The prince received the queen's advice with all possible respect, and her last sighs with an affliction that cannot be expressed without having seen it, and which nothing could equal but that of the king, his father, who was inconsolable in losing a charming princess with whom he had hoped to spend the happiest life that he could have desired.

Neither time nor reason could console the king, and, the sight of all the places in his palace where he had conversed with that charming person renewing his grief every day, he resolved to go traveling with a few companions. As he was a magician, however, he often abandoned those companions for several days, and sometimes for several weeks; but after having traveled, under different forms, in all the countries that awakened his curiosity, he returned to the place where he had left his retinue.

After having roamed for a long time from one realm to another without finding anything that touched him, he decided to transform himself into an eagle, and in that guise he cleaved the air, traversing a host of countries into which he had not yet been, and finally reached a region that he found very agreeable by virtue of the sweetness of the air one breathed there, caused by the odor of the jasmine and the orange-blossom with which the ground was covered.

Charmed by that odor, he descended to fly a little lower in order to see at closer range what was giving him so much pleasure. Finally, he perceived gardens below him that appeared to him to be of enchanted beauty, flower-beds planted in different fashions, charged with all the most beautiful flowers imaginable; fountains full of clear fresh water threw a hundred different figures into the air in as many jets of water, which rose up to a prodigious height. In another direction, waterfalls whose sound was appropriate to entertain melancholy were presented to his eyes.

There were also several canals lined with marble and porphyry, charged with small galleys and gondolas, on which gold and azure could be seen shining all the way to the oars. But objects even more brilliant caught the eyes. Several women of great beauty, clad in a manner to dazzle, by virtue of the quantity of pearls and diamonds with which their woven garments were decorated, filled the galleys and gondolas. It was the queen of the country, with her daughter the princess beside her, more beautiful than the day star, and all the ladies of her court, who had emerged from the palace in order to take the air as soon as the sun had set.

No mortal had ever appeared as brilliant as that adorable princess appeared then, and the king needed his eagle's eyes in order to sustain her splendor. He was so charmed by such a beautiful spectacle that he lost the use of his wings, and was stopped by a power that it was impossible to resist. He perched at the top of a tall orange-tree on the edge of the canal that bore that superb fleet, and from there he contemplated the attractions of the divine princess for a long time.

As an eagle that has the heart of a king is audacious, he formed instantly the design of carrying off the princess. He was so touched by her beauty that he anticipated that he could no longer live without possessing her. That design was great, and far beyond the strength of an ordinary eagle, but the king found forces in his art proportionate to his project, and being provided with them, he did not think any longer of anything but making it succeed.

He waited until the princess had emerged from the galley, and, seeing her slightly separated from her companions, he judged his time so well that he lifted her up into the air before her squire, who was preparing to give her his hand, had perceived him. The princess uttered cries and plaints so touching between the claws of her abductor that it would not have taken much for him to repent of his enterprise. However, as it would have been weakness to fail to complete the execution of such a fine design, the eagle continued to traverse the air with a rapidity that took away the means of making the princess understand the tender and respectful sentiments that he had for her.

When he thought that he was safe, however, he gradually lowered his flight and set the princess down gently in a meadow dotted with flowers. It was there that, after having asked her for a thousand pardons for the violence her had done to her, he explained that he was taking her to a flowery kingdom where he was the master, of which he wanted to put her in possession, with more authority than he had himself.

He neglected nothing to express his tenderness, and spared none of the oaths that lovers make in order to persuade her that it would be eternal. The princess, still frightened by the peril in which she had found herself, did not speak for some time, but when she had recovered her wits somewhat and saw that she was no longer in the arms of her dear mother the queen, penetrated by a profound dolor, she shed a torrent of tears.

The king, who loved her veritably, was touched by that. "Cease to be afflicted, adorable princess," he said to her. "I am only seeking to make you the happiest woman in the world."

"If you are telling me the truth, Sire," the princess retorted, "I demand the liberty that you have stole from me, or suffer that the violence you have done me today will make me regard you as my cruelest enemy."

She tried to appease him then, by telling him that if he asked the king her father for her, there was every appearance that he would obtain her, since, if he was a powerful king, as he said, her father would have no reason to refuse the alliance.

The king replied to the princess that he was in despair at seeing her so opposed to his design, but he flattered himself that he would render her more agreeable by taking her to a place where she would be respected by everyone, and where, he could assure her, pleasures would be born beneath her footfalls. At the same moment, he picked the princess up again, and in spite of the cries that she redoubled with all her might, he transported her with the same rapidity all the way to the capital of his estates.

He set her down gently on a lawn, and scarcely was she there when she saw emerging instantly from beneath her feet a palace of extraordinary magnificence. Its architecture was very beautiful and very regular; gold glittered equally outside and in all the apartments, which were ornamented with precious furniture. Everything that could flatter the senses and ambition was encountered there in abundance, and it was impossible to wish for anything that was not found there. The princess, who thought she was alone there, was agreeably surprised to see herself surrounded by a number of beautiful and very amiable young women, who hastened to compete with one another in serving her. A parrot with admirable plumage said the pettiest things in the world to her.

The king had resumed his natural form on arrival at that palace, and although he was no longer very young, he had what was necessary to please anyone but the princess. She was prejudiced against the prince by such a great hatred because of the violence that he had done to her, however, that although she saw that she was in his power and far from any hope of rescue, it was not possible for her to regard him as anything but her enemy, and she could only respond to all that he said to touch her with words full of her resentment.

The king hoped, however, that time might soften the mind of the princess, and that, not seeing any other man than him, she would become accustomed to him. He took the precaution of surrounding the princess's palace with an impenetrable cloud, and went thereafter to show himself his court, where everyone was in great anxiety, not having had any news of him for a long time. The prince, his son, and all the courtiers were overjoyed to welcome their king, for he was loved perfectly by all his subjects.

They were to have the displeasure thereafter of seeing him more rarely than in times past; he employed the pretext of affairs that he had found on his return to shut himself in his cabinet, but it was actually to be able to spend that time with the princess, whom he had the dolor of finding still inflexible.

Not knowing what remedy to apply to such a great misfortune, nor what the cause could be of the princess's obstinacy, he was afraid that, in spite of his precautions, she might have heard mention of the merit of his son, the prince, who was young and handsome and adored by the court for his benevolence. He was in a horrible anxiety, and could only find relief therefrom by sending his son away. He proposed to him that he travel, and gave him a magnificent equipage.

The prince visited several courts, where he stayed for various lengths of time, in accordance with how agreeable he found them, and finally arrived in the one where mourning was being worn for the abducted princess. The king and queen gave him a very gracious welcome. Time and the presence of an amiable young prince having lessened the dolor that the loss of the princess had caused, the pleasures of the court were gradually revived, and the young prince took full part therein.

One day, when the court was in the queen's cabinet, the prince, having perceived the portrait of a great beauty, was suddenly struck by it and demanded eagerly who it was. The queen, who overheard him, spoke for the young woman that the prince had asked, and said that it was all that remained of her dear daughter, who had been abducted, no one knew how or by whom. The queen could not talk about that sad adventure without shedding tears.

The prince was sensibly touched by that, and instantly promised the queen to search for the princess throughout the world, and not to take any repose until he had returned her to her hands. The queen assured him that she would receive such a singular favor with an eternal gratitude, and even said that if the princess were agreeable to it, she would give her to him in marriage, with the estates of which she was the sovereign. The queen was the heiress of a neighboring realm, of which the king approved of her disposing as she pleased.

The prince, more touched by the hope of possessing the princess than the kingdom he was offered, took his leave of the king and queen and set forth on his enterprise. The queen had given him a portrait of the princess that she wore on her arm, "in order," she told him, "that you do not lose the idea of her and do not have any difficulty in recognizing her when you encounter her."

The prince, already very passionate for the charming princess, of whom he had only thus far seen the resemblance, departed with his heart full of hope, and went in long stages to find the fay whom his mother the queen had recommended to him. He begged her to aid him with her art in such an important matter.

Having learned all the circumstances of the adventure, the fay asked for time to consult her books, and told the prince, after having thought about it, that the princess he sought was close by, but that it was too difficult to penetrate into the enchanted palace where his father, the king, was holding her, because he had covered it with a thick cloud. The only expedient she could imagine was to capture a parrot that the princess had, which she did not think impossible, because it sometimes went out and flew some distance from the palace.

The fay, who had a great passion to give pleasure to the son of a princess she had loved uniquely, went out immediately and tried to find the parrot. She came back shortly thereafter holding it in her hand, and immediately locked it in a cage. Having touched the prince with a mysterious wand, she transformed him into a parrot, and told him what he had to do in order to reach the princess.

The prince, well instructed as to how to be a parrot, went to the charming princess, whom he found to have a beauty hundred times greater than he had believed. He was so nonplussed that the princess was surprised; she was afraid that her parrot might be ill, and as he was her only consolation, she picked him up and caressed him, which reassured the prince and gave him the boldness to play his character well. He said a thousand pretty things, and the princess was charmed by them.

The king arrived, and the parrot had the pleasure of seeing him hated. When the king had gone, the princess went into her cabinet alone; the parrot flew in there and witnessed the laments she made regarding the persecutions of the king, who had begged her insistently to determine herself to marry him.

In order to console her, the parrot said a thousand things to her, in which she found so much intelligence that she sometimes doubted whether it was, in fact, her parrot that was talking to her so agreeably. He said even more forceful things, by which she was very astonished. When he saw that she was in the disposition he desired, he said to her:

"Madame, I have a very important secret to confide to you. I beg you not to be alarmed by the things that I am going to tell you. I am here to liberate you, Madame, and it is on the part of the queen, your mother, that I have come. To prove to you what I am saying, look at this portrait, which your mother gave me."

He took the portrait from beneath one of his wings. The princess's surprise was very great, but he she could not help conceiving hopes on the basis of what she saw and heard, because she had recognized the portrait as the one that the queen wore on her arm.

Seeing that he princess was not greatly alarmed, the parrot told her who he was, what the queen had promised him, and about the help he had already received from the fay, who had assured him that she would give him all the means of transporting the princess all the way to the cabinet of the queen, her mother.

When he saw that the princess was listening to him attentively, he begged her to permit him to appear before her in his natural form. The princess having made no response, he plucked a feather from his wing, and the princess immediately saw a prince of surprising beauty; she allowed herself to be flattered pleasantly by the hope of owing her liberty to a man who appeared to be so lovable.

The fay who had taken responsibility for the conduct of the adventure had made a chariot capable of containing the prince and princess and had hitched it to two eagles so powerful that they were capable of taking them to the ends of the earth. Having put the parrot she was keeping in a cage into the chariot, she charged the eagles with taking it as far as the widow of the princess's cabinet, which was done in a moment; the princess having climbed into the chariot with the prince, she was very glad to find her parrot there too.

As soon as the princess was in the chariot, she saw someone riding an eagle that was flying ahead of the chariot; she was astonished by that, but the prince reassured her, telling her that it was the good fay, to whom she was obliged for all the help that had reached her, who wanted to escort them all the way to her mother's cabinet.

The king, who had not slept tranquilly since the day when he first saw the princess, woke up with a start. He had just seen in a dream that someone was taking his mistress away. He resumed the form of an eagle and flew to her palace, where, not having found her there, he entered into a terrible fury. He returned home as quickly as possible in order to consult his books.

Having understood that it was his son who had stolen his precious treasure, he transformed himself instantly into a harpy, and, possessed by rage, he resolved to devour his son, and even the princess, if he encountered them.

He pierced the air with an extraordinary rapidity, but he had set out too late, and the fay, anticipating that he would follow them, had raised impetuous winds in the air behind them, which retarded his flight and gave the prince and the princess the time to arrive safely in the queen's cabinet. She was there, in an impatience of which she did not know the cause, as if she had had a presentiment of some extraordinary event. With what joy, as you can imagine, she received the princess she had regretted so much, and the amiable prince who had enabled her to see her again!

The fay also came to the cabinet, and warned the queen that the magician king, from whom something had just been stolen that was dearer to him than his crown, would soon arrive, and that nothing could protect the prince and princess from his fury, aided by his enchantments, if they were not married. As soon as they were united by the bond of marriage, however, he would be unable to do anything against them.

The queen sent a warning to the king immediately, and the marriage was made. The magician king arrived at the end of the ceremony; the despair that he was in at having arrived too late having troubled his mind, he appeared in his natural form, and tried to throw a black liquid over the married prince and princess capable of killing them, but the fay advanced a wand that she was holding in her hand, and turned the liquid back on the king who had just thrown it, whereupon he fell down, having lost the usage of all his senses.

The king in whose home he had just tried to carry out such a cruel vengeance, feeling deeply offended, had him picked up and put in prison. Magicians no longer having any power when they are in prison, the imprisoned king, when he came round, was very embarrassed to find himself in the power of a prince he had offended so gravely, but he was not subjected to any cruelty on a day of such great rejoicing.

The prince, having asked for mercy for his father, obtained it, and had his prison opened. It was no sooner open than the king was seen in the air in the form of an unknown bird; he only said as he departed that he would never forgive his son, or his neighbor the fay, for the cruel insult they had dealt him.

The fay was asked to establish himself in the realm where she was; she agreed to that, and transported her books and her secrets of enchantment there. She built a new palace there, which she made her residence; no one in the court thought any longer of anything but rendering thanks to the generous fay to whom they owed so many obligations, and enjoying the perfect felicity into which she had put the entire royal family.

The prince and he princess spent a long and very happy life together, and left in possession of the kingdom thereafter a posterity that was always covered in glory.

Prince Roger

There was once a Comte de Poitou who wanted to enable his eldest son to see the world, with a view to rendering him the most honest of men, and being informed on his return of several things that he was curious to know; but he was afraid that accidents might befall him, as often happens during great voyages, especially in those days, when the roads were full of thieves and in which the smallest matters were disputed by arms.

What precautions could be taken against such great dangers? He remembered having heard it said that Melusine, from whom he was descended in a direct line, had been a fay, and that she had left admirable secrets of enchantment and several instruments serving for particular usages in her art; that was an ancient tradition of his house. He began to wonder where he might find all of that, and judged that it must be in the tower of Lusignan, Melusine's former dwelling, where she still appeared from time to time, if the chronicles of Poitou could be believed

Impatient to find what he was looking for, the comte did not content himself with having the tower pierced in several places; he knocked down entire walls, so successfully that he found that treasure, hidden for so many years. It was a small chest covered with steel strips, the workmanship of which was so fine and delicate, and the material so shiny, that it was easy to see from all directions. The comte had no doubt that the secrets of the fay, his ancestress, were contained in that chest. He searched all its sides for a place where it could be opened, and not having been able to find one, he made the resolution to having it broken with blows of an ax.

That was a great pity, but what means was there of doing otherwise, except for renouncing all the advantages that might be obtained from the secrets? There was reason to judge that such a beautiful chest must contain things that were even more beautiful. Workmen were summoned, therefore, and the chest was broken—but what a surprise, when a light was seen to emerge therefrom that dazzled all the witnesses, and caused them such a great astonishment that no one dared approach it.

That light having gradually disappeared, the comte put his hand into the chest, and the first thing that he took out of it was a book, the binding of which was beautiful crystal, but a crystal pained in all the brightest and most splendid colors, imprinted in the substance in such a manner that they seemed natural; the pages were delicate polished gold and the letters were azure, the finest characters that had ever been seen.

Everyone was surprised by such a novelty, and the comte thought that he had found a book that contained nothing less than oracles. He read it eagerly, and found secrets of which he did not make the confidence to anyone, which apparently consisted of predictions of important events that would happen to Melusine's posterity, among whom there were kings in distant regions.

The comte also found in the chest a few mysterious wands and several gold rings, to each of which Melusine had attached some charm, and which she had locked in the chest in order to serve whichever of his descendants would be fortunate enough to find them. The precious stones and gold that were found there in abundance were counted as trivial, those who know the secrets of the fays having no need of them and never lacking them, so the comte shared those common riches liberally among all those who were present, only reserving for himself the charms of faerie, which he communicated to the prince his dear son, whom he sent away a few days later.

Above all, he gave him an ivory wand that had the power of metamorphosing anything it touched into anything that the person carrying it pleased. He also gave him golden rings that had the virtue of rendering invisible the persons who wore them uncovered; he gave him four of them, in order that he could make use of them on occasions when he was obliged to have two or three people with him.

With that apparatus and a magnificent equipage, the young Comte de Poitou departed in search of adventures. He covered ten leagues on the first day, and having left his equipage he went on with his squire alone and covered a further two leagues at nightfall. Having approached a castle, however, where there was a lady for whom he had a strong inclination, he left his horses at a hostelry on the road and went directly to the castle with his squire. It was there that he tested the charm of his golden rings for the first time, for he introduced himself into the lady's cabinet, without having been seen, although he had encountered many people on the way. He hid there until she was alone and in bed.

He had put his squire in a place in the house where he had told him to stay until he came to collect him. As the young cavalier did not relate the details of his adventures in his lifetime, no one knows what happened between him and the lady; what is known is that he left in the morning with his squire, apparently very satisfied by the night and having tested the power of his rings. He returned as quickly as possible to the hostelry where he had left his horses, had a light meal and went to join his equipage in the place where he had left it. People there judged that he had passed the night fortunately, all the more so because he went to sleep when he arrived and slept for several hours.

When he woke up he set forth after having something to eat; he took the road to Barcelona and traveled without seeking occasions to make use of all the fine secrets he possessed, which he was reserving for the court of Catalonia, where he arrived with his heart full of high hopes. That was not without reason, for he was as handsome as amour; it was not possible that he would not be desired; even without such fine means of deceiving the jealous, he would have found great facility in rendering himself happy.

He arrived in Barcelona on the day when the tourneys were commencing that the Count of Catalonia had organized for the occasion of the marriage of the princess, his daughter, which was to take place imminently. All the knights of all the courts of Spain, even those of the Moorish kings, were there, each at his most magnificent. The princess in honor of whom the fête was being held was more beautiful than the day star, and Prince Roger—that was the name of the young Prince de Poitou—was struck by the beauty the first time he saw her. Having learned who she was and that she was about to be married, he was annoyed; he would have liked to steal her from that fortunate rival. It was not that he wanted to marry her, for he had resolved not to limit to that court the adventures of which he was in search, but he was already jealous of the favors destined for the husband, and he would have liked them to be reserved for him.

He had himself introduced to the Count of Catalonia and the princess as a French knight in search of chivalric adventures, who had come to their court after hearing rumor of the tourney that was being arranged. He was thought handsome, and the princess soon began to look at him with a kindly eye; he perceived that and resolved to profit from it.

He retired to his abode to arm himself and presented himself in the lists with armor so beautiful that it attracted everyone's eyes, no one had ever seen any so splendid. He ran against all comers, and was always victorious. See what an advantage it is to have the protection of a powerful fay like Melusine! He won the prizes on all three days of the fête, and always received them from the hand of the princess he had found so charming. What a joy to be covered in glory! He won the admiration of all the spectators, and was further recompensed by the hands of amour, since it is true that the princess already had that for him.

When the combats had finished, he joined in with the conversations and the other pleasures of the court. He made use of his ring more than once in order to get close to the princess without being seen; he witnessed the insipid and tedious conversations that the prince to whom she was promised had with her; he found out easily that amour had no part in that marriage, which had only been made for political reasons.

He tried to discover what was happening in the heart of the princess; he was witness to frequent sighs and, convinced that they were not for the prince she was about to marry, he presumed that they could only be for him. He had no reason to doubt that, for the princess, who believed that she could only be heard by one person, who was her confidante, said:

"Oh, my dear, how cruel the fate of a princess is, seeing herself destined, by virtue of politics, to marry the person she likes least in the world. Was it necessary to enable me to see all the most amiable knights in the world, only to make me, after that, spend my life with the one who is the least amiable? Oh, how happy I believe I would be if I were to spend it with the one who was the victor over all the others, and who only received from my hand the least of the prizes that I would have liked to give him, so worthy do I find him of them all!"

Prince Roger, assured by that discourse that he was tenderly loved, was no longer occupied with anything but the care of telling her that he loved her too. He immediately hid his golden ring and, having rendered himself visible, approached the princess, who blushed at the sight of the handsome knight, as if she were afraid that he might have heard what she had just said. It was not that she would have been sorry if he had known it, but she would have been ashamed to have been the first to declare it.

The prince, who knew his society perfectly, and that it was for him to speak first, told her that he found himself very unfortunate in having come to the court of Barcelona just in time to witness the felicity of a prince who was perhaps not the most worthy of it, because he was not sufficiently aware of the value of a possession that only ought to be the recompense of a grand passion, which had only been accorded to him, it was said in court, because of the neighborhood of his estates.

"Is it necessary," said Prince Roger, "that the most lovable princess in the world does not have the power to choose? Is it not permitted to the one who might obtain her choice to dispute it?"

"No," said the princess, "my fate is settled, and I can only submit to it."

"But Princess," said the passionate Roger, "if you would permit the change, it might not be impossible to succeed in that."

"No," she replied, "it is not in human power, and I can never think of it."

"You could at least," said the prince, who had other designs than preventing her from marrying, "dispose of your heart as you wish, and if it is due to the man who knows the value of it, I would have the right to dispute it with all those who might have aspired to it."

"If I consulted my heart," the princess replied, "I would only be more unhappy; leave me I beg you, to follow a destiny that cannot change without exposing myself to too much misfortune; the Count, my father, is unshakeable in his resolutions, and this affair is too advanced for it to possible to break it. Leave me, I beg you, to my misfortunes, which will be less great if I do not see you again."

"I consent, lovable princess, to allow you to follow your destiny, provided that you will pardon me for a few tricks that I want to play on a lover who has not merited your tenderness, and that you will only know at the moment of their execution."

Those were the last words that Prince Roger said to the princess, who was in great anxiety. She did not know what tricks he was talking about, and she would not have suspected what he was meditating in a thousand years. He did not speak to the princess any longer, for fear that it might be observed; he only addressed her continually by means of gazes full of tenderness.

Great preparations were being made for the marriage of the princess; Prince Roger was a witness to them, and having entered invisibly into the nuptial chamber in the evening, when all the men had left, he saw with pleasure all the ceremonies that are ordinarily made in order to put the bride in the bed. It was then that the princess appeared to him even more beautiful and more lovable, and he conceived for her, at that moment, an amour that rendered him the most passionate of all men.

A short time afterwards, the groom appeared, and all the women withdrew. Prince Roger still remained invisible in the princess's chamber, jealous of the favors that she could not refuse to her husband, and he allowed him to get into the bed. Instantly striking him with his ivory wand, he caused him to fall into a profound sleep, from which only he could extract him by touching him with the same wand.

Then, charmed by the effect of his wand, and his heart filled with the most beautiful passion in the world, he wanted to profit from the trick that he had played on his rival; considering himself more worthy of the good fortune that he had in possessing such a lovable person, he tried to persuade the charming princess, to whom he rendered himself visible, confiding to her the secret of the tricks for which he had already begged her to pardon him.

The princess, very surprised to see the prince so close to her at a time when she had everything to fear if anyone discovered him, begged him insistently to go away.

"Have no fear, charming princess," he said. "You know my secret and that of my heart, but since I am unfortunate enough not to be able to possess you, at least permit myself to avenge myself on my rival for all the harm that you are going to make me suffer in not seeing you again."

The princess forgave him everything, on condition that he went away. Prince Roger obeyed her, but before leaving he struck the prince with his wand. It was already daylight; the sleeping prince woke up, but dared not trouble the repose of the princess, who, having need of it, was slumbering profoundly.

The same trick was worked several nights in succession, and the rumor having spread of the disgrace of the unfortunate prince, who went to sleep as soon as he got into bed, unable to prevent it no matter what care he took, the cause was sought and the conclusion reached that there must be an enchantment involved.

The princess, afraid that the secret might be discovered by some misfortune, begged Prince Roger to interrupt for a few days a commerce that had not been very disagreeable to her. Prince Roger was perhaps not sorry to have that complaisance on the part of the princess, and thus remained for a few days without thinking of any enterprise. He was, however, continually at court, where he enabled the desires of several beauties, for he really was made for painting, and was polished to the utmost perfection. As he was determined, however, to fly from conquest to conquest, he always sought out those who wanted to listen to him.

One day, believing that he had found a few dispositions of the kind he wanted in the heart of a very amiable young woman, he spoke passionately and was not repelled; he thought that was enough to be able to risk the enterprise. He made use of the means he had of being invisible to enter her bedroom while it was still illuminated, and when the lights were extinct he approached the bed. When he made a slight noise as he walked, however, the lovable person, not knowing who it was, began to scream desperately, which caused domestics to run to her aid.

At that moment, the prince was only thinking of running away as quickly as possible, for fear of being encountered and seized, even though he could not be seen. As he withdrew in haste his footfalls were heard; he was followed, and those pursuing him, not seeing anything, were so paralyzed by fear that the torches fell from their hands. Their astonishment was redoubled by the sound of the doors he opened in order to get out, and, not knowing by what enchantment they had heard running and doors opening without having seen anyone, they shouted for help and put the entire house into alarm.

That adventure being known the following day to the court and the city, everyone concluded that there were enchanters among the foreigners who had arrived in the city shortly before. People reasoned about the marvels that Prince

Roger had been see to perform, having always won all the prizes in the tourneys; reflections were made on the adventure of the newly married prince, and also on the assiduities of Prince Roger with regard to the princess over several days. That amiable person, whom he had wanted to surprise again, was asked what conversations he had had with her. She confessed a part of them—and from all that, it was concluded that he was an enchanter.

The Count of Catalonia allowed himself to be convinced, by everything that was put to him, that it might be true, and he ordered the provost to search for Prince Roger. The provost obeyed, but he arrived at his lodgings too late; he learned that the prince had departed a few hours earlier. He made his report to the count, who ordered him to mount up and bring him back, if possible, so curious was he to know what art he had used, but he expressly forbade that any harm be done to him. The count was a good prince, who would rather be ignorant of all enchantment for life than be instructed of them by shedding the blood of a man for whom he was commencing to have amity.

Prince Roger, who had anticipated that he would be followed, had made his equipage travel with great diligence, and he had remained behind with his squire, who, like him, had a gold ring to make himself invisible. He would have be able to transform the provost and his retinue in any manner he pleased, but he was the most benign of all princes, to the point that he would have been sorry to make a child weep, so he contented himself with approaching the provost, who was leading the way, and touching his horse with his wand, which he turned into a elephant.

The astonished provost threw himself to the ground, crying for mercy. His archers, as astonished as him, ran to his aid, although they were terrified of such a huge beast and the prodigy that allowed them to see it. They were also astonished to hear hearty laughter; that was Prince Roger, who had the malice to mock them, with his squire—after which he continued on his way, leaving the provost and his band to get out of the embarrassment as best they could.

As that adventure made even more noise, not without it being known in a matter of days, along with the preceding incidents, in every court in Spain, the prince believed that it would be prudent to pass over the mountains again and return to Gaul, with the consequence that, having rejoined his equipage, he immediately changed direction and headed for Navarre.

That was also the shortest route to return to Poitou, which he resolved to pass through only to give the comte, his father, the pleasure of hearing about his adventures, and soon after to take another road, in the design of seeking new ones. He had not been able to anticipate, however, that before reaching Poitou he would encounter a princess who would make him change all his projects of folly into a serious design to spend his life with her.

That was in Angoulême, where he arrived without intending to amuse himself seeking any adventure. He went on arrival to the court of the Comte d'Angoulême, where, having introduced himself as the son of the Comte de Poitou, he received a welcome such as one is entitled to expect of a neighboring prince and confederate of his father. The comte gave him an apartment in his palace and invited him to eat every day with himself and his family—which is to say, with Madame la Comtesse d'Angoulême, his wife, and two young princesses, their daughters, whose beauty was charming.

Although Prince Roger found them both very beautiful, he did not take long to differentiate between them; that was perhaps the effect of some sympathy, which caused him from that day on to form the serious design to please the elder and to renounce forever all the adventures that he had proposed to attempt by means of enchantments, only to think of meriting her be a thousand attentions and a veritable passion, which took possession of his heart at the first moment.

He was not the only professional seducer who had ever been fixed forever by a lovable person, but none had ever been reformed so promptly, or renounced, as he did so many means of succeeding in his gallantries; for, not to mention his enchantments, he was made for amour, so many charms were there in his person. He thought, however, that it was all too little for Princess Tullie—that was the name of the elder of the two Princesses d'Angoulême—and he would have liked to possess the attractions of all the men in the world and the empire of the universe in order to make a sacrifice of them to her.

Princess Tullie, by virtue of the effect of the sympathy I mentioned, to which much merit on either side almost always gives birth, also regarded him, from the first day, as a prince worthy of her. That had disposed her to listen to him favorably when he spoke. The prince did not take long to reveal the sentiments of his heart; she responded immediately that she would not be sorry if the Comte d'Angoulême, her father, were agreeable to his design.

Charmed by that response, Prince Roger talked about it to the Comte d'Angoulême, who was very satisfied by the proposition and declared that he would gladly accord his daughter to Prince Roger if the Comte de Poitou asked for her on his behalf.

Prince Roger, full of his passion, made the decision, in order to avoid delays, to go to Poitou himself, diligently, in order to obtain the consent of the comte, his father, which was a favor more precious to him than any other that he could ever ask him. He depicted his amour to him, and the merit to which it had given birth, so well that the Comte de Poitou, touched by what he heard, sent an ambassador in a matter of days charged with regulating the conditions of his marriage with the Princesse d'Angoulême.

Prince Roger was so impatient to see her again that he had scarcely had time to give his father an account of the adventures he had had by means of his enchantments than he returned them immediately, having no more need of them, since he only wanted to think henceforth of spending a tranquil life, loving faithfully a princess whom he believed to be the only one worthy of being loved eternally; which happened as he planned, for he married Princesse Tullie and spent with her the happiest life that had ever been seen to pass in marriage. From that fine union, many conquerors and heroes descended, who have worn crowns in another part of the world.

Fortunio

There was once a man who, having heart and spirit in mediocre fortune, did not believe himself to be inferior to any other. He sought in marriage a young woman who had, like him, a great deal of merit and mediocre wealth, and he married her. Although the two of them did not have a large fortune, they would have lived together very content with their lot if they had been able to have children, believing that to be the mark of the benediction of a marriage.

After desiring that for a long time in vain, having resolved to adopt one for their consolation, they were walking along a river bank one day when they perceived a cradle floating on the water. Curious to know what it was, they set forth in a boat; their curiosity was soon satisfied, for they encountered what they wished; it was a child who appeared to them to be marvelously beautiful, and a great hope, by virtue of the rules of physiognomy, of which they prided themselves in having some knowledge. As they held him to be their fortune, they gave him the name of Fortunio, brought him up and instructed him with all possible care.

The child having been born with the finest inclinations in the world, he did honor to the education they gave him, so well that he satisfied fully those from whom he received it, and consoled them for not having been able to bring children into the world. He even became so dear to them that they only thought of augmenting their fortune in order to be able to launch him in society and one day to leave him a considerable succession, in order to enable him to live with the splendor appropriate to his birth, as it had appeared to them to be by virtue of the richness of the swaddling-clothes by which he was enveloped.

During the time when they were occupied in that care, however, the amiable wife became pregnant, which did not diminish in any way the tenderness she had for Fortunio, nor that of her husband. They said to one another that if heaven was augmenting their family, it would also take care of augmenting their wealth, and that they would have reason to be satisfied if it gave them a son as amiable as the one they owed to fortune.

Heaven granted their prayers and gave them a son, such that was not possible to be prettier at birth. As he grew older, he became more lovable every day, and in addition to the contentment he gave to his father and mother he had a great deal of amity for Fortunio, whom he believed to be his older brother, and lived with him for a long time in great union. That would have lasted eternally if a young man who sometimes shared in their pleasures had not told him that he had reason to complain of the fact that Fortunio was treated with as much generosity as him, exactly as if he had been a child of the house, which he was not; that he was only a foundling whom his mother and father had adopted; but that, having been given, by virtue of his birth, the satisfaction that they had desired for so long, it was just that they did not lavish elsewhere caresses that were only due to him.

The child, prejudiced in that fashion, took the opportunity of the first petty argument that he had with Fortunio to reproach him for the fact that he was not his brother, that he was a foundling who was being cared for out of charity.

Fortunio, who had a noble heart, very surprised by such news, went to beg the person he had believed until then to be his mother to tell him whether it was true that he was not her son, and if it was, to make his brother shut up, who had sustained that he was not. She replied that he was, veritably, and that she would punish the little scatterbrain for having insulted him; but she did not say so affirmatively enough to convince Fortunio, who had such a great suspicion of his sad estate and pressed her so hard to speak positively that she was unable to hide it from him that it was true. At the same time, she assured him that he was no less dear to her than her own son and that she would always give him the same care.

As he was very well born, Fortunio was very grateful for the generosity that had been shown to him and that of which he was assured in future, but he was so touched by what he had just learned that he resolved immediately to seek throughout the world actions to perform that could efface the shame of his birth and procure him a better fortune. The person whom he had thought to be his mother, and who loved him veritably, did what she could to stop him, but, seeing that all her efforts were futile, chagrined to be unable to retain him, she heaped him with a thousand maledictions and even wished that if ever he went to sea, he would be swallowed by a siren.

Her husband, by contrast, who was more generous than her, approved of Fortunio's resolution and gave him money in order to provide an equipage. After assuring him of an eternal gratitude, Fortunio quit him and departed, uncertain of the route that he would take.

He had not gone very far when he came to a forest so dense that the sunlight had never penetrated it. He was at the entrance to that forest, in a great embarrassment, not knowing what to do, when he perceived a lion, an eagle and an ant, who were arguing as to the division of a deer that they had hunted and seized. The three animals had agreed prudently, in order to avoid a bloody war, to take for a judge the first human who passed by. As soon as they perceived Fortunio they approached him and begged him to make pace between them by regulating a difference they had regarding the division of the deer that lay dead between them, swearing that they would abide by his judgment without a murmur, even if it were unjust.

Fortunio, who was naturally audacious, replied without astonishment that he was very glad to have the opportunity to give pleasure to such honorable animals; one might have thought, on seeing him so bold, that he had been brought up among lions. He asked them whether they would accord him their amity if he judged equitably, and received a thousand assurances that not only would they love him, but that they would serve him wherever he might have need of them.

Charmed by their conduct, which appeared very honorable to him, Fortunio applied himself to the judgment of the important dispute, in such a manner that all the interested parties would be satisfied and he would be able to separate from them with their thanks—for, although he put on a brave face, he believed, as a man of common sense, that one of those animals, polite as it seemed, was not very good company for a man on his own. He worked on the division, therefore, and was so well able to give each of them what was to their taste, that the three satisfied animals gave him a thousand thanks, believing themselves to be fortunate to have encountered such an equitable judge.

When the polite compliments were finished, Fortunio thought about his journey, and leaving his new friends occupied in making their meal. As he was about to quit them, a fay appeared, so richly adorned that he had never seen anything so beautiful, He was surprised by that, and ready to prostrate himself, so much respect did the majestic appearance of the fay inspire in him. She had a hunting horn slung over her shoulder, which would have made him take her for Diana if she had not introduced herself as a fay whose palace was in the depths of the forest. As for the three animals, they knew her very well and respected her to the same extent.

The fay was curious to know what had happened in an assembly of creatures so different and so opposed. The lion spoke, and gave an account of the equity of the judgment that the human she saw before her had rendered, and begged her to be agreeable enough to use her power to recompense him for it. The fay praised Fortunio for the equity of the judgment he had pronounced, and the three animals for the just gratitude that they had for it; to oblige them all she gave Fortunio the power to take on the form of one of the three animals every time he had need of it and to quit it as he pleased in order to resume his own. She was even so touched by his justice and his good looks that she proposed that he spend a few days with her in her castle.

Fortunio, who was only in search of adventures, told the fay that he received the proposition she had made to him with great respect, and that he was ready to follow her. He spent a few days in the fay's palace, with all the pleasures that one can imagine, and only left regretfully, but the fay, who knew that he was destined for great things, sent him away after having made him considerable presents of precious stones and having give him admirable instructions for his conduct.

With those means of making people talk about him, Fortunio departed full of hope, and stopped at the first town, where he provided himself with an equipage. He went to several courts, where he had various adventures, and acquired a great reputation for valor in famous occasions of war that he encountered, the narration of which I shall put off until another time, in order only to talk for the present about the most celebrated and most fortunate of his exploits, since it enabled him to make the conquest of the most lovable princess of his century and a realm of which she was the heiress.

He arrived at the court of that princess at a time when her father, the king, had had it published in all the neighboring realms that, wanting to marry his daughter, he had resolved to give her to the man who could vanquish all the others in a tourney that he had organized to be held shortly.

Fortunio arrived in time to attempt a great adventure; he introduced himself to the king as a knight who was traveling the world in search of opportunities of war and adventures of chivalry. The king told him that he had arrived very appropriately, in order to witness a tourney he was holding in his court in a few days, and that it only depended on him to enter it, since no knight was to be excluded from it, apart from the fact that his good looks, which gave a high opinion of his birth, could enable him to be received anywhere. Fortunio replied to the king that he would strive to do nothing unworthy of the good opinion that His Majesty had of him. Then he asked the king for permission to go and make reverence to the princess.

The king ordered the captain of his guard to introduce him to her, and he received a very favorable welcome. The princess was the most charming person that he had ever seen, and on seeing her, he formed the design to conquer her or to shed the last droop of his blood trying. He was further encouraged in that by a few glances on the part of the princess that he believed to be favorable to him, and the thought of becoming agreeable to her by means of his profound respect and assiduity, while awaiting the day when he could conquer her by means of his arms.

In the following days he saw all the princes and knights arrive who were seeking to merit the princess or to die for such a fine design, and no more beautiful and nobler assembly had ever been seen. They all flocked around the princess and each would have liked to dispose her to offer prayers for him on the great day; some wanted to engage her to do that by means of the profound respect they rendered to her, and a few others by means of the passion by which they were so touched that they had the boldness to declare it.

Fortunio, the most passionate of all, was also the most respectful, and scarcely dared to allow the passion in his heart to be glimpsed in his eyes, so fearful was he of displeasing her; it was, however, to him that the princess would have wished the victory of which she was to be the prize, had she believed him to be a prince. There were moments when she thought he might be, or, at any rate, that he had a great merit that could equal any prince.

Finally, the day arrived that ought to determine her, or at least her fortune, and an infinite number of princes and knights were seen in the ranks.

The king had prescribed that they would draw lots to determine who would have the privilege of entering the lists first. He had established judges to determine that, and any difficulties that might arise between them. Several princes fought and destroyed one another successively. A neighboring king, valiant and strong, but known to be a prince devoid of morals and politeness, and ugly as well, entered the lists in his turn, and defeated all those who presented themselves before him. It was Fortunio's turn to fight him, but, nightfall being too close, the king postponed until the following day the decision of that great event, which the princess feared direly, for she saw herself in danger of falling into the power of a prince who horrified her by the reputation he had of being ferocious, and even more so by his frightful appearance. She saw no one but Fortunio who might dispute her with him.

The rumor had spread that Fortunio was very valorous. Several princes who had seen him in occasions of war had said so, but as she knew that he would be exposed against a man so redoubtable, she dared not hope to see him victorious. She would even have liked to let the prince know that, in the event that he felled the king she hated so much, she would have regarded it as a lesser misfortune to make the felicity of a simple knight. Agitated by those various anxieties, she was leaning out of a window in her palace, where she appeared to Fortunio to be a very afflicted person. He went to present himself at the door of her apartment, but he was told that she was not seeing anyone.

Touched by the affliction in which she had seemed to be, Fortunio had resolved to tell her that he would deliver her the following day from the trouble she was in. He went down into the street, and having wished to be an eagle, he became one, and flew to the window of the princess's cabinet. Having found her alone, he flew to her and resumed his natural form. She was frightened and screamed; her servants came running, and Fortunio disappeared; he had metamorphosed into an ant and had slipped into the princess's furbelow. No longer seeing anything, she sent her maidservants away, telling them that she had thought she had seen something but that she had been mistaken.

Still an ant, and hidden in the princess's clothing, Fortunio heard her uttering sighs, and even muttering a few inarticulate words, which enabled him to understand the horror she had for the king who had been victorious thus far, and the passion that she had to see victory snatched from him by a man who had touched her heart, although he appeared to be only a simple knight.

The ant had no sooner understood what was happening in the heart of the princess than it said to her: "Have no fear, charming Princess; the monster who frightens you will not possess you, and if you would be kind enough not to call your women again, you will see the man who will deliver you tomorrow, who is the man who respects you more than any other in the world. Don't be alarmed, therefore, Princess; he is about to appear before you."

Then Fortunio appeared before her and assured her that he would deliver her the following day from the subject of all her alarms. "And I shall," he said, "be only too happy to have served you, and happier still if, by all the cares of my life, I could merit the recompense that the king has promised to the victor."

After that conversation, Fortunio, having become an eagle again, flew out of the widow, by which the princess remained so frightened that she scarcely had the strength to get up from her armchair; she did not know whether she had dreamed what had just happened, and she said to herself: *It possible that I have found help in such a pressing need? Is it not a dream?* Fortunio had appeared so respectful and so amiable that it was not possible for her not to desire his victory, even though he was only a simple knight. The manner in which he had entered her cabinet and left it was what embarrassed her the most; she had often heard mentioned of the power of fays, and judged that one of them, touched by her misfortune, had doubtless sent her a defender.

In all the different anxieties into which she fell, unable to think about anything else, she decided to say that she was ill. In order to be able to wait in her bed for the day so much desired when someone would come to give her hope. She immediately called her women and sent word to her father that, with his permission, she would go to bed because she was afflicted with such a bad headache that it was not possible for her to see anyone. The king came, and having found that the princess had a head on fire, he ordered that she be left in repose, convinced that if she could sleep, her headache would dissipate.

It is easy to imagine that the princess, left alone, did not pass very tranquilly the night preceding such a great day, on which all the happiness of her life would depend. On the other hand, Fortunio was not without anxiety; he had to fight a prince redoubtable by virtue of his valor and has strength; but what can one not accomplish when one is guided by amour, when one has a great deal of courage and the protection of a powerful fay?

As soon as the lists were opened, Fortunio was seen to enter mounted n the finest horse that had ever been seen, covered in armor brilliant with gold and precious stones; he won the admiration of all the spectators, and the princess recognized him by the quantity of green ribbons with which he had made a knot around the harness of his horse and the green plumes with which he had charged his helmet, because he had asked her for permission to wear that color, which he had seen her wearing the previous day.

He was waiting thus in the career, in an exceedingly proud posture, when the vanquisher of all the others was seen to enter, who seemed to be surprised that there was still someone to be found who had the audacity to fight him after his triumphs, of which no one was unaware.

"Who are you?" he said to him. "What has made you as bold as to attack me? Were you not witness yesterday to the disasters of all those who dared to present themselves before me?"

"Only think of defending yourself," said Fortunio. "Today will not be as fortunate for you as yesterday was."

They separated then in order to charge at one another, and the first course put an end to the adventure, for Fortunio pierced his rival with a thrust of his lance through a fault in his breastplate, and caused him to bite the dust. As all the aspirants had already been vanquished, Fortunio waited in the lists in vain; no one presented themselves to dispute with him a prize that he had merited so well, since he had vanquished the vanquisher of all the others.

Immediately, great acclamations rose up among the people, and the heralds of arms, having entered the lists, conducted the fortunate Fortunio, to the sound of trumpets and drums, to the foot of His Majesty's throne, where, having dismounted and removed his helmet, the princes was charmed not to be able to doubt that it really was the man for whom she had already been destined by all the impulses of gratitude and a strong inclination that she had conceived for him on the first day of his arrival in the court.

The king, convinced, as I have said, that it was impossible that Fortunio was not of high birth, did not hesitate to extend his arms to him, saying to him: "Come, amiable stranger; here is the princess who is destined for you as the prize of such a great victory. You have vanquished in a moment the man who had not found any other knight capable of resisting him, and I think you have given great pleasure to the princess, my daughter, in removing from her a man who did not have as much to please as you, king though he was."

Turning to the princess, he said to her: "Here, my daughter, is a knight who belongs to you; it is for you to recompense him for what he has done to merit you; I want you to give him your hand in two days' time."

Fortunio threw himself at the king's feet and begged him to leave the princess the liberty of her choice and to give him the time to merit it by his profound respect, and by virtue of a few better actions in which he wanted to seek opportunities to perform for her glory. "I am," he said, "too unworthy for a great princess."

"No," said the king. "Is it not true, my daughter, that this knight would not be disagreeable to you?"

"I will have no difficulty," he princess replied, "in obeying Your Majesty on this occasion or any other."

The king was, therefore, obeyed without reluctance; the marriage was made, and was followed by fêtes and rejoicing that lasted for a month.

Fortunio spend a few years thus in the arms of amour, not finding anything for which to wish. The king having resolved to make war on one of his neighbor princes who had usurped the estates of one of his allies, and having prepared a naval army, however, Fortunio immediately asked the king to give him the command of it, saying that he wanted to perform actions that would make him worthy of the princess, whom he did not believe he had merited sufficiently.

The charming princess shed tears and would have liked to prevent that resolution, but the king, who liked glory, having approved of Fortunio's design, he finally embarked, after very tender adieux.

His pilot, however, having inconsiderately taken him into a part of the sea that is the empire of the sirens, their queen appeared out of the water with a numerous cortege, curious to see who was bold enough to traverse her estates without having asked her for permission. The queen was bored with only having tritons for lovers, and had often kidnapped men, whom she found a hundred times more amiable; it is therefore not surprising that, having been impressed by Fortunio's good looks, she conceived the design of capturing him, and made use of her art to that end.

She sang so sweetly that Fortunio, drawn on to the deck of his vessel, lost the usage of all his senses there. She had no sooner seen him in the torpor she desired than she approached and carried him away. What an affliction for the pilot and all the officers of the army! But as the harm was without remedy, it was necessary to turn the prow and return to give the king an account of what had happened. The pilot excused himself as best he could by the simplicity that had led Fortunio to lend an ear to the voice of the enchantress, in spite of the advice he had given him to beware, but Fortunio was destined to submit to the malediction that that been given to him by the person who had taken care of his education.

The king and the princess were inexpressibly afflicted by such a sad adventure, but the princess, inspired by the fay who had given her protection to Fortunio and to everything that belonged to him, did not lose hope. She had a secret presentiment that she would see her dear Fortunio again one day, and she resolved to go in search of him throughout the world. She wanted to take her son with her, who was the very portrait of his father, she could not take her eyes off him. The king, having yielded to her entreaties and consented to her departure, gave her the same ship and the same pilot who had guided Fortunio. When the princess had embarked, she ordered the pilot to take her to the place where Fortunio had been abducted.

The fay, who had inspired that enterprise in the princess, appeared to her in a very agreeable form, gave her three balls of an infinite value, and assured her that they would have the virtue of enabling her to see her husband, whom she loved so tenderly, but that it was necessary, when they arrived at the place where he had been taken, to give them to her son on three different occasions to appease him when he wept.

When the pilot told the princess that she was at the location that had been fatal to her husband, she ordered him to drop anchor. Her son having started to weep, she gave him a golden ball to appease him, with diamond plates attached to either side. The other two balls were a huge round emerald and a large round ruby. The little prince having immediately rolled the ball he had been given over the deck, a harmony emerged from it that astonished everyone and attracted the queen of the sirens from her palace, which was built on the sea bed.

The queen addressed the princess and said to her: "Give me that ball, Madame and I will be obliged to you."

The princess replied that she would gladly have given it to her, but that it was what she had to amuse her son when he wept.

"Give it to me," said the queen, "and I'll permit you to see the face of the person who is dearest to you."

"I'll give it to you with a good heart at that price," replied the princess, "but what guarantee is there of your promises?"

The queen swore that she was incapable of breaking her word, and that she would not even suffer anyone breaking it throughout her empire.

The princess believed her, and, having given her the ball, she immediately saw the head and shoulders of her dear Fortunio, but it was only for a moment. The queen dived again and made her lover dive with her.

The princess fell back into a great affliction at only having had a momentary glimpse of the person who was so dear to her. She took her son in her arms because he was her only consolation. The child, who wanted to be free on the deck, started to cry again. The princess gave him the emerald ball; he rolled it as he had rolled the first, and a harmony emerged from it sweeter than the first.

The queen of the sirens, more touched than she had been before, told the princess that if she would give her that ball, she would allow her to see her dear husband out of the water all the way to the knees. That was immediately done, but he was made to plunge again as he had before. The poor princess did not know what such an extraordinary adventure might promise. She had seen the person she desired so passionately to see, twice, but he had disappeared so suddenly that she had not been able to say a word to him, nor hear any from his mouth.

The princess had recourse once again to embracing her dear son in her affliction, and when the child cried desperately in her arms she finally gave him the third ball, which was a ruby. He rolled it over the deck again; it rendered a harmony a thousand times more touching that one can describe, and, the queen having emerged from her palace precipitately, cried like an extremely impassioned person: "Give me that ball too, and I'll grant you whatever you want."

"I ask you for my husband," replied the princess.

The queen promised to let her see him from head to toe, and told her that she would return him to her for one day.

As soon as the ball was given, Fortunio emerged from the water, his feet on the back of a triton. He metamorphosed into an eagle, and flew to the princess, where he immediately resumed his natural form.

The queen, in despair at having been tricked, dived again into her empire and ordered all the sirens and tritons under her domination to agitate the sea with all their power, in order to doom the ship that had stolen a man from her by whom she was still charmed, in spite of the indifference he had had for all the delights of her palace, of which she had rendered him the master.

Fortunio, who knew how far her fury would go, set sail as soon as possible, in order to get away from the extent of the offended queen's domination. He was soon outside it, and when he saw that he was safe he embraced his charming princess and his dear son tenderly, and gave caresses to all those who had come to contribute to his deliverance. The weather was so fine and the wind so favorable that the ship reached port in a matter of hours.

The king, informed of his daughter's good fortune, ran to meet her and his dear son-in-law, whom he was delighted to see again after a long absence. No one thought any longer, after such a happy event, of anything but giving fêtes to the people, in order to render the joy more perfect by making it universal. Fortunio related the marvels of the siren's palace, and emphasized to his charming princess the indifference with which he had received the caresses of that powerful queen in the heart of her empire. The princess redoubled her tenderness, to recompense him for such a rare fidelity, and they savored very sensibly the pleasure of seeing one another after a cruel absence.

Only one thing was lacking to Fortunio's felicity. He had always conserved a great passion to reestablish in his estates the prince who had been dispossessed; he asked the king for forces for that expedition. The king gave them to him and he marched against the usurper, defeated him in a pitched battle, and reestablished on his throne the prince who had been expelled from it.

That grateful prince, wanting to share his estates with him, begged him to remain at his court and to bring his wife, the princess, thereto. Sensing an extraordinary affection for him, he wanted to know the reason for it. Having examined his features and a mark he had under the left eye, it came to his mind that he might be a son that he had lost while still in the cradle, who had had the same mark under the left eye. That infant had been stolen during a disorder that the first prince of his blood, chagrined to see that he had a successor, had caused in his court. That evil prince had seized the child, who was bound in his cradle, during the confusion caused by the clash of arms, and had him thrown into the river.

The king, who believed that he had recognized his son, in whom blood said that he was not mistaken, pressed Prince Fortunio to say what he knew about the commencement of his life; he replied that he had been brought up be people who lived on the bank of the same river into which it was said that the king's son had been thrown. The king sent someone to fetch them; they arrived in a few days, and when they had declared that they had found Fortunio in a rich cradle at the same time when the loss of the young prince had occurred, the king recognized him as his son and had him proclaimed as the successor to the crown.

The news was carried to the princess, his wife, and the king, his father-in-law, and it is easy to imagine the joy that they had in seeing that fortune had caused them to find, in a hero who had merited the princess by his valor, a prince who also merited her by his birth. No one any longer thought, in the two kingdoms between which the prince and princess divided their life, of anything but celebrating such considerable events, and the merit of a prince who made their delight.

Those who had been the first cause of that, by saving the prince, who was about to perish in the water, were well recompensed for an action that enabled public felicity.

Prince Guerini

The kingdom of Lombardy was once governed by King Philippe, who, having neither gallantry nor ambition, spent his life as the simplest of his subjects might have done, in the tranquility that one finds with one's wife and children. He was only veritably occupied with the merit of the queen and the care of bringing up Guerini, his only son, who was a prince of great hope; if he had any other application, it was only for hunting, a pleasure that he took quite often, although it was always devoid of passion.

One day, when he was with a few of his barons, he saw a savage man emerge from a wood, who was so ugly as to instill fear; he ordered that he be arrested, but as it was necessary to fight in order to master him, the king shouted that he was to be surrounded, and that they were to refrain from killing him, for he had already cost blood to those who had been bold enough to approach him. However, when he saw that he was surrounded, he surrendered to the multitude and allowed himself to be put in chains.

He was taken away and kept in a narrow prison, where the king, curious to learn about the mores and opinions of savages, went to visit him every day with his court. He only wanted to retain him in his irons until there was evidence that he was domesticated and disposed to submit to the laws and customs of disciplined men, but as he could not see any appearance yet of that and he was afraid that if he allowed people to enter his prison freely someone might enable him to escape, he kept the keys to them himself. When he went away from the city he gave them to the queen to guard, and recommended her strongly not to allow them to be taken by anyone whatsoever.

Another time when he went hunting, his young son Guerini was gripped by curiosity to go and see the savage man. Having approached the window of the prison, were there was a iron grille, with an arrow in his hand of precious workmanship, the savage, who wanted to take it away from him, caressed him, in order to draw him close enough to be able to take it, as, in fact, he did. The young prince, very afflicted to have lost his arrow, begged him insistently to return it to him. The savage replied to him that, far from giving it to him, he would break it into pieces if he did not open his prison and give him the means to break his chains.

The young prince, to whom nothing was as dear as his arrow, for his most ordinary exercise was drawing the bow, wanted to get it back at any price. In addition to that, being humane, as one is at his age, he thought he would be doing a good deed by setting a prisoner free, especially the savage, who had not committed any crime; but he found great difficulty in disposing of the keys to the prison, of which he knew the queen took great care. He remembered, however that if she went to sleep after her dinner, which sometimes happened, as he had the liberty of entering her apartment at all hours, it would be easy for him to remove the keys.

That happened as he had foreseen. He immediately ran to the prison, carrying a bundle of keys, which also included that of the prisoner's chain. Thus, without reflecting that he was going to make his father angry, he set the savage free, who returned the arrow to his hands and fled as quickly as possible into the woods.

The queen, having woken up and not found her keys, was greatly troubled. She sent someone immediately to see whether the prison was open; they came back to tell her that it was, and that the savage was no longer there. She was in great affliction, dreading the king's first impulses of anger, which were violent. She wept, she cried, she threatened, and wanted absolutely to know who had been bold enough to enter her room while she was asleep. Her men told her that no one had gone in there except the prince, her son; they did not dare to name one of the squires whom they had also seen going in, who entered very familiarly in the absence of the king; that was a fact in which there was a mystery, and no one dared to pronounce his name.

Told that her son had gone into her room, the queen sent for him. He appeared immediately, and confessed everything that had happened. The poor afflicted queen, fearing the anger of the king more for her son than for herself, resolved not to expose him to the initial transports of the king's anger. She summoned two servants of the young prince whom she thought trustworthy and told them that he had committed a fault for which the king would have difficulty forgiving him and that she wanted him to go on a journey in order to give the king's passion time to calm down, that she was confiding him to them as two wise men, and that she implored them to think that she as putting into their hands what was most dear to her in the world. Then she gave her son a quantity of gold and gems of great value, in order that he would be able to appear in a good equipage wherever he went, and sent him away with great diligence, fearing that the king might arrive.

Thus, Prince Guerini left, but the king arrived soon after and, having found the prison open as he passed, he ran to the queen's apartment full of fury. She went to meet him and disarmed his anger by her submission and mildness. She told him that she alone was culpable, since she had not guarded the keys that he had confided to her well enough, that she had allow them to be taken by her son, whom she had not mistrusted, and, seduced by the entreaties of the prisoner, he had set him free. Then she had thought it appropriate to distance for a while from the eyes of an irritated father a son who had omitted a great fault, so she had sent him into the world in order to learn to be wiser.

Appeased by a punishment that he thought too great, the king only thought of sending people in all directions with orders to assure his son that he forgave him for the fault he had committed of opening the door of the savage's prison, and that he was greatly afflicted by the poor opinion he had had of him in despairing of parental generosity; that he implored him to return immediately, and to be persuaded that his father would die of chagrin if he was far away from him for a long time.

All the king's cares were futile, however, since all the people he had sent on campaign came back without having been able to discover what route his son had taken.

Meanwhile, Prince Guerini was still traveling with his two servants, almost without knowing where he was going. He could not be in worse hands than those of those two scoundrels, who had decided to kill him and share his riches. The execution of that detestable project was only deferred until the first wood, where they would have no witnesses to fear.

The prince, however, had a fortunate encounter, which preserved him from such a danger, which was that of a young knight, better built and better looking than all those he had seen in his father's court, who was mounted on such a beautiful horse and so richly equipped that he could only be regarded as a man who had come from a fine place, so the prince was disposed to receive very civilly the offer he made to keep him company. They entered into conversation on general maters, but because the prince did not know to whom he was talking he did not open up at first, and did not say where he was going or where he was coming from.

There was no need for Prince Guerini to identify himself, since the young knight knew perfectly well everything that had happened to him, because it had given him pleasure and he was there to express his gratitude. It was the savage man, whom the prince had set free, and who had had a very fortunate adventure since then. He had encountered a fay, one of those who seek to do good, and perhaps also to demonstrate their power.

That good fay, having found him asleep in the depths of a wood, had touched him with the wand she carried in her hand, at which he felt himself awaken with great pleasure, and even, so to speak, reborn; for he found himself with sentiments very different from those he had had thus far. Whereas before he had only respired blood and carnage, he no longer thought of anything but living a quiet life, ashamed of his natural ferocity. He even perceived that he had a more likeable face, and in spite of the self-esteem that always renders us content with our first being, he felt an indescribable joy at a change that he saw so considerable.

The fay, having metamorphosed him thus, had taken him to her palace, where she had retained him for a few days, but as she was a fay careful of her reputation, he had sent him away for some time, and had given him the means have an equipage, and a few secrets of her art, of which he could make use in order to travel the world with all the conveniences and pleasures of life. She was very generous, which had led her to instruct him, above all, to search for Prince Guerini, to whom he was obliged for his liberty with what had subsequently been given to him, making him understand that he could not do anything from which she would obtain more pleasure than avoiding ingratitude on all sorts of occasions. It was thus that she had sent him away, after having been well instructed, and had told him the route at he had to take in order to encounter his liberator.

That is how Prince Guerini began to receive the recompense for a good deed, which his compassion for another's woes had caused him to do. The knight whom he had encountered, whom the fay had caused to take the name Alcée, told him that, charmed by his intelligence and his manners, he had resolved not to quit him until he had taken him to a place where he might hope for agreeable adventures, for which he dared to answer, and that, with all the merit he could see in him, he could not fail to be loved in all the places he went. For that reason, he advised him to choose the court of a great king, where he might encounter adventures worthy of him.

The prince, who had nothing else in view, and who believed that he could see that Alcée was speaking in good faith, asked him to tell him which court he ought to choose. After some arguments, and a few reflections on the state of affairs of all the neighboring princes, they resolved to pass over the Alps in order to go to the court of the King of Arles, whose name was Godefroi, a prince who was generating a good deal of talk in society, as much because of his knowledge as his wisdom, and who was known to receive strangers very honorably. It was also known that he only had daughters, and Alcée told Prince Guerini that, good looking as he was, there was no fortune to which he could not aspire.

The prince, who was young and knew that he was highly born, conceived hopes easily; he immediately formed the design to please one of the Princesses d'Arles, and with his heart full of such a fine project, he and his companion traveled together, and eventually arrived at the court of Arles.

Sometime after their arrival, Prince Guerini introduced himself to King Godefroi as a knight who was traveling the world out of curiosity to see what was happening there. The king wanted to know who he was, but the prince, having said that he had reasons for hiding his homeland, only told him that his name was Guerini, that the knight accompanying him was named Alcée, and that they were two knights who had made a vow to seek adventures of chivalry and to learn what was considerable in the world. The king, who saw that they had such a good appearance and that they spoke with such assurance of those who were born among princes, interpreted the mystery they were making very advantageously for them, and, judging them to be of noble birth, did them great honor and had all his courtiers do likewise.

The two knights lived tranquilly thus at the court of Arles for some months, and Prince Guerini, who had his design formed, thought of pleasing the elder of the two princesses, but without declaring himself. As for Alcée, although he was not a prince, he had so much confidence in the science that the fay had conferred upon him, that he did not despair of pleasing the younger. The fay, however, who was jealous, would not easily have yielded to another such an amiable knight, whom she had only rendered such in order to for him make the delights of her palace from time to time.

Meanwhile, the courtiers, to whom the merit of the two strangers gave anxiety, having learned that they boasted of having a great deal of valor and that they were seeking opportunities to make it apparent, proposed to the king that he send them to combat some giants who were making all his subjects tremble, and which, after having caused great disorder in the plain from time to time, had retired into the mountains where no one dared go in search of them.

The king replied that he could not resolve to expose them to such great dangers, unless the desire for glory, for which they said that they were passionate, caused them to volunteer of their own accord for such a great expedition, in which he would have them assisted by those of his subjects whom he knew to be most willing to render him service. At the same time, he added that there was nothing that they ought not to expect of his gratitude, if they were successful in delivering his estates from such cruel enemies; and he confessed that he could only expect that good fortune from them, since his subjects, who had never seen war, were not appropriate for bold enterprises.

Alcée who had confidence in the protection of the fay, who had already done him so many favors, encouraged Guerini to that enterprise, and, seeing that he was having a great deal of trouble resolving to risk a peril that seemed so evident, he confided all of his secret to him. After having told him that he was the savage man, who had such a great obligation to him, and having informed him of those that they both owed to a powerful fay who had taken the under their protection, he declared to him how he had been warned of the plot of the two domestics, from which the good fay had wanted to preserve him by sending him to keep him company. As he had always observed them since, however, and that their will might have changed, he had not said anything to him about it; his opinion was that they should not let them know that they had been suspected, because it was necessary to reserve them in order to expose them to the first fury of the giant, which was a means of punishing them for their evil design from which some utility might be obtained.

The prince, charmed by Alcée's arguments, which he found so prudent, and filled with hope by virtue of the protection of a powerful fay, did not hesitate any longer, and they agreed that it was necessary to go and offer themselves to the king without wasting time.

What encouraged Guerini most of all was the passion that he had for Princess Pontiane and the generosity that she had had for a few days of allowing him to see a little tenderness in her eyes. For his part, Alcée, who found Princess Eleutherie charming, would have risked himself a thousand times to merit her, but he dreaded being thwarted by the fay, whom he knew to be extremely jealous. That did not prevent him, however, from volunteering gladly for the enterprise. He knew that at least the glory of it would remain to him eternally and that it would contribute to the satisfaction of Prince Guerini, of whom he was veritably fond.

They went, therefore, to offer their humble services to the king, to whom they promised to destroy the race of giants that was desolating his estates, or at least to drive them far away, if he was agreeable to giving them guides who could conduct them and inform them of the retreats that the enemies they had to fight had in the mountains. They also asked him to give them the liberty to choose fifteen or twenty men from the troops of his guard, in order to serve them in the expedition, in accordance with the circumstances in which they might have need of them. That was very few people for such a great enterprise, but the prince who was making it was very valorous, and Alcée assured him that the fay whose favorite he was would not abandon them in such an important occasion.

They both marched with that confidence, and a small troop, for an expedition that anyone else but them would not have undertaken with two thousand battle-hardened men. The giants were numerous, and a single one was capable of putting to flight a troop like the one that was going in search of them. They were men of prodigious stature and strength, and had faces so frightful that one could not even sustain their gaze; they were each armed with a club made from a thick tree branch, and they had never found men or animals that were able to resist them. They spent the night in caverns, the entrances of which they sealed with huge rocks, which they handled as they pleased. They thrived on blood and carnage, and the only garments they wore were made from the skins of lions and bears that they had defeated.

Those were the enemies that Guerini and Alcée followed by a small, poorly-seasoned troop, were attempting to destroy, which they would never be able to do without the helpful fay who had taken them under her protection. She appeared to them on the first day of their march, only visible to Guerini and Alcée; she made them knights, and gave them each an enchanted lance and a helmet for their only offensive and defensive arms. On each of the helmets, however, there was a carbuncle that, when left uncovered, launched streaks of fire so bright that one was dazzled by them to the point of no longer being able to discern anything, and that was what caused the doom of the giants.

Having arrived in the mountains with their little army, furnished with food supplies for several days, the knights perceived a cavern sealed by large rocks, which they approached very noisily. The giants, curious as to what was happening, emerged immediately. Guerini's two servants, who had had evil designs, fortunately thwarted, against their master, were exposed to them. What they had hoped happened, for the giants came to meet them, emerging from the rocks that enclosed them, crushing the two unfortunates; but they had no sooner advanced than the two knights attacked them without being discerned because of the light their carbuncles projected. The giants were pierced by lance-thrusts and retreated into their caves with terrible screams.

The same disgrace happened to several on the first day of the enterprise, and, those who had escaped death having assembled by night to hold council, they made a signal at daybreak with a kind of white flag to request peace. The knights sent two of their men forward, and two giants also advanced, and offered on the part of their entire company to retire deep into the mountains and to give assurances that they would never enter the plain, provided that they were left as masters in an expanse of the mountains that they demanded.

The treaty was made, on the basis of the authority given to Prince Guerini, on condition that two of the principal giants allowed themselves to be taken in chains to the court, that they would remain there for several years as hostages, and that Guerini could take away, as evidence of his victory, the heads of those giants who had died of their wounds; that was granted to him.

The prince then departed from the mountains, having made the giants retreat, in the execution of the treaty, within the limits prescribed to them, and having buried a few of their own men who had been killed on that occasion. The hostages were delivered, and the giants' heads, numbering ten, after which they resumed the road to the court.

The generous fay, who had contributed so much to the success of the expedition, had not asked Alcée for anything by way of recognition except that as soon as it was finished he would go to spend a few days with her, which Alcée had promised; and he went, wanting to avoid ingratitude, which he regarded as an enormous vice, in spite of the passion he had to see the charming princess again, whom he had formed the design to please. He also regretted quitting his dear Guerini, who begged him to take part in his triumphs, since he would have a great one for his victory. Alcée, who quit him with a dolor that can easily be imagined, assured him that he would see him again soon; thus, the two knights separated, after having embraced affectionately. Alcée went to see the generous fay again, and Guerini arrived at court, where he was received with the acclamations of the people, who were unable to express their gratitude.

The king and queen were so extremely grateful for what he had done that they assured him that they had no means of recompensing him for such a great one of which he could not dispose. Princess Pontiane gave him a welcome so favorable that he was charmed by it; she had been disposed to wish him well abundantly before his departure; a return so glorious determined her and her heart became very sensible. The ladies believed themselves to recompense the glorious actions, and some were seen every day who loved ugly and unpolished men solely because they had acquired some reputation by way of arms.

The king, who had conceived a great deal of esteem for Alcée, asked urgently what had become of him. Guerini replied that he would soon be at the court, but that a few indispensable duties had obliged him to make a journey that would only last for a few days. He rendered an exact account to His Majesty of the part that the brave knight had played in the victory. The king was very glad to learn that he would come to receive the testimonies for his gratitude; while waiting for him to arrive he did not forget any caress or good treatment that he could make Guerini, and also made considerable presents to those of his subjects who had distinguished themselves in that occasion, in accordance with the report that Guerini gave him.

Several days having passed in fêtes and continual rejoicing, Guerini was pressed by the king to declare the recompense that he had chosen. He asked for two more days to think about it; that was to seek an opportunity to speak to the princess. He found one, and having told her his birth, he then declared the great passion that he had for her, and that it was with a view to meriting her that he had undertaken the mission that he had just carried out; that it had had a success that satisfied the king, but not himself, he did not think that it was enough to have become worthy of her; that he would only ask, of all the recompense that the king offered him, permission to serve her until she was agreeable to granting him the only one that he could ever desire, which only depended on her.

To that, the princess replied that if it depended on her, the king could accord it to him whenever it pleased him, since he was the master of her will and she would obey him on this occasion without reluctance.

The prince, charmed to hear her speak so favorably for him, threw himself at the feet of the princess and swore to her that he would go beyond all imagination in order to render himself worthy of the happiness that she was according him. He told her that since she found it good, he would go to declare to the king what he had told her about his birth, and then the boldness that he had had of aspiring to such a great recompense for the little he had done for his service.

The king, having learned that Guerini was the son of a king, was very satisfied to have the opportunity to do nothing that was unworthy of him and the princess by giving her to a conqueror who was already so illustrious by virtue of his victory that he could not have refused him the princess even if he had only been a simple knight. The wedding celebrations took place a few days later and were followed by a felicity of a great many years.

Prince Guerini's credit was so great in that court that, a short time after his marriage, he obtained Princes Eleutherie for Alcée, and afterwards, to render his happiness perfect, he wanted to make him known to the king and queen to whom he owed the light of day, and thus divided the rest of his life between two courts, of which he and the princess made the delights, and where their posterity reigned for several centuries with great glory.

The Queen of the Isle of Flowers

In the realm of the Isle of Flowers there was once a queen who lost in full youth the king, her husband, whom she loved tenderly and by whom she was loved in the same way. That reciprocal tenderness had given life to two perfectly beautiful princesses, whom the queen, their mother, raised with all possible care, and she had the pleasure of seeing their charms augmented every day. The elder, in particular, at the age of fourteen, became incomparable in her beauty, which caused the queen some anxiety because she knew that the Queen of the Isles would be jealous of her.

The Queen of the Isles, who believed herself to be the most beautiful princess in the world, demanded from all beautiful young women a recognition of the superiority of her beauty. Impelled by that vanity, she had obliged the king, her husband, to conquer all the islands in the vicinity of her own, and the king, who was equitable and had only undertaken that enterprise in order to satisfy the queen, only thinking after his conquest of what might give her pleasure, had only imposed by law on all the princes he had subjugated the obligation to send all the princesses of their blood, as soon as they were fifteen years old, to pay homage to the beauty of the queen, his wife.

The Queen of the Isle of Flowers, who was aware of that obligation, thought as soon as her elder daughter was fifteen years old about taking her to the feet of the throne of the superb queen. The beauty of the young princess had already made so much noise that it had spread everywhere, and the Queen of the Isles, who had heard a great deal of talk about her, awaited her with an anxiety that as the presage of jealousy, by which she found herself gripped subsequently.

She was veritably dazzled by such a splendid beauty, and could not help agreeing that she had never seen anything so

228

beautiful, meaning that she judged that it was after her, for the self-esteem that possessed her absolutely, prevented her from believing that the princess was more beautiful than her. She even treated her quite civilly, in the thought that she would not take away her superiority. But the acclamations that all the men and all the women of the court gave the beauty of the princess caused the queen such a great chagrin that she lost all countenance. She retired to her cabinet, feigning illness, in order no longer to witness the triumphs of such an amiable rival. She had the queen of the Isle of Flowers informed that she could not see her again because of the indisposition that had overtaken her, and she advised her, furthermore, to retire to her estates and take her daughter, the princess with her.

The Queen of Flowers, who had once spent quite a long time at the court, had formed a friendship there with of one the queens maids of honor, who advised her confidently not to ask to take her leave of the queen and to think about getting out of her estates as soon as possible.

The maid of honor, who was a good person, and had premised amity to the Queen of the Isle of Flowers, was caught between the duties of friendship and the fidelity she owed to the queen she served; she thought she could make a just compromise by simply warning her friend, with whom her mistress had a discontentment about which she could not tell her. She thought she could simply advise her to retire to her estates without losing any time, and when she had done that, to prevent the princess, her daughter, from going out of the palace for six months, for any reason whatsoever. She promised her, in addition, to employ all her credit and all her industry in the meantime in order to calm the mind of her mistress, the queen.

The Queen of the Isle of Flowers, who had understood by her friend's mysterious speech that her daughter had a great deal to fear from the queen's vengeance, because she felt very offended by the great rumor that the beauty of the charming princess had generated in the court, took her back to her estates and took her to her palace in all diligence.

As she was not unaware how far the power extended that the secrets of enchantment gave the irritated queen, she warned her daughter that she was menaced by a great danger if she went out of the palace, recommending her with all her authority and all the tenderness of a mother not to do that without her permission, for any reason whatsoever.

The queen did not neglect anything to divert the princess, and only went out herself rarely, in order to render that long confinement more bearable by keeping her company in it.

The six months were about to expire, and on the last day there was a fête of great rejoicing, in a charming meadow at the end of the avenue of the palace, so that the princess, having seen the preparations for it from the window of her apartment and being very bored because she had not had the pleasure of a walk for such a long time, in a land covered in flowers everywhere, begged the queen to let go as far as the meadow.

The queen, who thought that the peril had passed, consented to that; she even wanted to go with her, followed by her entire court, whose members were charmed to see the princess who made their delights at liberty after a detention of six months, the reason for which the queen had not revealed.

The princess, delighted by the joy of walking along a path strewn with all kinds of flowers after having been deprived for such a long time, was a few paces ahead of her mother when—what a cruel spectacle!—the earth opened up beneath the feet of the charming princess and closed again after having engulfed her.

The queen fainted with dolor; the younger princess shed tears and could not quit the place where she had seen her sister disappear. That accident put the entire court into such great consternation that nothing similar had ever been seen. Physicians were summoned to help the queen, who, when she had been brought round from her faint by their remedies, had the earth excavated to abyssal depths. The most surprising thing of all was that no vestige was found there of any trace of the passage of the princess.

She had traversed the thickness of the earth very prompt-ly, and found herself in a desert, where she saw nothing but rocks and woods, without being able to perceive the slightest trace of human footfalls. She only encountered there a little dog of marvelous beauty, which ran to her as soon as she ap-peared and gave her a thousand caresses.

Astonished as she was by such a terrible adventure, she nevertheless took the little dog in her arms, which she found so pretty and affectionate. After having held it for a few mo-ments she put it down on the ground. Uncertain of which way to go, she saw the little dog walk away, turning its head con-tinually, seemingly inviting her to follow it. She allowed her-self to be guided thus, without knowing where.

She had not been walking for long when she found her-self on a small eminence, from which she discovered a valley charged with fruit trees, which bore flowers and fruits at the same time. She even perceived that the ground at the feet of the trees as covered with flowers and fruits, and saw in the middle a beautiful flower bed, and a spring bordered with grass.

She approached it, and found that the water was as clear as rock crystal. She sat down on the grass, where, over-whelmed by a misfortune that she could not contemplate with-out horror, she dissolved in tears, seeing everything to dread and not being able to foresee where the slightest assistance might come from. She could certainly see a remedy against hunger and thirst; she picked up fruits and made use of her white hand to take water and drink; but what help could she promise herself against wild animals? She could not rid herself of the thought that she was in danger of being devoured.

Finally, being resolved to all the evils that she could not avoid, she sought to muffle her dolor by caressing her little dog. She spent the day on the bank of the little spring, but when night approached her embarrassment increased and she did not know what to do. Then she perceived the little dog pulling at her dress. She did not pay any great attention to it to begin with, but, seeing that it was stubborn and that after having gripped her dress it took three steps, always in the same direction and returned a moment later to repeat the same movement, visibly seeming to want her to follow it in that direction, she allowed herself to be led that way.

Finding herself at the foot of a rock, she saw a spacious opening there, into which her little dog still seemed to be inviting her to enter by the same means that it had employed to bring her there. Surprised, the princess went into the rock, where she discovered an agreeable cavern illuminated by the radiance of the stones that composed it, as if by the light of the sun. In the furthest corner she perceived a small bed covered in moss. She went to lie down there, and her little dog immediately lay down at her feet. She was still in a new astonishment, at seeing things with which she was so unfamiliar. The reflections she made and the day's travails having overwhelmed her, drowsiness overtook her and she fell asleep.

When daylight arrived she was awakened by the song of birds that covered the branches of a few trees that were around the rock. In other circumstances she would have been charmed by it, for birdsong had never been so diversified or so melodious. The little dog, having woken up alike her, approached her feet with its affectionate little fashions, seeming to want to kiss them. She picked it up and went outside in order to respire the air, which was the mildest she could have desired, there being no more amiable climate under the sun.

The little dog stated walking away from her and coming back, as it had before, to take her by the dress. She allowed it to guide her, and it brought her back to the pleasant flower bed on the edge of the spring where she had spent a part of the previous day. She ate fruit there and drank water, by which she felt satisfied, as if by a god meal.

She spent several months like that. Not seeing any enemy to fear, her dolor gradually eased and her solitude became more bearable. Her little dog, so pretty and affectionate, contributed a great deal to that.

One day, when she saw that it was very sad, and it was not caressing her, she was afraid that it might be ill. She took it to a place where she had seen it eating a herb that she hoped might soothe it, but it was not possible to get it to take any. Its sadness lasted all day, and then all night, which it spent uttering great plaints.

The princess had fallen asleep, and when she awoke, her first concern was to look for her little dog, but she no longer found it at her feet, which it did not have the custom of quitting. She got up with great urgency, in order to see what had become of it. When she emerged from the rock she heard the voice of a man lamenting, and she saw an old man, who fled so promptly that she lost sight of him in a moment.

That was a new surprise for her: a man, in a place where none had appeared in several months; and the loss of her little dog surprised her as much as anything else. As it had been so faithful since the first day of her disgrace, she did not know whether the old man might have stolen it.

She was wandering around her rock, with a hundred different thoughts, when she was suddenly enveloped by a dense cloud and transported through the air; she did not put up any resistance, and allowed herself to be carried. She found herself, before the end of the day, not knowing where she had passed on the way, in one of the avenues of the palace where she had been born. The cloud had disappeared.

As she approached the palace she saw a sad spectacle. All the men she encountered were dressed in morning, which made her apprehensive that she had lost her mother, the queen, or her sister, the princess. When she was closer to the palace she was recognized and heard the air resounding with cries of joy.

The queen, alerted by the chorus of voices, ran to meet her sister and embraced her tenderly, telling her that she would give her crown back to her, which the people had obliged her to take after the death of the queen, their mother, which had happened a few days after the fatal accident that had caused her to disappear.

There was a noble contest between the two princesses, each wishing to cede the crown to the other, but in the end, the elder accepted it, on condition of sharing her authority with the princess who had surrendered it to her and who declared that she would not accept any part of it, being quite satisfied with the glory of obeying such a charming queen.

Having taken the crown, therefore, which was her right, the princess thought of rendering the last duties to her mother, and giving her sister a thousand marks of gratitude for the generosity she had had in yielding a crown of which she was in possession. Afterwards, being sensibly touched by the loss of a little dog that had been faithful to her for so long in her solitude, she ordered that a search be made for it in all the parts of the world that were own to her. Those she had employed in it not having learned anything, she was so afflicted that dolor bore her to say that she would give half her estates to anyone who could return it to her hands. Her sister, very surprised by such an extraordinary—not to say extravagant—resolution, employed a thousand reasons to oppose it, in vain.

The lords of the court, touched by such a fine recompense, departed in all directions, but came back like their predecessors having no agreeable news to give the queen. She fell into an affliction so excessive that she went as far as to publish that she would marry the man who brought her the little dog—without which, she said, to excuse herself, it was not possible for her to live.

The hope of such a prize, so unexpected, rendered the court deserted. While everyone was searching in all directions, someone came to tell the queen that there was a man of very shabby appearance in her cabinet with her sister, who was requesting to speak to her. She ordered that he be allowed to enter. He came in and told the queen that he had come to offer to return her little dog to her, provided that she kept her word.

The princess spoke first and said that the queen could not make the resolution to marry without the consent of her subjects, and that it was necessary to assemble the council in such an important occasion.

Having nothing to respond to the arguments of the princess, the queen gave an apartment in the palace of a man that had such a high pretention, and consented to submit to the deliberations of her council, which she ordered to assemble the next day.

When the princess was alone with the queen she represented to her so forcefully the wrong she was doing in proposing such a recompense for a little dog that she made her resolve to renounce such a bizarre design. Perhaps the queen was not sorry that a pretext had been furnished for her to break her promise to a man of such poor appearance.

The council having assembled the following day, the princess made it resolve that the ugly man would be offered great wealth as the price of the little dog, and that if he refused he would be banished from the kingdom without speaking to the queen again. The man refused the riches and withdrew.

The princess rendered an account of the council's resolution to the queen, and that of the man, who had withdrawn after refusing the riches that were offered to him. The queen said that all that had happened was in order, but that, as she was the mistress of her own person, she would leave the next day, after having returned the crown to her, to go and wander the world until she had found her little dog.

Frightened by the resolution of the queen, whom she loved dearly, the princess did not neglect anything to make her change her mind; she assured her with an unparalleled generosity that she would never accept the crown.

While they were having such a sad conversation, one of the officers of the queen's household presented himself at the door of her cabinet to inform her that the sea was covered with ships.

The two princesses went on to a balcony, and saw an army approaching the port under full sail. Having considered it, they judged by its magnificence that it had not come to make war. They saw all the vessels covered with a thousand marks of gantry; there was nothing bit flags, ensigns, streamers and silk banners of all colors. They were confirmed in that thought when they saw smaller boats approaching, which carried white ensigns as a sign of peace.

The queen had ordered that someone run to the port and go to meet that army to find out where it came from. She was soon informed that it was the Prince of the Isle of Emeralds, who was asking for permission to land in her estates and to come and offer her his humble respects.

The queen sent her principal officers to the prince's ship in order to give him her compliments and assure him that he was very welcome. She waited for him sitting on her throne, which she quit when she saw him appear; she even took a few steps toward him. That interview took place with a great civility on both sides, and the conversation was very witty. The queen had the prince taken to a magnificent apartment; he asked for a private audience and it was granted to him for the next day.

The time of the audience having arrived, the prince was introduced into the queen's cabinet; she only had the princess, her sister, with her. He approached the queen and said to her that he had things to say to her that might have surprised anyone else, but that she would easily recognize the truth of them by virtue of circumstances that were only known to her.

"I am," he continued, "a neighbor of the estates of the Queen of the Isles; mine form a peninsula which had a narrow passage to her realm. One day, animated by the passion I had for hunting, I followed a deer into one of her forests; I had the misfortune to encounter her, and, not having believed her to be the queen because she had no great retinue, I did not stop to render her what was due to her. You know Madame, better than anyone, that she is very vindictive and that she has an admirable power of enchantment. I experienced that immediately. The earth opened up beneath my feet and I found myself in a distant region, transformed into a little dog, and that was where I had the honor of seeing you, Madame.

"Six months having gone by, the vengeance of the queen not being complete, she metamorphosed me into a hideous old man, and in that state I was so afraid of being disagreeable to you, Madame, that I went to bury myself in the thickest part of a wood, where I spent a further three months; but I was fortunate enough to encounter a helpful fay there, who liberated me from the power of the superb Queen of the Isles, and told me everything that had happened to you, and where I could find you. I have come to offer you the homage of a heart that has known no other power that yours, Madame, since the first day that I encountered you in the desert."

After that speech, the prince continued to tell the queen that the fays, offended by the bad usage that the Queen of the Isles had made of the gifts of faerie, had taken them away from her.

Afterwards, the prince had several more conversations, in which the queen and he agreed to link themselves by eternal knots, and that resolution, having been made public, was received with universal applause. That was not without reason, for subjects never lived under such a mild domination. They enjoyed it for nearly a century, the king and the queen having governed them together and lived in a perfect felicity until an extreme old age.

The Favorite of the Fays

Galeran, a young gentleman of the city of Naples, nourished at the court, being suspected of having given bad advice to a young prince, the successor to the crown, whose favorite he was, fled with so much precipitation to avoid the anger of the king that he did not take anything with him. He was so afraid of being pursued that he traveled day and night until he was beyond the frontiers of the realm.

He had been riding for thirty-six hours without having eaten once or given fodder to his mount, so that he found himself overwhelmed by lassitude, and his horse could no longer put one foot in front of another. It was necessary, therefore, to stop, but, not finding any house in his path, he was obliged to go into a beautiful meadow in order to enable his horse to graze. He perceived that there were pomegranates and oranges in the hedge; he picked some and ate them, having nothing better, and having sat down in the shade, unable to resist weariness and slumber, he fell asleep, leaving his horse to wander.

A powerful fay whose palace was in a nearby wood, having come to walk in that meadow, perceived Galeran, who was profoundly asleep. Having found him very handsome, she sat down beside him in order to wait for him to wake up.

After having contemplated so much beauty for a long time, impatient to know whether he had a touching gaze and great charms in his mouth, which she could not judge in the state that he was in, she woke him up by pushing him gently with a wand that she was carrying in her hand.

Surprised to find such a magnificently clad person sitting beside him, Galeran got up, asked by what spell he found himself in such good company. The fay told him that, having found out about an unfortunate adventure he had had, she had come to offer him a secure refuge in a mansion of which she was the mistress, where he could stay for as long as he pleased, and when he wanted to leave, she would make sure that it was with whatever was necessary to him in all the places where he conceived a desire to go.

Galeran, who deemed himself exceedingly fortunate to have found so much generosity in a person he found so well made, told her that he was flattered to have had an opportunity to merit the favors that she was offering him, but that he would not neglect anything to render himself worthy of them. Eventually, the initial compliments having concluded, she invited him to climb into her chariot beside her, and took him to her palace, where she neglected nothing to render his sojourn there agreeable.

The cavalier, being gallant and polite, responded for a long time to the fay's generosity with great eagerness, but what almost always happens happened between them; the great urgency relented, and their conversation became languid. As a prudent individual, the fay judged that it was not possible to limit the ambition of a young man full of fire to the bounds of a mansion, and that it was necessary to let him seek to make people talk about him in a more extensive career. As she had wanted to know the details of the cause of his disgrace, she judged by the difficulties he made in telling her the secrets of the prince whose favorite he had been that he was incapable of a bad usage of the confidence she had in him.

Having found a young man as sage as he was amiable, she esteemed him as much as she had loved him, and, judging him worthy of every kind of happiness, she wanted to give him the means of appearing in society and making a great fortune there—but that was on condition that he swore always to be her friend, and to come to see her from time to time. Those agreements having been made between them, she sent him away, after giving him gold and precious stones, with an enchanted lance and armor, which was not done without a tearful response.

Finally, after tender adieux, he departed, and, not considering that he would be safe in any of the courts of Italy, he wanted to go overseas and to go to the kingdom of Epirus, where he knew that there was a warrior king who gladly received adventurers at his court who went to offer him their services, and who had a unique daughter the heiress of his realm.

Galeran had a heart naturally capable of grand designs, and, the fay having raised his hopes by the quantity of gold and gems she had given him, he provided himself with domestics and magnificent clothes in Italy and arrived at the court of the King of Epirus in an equipage that caused him to be judged a man of great condition. He went to introduce himself to the king, whose name was Marcian, and told him that, attracted by the rumor of his exploits, he had come to offer him his services, and begged him to regard him as a man who, when the occasion arose, would have as much zeal for the glory of his arms as those of his subjects who served him with the most passion.

The king, who found something in his physiognomy and his manners that marked grandeur, was curious to know who he was, but Galeran begged him to excuse him from naming his fatherland; he only told him that his name was Galeran and that he had strong reasons for not telling him anymore. The king, not wanting to press him any further, told him that he could see that he was from a good place and that he was very welcome in his court, where he would find all sorts of satisfaction. Galeran rendered him very humbly a thousand thanks and told him that he would await occasions of war, in which he begged His Majesty to employ him.

Princess Murcie, the heiress of the realm, was with her father, the king, and Galeran gave her a profound reverence. The king turned away to talk to someone, and in the meantime the young foreigner mingled with the courtiers, who paid him all sorts of compliments, competing to offer him their services, everyone hastening to offer him entries to the apartments of the ladies. He was introduced to the princess the same day by her maid of honor.

Galeran was enchanted by the beauty of the princess, and the gracious welcome she gave him completed rendering him the most passionate of men. He entered into all the parties and the most amiable societies of the court from that day on, and he was very assiduous toward the king and the princess, as often as he could be received in her company. There were tourneys in which he ran against all comers; he was always victorious and received the prize of victory from the hands of the charming princess.

How fortunate he would have deemed himself if he had dared to declare that he only entered the lists for the glory of the princess! He would have sustained against the whole world that there as only her in the world worthy of being served. He bore an emblem on his shield that could only be explained by the boldness he had of having raised his eyes as far as her; it was an eagle that had flown as close to the sun as it could, with the words: *I cannot be burned burn nor dazzled by its radiance.*

Galeran's assiduity with regard to the princess, his passionate gazes and the eagle on his shield informed Prince Pontian that Galeran had the audacity of thinking to please the princess. Prince Pontian was of the blood of the kings of Epirus via his mother, and, believing himself to be the most considerable man in the court and the closest to the crown, he had not judged that anyone would dare to dispute the princess with him; that is why he assumed that he had the right to punish, with all tortures, a foreigner who, being nothing but a stranger, had nevertheless had the audacity to become his rival.

He therefore attempted to punish him, and even to get rid of him by means of assassination, being certain that the death of a man devoid of relatives and friends, in a place where he was so powerful, would not cause him any embarrassment. With four or five well-armed men he placed himself in Galeran's path when he emerged from the palace accompanied by a single domestic, and would have fallen into an ambush that had been set for him if he had not encountered, at the door of the palace, a lady in a chariot who offered him a place beside her, telling him that she wanted to take him home in safety.

Galeran, preoccupied as he was with the attractions of the princess, was too young and too gallant to refuse the favors of a person who, judging by her retinue, seemed very considerable. He got into the chariot without knowing with whom. He had no sooner done so than he perceived that he had that obligation to a very well made woman. He also learned that he had a greater one than he knew, for she declared to him that he was in great peril, since a grandee of the court had resolved his doom, and was waiting on his route to kill him, but that she wanted to protect him, by taking him to a place where he would be secure for a few days, and where she would discuss with him the measures he would have to take to shield himself from the enterprises of his enemy.

Astonished by what he heard, not knowing what enemies he had to fear, Galeran did not resist in any fashion, and in spite of the reluctance he had to draw away from the princess, he allowed himself to be conducted blindly by a person of whom there was no appearance that he ought to be suspicious. She was a fay in the neighborhood of the court who, having discovered by her secret science the peril that an amiable man was in, had wanted to protect him, for the glory of doing a good deed, and perhaps also with a view to obliging a man she judged worthy of it, and whom she hoped to find grateful.

It was not the first time that the good fay had attracted friends by means of her benefits; she could no longer hope to do so by mean of her beauty. As she had a good deal of wit, she exchanged badinage with Galeran, and said the prettiest things in the world to him, about the fear he must have of finding himself abducted by a woman he did not know and being taken to a place where he did not know what company he would find or what welcome he would receive.

While saying things to him that might have embarrassed him, however the fay reassured him at the same time with a few caresses, to the point that it is even said that she put her hand under his chin. Galeran, who would have become bolder on any other occasion, dared not emancipate himself to any familiarity, not knowing whether he might be in the hands of someone above human nature, who was transporting him he knew not where. In sum, he wanted to wait until he knew with whom he was dealing and where she was taking him.

He was soon informed, for he arrived at a palace, which might have been named a palace of delights; he would not have found anything lacking there if it had been that of the princess he adored.

The fay gave her orders when she arrived, and several slaves immediately hastened to be the first to serve the slightest of Galeran's desires; all knees bent before him and he was obeyed before he had finished speaking. In sum, everything that can make the felicity of a mortal was at his disposition, since no pleasure was lacking, not even those that his discretion prevented him from publishing.

After having spent a few days thus, the fay, who understood reason very well, thought that it was time to return Galeran to a princess who was in great anxiety, not knowing what had become of him. The fay even took generosity further, for she employed all her power to add to his initial charms an air of beauty that he had not had thus far. She gave him gold and precious stones by the handful, and assured him that he could pursue his enterprise at the court boldly, that his enemies were ashamed of having formed such evil designs had had renounced them absolutely. She also assured him that any attempts that might be made against him with superior forces would never succeed. If two enemies that he had to combat had equal arms, she told him that she wanted to leave him the glory of overcoming them by his virtue, and that she would not interfere with that.

After that conversation, she sent Galeran away; he shed a few tears as he left, which he gave to recognition, for he was only veritably touched by the attractions of the princess, whom he was very impatient to see again.

As there had been great anxiety at court to know what had become of his, various speculations were made on his return about his absence, and people wanted to know what had caused it. The king having pressed him on that matter, he was obliged to respond that he had been obliged to make a short journey in order to see someone who came from his homeland, who had to talk to him about important affairs.

The princess embarrassed him much more; as she took more interest than anyone else in what regarded him—for she was very touched by his merit—she told him that she wanted absolutely to know where he had been and that he should take the time to render her an account of it.

Galeran, charmed by the anxiety that he saw on the part of the princess, and the order he had received to tell her what had happened, sought an opportunity to do so, and soon having found one he gave her an exact account of his adventure; he only neglected a few details of which a gallant man can never make mention, and which the princess understood very well without him talking about them. The opportunity was too good to be missed; Galeran exaggerated how much he had suffered in being distanced from her and depicted, in very vivid colors, everything that had happened in his heart since the first time he had seen her.

The princess replied that she would carefully refrain from complaining about the declaration she had made, since she had attracted it. "But," she continued, "don't go so far as to believe that I add faith to what I've just heard, and that I would approve if you were to mention it for a second time."

Galeran, who was afraid that she really might not want to listen to him another time, made her a thousand sworn promises of eternal servitude, and had no reason to repent of it, for the princess continued to listen to him with enough generosity, and only said him on quitting him: "Time will tell where you are telling the truth." That was not calculated to make a lover despair who had just spoken for the first time, so Galeran, very satisfied with that conversation, no longer thought about anything but seeking opportunities to have others, and explained himself, in the meantime, by means of assiduities and languid gazes.

Galeran was in that state when a herald arrived from the King of Sparta, who had just declared war. The King of Epirus declared that he accepted it, and that he would be found at the head of his army. He knew that the King of Sparta would be at the head of his, and he was so animated against him that he had it proclaimed in his court that he would give his daughter in marriage to whichever of his knights could put him in his power.

The hope of such a recompense inflamed all the young bravos of Epirus, and more than all the rest Prince Pontian and Galeran, both more touched by the beauty of the princess than the gleam of the crown of which she was the heiress.

The two armies set forth on the march a few days later and did not take very long to come to grips. Galeran found an opportunity before then to speak to the princess, and told her that she would never see him again if he did not bring the King of Sparta to her feet. The princess replied that she would be very satisfied to see him put under the power of her father a king who had often made war with a cheerful heart, and that she would say prayers for that.

Galeran, who was able to explain in its full extent what the princess had just said, departed full of ardor and hope. He remembered the obligation he had to the two fays, whom he had encountered in the most important occasions of his life; he would have liked passionately to encounter a third, who might have helped him in an enterprise on which the incomparable happiness depended that was promised to the vanquisher of the King of Sparta.

He was destined to be the favorite of the fays; a third presented herself to him who offered to fight by his side and to show him the King of Sparta, whom he would otherwise have difficulty distinguishing because he had four knights in his army with an equipage similar to his own.

Galeran already had an enchanted lance and armor, and the generous fay who wanted to share the peril of the day with him gave him a buckler that was proof against all arrows, but as it did not cover him everywhere, there was still enough danger in the expedition for there to be a great deal of glory in it. As soon as the battle commenced, Galeran and his faithful companion flew, without engaging, to where they had recognized the King of Sparta at the head of a squadron.

He had already felled two who had come to confront him, and was waiting a third who was charging him, lance lowered at the moment when the two squadrons were about to collide. Galeran advanced, removed the king's helmet with a thrust of his lance, and, having taken the bridle of his horse, pulled him out of the melee and took him prisoner. The king had broken his lance against Galeran's enchanted armor and, seeing himself devoice of a lance with his head bare, confined so closely than he could not draw his word, he declared that he was the prisoner of a knight who appeared to him to be invincible, and allowed himself to be led away.

That expedition made, the fay gave her hand to Galeran and told him that she would let him enjoy the victory, and that she only asked him to remember that she had wanted to serve him without interest, which he had not always encountered when he had need of help. The fay disappeared, and Galeran went to present his prisoner to the King of Epirus.

Prince Pontian, who had routed the King of Sparta's squadron, came running and claimed that he had a right to dispute Galeran's recompense, sustaining that it was him who had defeated the King of Sparta and that Galeran had only taken him prisoner because he had found himself abandoned by his squadron.

After a long argument, Galeran offered to sustain his right by arms in the presence of the two kings. Prince Pontian accepted the offer, and the King of Epirus ordered the combat for the next day. After haying employed the rest of the day pursuing his victory and carefully caressing in the evening the officers who had contributed the most to it, the latter spent the night in the repose one enjoys when one no longer has any enemies. The following day he witnessed, in the presence of his army in battle order, the combat that would decide such an important quarrel.

The two knights arrived almost at the same time, and immediately lowered their lances. It was difficult to recognize

Galeran, because he had not wanted to make use of his enchanted arms in an individual combat; he no longer had those he had carried in the battle, but it was possible to recognize him by his pride.

The two knights, animated by the prize of the combat, confronted one another like two lions, and having both broken their lances in the first impact, they began a combat with swords so terrible that they could only be regarded as valiant men; but Galeran was the more fortunate; he gave Pontian such a rude blow that he almost paralyzed his arm and caused him to drop his sword. The prince, without a weapon, was obliged to confess himself beaten and to yield the prize of the victory to a man that the princess judged in her heart to be more worthy of her.

The King of Epirus, who thought that crowns were only due to virtue, assured his own to Galeran by permitting him to marry the princess, his daughter. The marriage was very happy, and the king, very satisfied with the respects that his successors rendered to him, passed all the way to an extreme old age in great tranquility, and left his crown when he died to two persons who were the delight of their subjects.

Benevolent; Or, Quiribirini

There was once a king who appeared to be the most fortunate prince in the world. He possessed flourishing estates, the limits of which he extended by means of a war of several years, and he had acquired a reputation for being the most valiant and wisest captain of his century. He governed his subjects with so much mildness that they adored him, and to complete his felicity he had married the loveliest princess of his time, by whom he was loved tenderly. But as no happiness is perfect, the health of that lovely princess was so delicate that there was no reason to hope that she would live for a long time.

The king knew that, and was in mortal anxiety in consequence, continually occupied in seeking means to reestablish the health of the charming queen; he often conferred with her physicians and consulted all the chemists that presented themselves to him. He found no ordinary physicians or chemists, however, in whom he believed he could have confidence.

A woman of his court, touched by his embarrassment, told him that there was a man in his estates who, having been brought up by fays, possessed all the secret sciences in the utmost perfection; the difficulty was in encountering him, because he was always traveling, seeking opportunities to make use of his art in order to do good to all those who had need of being helped.

The king, having learned that he ordinarily resided in the depths of a forest that was not far from the court, sent people there, and he was found, fortunately, returning home after having been away from a while. He went with those who had come to fetch him, and, having learned what the king wanted of him, he asked for the liberty to consult his books. After having consulted them carefully, he knew that the king had a particular interest in a son who would succeed to his crown, and he devoted all his cares to fortifying the queen's health in order to render her capable of bringing children into the world.

As he had a perfect knowledge of simples, he chose them so well that he composed a broth that, in a matter of days, put the queen in perfect health. She became pregnant soon afterwards, and gave birth to a prince who was her perfect resemblance, and appeared in a few years to be ornamented by all the talents that can be desired to make a great prince. He was brought up with all the cares that can contribute to making heroes, and they were cares well employed, for the prince became incomparable.

The king and the queen were inexpressibly content on seeing a son and successor of such fine hope, but they did not enjoy that happiness for long; they both died in the same year, leaving that amiable prince the master of their estates and his own conduct. He was at an age when one cannot take a step without slipping, but he guided himself nevertheless and governed his subjects with such sagacity that he won their admiration.

One of his neighbors, who wanted to take advantage of his youth, declared war of him; the young prince put himself at the head of his troops and performed so many actions of great valor that he reduced his enemies to recognizing that they had attacked him recklessly and asking for peace, which he granted them on very mild conditions. After that, the great reputation that he had acquired being a sure guarantee that his neighbors would not attempt anything against him, and his subjects living in great tranquility, he devoted himself to hunting.

It was surprising that a young king, who had a large number of charming ladies at his court, seemed insensible to so many attractions; several of them formed thee design to please him, but it was in vain and they saw with astonishment a young and polished prince remaining indifferent in the midst of so many beautiful women with whom he had continual conversations.

The court was, however, very gallant in spite of the prince's indifference; the men and the ladies took part in all the prince's hunts, each of which was more magnificent than the last, and when the hunt was over all the other pleasures succeeded one another in turn; the prince alone was only touched by that he obtained from hunting.

One day, when he was pursuing a stag, the ardor of the chase having taken him far afield, he went astray in the forest and found himself in a small clump of trees that bore fruit and flowers. The place appeared very beautiful to him, and as he was contemplating it with pleasure he heard a noise behind him.

He turned his head and saw a man of very ugly appearance, who was pursuing a snake, sword in hand. The snake having taken refuge behind the king, as if in a place of safety, the generous prince gave it his protection and forbade the man to kill it; but the ferocious individual still continued his design. The justly irritated king went toward him, sword in hand, and put him to flight. Seeing him run away, the king did not deign to pursue him.

He was surprised, a moment later, to see the snake slithering ahead of him, turning its head from time to time to see whether he was following; the snake seemed to want to serve as his guide.

The king, curious to know what would happen, did indeed follow it, and saw it enter the clump of trees from which it had emerged. He approached a man who appeared to be asleep under a tree. The snake being dead, the man got up and threw himself at the feet of the king, thanking him for the life that he had just conserved.

Astonished by that prodigy, the king asked for an explanation. The man he had just saved from death told him that it was him who, by means of the secrets he possessed, had reestablished the health of the queen and enabled her to give birth to him. The king and queen, satisfied with his services, had accorded him their protection and had permitted him to make establishments in all the places in their estates that he cared to choose. He added that the late king had taken generosity far enough to have named him Benevolent to mark his satisfaction. Then he told the king that, when he was pursued by the cruel man he had seen with a sword in his hand, he had encountered a dead serpent and had transformed himself into it, thinking to avoid the fury of that implacable enemy, who had disembarked in a nearby port, his voyage having no objective but to kill him, from which he had only been saved by his protection; if he had been killed as a snake, it would not have been possible for him to reanimate his body.

The king was very curious to know how Benevolent could transform himself in that way and begged him to teach him to do it. Benevolent excused himself, but, pressed by the king, he made him hope that he would not hide anything from him when he knew that he had the necessary discretion appropriate to learn the secret sciences. In order to begin to satisfy his curiosity, he took him to a grotto that he had in the depths of a rock in the middle of a forest, unknown to anyone. He took the king inside through an opening that he made by touching the rock with a mysterious wand that he always carried in his hand.

The young king was surprised by the beauty of the dwelling; it was a palace in which there were several apartments on the same level, filled with all the rarities that can be imagined, at which he took great pleasure in gazing. Benevolent opened a cabinet in which the king saw a bow, a quiver and a bunch of arrows by which he was charmed. Benevolent then took him into another cabinet walled with mirrors, in which he caused to appear before him all the beautiful women in his estates, magnificently clad; but the king paid almost no attention to them.

Benevolent told him that if he was not touched by all the beautiful women from several foreign countries that he was about to show him, he would infallibly tell him all his secrets. The king saw pass before him, with great indifference, an infinite number of beautiful women, but finally, a princess of marvelous beauty appeared who was followed by her entire

251

court. She appeared further above all the ladies who were with her by virtue of her beauty than by virtue of the precious stones and all the magnificence with which she was adorned, and the king remained so nonplussed and attentive to gazing at the place where he had lost sight of her that he only turned his eyes away in order to ask who the charming person was, so distinguished by her beauty from all the others he had just seen.

Benevolent told him that she was a young queen who commanded in a very distant region. The king resolved instantly to send an ambassador to her to make a declaration of amour and propose that she come and make laws in a kingdom where she would be received with much respect. Benevolent warned the king that the proposition of marriage that he wanted to send might not be received as favorably as he expected. She had just refused to marry a prince, the son of a powerful king. It was true that the prince in question was a monstrous giant who could never be loved, but, being unable to make himself loved, it was to be feared, especially as his father, the king, was a magician and a wicked man, that he had obliged his son to besiege the queen since she had refused to marry him.

Benevolent then told the king that he was the cause of the siege dragging on, because he had been able, by means of his art, to keep the besieged queen's port free, by which she received the help of her neighbors, in spite of the efforts of the malevolent king, who had obtained from an allied king as wicked as himself a naval army to blockade the sea coast and the besieged city. That naval army being retained in harbor by continual calms, however, the wicked king had taken against Benevolent, whom he knew to be the cause of that. Having learned from his books where he was he had set forth in a sloop and had disembarked in order to find him and kill him— which he would have done but for the protection that fortune had sent him just in time.

Benevolent also told the king how he had been sent by the fays to thwart the designs of that king, whom they hated because he was wicked, and how they had given him, in order to carry out his mission, the art of enchantment by means of which he had made use in order to insinuate himself into the mind of the king, which he had done so well that, having become his favorite and his confidant, he had learned his most hidden secrets, and had since made use of the knowledge he had of them and the power of enchantment to thwart the cruel enterprises he made. The king, having perceived that, hated him mortally, and having no doubt, as I have said, that it was him who had stopped his naval army, he had sought him in order to kill him.

The king, knowing that Benevolent had the gifts of faerie, and knowing the evil designs of the wicked king against the charming princess, no longer thought about anything by means of protecting her from them. He begged Benevolent to help him, by means of his art. Benevolent told him that he only needed one secret, which he would gladly have confided to him if he had believed his heart to be free, but that he could not resolve to confide it to a young prince who had a grand passion, because he feared having the displeasure of seeing him overwhelmed by a thousand misfortunes if he had the fragility of revealing it. He admitted, however, that he had no other means of delivering the besieged queen.

The king made him so many oaths never to reveal that secret, that Benevolent finally decided to confide it to him. He told him, therefore, that by pronouncing the name Quiribirini, he would have the power to transform himself into whatever animal he wished, and that it was necessary in order to do that to take the bow that he had thought so beautiful and launch an arrow into the air with the intention of killing the animal of which he had need, which he should immediately lay at his feet.

The king took the bow, and having used it, he saw a fallow deer fall at his feet, which he had desired. Benevolent, who did not want to abandon the king, also launched an arrow with the intention of killing a fallow deer, and one immediately fell at his feet. They both said "Quiribirini," entered into the bodies of the deer, left theirs in the rocks and both ran into the forest in order to make a trial of the power of the charm.

After a short run they returned to the grotto, resumed their natural form, discussed means of helping the princess, and concluded that it was necessary to transform themselves into birds in order to be able to pass over the sea. Having done that, they fluttered around the fleet, which, finally having a favorable wind after a long delay, went to blockade the princess's port.

They went on ahead of the fleet and sought on arriving to see whether they might encounter the princes in her gardens. They were as fortunate as they had desired; they saw her, and saw her very afflicted; they even heard her say that she would rather kill herself then consent to marry the monster, who horrified her and who was besieging her. They alighted on the same branch in order to discuss the means of saving the charming princess, and agreed that Benevolent would take the body of a scorpion in order to go and kill the cruel prince, which was done as soon as the project was formed. Benevolent, having found a dead scorpion, animated the body and took it into the tent of the titan they had resolved to kill, and then into his bed. He stung him, which made his body swell up, and he died the next day.

As soon as Benevolent had completed his coup he left the scorpion he had taken, resumed the form of a bird and went to find the king, who was waiting impatiently in the garden where he had left him. As soon as the army knew that the prince was dead, detesting his cruelty and his injustice, the siege was lifted and the charming princess was left in repose. The general of the naval army, having learned that the siege had been lifted, set sail and took his ships back to the port from which they had departed.

Before leaving as a bird for the expedition that he had just completed, the prince had left orders for a naval army to be prepared, and having found it ready on his return, he departed immediately in order to go and try to please the princess whom he had thought so charming, and took his dear Benevolent with him.

His fleet was the most elegant that had ever been seen; every ship carried on the poop and all the masts silken flags of all colors, a thousand steamers and a thousand banners rendered the spectacle marvelously beautiful, and the air resounded to an infinite number of trumpets. The hull of each vessel shone with gold and azure, and if the army reeked of powder, it was iris powder, not gunpowder.

The king dropped anchor in that state within the queen's sight, and sent ambassadors to ask for permission to come and offer her his very humble respects. The queen sent all the grandees of her court to receive the king as he emerged from his vessel, and advanced on to the perron of her palace to wait for him.

No meeting ever gave such a reciprocal satisfaction. The king was charmed by the queen's beauty, which appeared a thousand times more touching that day. The queen, for her part found the king so good looking that she was disposed from the first moment to listen favorably to the propositions that he had come to make to her. She lodged him in a magnificent apartment, and the wedding was celebrated a few days later with an unparalleled pomp.

After having made her subject savor for a few months the mildness of the government of their new master, the queen consented to go with him to his realm, where she lived for a long time in great felicity, which was only equaled by that the king enjoyed. The subjects of the two realms were also very happy; they lived under the mildest and most amiable domination they could have desired.

The magician king meditated in his own estates the possibility of troubling such a perfect happiness. He was in despair at the death of his son, and seeing that the queen, whom he had aspired to enable him to marry, had married his enemy; after meditating for a long time he finally made his project of vengeance. He had a nephew who was handsome and well built, but as wicked as him. He assured him that he would be the inheritor of his estates, provided that he could succeed in avenging his son. He instructed him, giving him some of the secrets of his magical art, and sent him to watch for opportunities to execute his vengeance. The young prince promised his uncle not to neglect anything in order to satisfy him, and appeared at the court of the king he wanted to kill as a foreign knight who was traveling in order to discover what was happening in the world.

The king received him very favorably, and having found him very negligent, soon preferred him to all the lords of his court, and made him his confidant and his favorite. There was only one secret that the king reserved from him; he took an infinite pleasure in sometimes going to wander in Benevolent's grotto; the latter had absented himself in order to travel through the world seeking opportunities to make use of his art in doing good deeds. The king never took anyone there, and allowed it to be suspected that he was disappearing for some gallantry.

The favorite, who wanted to know all the king's secrets, in order to make use of them in the execution of his design, was afflicted by that. The king, who loved him, having the anxiety of seeing him sad and having asked him the cause, he replied that he was in despair at the scant confidence His Majesty had in him; that he could not console himself for seeing him make little journeys without taking him; and that he would gladly renounce life, which he could no longer value, since he knew that such an amiable prince, to whom he was devoted, did not love him and had no confidence in him.

The king wanted to make him understand that he had no reason to lament, since he was only hiding one unique secret which he was engaged by honor never to reveal. The favorite was not content with the king's explanation, and appeared afflicted to the point of becoming ill; the physicians thought that his life was in danger, and warned the king, who was so touched that he went to assure him that he would confide to him everything he knew and take him where he was accustomed to go as soon as he was cured. He begged him to take care of his health, if it was true that he had amity for him, because nothing would be able to console him if he lost him.

The favorite, who had appeared to be ill when he was not by means of the secrets of his art, was soon in a state to go with the king, who took him to the grotto, as he had promised. The king explained all the mystery to him and told him what it was necessary to do with everything he saw there; but the traitor had other designs. The king launched an arrow with the intention of killing a fallow deer, and one fell dead at his feet. He said "Quiribirini," entered into the body of the deer and left his own lying in the grotto.

The infidel favorite, instead of doing what he had promised, said "Quiribirini," animated the king's body and drew his sword in order to kill the fallow deer, which only avoided death by virtue of its speed.

The traitor, on arriving at the court, had been touched by the beauty of the queen, and, wanting to make use of the opportunity in order to play a cruel trick on her, he went to the palace in the form of the king, and claimed what the king had a right to claim. But the queen had conceived such a great aversion for the man she saw that she could not be persuaded to suffer that he lie down in her apartment. It was Benevolent who, although absent, inspired that aversion in her by means of his art of enchantment.

The pretended king rendered great respects to the queen, and did not want to be contradicted, with a view to gaining her subsequently, and in order that nothing would trouble that design, he ordered that all the fallow deer in the forest should be killed, and organized hunting parties every day in order to hasten that execution

One day, when the queen was present in her chariot, he encountered a fallow deer that always turned its head in the direction of the queen; he did not doubt that it was the one that he had the principal design of killing, and he pursued it with so much ardor that he obliged it to traverse a river to evade death. On the other side of the river it found a dead fish, said "Quiribirini" and became a fish.

The dogs having also crossed the river, the pretended king had no doubt that they had devoured the deer and returned from the hunt very satisfied, but the queen, who had left a little earlier than him, had retired to her apartment, and having said that she was ill, did not want to receive him there.

In the meantime, the veritable king, in the form of a fish, was having great difficulty knowing how he could get out of the water, it not being possible for him to live long in that element. Fortunately, he perceived a recently dead parrot on the river bank, which was still the prettiest in the world. He was careful not to miss the opportunity, said "Quiribirini," and, tired of being a fish, entered the body of the pretty parrot and flew into the palace gardens.

A nobleman of the state was walking there, while waiting to be able to enter the queen's apartment, whom he wanted to warn about the rumor spreading through society regarding her aversion for the king. The parrot had no sooner perceived him than it flew on to his hand. At that moment, someone came to tell him that people were being admitted to see the queen. He went in, and, delighted to be able to offer her a present that would be agreeable to her, he took the parrot to her.

But what a surprise! The parrot flew on to the queen's shoulder, approached her to kiss her and immediately flew to her dressing table, where it was heard to say surprising things.

The queen having gone into her cabinet with the lord, who had asked her for an audience, the parrot flew in there and formed a third party in the conversation. The king recounted the whole of his adventure, and they discussed together the measures that it was necessary to take to stifle the feigned king in such a manner that he would abandon the body that he occupied safe and sound. That was executed successfully and very promptly. The king, in the body of the parrot, said "Quiribirini," and reentered his own.

Benevolent, who had learned about the unfortunate adventure by means of his art, having come to the aid of the king and the queen, found them together and liberated from the traitor who had made them suffer. His advice was to punish the king who had planned that treason and he took responsibility for that, in order that no worry could trouble henceforth the felicity of a marriage so well matched of the two most amiable mortals there were under heaven.

They enjoyed it for a long time, and Benevolent was begged, in order to render it more perfect, to be kind enough to spend his life with them, which he granted; and for nearly a century he was the most accredited favorite that any prince ever had.

The Princess Crowned by the Fays

Once, a princess who had a great deal of intelligence and courage married a prince who lived as a private man in his estates, where his ancestors had reigned, and which a powerful neighboring king had usurped after the death of the last sovereign of the realm, who had been killed in the course of an enterprise in which three kings lost their lives on the same day.

The princess was no sooner married than she thought of inspiring in the prince, her husband, the design of remounting the throne that belonged to him. She insinuated the desire in him by means of continual discourse, making him understand that it was shameful to obey in a place where one had the right to command. Gradually, the prince appreciated her arguments, but the difficulties appeared to him to be immense. All the places in the usurped state were occupied by the usurer's troops, and all the governors were his natural subjects, although it was true that all the inhabitants of the usurped kingdom were in despair, having groaned under the yoke of proud and avaricious foreigners for a long time, who had rendered the domination of their king odious to his new subjects. What means of prevailing were there in those circumstances?

The sinews of any enterprise were lacking. The prince and the princess had sufficient wealth to live as private individuals, but to make a general revolution in a realm it is necessary to employ vast sums; it requires the provision of weapons and horses, and the engagement of the timid by the lure of gold. It is generally necessary to give wealth to all those to whom the secret of the enterprise is confided, in order that they cannot hope for a greater recompense than that given to their fidelity in advance. To whom could they have recourse in a necessity of that magnitude?

The princess had been brought up in a castle situated in the middle of rocks and woods, where she had heard mention of the power of fays; she knew that they had often transformed in several different ways the hunting equipage of the prince, her father, every time he got too close to the cavern where they made their dwelling, of which they did not want to allow any mortal to take cognizance. She thought that if she went to spend a few months in that castle, which was her heritage since the death of her father and mother, she might find a means of establishing communication with her neighbors, the fays.

That happened as she had foreseen; the circumstances in which that event occurred could not have been more favorable for the princess's designs.

A frightful ogre that lived in the same woods had been making war on his neighbors or a long time, and, only nourishing himself on carnage, had devoured one or two persons belonging to his neighbors the fays, which was contrary to the rights of the peoples, for there had always been a treaty of alliance between the fays and the ogres, much as we have with the Mohammedans, for the necessity of commerce.

Irritated against that detestable nation, the fays had determined to exterminate it, and the ogres, after a few encounters in which they had always had the disadvantage, finding themselves inferior in power and enchantments to their enemies the fays, had come to request refuge in the princess's castle. She had believed that it was humane not to refuse a refuge to unfortunates who had recourse to her.

The fays, whom their art informs of everything when they consult their books, having learned that the princess had given shelter to the ogres, send an envoy to bear their complaints to her and to tell her that, wanting to conserve their regard for a princess that they knew to be of great merit, they gave her warning that they could reduce her castle to ashes, along with their enemies who had sought refuge there, but that since they had the consideration for her that they believed was due to her, they hoped that she would throw them out immediately. They assured her that if she had need of them in any occasion of importance, she would find that they were very helpful neighbors. They also told her that if she knew the evil race that she had taken in, she would tremble to have guests who were incapable of any humanity.

The princess replied that she had only given shelter in her home in order not to refuse the plea that was made to her by people who seemed to be unfortunate; that she would send them away, and that she begged the ladies who had sent an envoy to her to permit her to go and see them in their palace, or at least to nominate a place where she could converse with them.

The most important of the fays, touched by the civility of the princess, came to visit her in a chariot drawn by animals of an unknown species, which each had four feet and four wings, and traveled at such great velocity that one could scarcely make out whether they were flying or only running rapidly. She was carrying a casket, of which she made a present to the princess, begging her only to open it after she had gone.

Benevolent fays like the one of which I speak do not make any visit without accompanying the honor that they claim to be doing with a few sensible marks of their good will. The princess received the visit and the present with great demonstrations of gratitude, with which the fay was satisfied, and told her that she was aware of the grand designs that she was meditating, which she was only mentioning in order to assure her that she would always find her ready to aid her therein, because they were full of justice.

The princess, who had been reliably informed that the cavern in which the fay had her palace was inaccessible to anyone that she did not wish to receive there, asked her for the liberty to me to see her there, and begged her to tell her which day would be convenient for her to have that joy, in order that she would be assured of finding her and not interrupting any of her occupations. The fay named a day, which the princess did not miss, and she was received at the entrance to the cavern by a dozen young fays, all exceedingly magnificent. They were clad in gold brocade, with bonnets charged with feathers and sprays attached with diamond buckles. They all wore the portrait of the great fay attached to a broad flame-colored ribbon, in the fashion of a necklace. Those twelve individuals received the princess with great respect, and conducted her to the apartment of the fay, who was reclining on a bed in which gold shone on all sides, with an eiderdown quilt.

She received the princess in that state in order to avoid the embarrassment of ceremonies. She had a large court composed of all the officers of her palace and all the fays of her family, who were all in great respect around her. Next to the bed there was a coral desk of matching pieces, topped with an enamel gold writing pad, with papers, books and instruments of enchantment. At the foot of the bed there were a few little dogs, and lower down, on cushions, parrots, dwarfs and monkeys—in sum, everything that serves for the amusement of aristocrats.

The princess was placed next to the fay, in an armchair of infinite price; it was embroidered in gold, heightened with a large quantity of pearls, everywhere they could be placed without inconvenience. As soon as the princess was seated, the initial civilities being over, everyone retired respectfully, to leave the princess and the fay the liberty to converse. When the two of them were alone, the fay recommenced the offers she had already made of her ministry in the great designs she knew the princess had in mind.

The princess thanked her for the rich present she had given her; that was the casket that the fay had left when she visited, which was full of precious stones of great value. The fay sad that she would always furnish them when she had need of them for designs as legitimate as hers, and gave her at the same time a casket full of gold coins, in order that she could make use of them right away while waiting to find a buyer for the gems. She also gave her parrots that were fays, in order that she could make use of them to carry news to people with whom she maintained intelligence and so that she could learn via such unsuspected spies everything that was happening in the homes of those she had reason to mistrust.

With those means of succeeding in her enterprise and all the advice and instructions that the fay had given her, the princess took her leave of her, assuring her of an eternal gratitude. She was impatient to see her husband again and put to work all the means she had of carrying forward a grand plan, which caused her to leave her castle after only being there for a few hours.

The prince had great difficulty in believing that first speech the princess made to him when she arrived, which is not surprising. Perhaps the reader will also have some difficulty believing the story I am telling. The prince, however, had so much tangible evidence of what the princess was saying that he resolved to tempt fortune; the gold and precious stones he saw, especially, were convincing proofs of what he heard. The parrots finished convincing him; they had conversations more rational than those of ordinary humans in the presence of people in whom they had confidence; everywhere else they only let poorly articulated and inconsequential words escape, like other parrots.

The prince, no longer doubting the power of the fay who was favoring his design, thought that there was no time to waste. In concert with the princess he sent one of the parrots, carefully instructed as to what it had to do, to stay close to the governor general of the kingdom, with orders to come back immediately if it discovered that he had any knowledge of the enterprise.

After going into the governor's garden, the parrot flew from one orange-tree to another for an hour or two, allowed itself to be caught, and was found to be so pretty and affectionate that the governor placed it in his cabinet, in a magnificent cage, from which it could emerge whenever it pleased. It made use of that liberty to fly everywhere that it saw the governor go, particularly when he had only one person with him, in such a fashion that he could not talk about any affair without it being known. When it had flown into the garden three or four times and always returned immediately, no one kept watch on it any longer, which gave it the facility to render accounts of anything new that it had learned to another parrot, which the prince sent from time to time to be informed. By that means the prince and princess obtained a thousand items of information, which enabled them to take certain measures for their enterprise.

The other parrots were employed in several places in the realm to carry and bring back news, and acquitted themselves with all the fidelity that could be desired. The gems were sold in the great cities and the money received for them, as well as that already provided by the liberality of the fay, was distributed with so much sagacity and so much good fortune that, the entire kingdom having risen up on the same day, the usurper's garrisons were disarmed almost everywhere, with so little bloodshed that there is no example among humans of a similar revolution being prepared and carried out with so much order.

The foreigners having been expelled, the prince and princess were crowned in the capital city, in the midst of the acclamations of all their subjects, who were charmed to see their legitimate master on the throne again, and a master so amiable that he could only be equaled in merit by the princess who had shared the cares of such a fine enterprise.

Restored to the rank of king and queen, the prince and princess thought that in order to protect themselves against powerful allies it was necessary to make alliances with potentates who had an interest in balancing the power of their enemies. They had no difficulty in succeeding; they had recourse to princes accustomed to sustaining the weak, and arranged a domestic alliance for the elder of the two princes who owed the light of day to them.

Those two princes promised a great deal in their early youth, but, the elder having belied it, the subjects preferred to obey the younger, and the proposed marriage as well as the crown was for him. When the princess destined to marry him arrived in the capital of the kingdom if which she was to receive the crown, she made her entrance to the sound of five hundred cannon shots fired alone the bank of the river that led to the palace. If that princess, who was one of the loveliest young women who had ever been seen was not as happy as it seemed that she might have been, it is because the king and queen who had caused the revolution by their wisdom were no longer alive, and the fay who had protected them had quit the realm since the loss she had had of such a lovable prince and princess, who had conserved throughout their lives a perfect gratitude for her favors.

The Unfortunate Fraud

There was once a king who had been married very young to a lovely princess that he loved tenderly. She gave him a son and a daughter, and died almost as soon as she had brought the latter into the world.

The king, left a widower while still very young, contemplated in his two children the image if the charming princess whom death had stolen from him. Only thinking about having them brought up well and governing his kingdom with the application demanded by a dignity that it always accompanied by great complications, he did not believe that it was possible to encounter a woman who had enough merit to replace the admirable wife that he had lost, and he lived in a great indifference, resolved never to make any other engagement. Satisfied to have a successor he deemed worthy of him, he judged that his subjects had nothing to desire, since it appeared that the blood of their princes would not be lacking. In order to render them even more certain of that, he meditated finding a young princess for his son, who could give him an alliance capable of fortifying him against neighbors jealous of his grandeur.

After having searched for a long time her learned that a young queen who possessed great estates had a unique daughter, and he judged by the account of her that he was given that nothing greater could be desired for his son. At the same time he learned that the queen was a young princess, widowed not long before, to whom, given her age, the inclination to marry again might easily come, and that she might have children, who would distance her daughter from the crown, for the realm over which she reigned was her heritage.

Then he made the reflection that it would not be a bad idea to think of rendering himself master of such a great realm by marrying the queen; but he had declared that he had renounced marriage, which embarrassed him, for he prided himself on keeping his resolutions. He was, however, curious to know whether the queen was beautiful, and he was assured that there was no woman in the world more beautiful. He took his curiosity further; he wanted her portrait and he searched for one among people of his court who had traveled. He found a famous painter who had an original, drawn by his own hand.

As soon as the king had cast his eyes on it, he paid the painter the price he asked and had it placed in his cabinet as a very rare item; he took great pleasure in looking at it, and in a matter of days the charming queen shook his resolution and inspired such a great passion in him that he had never had one like it. Unable to resist it, and no longer enjoying any repose, he made the only decision he could, which was to send ambassadors to the lovely queen to beg her to accept the gift of his heart and his crown.

The queen responded to the ambassadors that she received the proposition that the king was making duly, as a mark of his esteem for which she was grateful, but that she could not resolve to engage herself until she had found a considerable establishment for her daughter, the princess, whom she loved uniquely and from whom she could not be separated without an insupportable dolor. The ambassadors told the queen that the king had a son of the finest hope imaginable, and that there was every appearance that he would be very satisfied to see him marry the princess when she had he were of an age to be married.

The queen consented to that condition of marrying the king; the ambassadors had orders to give the queen whatever assurances she desired.

The marriage ceremony having been carried out, the queen was taken to the court of the king, her husband, and took the princess, her daughter, with her, in order to be brought up in her presence, with a view to her marrying the prince, assured that a process as lovely as her daughter would touch the prince's heart as soon as he was of an age to be susceptible to tenderness.

Heaven, however, had disposed otherwise; the prince conceived an invincible aversion for the princes as soon as he saw her. As he knew that he was destined to love her and marry her soon, he was wise enough to constrain himself to hide, as far as he could, the unjust aversion he had for a princes who appeared every amiable in the eyes of the entire court.

He confided to his sister the aversion he had for the princess who had been destined for him, and the resolution he had made to leave the court when he was pressed to marry her and not to return until she was married. His sister gave him all the reasons she could to turn him away from that design, but, not having been able to succeed, she obliged him when he wanted to leave to take her jewels in order to make use of them in such a great voyage.

After great arguments, he took them, and could not quit that lovable sister, who was so dear to him, without shedding tears. There was no remedy, however; all woes appeared to him to be petty at the price of the one he found in marrying the princess that everyone wanted him to marry, which he could only avoid by removing himself from the power of his father, the king, who would constrain him to it.

He departed, therefore, in order to evade what he envisaged as the greatest of misfortunes, with no equipage but his squire, and no other resource than his sister's jewels.

He had left a letter to the king on the table of his cabinet, in which he begged him very humbly to pardon him for the resolution he had made to travel until he had learned that the princess who had been destined for him was married. He was to be pitied, he said, for not having been able to curb his heart and his mind to obey his father and his king, to whom he owed so much respect, but that his star had caused him to be born to have an antipathy for the princess that he had never been able to vanquish no matter what efforts of reason he had employed. He admitted that it was a cruel and unjust prejudice, since the princess was very amiable and worthy of the respect of all those who knew her. He added that, never being able to love her, he would have been unhappy to spend his life with her

269

and to have to reproach himself for rendering a princess un-happy who merited finding a better destiny.

The king, informed of the prince's departure and his res-olutions by the letter he had left, sent people in all directions to try to bring him back, but in vain. The prince had made such great diligence that he was out of his father's estates be-fore the king knew that he had gone.

He traveled to several courts, where he had various ad-ventures, and finally found himself at the court of a young king in a country very distant from that of his birth. He was introduced to the king as a young knight who was seeking opportunities for war and chivalric adventures; the king re-ceived him very civilly, telling him that he was very welcome in his court and hoping that he would find it agreeable enough to be tempted to make a long sojourn there.

The young king was very fond of hunting, particularly wild boar, and he had forests where redoubtable ones were found, which he always brought down, but often at peril. A few days after the prince had arrived there was a famous hunt, which did not fail to find one; the king attacked the terrible boar, and when he had thrown his javelin at it and missed, the boar charged him and killed the king's horse. The king was obliged to confront the furious boar on foot, with his sword as his only weapon. He would have been in great danger if the young prince had not come to his aid and pierced the boar through the throat with a thrust of his javelin. The boar, sens-ing that it was grievously wounded, only became more ani-mated, and pursued the king. The prince dismounted, con-fronted the boar, and succeeded in killing it with thrusts of his sword.

The king was so touched by that action that he embraced his defender and assured him of an eternal gratitude. The king's officers and the courtiers who were searching for him arrived as the action finished, and the king, having mounted a horse that was put in his hand, called a halt to the hunt for the day. He told his courtiers, without omitting the slightest detail, about the obligation that he had to the knight who had come to his aid in such a timely fashion that he had saved his life.

From that day on, unknown as the young prince was, he had free entry everywhere and was as considered at the court as any of the nobles of the realm. Not long thereafter he was even more so, for he became the king's favorite, and his favor extended so far that the king did not hide any of his thoughts from him, nor anything that he wanted to do, and only separate from him when he went to see the princess, his sister, who had been brought up in a castle, in accordance with the custom of the land, which only permitted princesses to see their close relatives until they were married. That custom was observed with so much exactitude that none of the courtiers even entered the park of the castle for fear that the princess might encounter them while out walking.

One day, the king, as a singular favor, took his favorite into the park to see its rarities, and permitted him to remain there while he went to see the princess. The young prince was mounted on a rather skittish horse, and it would not have taken much for that to cost him his life. He had turned toward the place where he was to wait for the king and he was leaning over the neck on his mount, with the bridle slack, in a profound reverie, when the king suddenly arrived along a little path from an unexpected direction. The king had thought to have the pleasure of surprising his favorite, but it was at a very bad moment, for the umbrageous horse took fright, reared up, and the prince, surprised in his reverie, fell and was badly wounded in the head. The king, very afflicted by that, sent someone at full tilt to fetch the princess's surgeons, who found the prince's wound to be dangerous.

The king, fearing to cause him a fever by having him transporting a long distance, had him put to bed in an apartment in the princess's castle, where he came to see him every day, and continually spoke so well of him to the princess that she contradicted him and sustained that as many marvels as he described could not be true, that he was preoccupied with his favorite and that his preoccupation had fascinated his eyes, it not being possible that there was any man so perfect under heaven.

The king, piqued by the incredulity of the princess, told her that he wanted to convince her of the verity of what he had said by allowing her to see the knight of whom he was speaking as soon as he was out of danger. He added that she would be punished for her doubts and might perhaps find him too lovable. Then he told the prince that he wanted to accord him a favor that he had ever accorded to anyone before and was going to bring the princess to his room.

She was charming, and the prince, surprised by so much beauty and a great passion that gripped his heart at the first moment, controlled himself and thought seriously about hiding his surprise from the king, for fear that he might repent of the favor he had granted him and that it might be the last time.

The king brought the princess every day, and the prince was so honored, and thought himself so fortunate to see that adorable individual that what he feared most in the world was completing his curse, because he knew that his good fortune would only last as long as his illness. He was, however, recovering visibly, able to get up in order to take the air at the window.

One day, he was there holding in his hand a portrait of his sister, the princess. He thought there was a slight resemblance with the princess he adored, and wanted to see whether he was not mistaken. The king, who had come into the room quietly, surprised him in that occupation, and having seen a portrait garnished with valuable pearls, he suspected that he had a great passion in his heart. He looked at the portrait attentively, and found it so touching that he thought that he had instantly become his favorite's rival. He was afflicted by that, but it was not possible for him to resist it, the beauty he had see having made such a great impression on him that he was no longer the master of his resolutions.

The prince having tried to put the portrait into the pocket in which he carried it, the king begged him to allow him to consider it a little longer. The prince, who desired nothing so much as to see the king touched by it, abandoned it to him willingly. The king returned it after having admired it at length, and dared not ask who it was, for fear of learning precisely what he had already guessed: that his favorite was the most fortunate of men, in having been able to please such a lovely person, which he did not see any reason to doubt, since he had seen her portrait in his hands and jealousy made him judge by his own example.

Prejudiced in that manner, he left his favorite's room rather abruptly; he had come alone that day because the princess was slightly indisposed; he came back the following day with the princess, allowing her to see his favorite for the last time, whom he was taking back to the court because he feared causing murmurs among the courtiers by containing to give a stranger such a great favor against the laws of the state.

The prince, very afflicted by his cure, took his leave of the princess, but in a fashion so sad that she would have perceived, if she had been paying attention, that he was quitting her with a great dolor.

The king and the prince were equally pensive as they traveled, but the prince, having rallied, tried to speak to the king and was received with coldness. He was surprised by that, and examined himself, trying to determine the cause, but in vain. He had nothing whatever for which to reproach himself. He was even so well accommodated with all the courtiers that he did not believe that any of them could have thought of doing him a bad urn. That gave him the boldness to beg the king very humbly to tell him if his suspected him of having neglected respect in any occasion, or failed in the fidelity that he owed a great king who had heaped him with favors.

The king made no reply, but after having thought for a few moments, he begged him very urgently to let him see once again that portrait he had seen in his hands in the princess's palace. The prince gave it to him immediately, and the king, having considered it with great attention, suddenly turned to look at his favorite and asked him, very graciously, to confess to him honestly whether that was not a person he loved, and by whom he was loved.

The prince told him that it was indeed a person he loved, but that it was his sister. The king embraced him, and admitted to him ingenuously that he had conceived a great passion for her the moment he had seen her portrait, and that the cause of the coldness of which he had complained was that he was afraid of having him for a rival.

"I am full of joy," said the king, "to learn that I have nothing to dread, with regard to that charming person, from a man as amiable as you, and to be able, on the contrary, to hope to find you favorable to the design I have formed to ask for her in marriage.

The prince was charmed to hear the king speak, and thought that he ought to declare to him who he was, in order to extract him from the anxiety he might be in of not knowing to what alliance he was aspiring. Believing that he would give him pleasure by telling him that he was not meditating anything unworthy of his rank, he said that he was the son of a powerful king who, having no children but himself and his sister, could give the princess entire provinces for a dowry.

The king replied that he had nothing more to desire, in order to become the happiest of men, than the person of his sister, and that he would gladly renounce a dowry. Being impatient to know what he had to hope or dread, he resolved to send a pompous embassy, which would show his grandeur, to ask for the princess in marriage.

The prince assured him of the success of his embassy, provided that he did not give is ambassadors any knowledge of what he had confided to him about his estate, because if the king, his father, and the queen, his stepmother, knew that he was at his court and the treaty they had made, the discontent that they had with him was capable of making them refuse the princess.

The ambassadors departed, and the prince sent a courier to warn the princess about the subject of the embassy. He gave her an exact account of everything that had happened to him, and the merit and the passion of the king who was asking for her in marriage. The courier, who was the prince's squire, the only person to whom he could confide his secret, found the princess relegated to a castle to which she had asked for the liberty to go in order to remove herself from the reproaches and ill-treatment that the queen had made to her continually since the departure of the prince, of which she suspected her of having been aware.

The princess was still at the castle when the ambassadors arrived at the court. As she had been informed by the courier, who had arrived in advance of them, of the subject of their voyage, she expected news any day from her father, the king, but the queen, who had complete power over the mind of the king, had obtained that she would not be informed. She had also obtained that he would perpetrate the greatest fraud ever employed on ambassadors and the powerful king who had sent them, in renouncing the interests of his own blood by substituting another person for the princess, his daughter. She made him believe that he had the means of seeing again a son who was so dear to him by only showing them the princess who had caused his absence, whom it would be easy to make them mistake for the person for whom they were asking, provided that they acted diligently.

The king having given his consent to it, the intrigue was conducted so successfully that it succeeded, and the ambassadors, the marriage ceremony having been concluded, took away the queen's daughter in great pomp.

The princess on whom that fraud had been perpetrated, having been warned that the ambassadors had come to ask for her, impatient at not having heard from the king, send an assiduous man to the court to discover what was happening. Having learned on his return that the ambassadors had departed and had taken the queen's daughter to occupy the throne that was destined for her, she resolved to put everything to work in order to avenge the insult that had been done to her, she had recourse to a fay with whom she had some acquaintance in her retreat and who had assured her that she would

275

serve her with all the power that the art gave her in all the important circumstances of her life.

Meanwhile, the new queen approached the court to which she was being conducted, and the king, who came to meet her, not finding her similar to the portrait that his favorite had given him, took umbrage and, without wanting to listen to him, sent him to a castle to await the punishment for a deceit of which the king believed that he had been the victim. Having learned from his ambassadors that they had not seen any other princess at the court, he resolved to conclude his marriage in spite of the horrible repugnance by which he had been seized at the sight of the princess, so different from the portrait he had seen. He resolved to the same time to punish with the ultimate torture his favorite, who, he believed had played such a cruel trick on him, and sent an order to have him put to death.

The sad wedding was in preparation when the veritable princess that the king had had the design of marrying arrived at the court. She had had recourse to the fay, her neighbor, who had given her a flying chariot, in which she had been transported in very little time to the place where her rival was about to triumph. She presented herself to the court when she arrived, and the king, having recognized the resemblance to the portrait, had no difficulty in believing what she told him. She asked, with great urgency, for news of the prince, her brother.

The king confessed the orders that he had given and dispatched a revocation in all diligence, and a summons for the prince to come immediately to share the joy he had in having discovered the fraud that had been perpetrated and to see his sister, the princess, whom the king had found a hundred times lovelier than her portrait promised.

The preparations that had been made for the sad wedding to which the king had resolved himself for political reasons were converted into a thousandfold magnificence that he ordered, albeit in haste, not wanting to defer his happiness by a single day.

The princess who had perpetrated the fraud was treated with every respect. The king ordered the same ambassadors to take her back to her mother, the queen. The unfortunate princess asked that it should be immediate, to spare her the dolor of witnessing the triumph of her rival, which was executed as she wished.

The king was so satisfied to see himself on the eve of possessing the charming princess whom he had desired so much that he did not think of making any complaint about the trick that had been played on him. The favorite arrived, to render the king's felicity perfect by his presence—and his own, for the king, who knew about his passion for the princess, his sister, accorded her to him.

That day was quite remarkable, by virtue of one of the greatest revolutions that have every happened among human beings: four persons who were in despair found themselves, in a moment, at the peak of felicity. The two marriages were made and those four persons spent a long life very happily. The prince succeeded to the states of the king, his father, who died shortly thereafter, and his subjects lived in great contentment, seeing themselves governed by a king and queen who were goodness and wisdom personified.

The Inaccessible Island

A young princess of infinite beauty was the sovereign of an island where nothing was lacking that any human could desire; the houses there were covered in sheets of gold and the palaces paved with them.

The island's inhabitants lived in perfect health, each of them for more than a hundred years, and that long life was untroubled by lawsuits or quarrels; the games full of tumult that avarice has invented were not played there; people only thought of taking tranquil pleasures that cost neither worry nor anxiety.

The island had always been unknown to the rest of the human race; people were so happy there that no one wanted to leave it, and they did not want to receive strangers for fear that they might corrupt the innocent mores of the inhabitants. The people of those times, who had been so curious to make discoveries, had passed back and forth in the vicinity of the island without having had the slightest knowledge of it; nature had surrounded it with a chain of rocks that rendered it inaccessible, and only left one passage that led to an admirable harbor on the island; it was rather a pity that no one made any use of it, for a thousand ships could have been accommodated there.

Since people had stated searching for new habitations and had made so many marvelous discoveries, the princes of the island, who were aware of the power of several fays who had been living there since time immemorial begged them to prevent by means of their art those famously curious searchers from being able to penetrate their abode. The sole remedy that the fays had found for that was to surround the island with a cloud so thick nothing could be seen through it, and that was so successful that those who had already sailed within sight of the rocks having come back to seek a passage to see whether the rocks contained an island, did not recognize it any longer, having found nothing in the place where they thought they had seen them but a dense obscurity, which the keenest eyes could not penetrate.

For a century or two, the princes of the island had been curious to know what was happening on the continents, and their custom was to send spies from time to time to the lands of their nearest neighbors. They sent the most assiduous and cleverest of their courtiers, to whom the fays gave, by means of their art, the power of flying as far as they pleased, reposing from time to time on some rock. They had also given them the means of becoming invisible, by enabling them to wear robes as brilliant as daylight.

The convenience of sending people to neighboring lands had informed the inhabitants of the island of everything that was happening in the world, so well that there arose among them troops of politicians, or purveyors of news,[29] who reasoned as their peers reasoned in Paris about the designs and conduct of potentates, with the difference that those of the island were often more learned than the most enlightened of those that we know, who nevertheless have the boldness to decided the motives of pace and war, of which they do not have the slightest notion.

The princess, who was beginning to advance in age, became bored with the great tranquility in which she lived. She had seen, in the reports of her spies, that there was a very powerful king on the continent, who had acquired great glory

---

[29] I have translated *nouvellistes* as "purveyors of news," because that was the likelier intended meaning at the time when the story was written. It is not impossible, however, that the author had in mind the more recent meaning of "short story writer," and that the specific short story writer he had in mind was François Fénelon. The author of the present story might have written it with the calculation in mind that it was less likely to offend Louis XIV, if he happened to hear about it, than *Télémaque* or "Sans parangon."

at the head of his armies and a great reputation for wisdom at the head of all his councils, which had rendered him redoubtable to all his neighbors. He was so mild, so polite and so affable that he made the delights of his subjects; he kept a magnificent court, in which all pleasures abounded: carousels, tourneys, hunts, balls, music, plays, and sometimes good cheer occupied all the ladies and gentlemen of his court as well. In the midst of all that, he did not appear to want to make any engagement. He was, above all, the handsomest man in his court, but his beauty was accompanied by so much majesty and manners so elevated that he could only be taken for a hero. He had allowed all the painters who desired to do so to make his portrait, who had the liberty to work on it every morning while he was getting dressed.

The princess of the island, who knew that, charged one of her spies with bringing her one, and as soon as she had seen it, she was gripped by a sudden dolor because her island was unknown; the tranquil pleasures of her court appeared to her to be insipid, and she found all her courtiers infinitely inferior to a king of such fine appearance and such a fine reputation. She had read a few books full of great adventures, which had praised courage so highly that she could no longer hear talk of anything but heroes and heroic actions. In the end, she imagined that she would never be happy if the great king she esteemed so much did to think of marrying her. But how could that be achieved? She was unknown to him, and so was the island over which she reigned.

She summoned the fay who had the reputation of being the most knowledgeable of all those in her estates, and after having communicated to her the desire she had to make an alliance outside her island, and told her about the merit of the great king, she asked what means she could employ in order to make the dispositions she had for him known to him, and how she could give birth in him to similar ones for her.

The fay told her that it was necessary first of all to give him cognizance of the island, in order that he might acquire some curiosity to know what was happening there, not doubting that if he heard mention of the merit of the princess who gave the law there he would immediately have a great passion to possess her and her island.

It seemed, in fact, that it was the destiny of the great king to love the princess, since she was one of the most beautiful women in the world and he had never been touched by any other beauty, although his court was full of very amiable women. The princess, for her part, seemed to have reserved her heart for him, for although she had princes of her blood on her island, and several other noblemen capable of touching a young princess, she had always regarded them with great indifference.

In the end, the princess, counseled by the savant fay, resolved to send the last spy she had employed invisibly to the court of the great king. He flew there, as usual, by means of the art of enchantment, but he had orders to appear subsequently as a traveling foreigner. The princess had given him money and precious stones, of which he made use to dress in the manner of the country, and he was introduced into good companies.

After having sojourned there for some time, he found a means of acquiring familiarity with the people who were in the particular confidence of the great king. At table with one of them one day, where there were other foreigners, each of whom was arguing the merit of his own sovereign, he sustained that he had the honor of being under the laws of a princess whom it was more glorious to obey than it would be to command elsewhere. The argument becoming heated, he said that he could justify what he was saying, and, having shown a portrait of the princess that he carried in a locket garnished with stones of immense richness, it attracted the eyes of all those who were present, and then stood up in order to render a kind of homage to the beauty of the princess and contemplate her at closer range. He was immediately begged to say what part of the world was the birthplace of such a marvelous princess, but he made a difficulty about revealing his secret, and, out of discretion, they did not talk to him about it any longer.

The topic of the conversation changed, and when the meal ended, the rumor soon spread through the court of the surprising beauty of a princess whose portrait had been seen and whom no one knew.

The king, curious to know what he had only heard confusedly, sent word to the stranger who had it in his possession that he wanted to speak to him. The princess's envoy, who wanted nothing more, said everything to the great king that might give birth to a great passion to possess the princess and her island; the portrait, which he showed him, completed what his speech had commenced. The king, surprised by so many marvels, contemplated them for a long time without turning his eyes away, and if he did turn them eventually, it was only with a sigh, to beg the envoy, with great urgency, to tell him whether it was possible to see such a charming princess.

The envoy replied that anything was possible for a great king like him, and that the princess, who commanded in an island inaccessible to any other power, would render its approach facile for him, and that she already esteemed him greatly on the basis of the accurate accounts she had been given of all his great qualities. The king told him that if he facilitated for him the means of seeing a princess without whom he believed he was no longer able to live, he would have nothing to desire. The envoy replied again to the king that, believing that his sovereign would be agreeable to that, he would enable him to see her whenever he pleased, and that it was without hope of recompense, since he could only receive one from the princess to whom he had made an oath of fidelity.

After a secret conference with the king, the envoy of the princess departed in order to go and inform her that the greatest king in the world desired passionately to see her, and that he would come with a fleet of infinite magnificence if she were agreeable to rendering the passage to her island practicable.

The princess summoned the savant fay, who placed two diamond globes on the tips of two rocks to either side of the passage, which projected so much fire that all the sun's rays could not have conveyed more light. The envoy was dispatched to take the news to the great king, who set sail immediately, very impatient to see the princess who formed all his desires.

The rumor of that new discovery of an unknown island and a miraculous princess having spread throughout the world, a neighboring king jealous of all the prosperity of the great king resolved to dispute the possession of the princess with him, and set out to make the conquest of her and her island. The great king was no sooner at sea than he was followed by a formidable fleet. What he had to fear the most was that the king commanding it had a fay with him whose secrets were so powerful that nothing until then had been able to resist them; she had befriended the king she was with shortly before and had promised to set him above all his neighbors. The first opportunity that offered to prove her amity and her power was that of the conquest of the marvelous princess and her island, and the fay, not knowing that she would find herself confronting a power greater than her own, had promised marvels. The two fleets sailed on the same wind, following one another so closely that they approached the island at the same time.

The savant fay, who always had her eye alert to the interests of the princess, having learned by means of her art that the two fleets were approaching the island, sent a troop of dolphins to which she had imparted a few gifts of enchantment, and which, having encountered the great king's fleet, arranged themselves around his ship to serve as its pilot, and guided it into the harbor. It was a charming spectacle to see a troop of superb dolphins competing to travel in closer proximity to the royal vessel. On the contrary, the enemy fleet was afflicted by marine monsters and huge whales, which only allowed disagreeable objects to be seen, and to complete the disgrace, the wind became contrary to them while the great king's, under full sail, passed between the two rocks bearing diamond globes by way of beacons.

The king, seeing his projects failing, made reproaches to his friend, the fay, that she had failed him in his hour of need.

She excused herself as best she could, saying that some power superior to her own must have intervened, and, being able to do no better, she launched an infinite number of fireballs at the great king's fleet—but in vain; none of them surpassed half the distance there was between the two fleets. The king, in despair at seeing that he could not combat the great king, who was about to triumph in all his projects, had all sails hoisted in order to try to follow him, but a great storm suddenly blew up and dispersed his fleet. Some of his ships went to break up against the rocks that formed the island's ramparts and the one he was on was driven back toward the coast of his estates, while the great king entered the harbor of the island to the sound of a hundred trumpets.

What a pleasure it was for the marvelous princess to see from a balcony of her palace that overlooked the harbor a thousandfold magnificence that she had never known! The royal vessel, which appeared at the head of them all, was charged with ensigns, streamers and silk banners of all colors, and shining with gold and azure on all sides.

As soon as the great king had entered the harbor he sent ambassadors to the princess to beg her to approve that he set foot in her estates and permit him to come to offer her the homage of a heart that was filled with an infinite respect for her and a great passion to render him agreeable to her. The princess replied that she would see the king in her abode with a great deal of pleasure, and would await him impatiently. The king came ashore immediately, and, the princess having come to meet him as far as the door of her apartment, he found her a hundred times more beautiful than her portrait. The princess also found the king a hundred times above what she had expected.

The surprise was followed by discourse full of politeness, and the king was taken by the noblemen of the court to an apartment in which one could only cast one's eyes over precious stones or drapes of gold and silk, which composed all the furniture prepared to welcome such a great king.

A grandiose repast was served to the king, from which nothing was missing that could satisfy taste or sight. It had been prepared and was served by four young fays, each of whom wore a robe sewn with rubes; they placed delicious dishes on the king's table, some of which were unknown to him, in dishes whose material was a hundred times more beautiful than the finest gold. The sideboard was similarly laden with bottles of little known materials, as brilliant as the dishes. It is only known that there were two that were pearls so huge that it is impossible that nature had ever formed two similar ones. The king drank from a cup made from a single emerald a liquid more delicate than all the nectar and ambrosia that is served at the table of the masters of the world.

All the aforementioned magnificence and delights, however, only made the king pause momentarily. He entered incontinently into a cabinet, to which he summoned his ambassadors and sent them to tell the princess the reason for his voyage and to settle with her, if she had that agreeable design, the conventions and the time of their marriage—which is to say, to receive her laws, for that was the order that the great king had given his ambassadors.

The conventions having been soon regulated, the king saw the princess immediately and the marriage took place the following day. It was followed by an infinite number of days and years of an ever-perfect felicity.

After having stayed for a few months on the island, which he found delightful, the king took the princess to his estates, where he had her crowned in great pomp. Several of his courtiers were also married on the island, where they had encountered very amiable ladies, and were charmed to have the means of never losing sight, so to speak, of a sovereign who made the delights of all her subjects.

To recompense the savant fay for all that she had done for him, the great king wanted her to rule the island, which she agreed to do, she replied, in order to celebrate the name and the merit of a lovable king and queen and to carry out their orders punctually. Thus the inhabitants of the island, as well as those of the continent, who also obeyed illustrious sovereigns, savored for a long time the felicity there is in receiving laws dispensed with an exact justice, emanated from a throne brilliant with glory.

STORIES FROM *NOUVEAUX CONTES DE FÉES*
(1718)

The Little Green Frog

In a continent, the name of which has not reached me, there were two kings who were first cousins and neighbors, one named Peridor and the other Diamantin. They were protected by the fays but it is always necessary to say things as they are; the fays liked them much less than the princesses to whom they were married.

Princes ordinarily find it so easy to satisfy their passions that they need more virtues than commoners simply to be honest men, and the ladies of the court of a king find it cruelly difficult. Diamantin was more criminal, according to the fays. He abandoned himself more eagerly to his desires; and what was even worse, fundamentally, is that he testified more than scorn for the queen, his wife, whose name was Aglantine. What happened as a result? The fays punished him by causing his death. A unique daughter, whom he left in the cradle, inherited his kingdom; as she was not of an age to be able to govern herself, the regency was awarded with the consent of all the orders of the state to the dowager queen, Diamantin's widow.

That virtuous princess acquitted the task with as much wisdom as intelligence; only making use of her authority for the happiness of her people, she profited from the fortunate state of widowhood—of which so many good people are able to profit, to whom God gives a long life—in order to live with more restraint. Such a pleasant situation was only troubled by the absence of her daughter; the fays, for reasons known to her, did not want to leave her to raise that lovely daughter, whom they named Serpentine; that was a care for which they took responsibility.

As for the other prince, it is quite true that, in spite of the love he had for Queen Constance, and although he had never ceased to treat her very well, he could not avoid being suspected of a few petty gallantries. The fault, if there was one, was nevertheless pardonable because it was slight, so he was only punished indirectly—but would it not have been a thousand times milder to die than to see himself deprived of what he loved the most? Death robbed him precipitately of the queen, his wife; at the same instant he saw the object of his joy and his happiness disappear and felt reborn in his heart sentiments of amour for the queen sharper than any he had every experienced before.

His situation became cruel. Only one consolation remained to him, which was a unique son three years old, which the queen left him as a pledge of her love. He attached himself to him uniquely; the care of his education and that of the affairs of the kingdom were his only occupations. To speak sincerely, however, his dolor never permitted him to have a moment without the loss he had experienced of Queen Constance being present in his mind; while meriting from his people the surnames "the good" and "the just," he could not be refused that of "the sad." No one would surely believe that it was possible to live for fifteen years in a sadness equal to his. For myself, I have always been convinced that the fays furnished him covertly with the means of not succumbing to it.

The prince, his son, named Saphir, had responded perfectly to the education that the sad Peridor had given him. He was, to speak without any prejudice and without any habitude of the beautiful epithets that are ordinarily added to the name of prince, accomplished. He face, utterly charming as it was, merited far fewer eulogies than his character. He was born gentle, and his intelligence, ornamented by a good deal of knowledge, as accompanied by a lively and agreeable imagination.

When he had attained the age of fifteen, the fays feared that the tenderness toward which he was naturally borne, might be an obstacle to the designs that they had for him. They therefore placed, without affectation, in a very agreeable cabinet to which Saphir often retired, a mirror that was simple in appearance, since it was only bordered by a black frame, like those once seen in Venice, which our forefathers like so much.

It was some time before the prince paid any attention to that new item of furniture. The day when he noticed it, simple surprise engaged him to look into it. With what astonishment he perceived in that mirror, instead of his own face, that of a young woman as beautiful as the most beautiful day. She had just emerged from childhood, and the beautiful bloom of youth covered the most agreeable features in the world. The handsome Saphir was struck by them. Who would not have been?

The charm of that marvelous mirror did not consist only in rendering such a beautiful portrait faithfully; it also depicted, with the same exactitude, all the actions of that incomparable beauty, and produced at every moment scenes all the more agreeable because the most beautiful person in the world was the dominant figure therein.

As one might think, that miracle seduced the heart of the young prince. He became recklessly amorous of so many charms, so much mildness and so much sagacity; all his occupations ceded to that of being constantly witness to the most frivolous occupations of the unknown beauty; he could not be extracted from his cabinet. It was, it must be agreed, a great relief for his troubles to see someone he loved at any hour, but after all, he could not imagine what the end of such an adventure might be, and his mind often revolted against the sentiments by which he heart was intoxicated—but what can the reflections of the mind produce in opposition to the sentiments of the heart?

Sensible as he was to that uncertainty, a new subject of anxiety tormented him even more cruelly. Scarcely a year had gone by since he had acquired his faithful mirror when one day, on considering it more attentively, he thought that he discovered a second mirror perfectly similar to his own, which had the same property. He was not mistaken; the unknown beauty had not possessed it for long, and was no longer occupied by any care than looking into it.

What do a lover's eyes not see! Saphir had deduced that the heart of the beauty had become sensible; he had even perceived in her the changes that only amour can operate in persons previously indifferent. It was not difficult for him to divine the cause of that miracle, or why the new mirror was consulted so frequently; but no matter what trouble he took, it had not yet been possible for him to distinguish what was happening therein. The mirror was always disposed in such a fashion that the lovely person by whom he was enchanted was placed when she looked into it between him and he object that occupied it, and in consequence, she hid it from him completely. He had only distinguished enough not to be able to doubt that the face of a man was depicted for her, but that was sufficient to ignite the blackest jealousy in his heart.

Is it necessary that a passion for which we are so veritably born, a passion authorized and admitted by nature, should have such sad and painful objects in order not to be extinguished? Alas, it is only too true; I am quite sure that, in spite of all the charms with which the person in the mirror was endowed, without that jealousy, without the trouble, the impatience and the oaths that Saphir uttered at never being the witness of the gazes that they directed at one another, his amour would not have been as constant as it was. At any rate, the fays wanted it thus; presumably, they had their reasons.

I have related quite accurately, it seems to me, the sad state to which King Peridor was reduced; I have also said that he had not known any pleasure for fifteen years; his son must therefore have been eighteen, and for three years he had been making constant use of the pretty mirror. At the end of that time a malady of languor took possession of Peridor; it soon gave rise to fear, with good reason, for his life. His son, his household, his capital and his entire kingdom experienced an anxiety and a dolor so intense that I shall not tempt to describe it; that description could only sadden the reader and me.

The sad king, throughout his illness, talked about nothing but the queen and the chagrin he had for having offended her. Eventually, the hope of seeing her again was the sole consolation that he experienced. All the faculties, all the empirics and charlatans, had attempted in vain to cure what the waters, in the last place, and all the possible remedies that had preceded them, had failed to achieve. Finally weary of all the futile words and all the citations, as many Greek as Latin, that were produced at every moment to prove that he was ill, at the end of all complaisance, he obtained that he be left alone in his room, and that no one would come to trouble him there.

One of his greatest woes was a considerable oppression, which scarcely left him the faculty of breathing. He had therefore ordered that the windows be left open, in the design of having a little more air.

Scarcely had he been alone for a few minutes than a bird with dazzling plumage came, after fluttering for some time, to alight on the window-sill. Its plumage was sky blue and gold, its feet and beak ruby red, but so highly polished that one could not sustain the sight; its eyes effaced them with their glare, the glitter of the most brilliant diamonds. On its head it had a crown; in truth, I don't know what it was made of, but I know for sure that it was brighter than all the rest. Comparisons are lacking to enable you to imagine how agreeable and well-disposed its breast was. As for its song, I cannot say anything about it, for the bird did not sing; it only looked at the king, and that gaze returned all his strength.

The bird did more; it flew into the room, still staring at the king, and every glance was a further confirmation of health. Peridor found himself well, such as he had been before his illness; he got up, unable to resist the desire to render himself master of such a beautiful bird, to which he was also indebted for his entire cure. He tried to catch it, but, lighter than a swallow, the bird was able to evade him.

Peridor rang desperately, with all his strength; people came in a crowd. He paid no heed to the joy or the surprise that his entire court, who adored him, wanted to express at the return of his health. He described rapidly the bird that he had seen and ordered that it be pursued, that they go down into the garden and that nothing be neglected in order to bring him his only desire. People ran in haste in all directions, on foot or on horseback; all the bushes were beaten, all the bird-catchers in the kingdom sent out on campaign. Peridor was so beloved, and the recompense he promised was so considerable—those two motives have always been so powerful in making people act—that in no time at all, everyone, great and small, was in the fields, and the cities were deserted.

All that great stir produced, as usual, nothing but tumult and a great deal of noise; the bird was not found, and, what was even more afflicting, a few days later he king fell back into the same state and was soon seen, with chagrin, to be at the final degree of languor.

Saphir, penetrated by the most intense dolor, for he was the most affectionate son one could encounter, convinced that sentiment facilitates research, flattered himself that he could do better than anyone else. Why should he hope so? Because he had more desire to encounter it. He departed, whatever could be done to prevent him; his household wanted to follow him. He had not formed any project that determined him to take one road rather than another. The retreats that he thought most favored by birds were his only guides; he beat all the hedges and all the bushes; he questioned all the people he found in his path; in sum, he did everything that a sentiment as good as that of wanting to save a tenderly beloved father's life can dictate, but the more he searched, the less he found. His impatience equaled his attachment.

He arrived in one of the most immense forests in the world; the cedars that composed it, respectably by virtue of their antiquity, raised their heads to the clouds, and those superb heads were borne by the straightest stems imaginable, In spite of the shadow that such fine trees spread over the earth that produced them, that earth was ornamented by soft grass, dotted with the rarest flowers. All those things persuaded Saphir that the beautiful bird must have such a delectable abode for its retreat; with that idea, he made the resolution not to quit that forest, of which he would examine every nook and cranny. He resolved to explore it in all directions; he imagined more, having nets pained in all colors in which the bird had been described it him, convinced that one easily captured by something that resembles oneself. Not only did he have with him experienced bird-catchers, but his entire retinue excelled in that profession. Independently of the love that Peridor had attracted, does not a courtier have all métiers?

After having traveled for part of the days, as he usually did, Saphir felt pressed by thirst. Fortunately, he perceived a spring, agreeable in its rusticity, the clear and lively water of which promised a complete satisfaction. He took a cup from his pouch—that is a precaution that no traveler ought to neglect—but as he tried to fill it, a little green frog, much prettier than a frog ought to be, jumped into the cup. He tipped it out, scantly touched by its charms, but it made a new jump, swifter than the one before.

Tormented by thirst, and his mind anxious, Saphir was about to throw it away with a sort of impatience that was fundamentally quite pardonable, when the little frog, looking at him with the most beautiful eyes in the words, said to him: "I'm a friend of the bird; be careful. Your thirst troubles me; drink, and listen to me afterwards."

When the prince had slaked the thirst that was devouring him, he obeyed the pretty frog, which ordered him to sit down and rest.

"Now," it said to him, "follow point by point what I'm going to order you to do, Reassemble your retinue; establish it in a hamlet you'll find a short distance from here, which is sufficient to accommodate it. Follow on your own, without anyone accompanying you, a broad road that you will find to your right, marching southwards. The road is long, planted with cedars of Lebanon. At the end of the avenue, a superb castle will appear before you. Take this little grain of sand"— it presented it to him as it spoke, with an infinite politeness and grace—"put it on the ground as close as you can to the door of the castle; it will have the virtue of making it open and putting all the inhabitants to sleep. Then go straight to the stables, without occupying yourself with anything but what I command you to do. Choose the most beautiful of all the horses, mount up promptly, and come and find me here as quickly as possible. Adieu, Prince, I wish you luck."

Having said that, the little frog plunged into the water, and did not reappear.

The prince, filled with a hope that he had not had since his departure, did what had been prescribed to him. He left his followers in the hamlet, found the road that had been indicated to him, followed it on his own, eventually arrived at the door of a castle that seemed to him to be superb—and rightly so, for it was made of crystal and all its ornaments were solid gold. He paid scant attention to those beauties, and sowed his grain; the door opened; everyone, as the frog had predicted, was asleep.

Saphir went straight to the stables; he had already made the choice of the most beautiful of the horses by which they were filled when he perceived, next to that fine animal, the richest harness that has ever been seen. He did not doubt for a moment that it was the equipage of the mount destined for him, and without imagining that he was doing the slightest harm—in fact, who takes the horse can surely take the saddle—he put it on the back of the superb charger.

Instantly, all the people in the castle woke up; they threw themselves upon him, and he was duly arrested, everyone crying "Stop, thief!" He was taken before the lord of the place who, prejudiced by his good appearance rather than what he said, was kind enough to give him permission to withdraw. I am told that he had explained that, being very fond of the cavalry, he had wane, while waiting for the people of the castle to

294

take up, to do a few exercises on the horse on which he had been found; that reason, frivolous as it was, was found to be good, and the proof is that he was released. It is necessary not to raise needless difficulties; nothing can be said against that which succeeds.

Very sad and afflicted, Saphir returned to the spring, where the frog treated him very badly.

"What do you take me for?" it said, angrily. "Do you honestly believe that it was just to chatter that I gave you the advice from which you have profited so poorly?"

The prince's dolor enabled his apologies to be received, and the good little frog, having allowed itself to be softened, gave him another small grain, but this time it was gold. It recommended him to do the same things as the first time, with the single difference that, instead of going to the stables that had been so fatal to him, it told him to go into the castle as quickly as he could, follow the sequence of apartments until he found a room filled with perfumes, in which a sleeping young woman of perfect beauty would be presented to his eyes; he was ordered to wake her up and take her away immediately, whatever she might say to oppose his design.

The prince carried out the frog's orders point by point, and everything succeeded again; the door opened; all the inhabitants of the castle seemed to be plunged into the most profound slumber; he found the young woman lying between two sheets, and her beauty appeared to him to be admirable. He woke her up, begging her, in a sufficiently determined fashion, to go with him; the beauty consented to that, albeit with some difficulty: "On condition, sir," she said to him, "that you only permit me to put on my skirt. What would people think of you and me," she added, "if they encountered you giving our hand to me politely, while I was in my chemise?" That proposition appeared to Saphir to be too natural to be refused.

The beauty had no sooner touched the fatal skirt, however, than the whole household awoke and, much more seriously than the first time, the prince was arrested and tied up. He was so troubled by the fault that he had committed, so annoyed by his stupid complaisance and so disconcerted that he did not know what to say to justify himself.

For myself, I have always thought that the fays seduced the judges; in fact, how could he be excused, and what punishment did he not merit, having been caught *in flagrante delicto* as he had, and what is worst, in recidivism? At any rate, he was put out of the door with sufficient politeness—but what caused him a much greater embarrassment was the dread of seeing the frog, his benefactor again. How could he resolve to appear before it after what had happened?

He finally made that decision, but it was with infinite difficulty. The frog scolded him, lectured him and went, as they say, over the top. The prince begged its pardon, representing that it was very difficult to refuse a pretty young woman, who, in addition, is willing to go with one, the simple permission to put on a skirt.

"It is necessary, in a word, to do what I order," the pretty frog told him, angrily.

After many apologies and regrets on Saphir's part, it rendered again to his pleas, and, having calmed down completely, it gave him a little grain of diamond.

"Go back to the castle," said the frog, "sow the grain of diamond at the door, but don't think about the stables or the rooms; they've been too fatal to you. Go straight to the garden, go under the portico that faces an arbor, in the middle of which is a tree with a golden trunk and emerald leaves. Perched in that tree you'll find the beautiful bird for which you're searching with so much care; cut off the branch on which it's reposing and bring it to me immediately. But I warn you, as a good friend, that if you get distracted, as you've already done twice, you'll have no more resources to hope for, either from me or anyone else."

Then, as usual, it hid under water, and the prince, struck by its last threats, departed with the resolution not to merit them. He found everything as it had been announced to him: the portico, the arbor, the superb tree and the beautiful bird profoundly asleep on one on its branches. He cut it, and although he saw beside it a golden cage that was marvelously suitable, it seemed to him, to take away his prey with more assurance, he made no use of it, and returned to the spring, walking on tiptoe and holding his breath for fear of waking the beautiful bird.

How astonished he was when, instead of finding the spring, as he had hoped, he perceived in the location it had previously occupied a little palace, rustic, to be sure, but built in the best taste, and on the doorstep of that pleasant retreat a charming person, the sight of whom put him beside himself. The reader will not be surprised by that, since it was, in fact, the unknown woman of the mirror.

"What, Madame!" he said, no longer knowing what he was doing or saying, so emotional was he, "It's you!"

The beauty blushed and said "As for you, sire, your face is well known to me, but I believe that you're seeing me for the first time."

"Oh, Madame," he replied, "I have passed many days and moments admiring you."

That commencement of conversation was followed by the detailed relation of what had occupied our two lovers until then; they communicated reciprocally without hiding anything, everything that had happened to them. They had detailed communications in which the mind, submissive to the heart, only hears the organs of sentiment. In sum, the deeper they delved the more convinced they were that that they were each the object of the attentions they brought to their mirrors. In admitting their anxieties and their jealousies, they admitted all imaginable amour for one another.

After a few minutes of the most tender conversation, the prince could not help asking the unknown beauty by what fortunate adventure she had come to be in the forest. He begged her to tell him what had become of the spring and implored her above all to give him news of a frog to which he was indebted for his good fortune, to whom he had promised to bring the beautiful bird—which, parenthetically, was still asleep.

"Alas, Sire, you see that frog before you," she said, with an embarrassed expression. "My story won't take long. I don't know either my birth or my homeland; I only know that my name is Serpentine; the fays who have taken care of me since I have been in the world have never wanted to inform me of one or the other. They have neglected nothing for my education, and their generosity for me has been excessive. I've always lived in retreat, and for two years I confess that it hasn't been difficult for me to sustain. I had a mirror, Sire…"

Blushes and timidity prevented her from saying more, but she only interrupted herself and resumed with vivacity. "You know that the fays want to be obeyed, and without reply; yesterday, they changed the little dwelling that you see here into the spring of which you asked me for news, and, having metamorphosed me into a frog, they ordered me to tell the man who came to the spring everything that I have told you with exactitude. But Sire, when I saw you appear, how painful it was for me, especially with the impressions of which my heart was full, to appear to your eyes in such deformity! In any case, it was necessary, and cruel as it seemed to me, it was necessary to submit to it. I desired your success, not only for your interests, sire, but also in regard to my metamorphosis, which was only due to end when you were the master of the beautiful bird; I have absolutely no idea what made you desire its possession."

Then Saphir explained the interest of his father's health, and everything that has been related previously.

Serpentine was saddened by the story, and her beautiful eyes filled with a few tears. Saphir pressed her tenderly to inform him of the reasons for such a prompt change.

"Oh, Sire, you know nothing about me but my face and a few actions of which your mirror has informed you. I agree that those actions, utterly indifferent as they might be, denote in general the sentiments of the heart; but I know nothing of my birth, and I learn that you are the son of a king. I see, furthermore, that you merit being; what will become of me, unfortunate that I am?"

298

Saphir protested everything that excessive amour can say in such circumstances, but the lovely Serpentine always replied: "Sire, I love you too much to engage you o make a marriage that is inappropriate to you. I shall have a great deal to lament, but I shall not change my sentiments. If the fays, informing me of a birth about which, until now, I confess that I have had no curiosity, do not prove that I have an extraction worthy of you, Sire, whatever sentiments you have inspired in me, I shall never accept the offer of your hand."

They were at that point in their conversation, which would not have terminated so promptly, when a fay appeared in her ivory chariot, accompanied by a very beautiful woman, who was no longer in her early youth. The beautiful bird woke up then, and, hopping on to Saphir's shoulder, which it never wanted to leave, it made him all the caresses that a bird can make.

The fay told Serpentine that she would be content with her; then she expressed a thousand amities to Saphir, and introduced him to Aglantine, his aunt by marriage, for the woman with her was, in fact, Diamantin's widow.

After a few embraces, the fay, with a thrust of her wand changed her vehicle into a four-seater vis-à-vis ; she placed herself with Aglantine in the back, Saphir—who still had the beautiful bird on his shoulder—and Serpentine in the front. The fay instructed the prince's equipage by way of one of her pages that it could return to Peridor's court in small stages, and that the beautiful bird had been found. After that small attention she made her chariot take off. In spite of the speed with which the journey was made, Saphir and Serpentine were agitated by all the thoughts to which the pleasure of seeing one another and the end of their conversation could give birth in them, for nothing equals the promptitude of the thoughts of lovers.

In that mental situation they arrived at the palace of King Peridor; he had been carried into an airy vestibule, where it was believed that he might reach his last breath and any moment. As soon as the chariot was a certain distance away, the beautiful bird took flight and came at full tilt to fall upon the ailing king; it rendered him a health in which Constance was even more interested than him; it was, in fact, her, who resumed a face that her dear Peridor had not been able to forget. She testified to her husband and her son the contentment she experienced in seeing them again, and at the same time she assured the fay of her most intense and tender gratitude.

She was expressing all those sentiments at the same time, with the disorder of excessive joy and surprise, when another chariot was seen arriving through the air. It was the equipage of the other fay, for it ought to be remembered that I have always said that there were two. She brought with her Diamantin, whom she had punished by absence and imprisoned in a castle between four chairs, from which he had not budged, and who, more passionate than ever, and in the firm resolution to be faithful, found Aglantine more beautiful than he had ever seen her. Their reconciliation was as tender as it was sincere.

In the midst of so much gratitude and contentment, our young lovers were in a perplexity difficult to express, when all of a sudden, the fays, taking Serpentine by the hand, said to the kings and queens: "You have not asked us who this beauty is. The excess of your joy excuses your lack of curiosity." Then she said to Serpentine, showing her Aglantine and Diamantin: "These are the people who gave you the light of day."

The nobility of her sentiments, and the vivacity of the movements of her heart, caused her at those words a joy that only Sapir could dispute. After the tender embraces of a reunited family, the fays proposed the marriage of Serpentine and Prince Saphir, which was generally approved. Their hearts were always faithful subsequently.

The fays witnessed those three marriages—for there were, in fact, three of them; I do not believe that anyone can dispute that with me—and everyone was content and sage thereafter.

Peridor and Diamantin, heaped with the good will and the favors of the fays, wanted their story to be made public, in order that it might serve for the instruction of all people, and in order to give a further mark of their gratitude, they had the stories of Faerie that had happened in neighboring realms collected, and it is a part of those tales that compose this little volume.

The Flying Ship

Several centuries ago, all the princes of the earth, as well as their subjects, fatigued by the tyranny that fays exercised incessantly, resolved with a common accord to declare war on them. They were convinced that their power ordinarily caused great evils, and was only beneficial for very few people. And how was that done? Most often, it was on conditions so rigorous that it was necessary to be delivered to the most terrible ordeals before succeeding in accomplishing one's desires, and sometimes before obtaining the slightest favor.

The fays were immortal then, as they are today, but they were nevertheless submissive to that fatal day every week when, appearing in the form of some animal, they were exposed to the insults of their enemies. At the moment of their metamorphosis all their power vanished, and, subject to the same poverties as the beasts whose form they had been obliged to take, it was only by fleeing or hiding that they could escape the outrages in preparation for them. In spite of all the precautions they took, however, they were often surprised, and all the aforementioned kings took advantage so successfully of the advantage that the day fatal for the fays gave them that in a short time they perished in large numbers and were reduced to making the decision to retreat.

They were rather irresolute about the choice of a country where they could live together without mingling with any mortals when one of their number, who surpassed the others in prudence and industry, offered an opinion that was universally applauded. She proposed the construction of an enormous vessel of extremely light wood, the external surface of which would be covered by ostrich plumes. Those plumes ought only to be attached to the hull of the ship by the end of the quill, in order that the air, by agitating them, would sustain the machine and cause it to progress in a rapid and certain fashion.

The interior of the great vessel ought, according to the plain, to be lined with the skins of swans; and two phoenix plumes, so dazzling that they had the virtue of rendering invisible everything that surrounded them, ought to be attached to the poop and the prow of the beautiful machine, in such a fashion that nothing in the world could separate them from it.

As soon as the design of that vessel was approved, the work was complete; the simple wish of the fays sufficed for its execution. They embarked in haste, firmly resolved not to determine their residence until they had examined the whole word with the greatest attention. They were lifted up instantly, without the ship making the slightest movement, and no mortal has been able to boast of having seen their embarkation.

When they had reached the highest region of the air, the vessel traveled with perfectly smoothness, as it would have done on the calmest and most placid sea. The stars appeared in that place with a splendor that was never obscured, which one cannot imagine in our hemisphere; their glare did not cause any dazzle and their proximity was not inconvenienced by their heat. When one looked at the earth through that immensity of air, it resembled a sad and tenebrous chaos, which would naturally inspire no regret in persons who had abandoned that abode.

But what cannot habitude achieve? They fays had been too long accustomed to the habitation of the earth; they valued their art too much, which could only be exercised on humans, to resolve to separate themselves from it entirely. Nor did they want to be distant from the vicinity of the heavens. Torn between those two desires, which appeared to them to be incompatible, they were assisted by encountering a mountain, against which their vessel was in danger of breaking.

That mountain was the only one in the world that rose up to such an excessive height. The precipices that surrounded it rendered it inaccessible; the summit far exceeded the denser air; in consequence it was exempt from all bad weather; but the closer the slope of the mountain approached the earth, the more it was covered by snow and ice. The fays amassed them in one place and used them to construct a vast and very high hall. The cold and the tempests were forbidden to approach that entire section in future; flowers and fruits took the place of frosts and the zephyr had orders never to cease to embellish them. The situation of the summit of the mountain was admirable and delightful, but unfortunately, its area was small in extent.

The fays organized the terrain, therefore. In the middle they placed a basin of a precious substance; they gave birth there to a spring that would never dry up, the water of which would spread out incessantly, by means of agreeably distributed cascades, over the flowers and fruits with which the mountain was henceforth clad. That water, which participated in the celestial matter with which it was mingled, was much purer that that we use down here; furthermore, it had the property of procuring the immortality and maintaining the beauty of the persons who bathed in it, at the same time as it procured a perfect health for those who made use of it as their beverage. In a moment, the fays erected a magnificent palace on one side of that spring, where they established their dwelling, and that palace was placed symmetrically with the aforementioned hall.

The fays had made that hall a place of enchantment; they had converted its walls, which had previously only been masses of ice, into diamond, and the sun, by virtue of its proximity, had finished giving them solidity without altering their transparency. That was, however, one of the least of the prodigies that rendered the hall marvelous and worthy of being inhabited by the gods. When one entered it and looked upwards, the movement of the heavens was developed with the same clarity as if one had been in the sky; similarly, when one looked downwards, one could distinguish the immensity of the sea and the entre earth; one could penetrate all the way to its entrails. As for the walls of the beautiful hall, they represented by turns, In accordance with the will of those considering them, all the individuals inhabiting the world. Not only were

304

their faces depicted naturally, but all the actions presented there were retraced with the most exact verity.

To the miracle of sight was added that of hearing. Without the latter article its curiosity would have been lacking something. In the same place, therefore, several sorts of instruments were found ranged on ruby tables, which produced the same effect for conversations as the walls did for visible objects, so that, in knowing the faces, it was also possible to know the character of their hearts and minds. In order to operate the instruments, it was sufficient to order the one whose sound one preferred to bring the words that the persons about whom one was curious were speaking; the instrument obeyed immediately, with a great deal of fidelity and melody. It had, in addition, the advantage of only rendering it intelligible to the person interrogating it, in order not only to be discreet but also not to be an obstacle to those who might have a similar desire at the same time.

The fays found themselves in the obligation of employing the utmost industry in order to live easily in such a small area. Furthermore, it was necessary for them, in order to come safely to earth, when they desired to do so, to render themselves unrecognizable by changing their form; otherwise, what hope could they have had of exercising their talents freely? That last expedient was to reduce their stature to the height of the smallest children, while nevertheless conserving the proportions of the best made adults. They also gave their skin a hardness approaching that of stone and covered that skin with a varnish that allowed the pallor of their complexion to be seen and the rouge with which they liked to adorn themselves. By that means, their beauty became splendid and very solid.

When they had a desire to come into the world they presented themselves before the walls of the hall; they passed in review all the persons, especially the prettiest children, that were then on earth and determined, on the basis of the physiognomy, to attach themselves to them, sometimes in order to harm them, and sometimes to give them pleasure. In sum, they acted in that regard as almost everyone does, following the prejudices of hatred or inclination.

On arrival on earth they ordinarily forbade themselves the usage of speech. It was, therefore, only children who would have consideration for them, but it was unimportant to them by what title they entered palaces and the simplest houses, provided that they were, in fact, received there. Their complexion had, as I have said, a whiteness, a redness and a polish above the natural and their adornment was always very carefully chosen. Children amused themselves dressing and undressing them; they became common in society; they were found everywhere. It was therefore necessary to chose a name for them, and people gave them that of Doll, in memory of an empress on the same name,[30] who became famous by virtue of the continuous application she had had all her life to making up her face and ornamenting herself. Dolls, received in the world without anyone having the slightest suspicion of them, did all the good and evil they wished without either being attributed to them, and it appears that they still conduct themselves in the same fashion, in spite of the prejudice people have that their power is finished and that their bodies have been converted into inanimate plaster.

At any rate, seven or eight thousand years ago, one of the fays, whose treasures are inexhaustible—the same one who, as everyone knows, had raised to royalty by a bizarre route a young woman of mediocre condition whom she had taken in

---

[30] The *Cabinet des fées* text has a note at this point, presumably inserted by the author, to explain (in jest) the origin of the French *poupée* [doll]: "Sabine Poppée, the second wife of the Emperor Nero, famous for coquetry and the care she took for the conservation of her beauty. Some people attribute the invention of make-up to her." The reference is to Poppaea Sabina the Younger (30-65 A.D.), who was, like every other wife of an emperor, snidely slandered by Roman "historians" in much the same way that the mistresses of French kings were slandered.

amity—resolved to seek again some occupation worthy of her. She entered the hall and, having at down negligently on a sofa facing one of the walls, she was struck during the review she made of the human race by a little princess four years old, whose beauty and charms surpassed anything that had ever been seen. She consulted regarding her intelligence a sort of violin, which reported speech so brilliant and jovial that she judged that she was nothing less than perfect. The princess, her mother, who was very young, very beautiful and very witty, charmed her no less.

She felt ready to fly toward that amiable family, and nothing put any obstacle in her design except the discovery she made, to her chagrin, that there was no further perfection to give them. She could not, however, resolve herself to being unnecessary to them; when one is keenly interested in people, only easily distinguishes how one might be useful to them. She perceived that their fortune was not proportionate to their birth and their merit; that the little princess had a brother to whom all the wealth of the house belonged, and that, in consequence, she might have great need of her assistance in future—for in those remote times, the fay of treasures was necessary and desired in the world.

That discovery determined the fay to depart, but in order to be received more favorably by that amiable child, she found the means of being sent by an aunt whom she loved very much. That aunt spent her life retired in a desert, and only saw her niece very rarely. She was delighted to have such a present to give her, and no one had been able to tell me which of them had the greater pleasure, in giving or receiving. The aunt dressed the Doll in clothes similar to her own, and those of the persons with whom she lived in her desert.

The little princess received the present; she called the Doll her aunt and gave her amities and caresses, as if she were indeed her aunt. The rest of the house gave her a welcome no less warm, and was so content with it that she engaged one of her sisters to come and keep her company. The later consented gladly, and was given by the same hand in the same costume.

The two fays, unable to add anything to the graces of the princess, applied themselves to inspiring her with a courage capable of resisting all the misfortunes of life. They did the same favor for the mother, and as the child was at the age when the education of children begins, the fays rendered her very knowledgeable in a short time without putting her to the trouble of studying; her vivacity would never have become accustomed to that difficulty.

When she had attained the age of twelve, they took her away one night in the launch of the ship whose description has been given. Ostrich plumes gave it the same lightness. They took her into the beautiful hall that might be called the mirror of the world. Then they passed in review before them all the kings of the world, with the design of knowing which one she found most to her taste. The princess dared not make a choice to begin with; it appeared that that would wound her modesty in some way. Finally, after an absolute command, she noticed a young king, and it was the same one that the fays destined for her.

They had heaped that prince since his birth with their most precious gifts; they had rendered him extremely lovable, and he still had a free heart. It only a matter of inspiring desire in him equal to the one to which he had given birth. The fays caused a portrait of the princess to fall into his hands; that was not very difficult for them, and the prince fell madly in love even more easily. Although he was in earliest youth, his sagacity and his extraordinary merit rendered him the absolute master of himself and his estates; thus, he did not want an ambassador to negotiate the affair that was to him the most important in the world; he came in person, with a court and a pompous equipage, to ask for the hand of the princess. He had no difficulty obtaining it; even in those remote times it was no longer merit alone that determined fortune.

That happy event appeared incomprehensible to everyone; no one knew to whom the little princess and her mother could have such an obligation. They alone, who were in the confidence of the fays and took advantage of their benefits every day, had knowledge of it.

The flying ship, which the fays had conserved preciously in a grotto in the mountain, was given to the newlyweds, who rightly preferred that equipage to any other to go to their kingdom. They were received there with acclamations and a joy that is indescribable, and which did not relent with time. The ship always remained with those two amiable spouses, along with the power to take aboard anyone they wished, and that of being visible or invisible. It will be remembered that, in order to do that, it was only necessary to cover and uncover the phoenix feathers at will.

The newlyweds went in their beautiful vehicle to pay a visit to the aunt who had given the Dolls. They no longer wanted to permit her to live in her desert; they took her away with them. They did more, and associated her with all the privileges accorded by the fays. The one that touched her the most was the pleasure of bathing with her sister and her niece in the celestial water that communicates immortality. That circumstance allows the well-founded judgment that the company still enjoys all the felicity that has just been depicted, and they are perhaps diverting themselves at this very moment traveling through the air on the flying ship—and some day, the phoenix plumes, differently placed, might permit us to see them pass by.

Prince Perinet; Or, The Origin of Pagodas

Almidor, the king of a part of India, fell in love with a beautiful princess, whom he married with all sorts of magnificence. The short time that the two new spouses lived together they spent in perfect union, the reason for which is simple: they had nothing to desire, and, in consequence, nothing for which to reproach one another.

The queen had become pregnant at the commencement of the marriage, and the king waited impatiently for her to bring the fruit of their amour into the world. She finally gave birth to a handsome prince, who was named Perinet. Almidor was savoring a perfect joy when one of the queen's women came to tell him that she was approaching her last hour. He did not run, he flew to the apartment of the princess, whom he found ready to render her last sigh. As soon as she saw her dear Almidor, she held out her hand and said to him, in a halting voice: "I'm leaving you a son who, I hope, will console you for my death. If you love me, you will never remarry."

She would have said more, but inhumane fate closed her mouth forever.

The king abandoned himself to all the regrets that the loss he had just suffered necessarily demanded of him. He shut himself away with his dear Perinet, whom he held in his arms and moistened at every moment with his tears. When the excess of his dolor had eased slightly, he showed him to his people and was only occupied with the care of governing well

A few years went by in that fashion; the little prince was then six years old, and the king brought him up with all the care and tenderness merited by such a lovable child, who was dear to him.

One day, the entire court was walking on the sea shore, in a delightful garden irrigated by an infinite number of springs of the finest water in the world, which was only formed by compartments of flowers and lawns, arbors and enclosures covered with exquisite fruits. Suddenly, they saw a fire rise up over the surface of the sea, which, although it was calm everywhere and there was not the slightest wind, floated over the surface on the waves with incredible speed, and which grew to the point that when it stopped, close to the shore, it appeared to be a blazing mountain.

Everyone gazed at that prodigy with an astonishment mingled with admiration, but they were very surprised when they saw a small boat emerging from the heart of the flames, drawn by two swans whiter than snow, in which a woman of dazzling beauty was seated. When the boat was within voice range, the beautiful woman addressed the king and said to him: "I am the fay Manipe; I have always been interested in the princes of your house. A misfortune is threatening you, but you can prevent it. You will be separated from your son. Before he reaches his fifteenth year he will be abducted in your own estates; make the decision in that regard that your prudence dictates."

She disappeared at that moment, and left the entire court in a dolor as sharp as if the prediction had already been fulfilled.

Almidor withdrew, overwhelmed by sadness, and no longer thought of anything but means to avoiding such a misfortune. In the end, he judged that only his sister, the Queen of the Fays, was capable of preserving him from it. Without deliberating any further, he took his dear Perinet to the palace of that princess personally. She received them both with all possible affection and amity. When the king had informed her of the reasons that obliged him to put such a precious deposit in her hands she said: "I accept with all my heart; be sure that, sensible, as I ought to be, to the confidence that you are testifying in me, I will have all the attentions for your dear nephew that he merits. Yes, I promise you: as long as he is in my realm, nothing will happen to him that can cause you the slightest pain."

Almidor, charmed by his sister's generosity, returned home satisfied.

The Queen of the Fays was no longer occupied with anything but procuring her nephew all the diversions appropriate to his age. She had no children; she therefore regarded him as her own son, and loved him with as much tenderness as if he really were. As the same time as she exhausted her art in enabling the young prince to spend delightful days, however, she was even more attentive to procuring him an education worthy of his birth. Clever masters were summoned from all directions to teach him music, dancing and all the exercises that form the mind and the body. In short, she had him taught everything that a prince ought to know thoroughly, and wanted him at least to have a smattering of what a man of a certain rank is not permitted to be entirely ignorant.

Hunting ordinarily occupied Perinet; when he returned he always found some new pleasure. The queen had the most beautiful young women in the world with her, among whom there was one who was even distantly related to her; she ordered her to put everything to use to appear lovable in Perinet's eyes.

That young woman was named Ticie. She obeyed the fay's orders without difficulty. For some time she persuaded herself that obedience alone had a part in the cares she took to make herself loved, but gradually, she perceived that there was also something in it that was unknown to her, and she soon fell into a languor that rendered her unrecognizable to herself. She sought the cause, and discovered, but too late, that she had the most violent passion for the prince.

On the contrary, Perinet received her urgent attentions with a coldness capable of making her die of dolor. He did not know amour as yet and it was not born for Ticie. The young woman made every effort to cure herself of the cruel amour that tyrannized her, but it was futile. She was no longer the mistress of her heart.

Vengeance is so sweet that it has attractions for a scorned woman; Ticie no longer thought of anything but persecuting her lover, since she had not been able to make him love her.

Nortandose, the Prince of the Blue Isle, had not been able to resist Ticie's charms; he had been madly in love with her for some years. He was one of the great magicians of his time; it was to him that Ticie had recourse. She confided her secret to him, and promised him that if he would help her to avenge herself for the prince's scorn, her heart would be the recompense for her services. The Prince of the Blue Isle received Ticie's propositions with all the joy that hope can give to a man in love.

It was necessary to draw Perinet outside the fay's realm, for it was impossible to harm him in her estates, and Perinet was guarded with an extreme attention. Nortandose flattered himself that he could overcome the difficulties.

The prince often went hunting. One day, when he was pursuing a stag, an animal more terrible and more singular than one can describe presented itself to him. The monster was as big as a bear; it had three heads the size of that of an ox; six frightfully hissing snakes, capable of frightening the most determined men, formed its six tails. That frightful beast threw itself on the dogs and devoured them all in an instant. A mortal fear seized all those who were following the prince; they abandoned him, but he, only consulting his courage, approached the monster intrepidly and threw his javelin at it with a sure hand.

Although it was invulnerable, the monster immediately ran away. Perinet did not lose sight of it, and attached himself to its pursuit, charmed to have found an opportunity worthy of his valor.

The frightful animal would doubtless have led him out of his aunt's estates, to the place where the enchanter was waiting, but another marvel stopped him when he was near to emerging from them. He perceived several women walking near a castle, in a little juniper wood. There was one to whom the other women were rendering their respects, and it was that one who attracted his gaze and whose extreme beauty caused

313

him to pass in a moment from the keenest admiration to secret movements that were entirely unknown to him.

He approached that pleasant company. Princess Zainzinette—for it was her that he had remarked—looked at the prince in her turn with an astonishment that he perceived. They both had too much intelligence not to know what was happening in their hearts. They thought, therefore, that there was no need to make a mystery of it. They said everything to one another that the commencement of a violent passion can inspire, and made arrangements to see one another every day in the same place.

For some time the two lovers savored all the sweetness of amour without experiencing its pains, but alas, there are no durable pleasures. One day, when Perinet had been to visit Zainzinette, and was coming out of her dwelling more amorous than he had ever been, the Queen of the Fays came to tell him that Almidor was approaching his fatal term and wanted to have the consolation of embracing his son before dying.

The prince, duly afflicted, set forth immediately. The fay had given him a liquor, the effect of which was so marvelous that as soon as Almidor had made use of it, his health was restored in a surprising manner. Independently of the remedy that he had taken, the joy of seeing once again a son he loved contributed not a little to his recovery.

He was on the point of sending that dear son away again, in order to avoid the misfortune by which he was threatened, but so little time remained before the prince reached his fifteenth year that he could not resolve to be separated from him; he thought it sufficient to have him guarded with extreme care.

Finally, the day of the prince's birth arrived, and the king, delighted to see the term accomplished of the misfortune that had been predicted, wanted to celebrate such a happy day. He gave the most brilliant and elegant fête of which mention has ever been heard, on the sea.

The diversions had not yet concluded when Perinet, under the pretext of fishing, but in fact to rid himself of the importunate courtiers and dream at liberty about his dear

Zainzinette, set forth alone in a small boat. He had already caught several fish without paying any great attention to them when he perceived one of extraordinary form. Its scales were gold and blue and its eyes resembled two carbuncles. That fish came to bite his hook, but was not caught by it. The prince would have given all he possessed in the world to have it; he would have had great pleasure in making a present of it to Zainzinette. He had already resolved to send it to her post-haste. But the beautiful fish drew away as he pursued it, and he drew away from the shore so far himself that he lost sight of all the people who, following the custom of courtiers, were occupied in the same exercise.

Then he felt his boat sinking into the sea. It was necessary to be as courageous as Perinet not to be frightened by such an accident, but he did not know fear. He stated swimming, determined to reach the shore. Imagine his astonishment when he saw a man with a horrible face coming toward him, mounted on a huge toad. The frightful man seized him, placed him in front of him on his saddle-bow, without pronouncing a single word, and the toad immediately started swimming with an extreme speed.

A few moments later, all three of them arrived at an island that only appeared to be inhabited by terrible beasts. It was confided to the guard of two lions, two bears, two elephants and four tigers. The master of the toad, after having muttered a few words between his teeth, put his hand on the prince's head and at the same moment, he was changed into a teapot.

It is easy to deduce that that ugly gentleman was the Prince of the Blue Isle, who, in order to please Ticie and defeat a rival, had just given that form to Perinet. Immediately, he flew away to receive the prize of the malevolence he had just committed; but Ticie, who had been unable to banish the handsome Perinet from her heart, could not even look at him. She banished him from her presence, heaping him with insults.

The sad teapot, abandoned on the island by Nortandose, advanced a few steps without any encounter, but on entering a little wood that he found on his route he heard voices that proved that the place was inhabited. Society is a consolation in misfortune, so the prince continued his route; but nothing could equal his surprise when he perceived porcelain bowls, urns, jugs and cups conversing together.

As he advanced to listen to what such individuals might be saying, he was perceived by all the crockery that he had before him. They asked the teapot what misfortune had reduced him to that state, and he told them that he had been captured at sea by a huge ugly man he did not know, that the ugly man had made him mount a toad and had metamorphosed him in the fashion they could see when they arrived on the island.

By the description he gave of his persecutor, a jug spoke and told him that his enemy was Nortandose, a genius of the most vulgar species, who had a passionate love of porcelain, and transformed in that fashion anyone who had the misfortune to displease him.

Meanwhile, Almidor, not seeing his son return from fishing, felt all that anxiety and floor can cause one to experience, and the entire court imitated him. The good king sent everyone on campaign, and ran in different directions himself searching for the prince, but all his efforts were futile. He had recourse to his sister. Although her power was incontrovertibly great, it did not extend as far as extracting the prince from the place where he was. She promised, however, to give him all the aid that she could.

Immediately, he transported herself to the Blue Isle—or, rather, the Isle of Porcelains, for it was known by both names. In spite of her great knowledge, she would never have recognized the unfortunate Perinet if the beautiful yellow teapot had not whispered to her: "I am your unfortunate nephew, who is suffering more than anyone has ever suffered; the state in which you see me is not what afflicts me the most, but I am separated from the beautiful Zainzinette, and without her, I cannot live."

The queen was touched by the state to which the most beautiful prince on earth had been reduced; she promised to

316

satisfy, as soon as she had the power, all the wishes that he might form. Perinet asked her for the sole favor of having news of Zainzinette every day. She granted him that satisfaction, very consoling for an absent lover, and to that effect, she made him a present of a little brown and white spaniel, which she ordered to report to the prince continually everything that his mistress was doing. That spaniel was the prettiest animal that had been seen to date; all the porcelains became madly fond of it and could not go a moment without playing with it and without saying all the stupid things that women say all too frequently to its peers. Perinet, to whom the dog had been given, had difficulty finding moments in which to satisfy his curiosity regarding Zainzinette.

After the fay had given him such a fine present she tapped her wand three times and a palace formed in the middle of a garden, both worthy of the Queen of the Fays. The porcelains of the island were ordered not to quit the prince, and to afford him all the pleasures that might be capable of distracting his chagrin. To attach them more strongly to his person, the fay told them that he was destined to put an end to their misfortunes.

All the porcelains, being thus united, followed the teapot, which marched at their head with gravity and led them into the new palace. It was made of white porcelain, enameled with the ancient blue that that is beginning to become so rare and precious. All the porcelains found precisely the number of apartments there that were necessary to them. The one that the prince chose was ruby, speckled with emeralds; his cabinet was diamond, paneled with sapphires. That room was a place of assembly, were they were only occupied with amusing Perinet, whose only concern was his dear Zainzinette.

After having made that fine establishment, the fay went to find Almidor, and told him everything that had happened. "There is no other resource in your misfortune," she said, "and no other means of ending it, than that of exposing on the sea, in a ship, a young virgin. If she is such as I ask, the vessel will go of its own accord, without a pilot, to the place where the prince is captive. Don't embarrass yourself with any other concern than finding her. It will be that virgin who will enable your son to resume his amiable form.

All the most zealous fathers and mothers came immediately to present their daughters. Not a moment was lost; the first of them was embarked on the ship, but scarcely had the vessel set sail that it returned to the port. That day, more than a hundred experienced the same destiny. Either because the wind was not favorable or, in sum, they lacked something, they all returned to the place from which they had departed.

In despair at not being able to find, in a realm as large as his, a young woman of the sort he needed, the king had recourse to his sister again. After she had searched hard in her old books, she told Almidor that only Princess Zainzinette could deliver the prince. Immediately, the king sent envoys to Queen Mindamire to ask her for her daughter, Princes Zainzinette, for Prince Perinet. Mindamire had wanted that alliance for a long time, but she desired it all the more since her daughter had confided to her the amour she felt for the prince.

For all sorts of reasons, therefore, Mindamire received the proposition with great pleasure. She went to look for Zainzinette immediately, for she had retired since she had lost her lover to a country house where she abandoned herself to her dolor. She informed her of the reason for her visit and the intention she had of taking her to Almidor personally. The joy of the princess was inexpressible. She went with her mother to the estates of the king, who received her as the liberator of his son.

Without wasting a single moment, she boarded the ship, fatal thus far to so many beauties. The entire court and the people of the city were on the shore, but the spectators were agitated by very different sentiments. The parents and friends of those who had not been able to carry the adventure through, and the latter above all, as can easily be imagined, desired that the vessel would be as unable to set sail for Zainzinette as it had been for them. The few—small in number, in truth—who were good citizens, flattered themselves, albeit feebly, with the hope of success. The greater number lamented in advance the fate of the beautiful Zainzinette. In sum, everyone was attentive to the great event, when the sails were seen to deploy of their own accord and the ship set sail with such great velocity that it was lost to sight in an instant.

The princess sensed a joy that would be difficult to describe. She was about to see her lover again; she alone in all the world would be able to free him from the unfortunate fate he was experiencing, and to complete her happiness, she was giving him at the same time a striking proof of her fidelity.

It was night when the vessel moored at the fatal island, but Zainzinette disembarked anyway, so great was her impatience. Scarcely had she descended to the shore than she saw a little girasol chariot coming toward her, the wheels of which were topazes. It was drawn by six glow-worms; a laughing child as beautiful as the day was guiding the vehicle. As soon as he had perceived the princess he got down, went toward her and, taking her by the hand, he helped her mount the chariot, placed her in the back and set himself at her feet. The chariot moved off at such great speed that she did not have time to make the slightest reflection on what was happening. In an instant, she arrived outside a superb palace, and it was there that the pretty vehicle stopped abruptly.

Singularity, always more piquant in human eyes than magnificence, distinguished that admirable habitation. It was built of red and blue butterfly wings, and the furniture was made of the most beautiful spider-webs, embroidered with gold. As soon as Zainzinette had entered it she ran everywhere, calling: "Perinet! My dear Perinet!" for she had no doubt that this was the place where he would be shown to her eyes.

When she had traversed several rooms she was stopped by a woman even smaller than the child who had just served as her coachman. That dwarf of sorts cried: "Stop, beautiful Zainzinette, and listen to me. You are searching for Perinet in vain. My father, the Prince of the Blue Isle and master of this realm, has charged me with meeting you, in order to assure you on his part of the most violent passion you will ever inspire. The fear of displeasing you has prevented him from presenting himself; he has not dared to appear before you after the trick he has just played on you, for he is the one who adopted the form of a child to bring you here and prevent you from reaching the palace of porcelains."

At this speech the princess felt the most intense dolor. She could not constrain herself, and in her anger she said everything that despairing amour can pronounce so well; after which she fainted in the arms of the dwarf, who carried her to a magnificent bed.

Nortandose was as afflicted as he could be by the state in which he found Zainzinette. He reproached himself for his cruelty, and was even on the point of taking the princess back to the place where he had found her, but unfortunately, he remembered then the good grace with which she had embarked, and the marvelous beauty by which he had been dazzled the first time he had seen her. In sum, he remembered at that moment everything that amour had caused him to feel, for, unfortunately for poor Zainzinette, he had been abroad on the sea when she had embarked to deliver the handsome Perinet. After making all those reflections, which occupied him for a long time—for the story reports that he required a long time to reflect—he decided that he could not separate himself from a person who had seemed so beautiful and had become so dear to him.

The dwarf, his daughter, employed her cares to bring the princess round from her faint. She was as good and has gentle as her father was cruel and malevolent. "Beautiful Zainzinette," she said to her, when she had recovered her senses, "moderate your affliction, and calm your tears; my father—I could cite you a thousand examples—is the most inconstant of men; he often looks indifferently in the evening at what he loved recklessly in the morning; ought that alone not reassure you? If, however, he persists in his evil designs, I want to help you; I can do it, rely on me."

But nothing consoled Zainzinette; she only opened her mouth to say: "Let me die, since I cannot see Perinet."

She spent several hours in that cruel state, and, although it might appear difficult to believe, Nortandose had the discretion not to appear before her, for fear of irritating her. That restraint was perhaps the only one he ever had in his life. As for the dwarf, she was so touched by the misfortunes of the princess that she promised to get her out of her father's hands, provided that she was able to give some relief to her dolor. Zainzinette recognized that she was speaking with sincerity; she therefore followed her advice, yielding to hope, and moderating her tears and groans. They agreed together that she would permit Nortandose to visit her, and that she would make every effort not to allow the extent of her aversion to become apparent.

The Prince of the Blue Isle was easily deceived; he seemed transported by the good will that he imagined he was receiving from the princess. Every day he gave her magnificent diversions and prepared new fêtes for her. His self-esteem easily persuaded him that he would soon be the happiest man in the world. He was finally obliged to go and take care of various new arrivals, including some noblemen of his realm, and his daughter, to whose guard the princess was confided, took advantage of his absence to keep her promise.

Before separating from Zainzinette she made her a present of an entirely blue robe, which covered her from head to toe. That disguise, although simple, facilitated her flight, for the inhabitants of the Blue Isle wore no other color. She accompanied that present with that of a small white wand, which would guide her straight to the palace of porcelains; she implored her to trust it entirely, embraced her tenderly and said: "I hope that your journey will be as successful as I desire."

Without knowing where she was going, Zainzinette followed the wand exactly, which always preceded her by a short distance. She walked for six months, not without experiencing unimaginable fatigues, or without despairing sometimes of ever finding her lover.

Finally, one day, she perceived a castle upon which the sun's rays were falling vertically. It was so brilliant that her eyes could not sustain the glare; that marvel redoubled her curiosity. When she was within a certain distance her astonishment became even greater. Porcelains of every species came to meet her. Two jugs offered to take her hand; two cups carried her robe; a host of bowls preceded her, followed her and paid court to her. In the midst of the honors she received, a yellow teapot pierced the crowd by which she was surrounded, stopped in front of her and said, in a most passionate tone of voice: "It's you, my dear Zainzinette, who is willing to see Perinet is the deplorable state he is in."

She could not mistake her lover's voice; she took him in her arms with transports of infinite joy.

The prince was ashamed of appearing before his mistress in such a baroque form; he dared not proffer a single word, and made nothing heard but sighs.

Zainzinette perceived that, for lovers perceive everything. "What, my dear Perinet?" she said to him. "You don't express more pleasure at seeing me again? Do I have to fear other changes in you than that of your form?"

"When one loves you," replied the prince, "can others arise? Nothing equals the shame and dolor I am in."

"You judge my tenderness poorly, my dear Perinet," the princess replied. "Whatever form you have, you are always equally dear to me."

That speech on the part of Zainzinette reassured the teapot, and enabled him to say everything that amour and gratitude can inspire in a lover.

When they had arrived in the palace, the princess went through it, admiring its magnificence. Then she came to lie down in Perinet's room. It was there that the porcelains all gathered in order to pay her the most polite and agreeable compliments, only speaking to her about her lover's dolor throughout the time he had been separated from her. They told her how the little spaniel had informed them of all her steps, and Perinet then told her in exact detail everything that she had suffered on the way, and the mortal anxieties that he had suffered in consequence.

The subject-matter was excellent for a tender and sincere lover, so he took advantage of it, but when the conversation was in full flow—which must have been a very singular spectacle, the little dog came running with so much rapidity that it nearly knocked over ten or a dozen porcelains, at least. After having recovered his breath, he told the company that Nortandose was on the steps of the palace, that he was infallibly about to enter, and that what persuaded him of it was that since he had lost the princess he had not ceased to search for her in all the places where he believed he might encounter her.

That news caused a general alarm. The little spaniel demanded silence, and addressed the teapot in these terms: "Prince, it only depends on you to make your happiness; the enchanter will soon appear in the palace. He can only be wounded on the summit of his head; remember that an opportunity missed might never be found again."

With those words, the little dog disappeared. As can easily be imagined, its departure afflicted the whole assembly, for they had no other resource, and what the spaniel had just said made them think that it knew a means of liberating them from the tyrant. A thousand were proposed, all at the same time, without any having the time to be approved. The porcelains were overwhelmed by sadness when Zainzinette suggested that it was necessary to place the teapot, whose courage and resolution she knew, one the ledge above the door of the room, which Nortandose would doubtless enter, and that the teapot had to choose its moment well enough to fall vertically on to the magician's head.

The porcelains approved the princess's advice, all the more so as they could not think of anything better. Zainzinette picked up her dear teapot herself, kissed it a thousand times, and placed it in the middle of the ledge, after which, all the porcelains arranged themselves around her, very anxious about the outcome of an event that was of such great importance for them.

Scarcely were they in order than the Prince of the Blue Isle was heard at the top of the staircase. He went from room to room, searching everywhere for Zainzinette. He eventually reached the one where she was, but scarcely had he set foot over the threshold of the door that the teapot precipitated itself on to the top of his head; from there it fell to the floor, where it shattered into a thousand pieces.

At that sight, Zainzinette uttered an agonized scream, and fell in a faint; but Perinet, who resumed at the same instant his charming form, the only one that had ever made an impression on her heart, easily brought her round.

At the same moment, all other porcelains recovered the forms they had had before their metamorphosis. Never had such a large number of pretty women and good looking men been seen at the same time, for the charms with which they were seen to shine only ceded to those of Perinet and Zainzinette. Those two illustrious liberators had no more doubt about the death of Nortandose, but what was their surprise when they realized that he had been changed himself, into a porcelain pagoda. That pagoda did not have, as they had had, the liberty of speaking and walking; it only had a certain movement of the head, which was still menacing them.

In the midst of the homages and thanks that he was receiving from all those whose liberty he had just procured so generously, Perinet was only sensible to the caresses of his dear Zainzinette. She held him tenderly embraced. Charmed to see one another more beautiful than ever, they were savoring an infinite joy, which the witnesses of their happiness shared wholeheartedly with the objects of their own tenderness.

They were still on the fatal island, however, and they had experienced so much chagrin there that it was prudent to get away from it as soon as possible. The prince voiced that opinion, and all together they took the road to the sea. There they found the monsters that guarded the island, and which opposed their passage, hurling themselves upon them in order to devour them. They had no weapons and they were unable, in consequence, either to repel them or defend themselves.

In a situation so desperate, they were obliged to return to the palace, gripped by a dolor without example. "Our misfortunes are not over," they said. "We have only resumed our original forms in order to see those we love die more cruelly. What help can we hope for against hunger?"

They were agreeably surprised, however, when they found, on returning to the palace, several tables covered with the most delicious dishes. They took advantage of it with an enviable appetite, like a troop that had not eaten for three hundred years. The most exquisite liquors flowed abundantly of their own accord into goblets and cups of inestimable price, and presented themselves to the hand as soon as one felt thirsty.

Perinet had no doubt that he owed that obligation to his aunt, the Queen of the Fays. For the present, all the members of that good company were easily consoled for being obliged to live in such a beautiful place, where they did not lack anything. Zainzinette and Perinet asked for nothing better than to live there for a long time. What had they to desire? They loved one another passionately; they would see one another all the time, and nothing would distract them from their pleasures.

When the meal was over, they went for a walk in the beautiful garden mentioned previously. Scarcely had they entered it than they saw a chariot appear in the air, which caused them a great fright. Those who have suffered always dread some new misfortune more easily than anyone else.

The vehicle was extraordinary in form; palm leaves formed it and swallows were drawing it. As it descended, they distinguished a woman, who was soon recognizable as the Queen of the Fays. She had the little dwarf, Nortandose's daughter, beside her. Perinet ran to her; she received him with all imaginable tenderness, and, having placed him beside her with his dear Zainzinette, the rest of the company was placed in a following carriage, drawn by six wild ducks.

On the way she told them that she was the one who had changed the enchanter into a pagoda at the moment when he rendered his soul, and she assured them that all those who landed on the island and who had evil designs would experience the same destiny. It is to that punishment—or, rather, to that justice—that all the beautiful pagodas we see every day are owed.

Scarcely had she finished speaking that she arrived in Almidor's kingdom. That prince was waiting on the sea shore; his joy in seeing his son again was inexpressible. He did not want to delay any longer; he enabled him to marry Zainzinette right away. The wedding was magnificent and the fêtes that followed it very agreeable. The fay, at Zainzinette's request, rendered Nortandose's estates to the dwarf, and the goodness of her heart enabled her to experience, throughout the time that she lived there, the solid pleasure of rendering her people happy—quite different from Ticie, whom hazard conducted to the Isle of Porcelains, and who was one of the first pagodas of Nortandose's court. How many people there are in the world that I would send to travel to the Blue Isle if I could!

Rose-Red, White and Black

The eldest son of a great king was walking all alone in winter in a country covered with snow. He perceived a crow on which he exercised his skill. The bird fell dead in the snow and tinted it with its blood. The sheen of its black plumage, the whiteness of the snow and the redness of its blood produced an assemblage of colors by which the prince was struck. That idea took such possession of his mind that it was no longer possible for him to expel it. Gradually, it gave birth in his heart to a violent passion, which, entirely imaginary though it was, would not permit him to believe that he could be happy until he had found a person whose rose-red and white complexion was heightened by perfectly black hair.

He was absorbed in his profound reflections when he was distracted by a voice that said to him: "Go, Prince, into the Empire of Marvels. In the middle of an immense forest you will find a tree laden with apples larger and more beautiful than they are ordinarily. Pluck three and be master of yourself sufficiently not to open them until you return; they will offer you a beauty such as you desire."

The empire that was indicated to him was distant and difficult of access, but nothing could prevent the prince from undertaking such a voyage. He set forth within the hour, crossed the seas, and explored the entire forest with an infinite care. In brief, he found the tree. He plucked the three beautiful apples, and, unable to resist the curiosity that was tormenting him, he opened one. Instantly, a woman emerge from it so marvelously beautiful and so much to his taste that he was gripped by admiration. Far from being favorable to him, however, the beauty looked at him with an angry gaze and complained that he had abducted her from her home. She disappeared at the same moment.

The impatience to which he had just succumbed ought naturally have caused him to despair, but as he had a mind susceptible of consolation—a fine gift of heaven—he easily flattered himself that he would be able to repair his loss in the two apples that remained to him. Filled with that pleasant hope, he resolved not to open them until he had returned to his homeland.

Often, the saddest experiences are incapable of correcting a small fault. The impatience of the prince was again stronger than his reason; for a second time, he was unable to resist the desire to open one of the apples.

He was then at sea. One does not ordinarily experience any dissipation on that sad element. There are few people, therefore, who would not have done as he did in a similar situation. He imagined that by covering exactly by the vessel on which he was embarked, the beauty would not be able to escape. He opened the second apple, and, just like the first time, a woman of incomparable beauty emerged from it, who testified to him just as much discontent, and in spite of all the precautions the prince had taken, she disappeared, as her predecessor had done.

Those two experiments were just sufficient to render the prince sage. He arrived in his homeland therefore, and when he had opened the only apple that remained to him, a woman emerged from it as beautiful but milder than the other two. He married her immediately, and found himself the happiest of men.

Sometime after his marriage an important war obliged him to separate from his rose-red, white and black beauty. The queen mother, in whose hands the young princess remained, had never approved of the marriage. She caused her to die cruelly and had her body thrown into the castle moat. To complete her wickedness she substituted for the unfortunate princess a woman over whom she had an absolute power.

The prince, on his return, was astonished to find a wife so different from the one he had quit, but the queen assured him positively that the woman she presented to him was his wife. She agreed with all the apparent differences he found, but attributed that metamorphosis to the consequences of an enchantment.

In fact, the circumstances in which the young woman had been found by the prince gave a sort of plausibility to that discourse. In the end, either out of mildness or lack of mistrust—for honest men do not know it—the prince believed what he was told. But nothing was capable of curing him of his original passion. He spent days and nights dreaming, and often spent entire hours leaning on one of the window sills of his palace.

One day, when he was in that sad occupation, he perceived a fish in the moat, whose brilliant scales mingled red, white and black. That object struck him; it was not possible for him to take his eyes off it. The queen mother, thinking that the marked attention in question was a sequel to his original passion, resolved once again to destroy its object. She ordered, secretly, the woman who was playing the role of the princess, and who was pregnant, to say that she had an extreme desire to eat the fish to which the prince was so attached. The fish was caught and served to the pretended queen, and the prince fell back into his previous melancholy.

He was relieved a second time by the sight of a rose-red, white and black tree. The tree was of an unknown species; no one had planted it or brought it. It had come of its own accord; it had been seen suddenly to be born at the place where the scales of the fish had been thrown. The beautiful tree gave the same pleasure to the prince and, in consequence, the same jealousy to the queen mother; its doom was immediately decided, in spite of the opposition and regrets of the prince.

The beautiful tree was uprooted and burned, but a superb castle, built of rubies, pearls and jet, which the ashes of the tree instantly produced, caused the three colors that the prince had always loved to revive again. They appeared then with a brightness that enraptured him.

The efforts that were made to enter that beautiful house were futile for a long time. The doors being locked, he was content to gaze at it incessantly, and remained for several days in that occupation, which reminded him of the object of his desires.

His perseverance was eventually recompensed; the doors opened; he entered the palace, and after having traversed several apartments, in which the furniture responded to the richness of the exterior, he found, in a cabinet more magnificent than any other room in the rest of the palace, the first wife, with whom he had been so much in love, and whose memory was so dear to him.

She reproached him for everything that she had suffered by virtue of his excessive facility, but at the same time, she expressed the joy she had in seeing that he merited a pardon that she had such a great desire to grant him.

The prince, his mother and the wife who had been substituted no longer troubled the union of the two spouses; they lived very content with one another, as well as their fortune.

Alphinge; Or, The Green Monkey

There was once a king who was married twice. His first wife was endowed with an infinite beauty and merit; unfortunately, she died shortly after the marriage while bringing a little prince into the world. The king was sensibly touched by the death of the queen and the only consolation he received in his dolor was that of seeing and embracing his son. The prince merited his attachment, not only by the resemblance that he had to the queen, his mother, but also because he was himself the most beautiful and the most lovable creature in the world.

It was the custom in that country to have a name given to children by some considerable individual. For that ceremony the king chose a neighboring princess renowned throughout the world for her intelligence and great wisdom. She was commonly known as the Good Queen. She came to the king's court, therefore, gave the little prince the name of Alphinge, and conceived thereafter an amity for him that was useful to him later.

Time effaces the greatest dolors. Scarcely a year had gone by since the death of the queen when the king not only had a desire to remarry but put that desire into execution. He married a princess who could not be refused beauty, but it would have required a great deal for her to possess all the virtues with which the late queen had been ornamented.

The new wife became pregnant shortly after her marriage and gave birth very fortunately to a boy. Scarcely did she find herself a mother than she became a stepmother in a complete fashion, for she conceived an extreme aversion for little Prince Alphinge, who added every day to the charms of his person those of a marvelous intelligence. The applause that was given to him redoubled in the queen the base jealousy that no benevolent heart has ever felt. She dissimulated her sentiments so well, however, that the king had no knowledge of it.

331

Finally, however, almost no longer mistress of herself, she sent one of her most faithful domestics to find the Fay of the Mountain. That fay, with whom she had a close liaison, had promised to second her in all her projects, whatever they might be. The queen requested, via her courier, that she conjure the undoing of Prince Alphinge, her hatred for him having reached its peak, all the more so as he was an insurmountable obstacle to her own son succeeding to the crown. Everything that a furious stepmother born wicked can write on that subject was in her letter.

The fay replied to her that, eager as she was to satisfy her desires, it was impossible for her to attempt anything against Alphinge, because a superior force more powerful than her own protected the prince; she did not know the principle of it, but she could not doubt the futility of her knowledge on this occasion.

In fact, the Good Queen was watching more attentively than ever over the conservation of Alphinge. She was still in her distance estates, but as her knowledge extended over everything most secret that was happening in the world, and absolutely nothing was hidden from her, she was not unaware of any of the evil designs of the queen. She had, therefore, sent the prince a ruby of an extraordinary size and beauty, recommending him to wear it day and night. Her orders were followed exactly, and by that means, the prince was shielded against anything that might be attempted against him.

That talisman only had virtue, however, as long as Alphinge remained in his father's estates. Everywhere else it was devoid of force. The Fay of the Mountain informed the queen of that. From then on, that princess no longer thought of anything but means to send the lovable Alphinge away. She made several attempts that were futile, but in the end, hazard did for her what all her intrigue had not been able to produce.

The king had a sister married to a powerful prince who reigned in estates rather distant from his own. That sister conserved a very tender amity for her brother; she often received news of him, and obtained an infinite pleasure in the relation of everything that was happening in his court. The stories she was told about Prince Alphinge filled her with admiration; they gave birth to such a great desire to see her amiable nephew that she begged her brother to agree to him spending some time with her, She accompanied her pleas with the most pressing entreaties.

The king, in the interests of politics rather than sentiment, would never have granted that favor, but the queen pressured his mind so well that, without him having the slightest suspicion of the motive that made her act, he finally consented to that journey, and no longer thought about anything except determining the day of the departure and arranging an equipage appropriate to the birth of his son. He was then fourteen years of age, and it can be said without flattery that nothing comparable to him had ever been seen.

It was the custom in those days that ladies of the highest condition served as nurses to the children of kings. Prince Alphinge had been nursed by a lady who combined the grandeur of her birth with a virtue as solid as it was amiable, which distinguished her among all the women of her time. She had not only nursed the prince, but had even raised him until the time when he had been removed from the care of women, and then it was her husband who had been given to him as a tutor. Thus, she had never been separated from Prince Alphinge, and she loved him with a tenderness equal to the one she felt for her unique daughter, named Zayde. The graces and virtue of that charming person made the happiness of the parents to whom nature had given her. For his part, the prince was not ungrateful for the amity of his nurse; he had for her all the sentiments that he would have had for his mother.

When the question of the journey arose, it is easily understandable that the amiable family in question wanted to go with the prince; he therefore set forth accompanied by the people to whom he was most attached in all the world.

He traveled through his father's estates without any accident befalling him, but after he had crossed the frontier and he was traversing a plain of sand in insupportable heat, he went into a wood that he found on his route. The prince then complained of a thirst that had been tormenting him for several hours. In spite of the rarity of springs, one was found and water was brought to the prince. As soon as he had tasted it, he leapt down from the carriage and disappeared from the eyes of his court. It was in vain that, dissolving in tears, all the members of his retinue searched for him in all directions.

They were making the woods and the rocks resound with their cries when a huge and stout black monkey appeared on the tip of a sheer rock, and said to them: "It is in vain, poor desolate people, that you are searching for Prince Alphinge. Return to the country you have quit and only hope to see him again after having failed to recognize him for a long time."

They did not understand those words, and returned with an incredible dolor. When the king learned that news he was so afflicted by it that he died soon afterwards.

The queen had an immeasurable ambition; she was delighted to see the crown on the head of her young son without anyone being able to dispute it with him. She governed the state with him, and as authority does not admit constraint, her evil nature soon developed, and no one in the realm was able to doubt that she had caused the death of Prince Alphinge. It is even certain that, without the consideration people had for the king, her son, who was a very well born prince, the revolt would have been general.

Meanwhile, the nurse of the unfortunate Alphinge lived retired in her home, in a profound sadness; her daughter was then aged fourteen and was becoming so beautiful every day that she caused the admiration of everyone who saw her. She regretted the prince, whom she had loved since she had begun to know him, and recalled with pleasure the returns of tenderness that she had received from him. That pleasure was succeeded by sadness, and I know from a reliable source that she spent entire days weeping with her mother. As for the queen, she no longer thought about anything but procuring diversions for the young king, her son.

That prince was extremely fond of hunting, and it was a pleasure he took very often, accompanied by all the youth of the kingdom. One day, when he had a large party, in order to give evidence of his courage and skill against lions, tigers and the most furious animals with which the forests of that country were filled, after having hunted all morning he came to rest in a wood on the edge of a small river, where the hunt's repast was prepared under a magnificent tent.

While he was at table he saw a monkey in a tree, the color of which was the most beautiful green in the world; it was gazing at him fixedly, in a manner so tender that it made an impression on him. He forbade his men to do anything that might frighten it. The monkey, seeing the attention that was being paid to it, leapt from branch to branch, which such grace that everyone was occupied by it. They maintained the greatest silence, in the fear that it might not allow itself to be caught. Gradually, however, it drew nearer to the company, and the closer the range at which they saw it, the more agreeable its gaze and attitude seemed.

The king offered it something to eat; it took it graciously, and even came on to the table. Finally, the king received it on his knees, and took it away, charmed to have made such a discovery. He did not want to confide its guard to anyone but himself, and he took all the care of it imaginable, which is easily believable, since there was no longer any talk at the court of anything but the green monkey.

One morning, when Prince Alphinge's nurse was in her apartment with the beautiful Zayde, the monkey came in through a window that it found open; it had escaped from the king's apartment. Their first movement was fearful, but the little animal came toward them in a fashion so mild and insinuating that they soon recovered from their fear, and a moment later they experienced tender feelings, without being able to divine the reason for it.

The green monkey had been with them for some time, making them all kinds of caresses, when someone came on the king's behalf to ask for its return. They tried to take it, but it made cries so plaintive that Zayde and her mother were touched by them. They went to beg the king to leave it with them for a little longer, and he granted them that. It therefore stayed with them for a while, and often came back subsequently. Every time it was taken away it manifested an excessive dolor.

One evening, when they were in the garden sitting on the edge of a fountain, taking the air, the little money looked at Zayde, whose beauty was incomparable, with such a sad and passionate expression that they did not know what to think. Their surprise was even greater when they saw tears falling from its eyes. They were moved by that; Zayde could not reconcile herself with what was happening in her heart, and in spite of all the aid of reason, she felt herself drawn away by a sentiment of which she was not the mistress.

One day, she was out walking with her mother; after having walked for some time they rested in a jasmine arbor, and the conversation naturally fell upon what they had remarked in the little monkey. The mother said to Zayde: "I can't hide from you any longer, my dear daughter, what I have in my heart. I've done what I can to banish from my mind the idea that it was Prince Alphinge that we saw in that strange form, but my efforts have been futile; the idea torments me incessantly and never abandons me."

Scarcely had she finished speaking than she perceived the pretty little monkey, which, by means of tears and gestures that agreed with their discourse, seemed to be confirming their suspicions.

After that, Zayde's mother saw the Good Queen in a dream, who said to her: "Cease weeping and do exactly what I am going to prescribe. Go down into your garden, walk as far as the foot of the great myrtle in the shade of which your daughter often sits. Lift up a small marble tile; you will find a crystal vase full of a liquid that is the most beautiful green in the world. Take that vase; have what occupies you most placed in a bath covered in roses; when it is in, rub it with the green liquid. That is the one and only means of recovering Prince Alphinge."

At those words, she woke up, very astonished. She got out of bed immediately and went down into the garden, carried out the orders that the Good Queen had given her, and found exactly what she had indicated. Then she ran to wake her daughter, who, as you can imagine, she no difficulty getting out of bed. With what hope and vivacity she helped her mother in the care she took in preparing the bath—for neither of them wanted their maidservants to have the slightest knowledge of what was happening. The beautiful Zayde went to pluck the roses, and contributed ardently to everything they had to do. When everything was ready, they put the monkey in a jasper basin. It submitted to everything that was wanted of it.

While it was in the bath, the mother, as she rubbed it with the liquid as ordered, talked to her daughter and continued recounting the dream by which she had been so struck. The monkey, as it had done a thousand times, entered into the conversation by means of glances and nods of the head placed so appropriately that they hoped for the success of their enterprise at any moment.

They did not have to wait long; suddenly, they saw the skin of the monkey fall away, and Prince Alphinge appeared to their eyes, the most handsome and most lovable of all men.

Zayde, who had turned away while he was putting on a robe, was in a state difficult to describe. I leave it to those who have loved tenderly to imagine what she felt when she realized that she had not been able to help loving him in the form of an animal; for it was true that she loved him, and that love did not diminish on seeing a young man of sixteen, more handsome and more charming than Amour himself. I shall not attempt, for the same reason, to report what happened between the two lovers. What one thinks calmly is too far below those tender verities.

The mother was still the witness of their conversation. For her part, she experienced the transports of an excessive joy; she could not weary of admiring the prince and of making him relate his adventures and the difficulties he had endured in the woods and the deserts, exposed as he had been to hunger, thirst and all the insults of the atmosphere.

He admitted that the intelligence and reason that had been left to him by virtue of malevolence had augmented them greatly, and that, without the consolations he had received from his godmother, the Good Queen, he would have succumbed a thousand times, but that she had often come to visit him and had given him all the help that he could receive in such an unfortunate state. She had always enabled him to hope that he would see an end to it. In the end she was the one who had shown him the way in order to reach the place where he had found the king, his brother.

They spent several days and nights in those charming conversations, but eventually, Zayde's mother, whose heart and mind were very noble, thought about means of replacing the king on the throne that belonged to him.

For her part, the queen was experiencing great anxieties. The sight of the little monkey had troubled her greatly; ever since her son had brought it she had only been occupied with means of killing it, not doubting that it was Prince Alphinge. Her suspicions were confirmed by the Fay of the Mountain, who warned her about everything that had happened. Tearfully, she ran to find her son.

"I've been informed," she said to him, "that there are ill-intentioned people in your kingdom; they have created an impostor in order to dethrone you; it's necessary to have him killed in order to assure your tranquility." She could not and did not want to admit the truth.

The king, who had a good deal of courage, assured the queen that he would soon punish the guilty parties. He sought information carefully as to what had given rise to the rumors that were circulating. He could not believe that a widow—for the husband of Zayde's mother had died shortly after the loss of Prince Alphinge—and a young beauty deprived of the means necessary to excite a revolt could form such a great project. He resolved to go to see them, accompanied by enough men not to be at any risk. Neither the queen nor any of his confidants were aware of his design. He chose the middle of the night to carry it out.

He went into the palace; the first doors were still open, but when he arrived at those of the apartments he knocked rather violently. The ladies, who were conversing with the prince in a large cabinet, were extremely surprised by such an unexpected visit; they begged Alphinge not to show himself, but he had a great deal of difficulty according them that satisfaction.

Their astonishment was even greater when the doors were opened to see the king, followed by a part of his court.

"I know," said the prince, addressing Zayde's mother, "that you have formed designs against my person and my estate. I have come to clarify the matter with you. I only ask you to tell me the truth."

As they were preparing to respond to him, Prince Alphinge, who had not missed anything of the conversation, suddenly presented himself and said: "I am the one who will inform you; recognize me, my brother. He spoke, and showed so much grace and majesty that the king and all those who were with him remained motionless. As for Zayde and her mother, they thought they would die of fright at the peril he was risking.

Finally, the king pulled himself together and, not being able to mistake the prince, since it was only two years since he had last seen him, he embraced him, saying to him: "Yes, you are my brother, and to confirm it more fully, come and remount the throne that belongs to you. I have no further claim on it, since I have found you again." Then he kissed his hand, with a great deal of respect.

The prince embraced him tenderly. Then they went to the palace of the kings; it was there, in the presence of all the noblemen of the realm, that Alphinge received the crown from his brother's hands. In order to finish removing all doubts, in case any remained, he showed him the ruby that the Good Queen had sent him in his childhood. While they were looking at it attentively, it split with a loud noise. At the same instant, the queen died. She had shut herself away, unable to bear witnessing the happiness of a prince she had so cruelly persecuted.

Alphinge no longer had any cares by that of going to express his gratitude to his dear nurse and the beautiful Zayde, whom he married that same evening. The Good Queen arrived as the celebration of the wedding began, and the contentment of the new king was complete. She revealed all the conduct of the wicked queen, and assured him that henceforth he would no longer have anything to fear from the Fay of the Mountain; she could no long harm him, and the split ruby was proof of that. She spent some time with the newlyweds, and then retired to her estates.

King Alphinge governed his kingdom with all the prudence and mildness imaginable; he was adored by his subjects and tenderly loved by his family, and he always regarded the prince, his brother, as an associate of the crown.

This story is so famous, and the memory of King Alphinge so commendable, that it is told to children in their earliest youth, the palaces of kings are ornamented with paintings representing his adventures, and princesses take pleasure in retracing them with the needle in their richest furnishings.

The Satin Physician

There was once a very rich man who only had two daughters from all his marriages. The older was a shocking figure; she was cross-eyed and hump-backed; by way of recompense she had a great deal of intelligence, but it was a cunning and malevolent intelligence; it should not be difficult to believe that her flattery and her complaisance had gained her the entire confidence and good graces of her father, the king. The younger, by contrast, was admirably beautiful and her character was charming. Many people—they were neither courtiers not lovers, according to what I have been told—did not know whether to give preference to the charm of her intelligence or the graces of her face.

A young emperor was a neighbor of that country. He was only twenty years old, but at that scantly advanced age he had performed worthy deeds of a great captain and soldier, so bold, and at the same time so brilliant, that he could easily have rendered himself master of the world. Fortunately for the repose of the world, moderation appeared as his good side; he accorded peace to his neighbors, and his subjects pressed him, with reason, to give them an empress.

The two aforementioned princesses were the only ones of an appropriate age or birth that he could choose. He sent his ambassadors to ask for the elder, as was customary, for he was absolutely unaware of the looks and character of the two sisters. As he only wanted to marry in order to live happily with a woman he loved, however, he resolved to judge for himself before engaging himself in such a terrible knot. Sometime after the departure of his ambassadors, he came to find them incognito, with the unique design of seeing the princesses; whatever diligence he made, however, the request for the older princess had already been made when he arrived.

His journey had not been kept so secret that the king had not been informed of it; he therefore prepared to receive him with all possible magnificence, while still conserving his incognito. The ambassadors introduced the emperor to the king under the name of one of the princes of his court; the king received him as such.

There was a ball in the evening; the young emperor saw the two princesses there without any obstacle. The deformity of the figure and the acidity of the character of the elder shocked him to the point that he would not have wanted to marry her if she had ten kingdoms for a dowry. On the contrary, he was so vividly touched by the intelligence and the charms of the younger that he would have divided his empire with her even if she had been a simple shepherdess, and from that moment on his heart no longer belonged to him.

His repulsion for the elder princess and his attached to the younger became so intense at that first meeting that it was with great difficulty that he rendered the hunchback the appearance of homages that his heart rendered internally to the younger. But all the discoveries he made in the following days rendered his passion to violent too be hidden, and all his cares and desires finally declaring themselves for the younger, he let her know the passion that he felt for her and made her party to the project he had formed to ask his father the king for her— something that could happen—provided that she wanted to give her consent to it. The young emperor was made in such a way as not to have any difficulty obtaining amour.

He had asked his ambassadors to defer their leave-taking audience for a few days, and when it was no longer in their power to delay any further they went, on his orders, to ask for the younger princess. One must remember at this point the prejudice and blind amity that the king had for the elder princess. He was, therefore, so annoyed by the ambassadors' compliment that he had difficulty containing himself when he received them. As soon as the time of the audience had expired—for princes have always had an etiquette—he went to see his elder daughter in order to tell her about the insolent request that the emperor had just made for her sister.

"I can see," he added, "that what we have been told about the judgment of this young emperor is not true; the solidity of his reflections and a wisdom in advance of his years have been praised to us, but I cannot help disparaging them infinitely, since weakness has allowed him to be surprised by the beauty of the young princess."

The result of the council held between the father and daughter was a decision to the beautiful princess to a province so distant that the emperor could never see her. It was the sole means of making him change his conduct and rendering him more reasonable, in their way of thinking.

The cunning princess pretended to try to calm her father's mind; she affected to be sensible to the discontentment that her sister would experience; in sum, she neglected nothing that a deceptive and offended woman can put into practice, and ended that good advice by persuading him to imprison the young and lovely princess in a tower in the desert, representing to him that it was the only place in the kingdom where the young emperor would not be able to approach her.

Those who are offended ought, it seems to be, to be more recognized in society than in fact they are, and that is easily done, for they affect a marked indifference that ordinarily characterizes them, and always ought to give them away. The hunchback, who persuaded her father of everything she desired, had no difficulty making him understand that she did not care about the preference that the emperor had given to her younger sister, that it was necessary to testify indifference for that new choice, and that it was necessary, in consequence, to continue the diversions that had been prepared. The king approved of the advice of his wily daughter; he did not perceive that jealousy and the desire for vengeance were the only motive making her act. He therefore gave the necessary orders to make the fêtes even more brilliant.

A day was determined for the abduction of the princess, and the whole court was told to meet at a place in the forest in hunting costume. The ladies and cavaliers were ordered to go there separately. The emperor and the young princess had formed such pleasant ideas about that party that they waited for the day when it was to take place with great impatience.

The king came to the rendezvous with the emperor. Imagine the latter's surprise and the disturbance by which his mind was agitated when he did not find the princess among the ladies of the court. The first glance, which so rarely imposes upon lovers, did not deceive him. She had, however, departed long before him in order to go to the same place. The anxiety of the prince was at its height when he saw the hunt begin without her. He sent those of his men who had accompanied him in all directions to discover news of her, and spent the day searching for her himself and regretting her. When the hunt was over he came back overwhelmed with chagrin and the cruel agitation that amour enables one to experience.

One of the men he had sent to look for her had encountered the princess's carriage, accompanied by several cavaliers who were guarding it with the greatest exactitude; he had followed it all the way to the tower in the desert, but all that he had been able to observe was that the carriage had emerged from that horrible solitude empty. It was easy to deduce that the princess had remained imprisoned in that frightful retreat. The news that he came to bring the emperor penetrated that prince with the most intense dolor. He departed immediately, after having given his ambassadors an order to declare war on the king the next day if he did not set the princess free.

Scarcely had he arrived in his estates than he raised a powerful army, made it advance with diligence, and rendered himself master of the frontier without the enemy even having thought of mounting a defense.

As he quit the place where his amour had been born he had written a very tender note to his adorable princess, and had charged one of his favorites, who was as adroit as he was affectionate, with the care of delivering it. The latter had examined the surroundings of the tower in the desert with so much exactitude, and had obtained information so cleverly of

the place where the princess was lodged, that he finally discovered a small window in her bedroom that overlooked an
area filled with brambles where no one went.

The unfortunate princess was so prodigiously constrained that she was not even permitted to take the air at that
little window, although it was the only one that let daylight
into her room. The nurse of the hunchbacked princess had
been chosen as her governess; she was a woman who was said
to be directly descended from Argus. It was said that, like him,
she had one eye that never went to sleep. In addition to that
importunity she was a nasty creature in every respect. She did
not quit the princess for a single moment, and the unfortunate
beauty experienced a hindrance and an affliction that was all
the harder to bear because she had almost no hope any longer
of receiving news of her lover.

One day, when the inconvenient watcher was shut in her
cabinet, occupied in writing to her fine pupil, the hunchbacked
princess, in order to give her an account of what the young
princess had done and said since she had been in prison, the
unfortunate beauty took advantage of the moment of liberty
that the absence of the Argus gave her to get some air by looking out of the window briefly. She perceived a man hiding
among the thorns, who advanced as soon as he saw her and
showed her a letter. Immediately, she threw down a thread, to
which he attached the note. I leave it to the imagination to
judge the promptitude with which she pulled it up.

Fortunately, she had time to read it before the nurse
emerged from her cabinet, having finished her dispatches. It is
impossible to describe her joy. The same circumstance that
had favored her that day furnished an opportunity the following day for her to be able to respond. She made use of a page
from her notepad, which she threw to the man who had sent
her the note.

The emperor, charmed to be able to send his news and
receive that of the princess, resolved to go to the tower in the
desert himself, at the risk of whatever might happen, even if it
was only to see the person he adored for a moment. He sent

his faithful messenger back to ask for her permission, by means of a further note, and in the meantime, he gave the orders necessary for his absence not to alarm his army.

The princess replied to that second letter that she would be delighted to see him, but that she implored him not to expose himself to such a danger, all the more so as the vigilance of the aged nurse might perhaps render his voyage futile. She added, however, that she could not help informing him that the pitiless governess sometimes spent a quarter of an hour in the morning writing, and left her alone then.

The emperor was too amorous to be stopped by the most invincible obstacles. He was determined to confront all perils, but resolved nevertheless to attempt to put the watcher to sleep, in order to be surer. To that effect he sent the princess a soporific powder. He departed shortly after his favorite, and arrived by night in the brambles; the favorite guided him to the foot of the tower.

For her part, the princess, having put the Argus to sleep by means of the powder, appeared at the window as soon as she heard the signal that had been agreed. Her heart was so divided between dread and joy that it would be difficult to say which of the two passions dominated her more. As for the emperor, he was only occupied with the pleasure of seeing his dear princess again. He begged her with so much insistence to permit him to enter her apartment that she could not refuse him that favor. She threw down the end of a cord that she had composed with several knotted ribbons, and by that means she pulled up the silken ladder that the emperor had sagely brought with him.

No sooner was it attached to the sill than she saw the emperor arrive in her room. Their conversation was one of the sweetest and most tender. It is necessary to have experienced the same sentiments, and to have been in a similar situation, to be able to imagine all that they said. Their farewells were even more touching; they separated with dolor when daylight no longer permitted them to remain together.

Having detached the ladder and closed the window, the princess went to bed, believing that it was impossible for the old woman, who was profoundly asleep, to know anything about what had happened. However, the latter had seen everything by means of that ever-open eye; it was, fundamentally, an infirmity that had been falsely attributed to a relationship with Argus. It is true that her curiosity and her importunity, combined with that infirmity, had sufficiently authorized that fiction. At any rate her first concern, as soon as it was light, was that of writing to the jealous princess and relating to her in the most exact detail al the circumstances of the meeting of the two lovers.

The malevolent hunchback learned that news with fury, and, no longer putting any limits on her resentment, resolved to avenge herself rudely for the scorn that the emperor had shown to her pretended charms. In order to have the leisure to execute her pernicious designs, she instructed her nurse not to give any indication of having perceived what happened. She had a kind of trap constructed in such a fashion that the emperor, in passing through the baubles at the foot of the tower would trigger its springs, which would not only catch him, like a mouse in a mouse-trap, but would also launch a large number of poisoned darts, which would pierce all parts of his body. That fatal machine was constructed in a few days and placed without the beautiful princess having the slightest suspicion of it.

The emperor pressed by an impatience that only amour can inspire, came that evening even earlier than usual. As he approached the tower he heard the princess uttering one of the loud burst of laughter with which youth contents itself, unknown to any other age. He advanced precipitately in order to make the customary signal. Fortunately, the mechanism was only partially triggered, so that only a few darts departed from the detestable machine, which nevertheless inflicted wounds sufficient to make the prince fall backwards, covered in blood.

His faithful squire, who had never wanted to abandon him, carried him into a nearby wood, where the rest of his retinue was waiting. His wounds were bandaged and he was put on a stretcher, which was carried away with diligence in order to get him out of enemy territory. The surgeons found that the wounds were not mortal, but however great the pain that he felt was, it was less sensible to him than the memory of the laughter of the princess, at a time when he was treated so cruelly.

For her part, the princess was in the cruelest anxiety; on the evening that had been so unfortunate for the emperor, she had experienced the joy that the heart's contentment gives. A little monkey of which she was very fond made a grimace so singular on hearing the old woman snore, that the princess, at the age when gaiety is so natural, had allowed the burst of laughter to escape by which the emperor had been struck as he approached the tower. The usual time for the signal arrived, and she was very surprised not to hear the emperor or anyone on his behalf. She was even more so when the old woman, whom she had believed to be fast asleep, obliged her to go to bed immediately, and since that time she had not taken her eyes off her.

She spent a fortnight in an affliction and an anxiety that nothing could equal. At the end of that time the nurse went into her cabinet in order to dispatch her usual correspondence; she had left the key in the door and the princess locked it so adroitly and so promptly that the old woman only perceived it when the letter was written.

The first movement the princess made was to run to the window. What became of her when she saw the darts and the blood on the brambles! She was no longer mistress of herself, and, not doubting her misfortune, she wanted to throw herself out of the window in order not to survive her lover. A second reflection, which was not incompatible with the purest hero-ism, caused her to make the decision to make sure of the mis-fortune of everything she loved before going to such an ex-tremity.

In that design, she got out of the tower. Desperation is an intoxication that facilitates the most impracticable things. Fortunately, when she was some distance away from the prison she was fleeing, she encountered the husband of her own nurse, who was coming with the intention of rendering her some service, or at least to obtain news of her. The princess did not hesitate for a moment to make herself known to him. She implored him to go in search of male clothing, and in order to give him time to carry out that commission she went to wait for him in the deepest part of a nearby wood, which she indicated to him.

The good man carried out her orders faithfully; he was not long in doing so—attachment and amour do not ordinarily allow commissions to languish. She put on the clothes that he presented to her and put those she had been wearing into a bag that the good man put on his back. That clothing suited her perfectly and, according to the custom of all heroines, was covered in precious stones.

In that state they set off together for the emperor's estates. As one can believe, disguised as she was and in fear of being pursued, she slept under the stars.

One day, she found herself in a delightful valley, irrigated by a spring that was no less agreeable; she chose that place to spend the night. At daybreak she was worked up by a charming voice. That singularity surprised her, in such a solitary place. She advanced in the direction of a myrtle wood, from which she thought the voice had emerged. She perceived a young child, who was wearing a quiver and had an ivory bow in his hand. He was charmingly beautiful, and she might have taken him for Amour, but he did not have a blindfold.

The beautiful child, reading her thought, told her with an agreeable smile that she ought not to be surprised not to see him with a blindfold over his eyes; that, his arrows only giving birth to innocent desires and purified flames, he needed for that reason a more penetrating sight, in order to discern hearts capable of receiving them. In that he was quite different from the other Amour, who caused so many criminal desires, and for whom a blindfold over the eyes was absolutely necessary, in order to serve in some fashion to excuse all the crimes, injustices and disorders that he caused in the world. To that panegyric he added that, having given birth to the pure and tender amour with which she and the emperor were burning, he was obliged to aid them in their misfortune. He therefore gave her a little bottle of an admirable balm, recommending her to find a means of putting it on the emperor's wounds.

"You are only two days from his abode," he added. "Don't waste any time; although you will find the emperor without hope of a cure, trust in amour."

The princess thanked the beautiful child, her heart so swollen and her eyes so bathed with tears that anyone who saw her would have been moved to compassion. She woke up her nurse's husband promptly, and set off diligently along the road to the place that the Amour had indicated to her.

Finally, she arrived in the city so much desired. She went straight to the castle. Her manner was so majestic, in spite of her disguise, that the first person to whom she spoke—it was an honorable shopkeeper—was only too glad to offer her an apartment. The princess asked for news of the emperor with an urgency that can be imagined; she was told that he was at the last extremity.

With a boldness that only confidence in amour can give she decided to pass herself off as a physician, and answer with her head for the prince's cure, only asking for a few days to restore him to full health.

In order to appear in the court with more splendor, the charming new physician resolved to have a satin costume made. The merchant furnished her, so she said, with the finest in the city; a tailor took her measurements he was generously paid, and the costume was ready in two hours. The pretty physician then purchased a mule, for which he had made, with the same diligence, a blanket of satin similar to that of her robe.

While the work was being done, the physician asked the merchant a hundred thousand questions, and asked above all whether she knew anyone in the emperor's household. She replied that he could be tranquil on that score, because an officer at the gate was a brother of the cousin of one of her friends, and that officer was the first cousin of the secretary of the captain of the guard. The physician told her that she could assure everyone she knew that, in response to the rumor of the emperor's malady, a foreign empiric had arrived, who would answer for his cure on pain of being burned alive if he did not succeed in his enterprise.

The merchant, who had gossiped a hundred times about less important matters, ran to the castle to talk about the foreigner who was lodging with her, her head increasingly heated by her tales; her empiric had effected cures before her eyes more difficult than that of the prince. Finally, she repeated so many times that her physician would answer with his head for the emperor's cure that her discourse made an impression on all the courtiers.

Physicians, who do not like other healers than themselves and their own kind, protested in vain that the empiric was a madman and that the offer he was making was sufficient to prove it. Some of their patients believed them, but all the officers of the palace responded, with reason, that since they had confessed that their own art no longer furnished them with any resources, there was no risk in listening to the empiric and that they wanted absolutely to have recourse to him. It is necessary to know that the emperor's wounds, which had not been judged mortal to begin with, had become so because of the terrible effect of the poison with which the darts had been armed.

They went to see the physician, therefore, and implored him with tears in their eyes to employ his remedies to cure a prince adored by his subjects. He did not have to be begged; he mounted his mule with his equipage. The soldiers and the inhabitants, seeing both covered with satin, said: "There goes the Satin Physician," and his arrival at the castle was announced by that name, which stuck.

He was taken to the hall, where the captain of the guard as waiting to judge by his face, his discourse and his deportment whether it was possible to have any confidence in him. He found him, although extremely young, to have an appearance so noble, so honest and so fortunate, and a bearing so modest, sage and polite, that he undertook warmly to enable him to see the emperor, and achieved that in spite of the cabal of the physicians and their partisans. It is necessary to admit, however, that fatigue and dolor had diminished the splendor of her beauty considerably.

As soon as the emperor had perceived the physician and had heard the sound of his voice he was touched by a particular inclination for him, and acquired confidence in his remedies. The Satin Physician repeated what he had already told others modestly about his great knowledge, but he added that he did not want his conduct to be criticized or examined; and for that reason he would not suffer that there was anyone else in the emperor's chamber but his favorite squire.

The more the emperor listened to the Satin Physician the more his heart engaged him to abandon himself blindly to his remedies, and he therefore ordered all his officers to withdraw. The physician applied his balm that very day to the emperor's wounds, and the prince received such a great relief from them that he spend the entire night in slumber. The following day, the physicians, as well as the entire court, were surprised to find him in such good condition. After he had taken some nourishment, the Satin Physician again wanted no one to remain in the patient's chamber.

He removed the initial dressing and applied his balm to the prince's wounds for a second time, with such success that the following morning, he was almost healed. Thinking about the cause of his illness, however, chagrin took the place of his dolor; the voice and face of his new physician recalled to him forcefully the memory of a princess he believed to be perfidious. He sighed, and even allowed a few tears to escape him.

The Satin Physician perceived that, and told him that he recognized in him a malady other than the one for which he had been summoned.

The prince replied: "I can see that you have more than one expertise, but it is impossible for you to cure me of the malady that you have just discovered in me."

The Physician begged him to set his mind at rest, and assured him that before quitting him, he would cure his chagrin as well as his wounds.

The new Physician possessed that talent of speech to an eminent degree; he not only had the art of persuasion but he also had the fortunate talent of knowing how to amuse his patient with the pleasure of light, lively and witty conversation. The police ought to forbid physicians to be harsh and surly.

With such aid it was easy for the Satin Physician to insinuate himself into the emperor's mind and obtain his confidence. He became his confidant, and the prince, confessing to him the excess of passion that he had had for the princess, could not hide it from him that he still loved her madly, ingrate and perfidious as she might be; for he believed her to be an accomplice to the treason to which he had been subject, although that cruel prejudice had no other foundation than the burst of laughter he had heard at the moment when he had been wounded.

Lovers are always borne to all extremities because of the merest bagatelles, so I exhort them, as hard as I can, not to be affected any longer by trivia that might destroy their passion, but to take nothing to heart and not to allow themselves to ignore any impression.

The Satin Physician listened to what the prince said with a pleasure mingled with dolor; he could not help sighing several times. He did everything he could to persuade the emperor that there was every appearance that he was mistaken in the judgment he had made of the princess. He alleged, in vain, very good arguments to justify her, for the prejudices of jealousy and discontentment are difficult to efface from the mind.

Finally, the Satin Physician spread his precious balm over the emperor's wounds for the last time. He slept profoundly, and the physician did likewise.

The following morning, the princess made the decision to appear in her natural state. She woke up early, quit her satin robe in order to put on her ordinary clothing, put on her jewels, and did not neglect any attention to her adornment that could not only allow her to be recognized but also render her brilliant in the eyes of her lover and all his court. She had just finished dressing when the emperor woke up.

He found himself then in a health so perfect that he did not feel the slightest weakness. He was so wide awake that his situation seemed to him to have been a dream, and what confirmed him in that thought was the sight of the princess, who came to draw the curtains of his bed personally. Then she told him the detail of the various situations in which she had found herself since their last conversation in the tower in the desert, reproaching him tenderly for the unjust suspicion into which he had allowed himself to fall.

The emperor threw himself at the feet of the princess, and did not neglect anything of what could be said to mark his gratitude and the violence of his passion. In the meantime, the principal individuals of the court were in the antechamber, awaiting the success of the remedy.

The emperor wanted them to know the obligation that he had to the Satin Physician. He had the door to his chamber opened. Their astonishment was extreme on seeing him enjoying a perfect health. Like the good courtiers they were, they entered precipitately in order to give thanks and eulogies to the Satin Physician, but imagine their surprise when, instead of the empiric, they perceived the most beautiful princess in the world! The emperor told them that in thanking his physician they could salute their empress at the same time. He wanted to give orders immediately for the ceremony of their marriage, but the princess begged him to wait sagely for the agreement of her father, the king.

The emperor's army, indignant at the treason that had been perpetrated against their prince, had pushed its conquests with as much success as courage under the orders of a skillful general. The king, the father of the two princesses, was trapped without any resource in his capital city. The siege was formed, and the earthworks were being carried forward with a great vivacity.

In spite of the care that was being taken to seal the place completely, the rumor of the emperor's singular cure and the quality of his physician spread into the besieged city. The malevolent and jealous princess, whose temperament was the most choleric, experienced such a sharp dolor on learning that her sister and the emperor were on the point of being happy, and was so chagrined by the failure of the obstacles she had brought to their happiness, that she choked to death.

The king was penetrated by her death; in his first transports he had the elder princess's nurse burned to punish her for the scant care with which she had guarded the younger princess in the tower in the desert.

The king's dolor commenced to ease, and he was in a better state to recognize his injustice when the emperor's ambassadors arrived to offer him peace on such advantageous conditions that he was only too happy to accept them, as well as the request they made him for his daughter on behalf of their master, the emperor. He even wanted to be present at the marriage ceremony, which was held with as much joy as magnificence; but remorse rendered life so insupportable to him—fundamentally, he had a good heart; only the bad advice of his daughter had perverted it—and he was so afflicted by having loved a person so unworthy of love and having tormented the object that merited his amity more, that it was not possible for him to survive such painful chagrins.

As for the two spouses, they experienced the fate of persecuted lovers; they loved one another all the more tenderly for it, and lived happily in all circumstances.

The Rainbow Prince

There was once a king who was married for a long time without having any children. He finally obtained from heaven a daughter of such great beauty that he could not think of giving her any name better than More Beautiful than a Fay.[31] The good prince did not realize that such a name would necessarily attract the redoubtable hatred of the fays to the child. In fact, they were no sooner informed of that prideful name than they formed the design of seizing the person to whom it had been given, resolved to torment her cruelly, or at least to hide her from the gaze of humans.

The oldest of the entire corps was charged with the care of that vengeance. That fay, whose name was Lagrée, was so old that only one eye and one tooth remained to her, and she was obliged to soak them overnight in a fortifying liquid. At the same time, she was so malevolent that she was only occupied with the dismal care of carrying out the black and malevolent wishes of her companions. With as much experience of evil intention as she had, it was not difficult for her to abduct More Beautiful than a Fay.

The little girl, who was then only seven years old, nearly died of fright when she found herself alone, in the power of such a hideous person. She was slightly reassured, however, when, after having traveled for about an hour underground, she found herself in a superb palace surrounded by magnificent gardens, and when she perceived that her dog and her cat had come with her.

---

[31] There is a story by Mademoiselle de La Force featuring an eponymous princess of the same name, but it is a very different story, although there are some slight similarities in the plots of the two tales.

The old woman took her to a rather pretty room, which she gave her for a residence. Showing her a fireplace, she ordered her to maintain a continuous fire there and to be careful, on the eyes in her head, to conserve without breaking them, two glass phials that she confided to her care.

After giving those two orders, with the accompaniment of the most terrible threats, the old woman went away and left the little girl quite content in being able to walk around the palace and only having two functions, which did not seemed to her to be difficult to fulfill.

She acquitted them very exactly for several years, and became so accustomed to the solitary life that she forgot her father's court completely.

One day, when she was amusing herself playing next to a beautiful fountain placed in the middle of the gardens, the sun's rays falling upon that clear water formed a rainbow, the splendor and beauty of which surprised More Beautiful than a Fay. A voice emerged from the rainbow, which charmed her even more. The voice appeared to be that of a young man. By the mildness and the charm of what he said, it was impossible to dispense with forming the most agreeable idea of his face, but only the imagination could work in that occasion, for the person was invisible.

The beautiful rainbow told More Beautiful than a Fay that he was in early youth, that his father was a powerful king, and that Lagrée, in order to avenge herself on his parents and afflict them, had deprived him of his natural form for some years and had imprisoned him in this palace; that his penitence had been very difficult to sustain at first; but that he could not conceal from her that he dreaded seeing it finish since he had had the good fortune of seeing More Beautiful than a Fay, whom he had been bold enough to love. He added many things to that declaration even more gallant, to which More Beautiful than a Fay was all the more sensible because the gentle seduction of tender words was an entirely new pleasure for her.

The prince could neither appear nor make himself heard except in the form of a rainbow. It was therefore necessary for the sun to appear and for him to find water in order to produce that agreeable apparition.

More Beautiful than a Fay did not waste any of the moments when she might be able to see her lover. One day, the conversation became so interesting and the moments appeared to her so brief, that the fire that had been confided to her went out. On her return, Lagrée perceived that negligence, and, far from testifying resentment, she seized that pretext joyfully to exercise all her rage against the beautiful child who was her prisoner.

She commanded her, therefore, to go early the following morning to ask Locrinos for fire to reignite the one she had allowed to go out. Locrinos was a cruel monster who devoured everyone he encountered, especially young girls. More Beautiful than a Fay obeyed with an infinite meekness, and, without having been able to bid adieu to her lover, she went to Locrinos's dwelling as to certain death.

As she was going through a wood, she was told by a bird to pick up a pebble as shiny as a star, which she would find in a nearby spring, and to make use of it when the time came.

More Beautiful than a Fay followed that advice, continued her journey, and arrived at Locrinos's house. Fortunately, she only found his wife there, who was alone in the house. She was touched by compassion at the sight of the young princess—one of the great advantages of beauty is the interest it can inspire—but the monster's wife was even more struck by the gleam of the pebble that she presented to her. She gave her the fire, therefore, and, in gratitude for the beautiful stone she had given her, she made her a present of another, of which she told her that she might be able to make use one day; then she sent her way without having done her any harm.

Lagrée showed as much surprise as discontentment at such extraordinary good fortune, and More Beautiful than a Fay waited with extreme impatience for the moment when she could tell the Rainbow Prince what had happened to her, and express the joy that she had in seeing him again. She was not telling him anything new, though; he had already been informed of her adventure by a fay who was one of his relatives and who protected him.

The fear of exposing everything he adored to new perils caused him to imagine a more convenient way than the one he had had thus far to converse with her. More Beautiful than a Fay employed it every day with success. She placed on the window of her bedroom, in accordance with the instruction she had received from her lover, a bowl full of water. The rainbow formed in the bowl as it had in the fountain, so, More Beautiful than a Fay did not have to go far, in order to see her lover, from the fire or the two phials, in which the fay soaked her tooth and her eye. For some time they took advantage of every instant of sunlight to have the tender conversations that render days so short.

The Rainbow Prince came to the rendezvous one day in the most profound sadness. He had learned with despair that he was about to be banished imminently from that beautiful place, without knowing precisely where on the earth he was to be taken. The dolor of the two lovers is easy to imagine. They did not allow any of the sun's rays to escape, and arranged to meet again the following day.

The following day finally arrived, but the weather was unfortunately cloudy. After a few hours of an impatience that only amour can know, the sun was uncovered momentarily. More Beautiful than a Fay ran to take advantage of it, but it was with such a great vivacity that she spilled all the water from the bowl that she had prepared the day before. She could not find any other except that in the two bottles confided to her care. It was a matter of seeing her lover one more time before a separation. She did not hesitate, therefore, to break the two phials, and the rainbow formed.

It is necessary to know that the use of speech that was granted to him was attached to the brightness of the colors. Their adieu was full of tenderness; the prince made his mistress the most sincere and the most eager protestations; he promised not to neglect anything in order to extract her from the place where he was constrained to leave her, in order to unite himself with her by means of a marriage to which he begged her to consent. More Beautiful than a Fay swore in her turn that she would never have any other husband and that she was ready to risk death in order to find him again.

The destiny that was separating them so cruelly did not permit them to make their adieux any longer. The Rainbow Prince vanished, and More Beautiful than a Fay, beside herself with dolor and resolved to attempt anything, took her dog, her cart, a branch of myrtle and the stone that the wife of Locrinos had given her. What boldness does veritable amour not inspire on certain occasions?—for it is certain that the young princess set forth without any other equipage and without any other guide than hazard and despair.

When she returned Lagrée perceived the flight of her prisoner; she became furious, and ran after her immediately. She caught up with her at exactly the time when the unfortunate girl, overcome by lassitude, wanting to take a rest, had lain down in a cavern that the stone she was carrying had just formed for her. The little dog, which was mounting guard over its mistress carefully, bit Lagrée in such a sensible fashion that, instead of seizing More Beautiful than a Fay, she bumped into the cavern and broke her only tooth.

Before she had recovered from the pain and rage that the accident caused her, the young girl had the leisure to escape and to cover a good deal more ground. The dream of such an urgent peril made her forget her lassitude for some time, but, finally succumbing, she let herself fall, no longer able to sustain herself. Hazard enabled the myrtle branch she was carrying to touch the ground, and immediately, that branch made her an arbor, where she hoped to sleep tranquilly.

For her part, Lagrée, who was only occupied by the desire for vengeance, had set forth in pursuit of the unfortunate princess again. She arrived just as she was falling asleep. The cat, which had climbed on to one of the branches of the arbor, was no less help to its mistress than the little dog had been a few hours before. It leapt at Lagrée's face, tore out her only eye, and thus delivered More Beautiful than a Fay once and for all from the persecutions of the pitiless fay.

Scarcely had she seen herself relieved of such a great anxiety, however, than she experienced the horrors of hunger and that of fatigue. She was on the brink of succumbing to them. Finally, half-dead and in a frightful state, she arrived in the vicinity of a little green and white house.

A beautiful lady dressed in those two colors, who was its mistress and only inhabitant, received her there with all imaginable kindness. After a long supper and a long sleep in the best bed in the world, the green and white lady predicted to More Beautiful than a Fay that after great difficulties, she would attain the goal of her designs. When she embraced her and bid her adieu she gave her a walnut, which she told her only to open in case of urgent need.

After having endured many fatigues, More Beautiful than a Fay was received in a house and by a lady exactly similar to the one she had already found. She also received a present there, on the same conditions, but instead of a walnut she was given a golden pomegranate.

The sad and fatigued princess was again obliged to continue her journey with incredible difficulties, and she was received a third time in a house similar to the other two that she had already encountered on her route.

Those houses belonged to three sisters equally endowed with talents of enchantment and faces and a humor so similar that they also wanted their dwellings and their garments to resemble one another absolutely. They were only occupied by the care of helping the unfortunate; in sum, they were as mild and benevolent as the defunct Lagrée has been cruel and malevolent.

The third fay consoled More Beautiful than a Fay, implored her not to give up, and promised to recompense her for her pains. She accompanied her speech with the present of a rock-crystal bottle with an order only to uncork it in absolute necessity. Our heroine thanked her with the mildness and affection that sadness and hope can inspire, and drew away, her head filed with the most agreeable thoughts.

The road that she followed led her a few hours later into a charming wood. One respired a pure air there, perfumed with the sweetest odor. She had not taken a hundred steps in that beautiful place than she perceived a silver castle attached to four huge trees; it was suspended by long, thick chains of the same metal, and so delicately balanced that it was agitated by a soft breeze that only made the noise required to maintain a peaceful slumber.

The hope of seeing an end to her troubles was redoubled by that sight, apparently by virtue of a secret presentiment, but those same hopes relented slightly when she realized that the castle was in mid-air and had neither a door nor windows. She had no doubt—I have no idea why—that the moment had come to make use of the walnut she had been given. She opened it, and a doorman came out of a stature proportionate to the place where he had been confined. There was a golden key hanging from his belt attached to a short chain; the key might have been half the size of a pin.

More Beautiful than a Fay made use of one of the chains that was hanging down to the ground to climb up to the silver castle as she might have used a ladder. She held the little doorman in her hand, and, in spite of the apparent disproportion of his stature, he opened an imperceptible door, which became large enough to allow More Beautiful than a Fay to pass through. A marvelous hall composed the interior of the castle; it only received light from the golden stars and gemstones attached to its vault. In the middle of the room there was a cot, whose fabric was dyed in the same colors as the rainbow, and that bed, sustained by golden threads, followed the same movements as the castle, in such a manner as to procure sleep delectably.

It was on that beautiful bed that the Rainbow Prince, much more beautiful than all the things that surrounded him, had been asleep since he had been separated from everything he loved. Without such an enchantment, his dolor and his amour would not have allowed him the slightest repose, and the presence of his mistress would then have transported him with joy.

More Beautiful than a Fay, in spite of all the presentiments of her heart, dared not surrender to the pleasure of gazing at the person who appeared to be the master of that singular and voluptuous habitation. She dreaded not finding, in the face that was beginning to charm her, the sentiments and the sound of the voice of the man she loved. Without giving herself time to disentangle the various agitations of her soul, however, her self-esteem was offended by the indifference and insensibility with which she was received.

She related twenty times over the difficulties and fatigues that she had endured, and although she was speaking in a very loud voice, the slumber of the prince did not appear to be interrupted. She had recourse to the pomegranate; all the seeds that it contained were as many tiny violins, which, when it was opened rose into the vault and immediately composed a charming music, soft and full of melody. The prince did not wake up entirely, but he opened his eyes slightly and, in consequence, became infinitely more beautiful.

More Beautiful than a Fay, becoming impatient at not being recognized, employed the last present that she had been given. She opened her bottle, and a tiny siren emerged, who had the violins fall silent and sang into the ear of the prince everything that his mistress had suffered in order to come to find him. She added a few slight reproaches to her stories, and then the prince woke up entirely.

Transported, he threw himself at the feet of More Beautiful than a Fay. At the same instant, the hall opened on all sides, and a golden throne covered in precious stones rose up in the middle. A court as superb as it was numerous appeared then, which preceded several chariots of an extraordinary beauty, filed with the most beautiful and the best adorned ladies. At the head of the chariots there was one that surpassed all the others in its magnificence. It was easy to judge that the lady who was sitting in it on her own was the queen of that court.

The lady was even more beautiful than she would have been in early youth. She was the mother of the Rainbow Prince. She told him that his father was dead and that the anger of the fays was appeased, so that nothing any longer prevented him from coming to govern faithful people who only wanted his presence. She added to that declaration all the caresses that can be imagined.

The court, which was present at that conversation, testified all possible joy and affection to its new king. He would have been delighted at another time, but he was uniquely occupied by the desire to declare More Beautiful than a Fay the queen of the estates that had just been offered to him. He had decided only to show his new court the charms of More Beautiful than a Fay in order to have his choice approved, but the three green and white sisters arrived then, when they were least expected. They declared the birth of More Beautiful than a Fay, and by means of that speech rendered the applause of the court absolutely general and unanimous.

The queen mother had the two lovers mount her chariot, and conducted them to the capital city. All the inhabitants received them with acclamations and cries of joy that cannot be described. The marriage was celebrated the same day, and did not bring any diminution to their amour; even the years did not destroy either their beauty or their tenderness. They lived for several centuries, always loved by their subjects, and left children who inherited their perfections and their good fortune.

CLASSIC FRENCH FANTASY

Honoré de Balzac. *The Last Fay*
Gabrielle-Suzanne Barbot de Villeneuve. *The Naiads   Beauty and The Beast*
Chevalier de Béthune. *The World of Mercury*
Jean Carrère. *The End of Atlantis*
Charlotte-Rose Caumont de La Force. *The Land of Delights*
Félicien Champsaur. *Pharaoh's Wife*
Jacques Collin de Plancy. *Voyage to the Center of the Earth*
Gaston Danville. *The Perfume of Lust*
Comtesse D.L. *The Tyranny of the Fays Abolished*
Paul Féval. *Anne of the Isles*
Charles de Fieux. *Lamékis*
Judith Gautier. *Isoline and the Serpent-Flower*
Nathalie Henneberg. *The Green Gods*
Gustave Kahn. *The Tale of Gold and Silence*
Edmond Haraucourrt. *Dieudonat*
Marie-Jeanne L'Héritier de Villandon. *The Robe of Sincerity*
André Lichtenberger. *The Centaurs; The Children of the Crab*
J-M. & Randy Lofficier. *The French Fantasy Treasury 1-3*
Charles Lomon & P.-B. Gheuzi. *The Last Days of Atlantis*
Maurice Magre. *The Marvelous Story of Claire d'Amour; The Call of the Beast; Priscilla of Alexandria; The Angel of Lust; The Mystery of the Tiger; The Poison of Goa; Lucifer; The Blood of Toulouse; The Albigensian Treasure; Jean de Fodoas; Melusine; The Brothers of the Virgin Gold*
Marie-Madeleine de Lubert. *Princess Camion.*
Camille Mauclair. *The Virgin Orient*
Hippolyte Mettais. *Paris Before the Deluge*
Victor-Emile Michelet. *Superhuman Tales*
Henriette-Julie de Murat. *The Palace of Vengeance*
Charles Nodier. *Trilby   The Crumb Fairy*
Edgar Quinet. *The Enchanter Merlin*

Henri de Régnier. *A Surfeit of Mirrors*
Restif de la Bretonne. *The Fay Ouroucoucou* (2 vols.)
J.-H. Rosny Aîné. *Pan's Flute*
Marie-Anne de Roumier-Robert. *The Voyage of Lord Seaton to the Seven Planets*
Nicolas Ségur. *Penelope's Secret*
Kiurt Steiner. *Ortog*
C.-F. Tiphaigne de La Roche. *Amilec   Giphantia*
Simon Tyssot de Patot. *The Strange Voyages of Jacques Massé and Pierre de Mésange*

www.ingramcontent.com/pod-product-compliance
Lightning Source LLC
Chambersburg PA
CBHW030357030726
47497CB00002B/373